I0822866

OldTown

Fly, Sparrow, Fly

A. K. Frailey

Hardcover Edition

Cover Design: A. K. Frailey and James Hrkach

ISBN 979-8-9874047-8-2

The Writings of A. K. Frailey

Books for the Mind and Spirit

https://akfrailey.com/

Contact

akfrailey@yahoo.com

Historical Science Fiction Novels

OldEarth ARAM Encounter

OldEarth Ishtar Encounter

OldEarth Neb Encounter

OldEarth Georgios Encounter

OldEarth Melchior Encounter

Science Fiction Novels

Homestead

Last of Her Kind

Newearth Justine Awakens

Newearth A Hero's Crime

Short Stories

It Might Have Been—

And Other Short Stories 2nd Edition

One Day at a Time and Other Stories

Encounter Science Fiction

Short Stories & Novella 2nd Edition

Inspirational Non-Fiction

My Road Goes Ever On—

Spiritual Being, Human Journey 2nd Edition

My Road Goes Ever On—A Timeless Journey

The Road Goes Ever On—A Christian Journey Through The Lord of the Rings

Children's Book

The Adventures of Tally-Ho

Poetry

Hope's Embrace & Other Poems 2nd Edition

Audible Versions Now Available.
Check book details on Amazon
for current listings.

Fly, Sparrow, Fly

Frail life born into a harsh wind world,
While Spring leaves swirl.

Tiny and helpless,
Shivering, you wait, powerless.

Mother's sweeping flight, father's chirping might,
Swooping near, then far, far away,
Trusting providence every day.

Grow, Sparrow, Grow

Summer Time
Under a brilliant sun,
Long days,
Mild nights.

Small bones, fledging feathers, expanding wings,
A distant call, the blue sky sings,

Of Wonder!
Of Joy!
Updraft of Hope.

Fly, Sparrow, Fly!

Build your own nest,
Make it the best,
To your own self be true.

Colors brighten, days darken,
Winds rise, green things die.

Autumn warns of winter frost,
Daring — Prepare or be lost!

Little birds grown must adapt or flee,
Not for the weak to wait and see.

Beware, Sparrow, Beware

Ice, snow, and cold winds blow.
Barren lands
Nowhere to go
Alone in silence

Be Brave
Be Strong
Do not Despair.

Fight the icy blast,
Scrounge for each repast,
Huddle under wing,
Let the furies sing.

Survive, Sparrow, Survive

Long past dreamy hopes of dawn,
The sun shines, breezes blow in a new song.

A revived spirit rises from your depths,
Hope blooms with flowers blessed,

On a new day,
You find your way.

No longer alone,
Flying becomes dancing as your skills you hone.

Your nest has room for more.
Go and find them,
Those who'll be
Your nestmates, your loves, your family.

Fly, Sparrow, Fly!

TABLE OF CONTENTS

CHAPTER ONE 1

CHAPTER TWO 25

CHAPTER THREE 46

CHAPTER FOUR 80

CHAPTER FIVE 109

CHAPTER SIX 133

CHAPTER SEVEN 159

CHAPTER EIGHT 180

CHAPTER NINE 203

CHAPTER TEN 228

CHAPTER ELEVEN 261

CHAPTER TWELVE 292

CHAPTER THIRTEEN 313

ABOUT THE AUTHOR 319

Chapter One

How Rhona Tried to Save a Broken-Winged Bird and Had to Enlarge Her Life Vision

Early September

Rhona tried to rub dried garden dirt off her hands but gave up as a black-haired doctor with a grave expression entered the hospital waiting room. The dirt didn't matter. Her niece's life did. Her gaze fixed on the Mediterranean-looking man in the blue scrubs, far too young for a surgeon, she thought. Surely, he could see that they were all waiting anxiously.

Whether he saw or not didn't seem to matter. He intercepted a nurse in a matching blue uniform and spoke softly, stuffing his hands into large pockets.

The pretty blond woman checked her chart and started talking, her eyes darting from the chart to his face as if to make sure that he didn't disappear while she was reviewing her notes.

Rhona's husband, Dermid, wrapped his arm around her shoulders and attempted a comforting side hug. It didn't help. Nothing made sense. Her world had crashed, and time had shifted. From a bright autumn afternoon in the garden, gathering the last of the tomatoes and peppers for a final batch of salsa, to this moment, no discernible connection could be made.

Her brother-in-law, Zhang, had called, hysterical, talking much too fast. As owner of the largest automotive dealership in the county, selling and leasing cars to enterprising companies across the nation, Zhang was one of the most successful and unflappable men she knew. Why, the man could sell a Ferrari to a funeral director. Seeing his name pop up on her phone sent shock waves over her nervous system. Zhang never called her. They barely ever spoke.

His voice had jolted through her as she started jogging to the house. "There's been an accident. Nia was taking the kids shopping after they finished classes, and they went off the road. Andy is fine, just a few bruises, but Nia is pretty banged up, and Syn's got a dislocated shoulder and a broken arm. She wasn't wearing a seatbelt!"

Rhona could imagine his headshake even as her heart raced, and she picked up her pace, taking the porch steps two at a time, unmindful of the fact that she wasn't a spring chicken anymore.

It didn't take long to jog through the house and enter her husband's office. She waved frantically to get Dermid's attention away from the computer screen where he was undoubtedly trying to wrangle sense out of some high school student's idea of an algebra solution.

Abruptly, saying he had to go, Zhang ended the call.

Refocusing, Rhona pressed one hand against her chest, trying to keep her heart from sending her into cardiac arrest, and explained the situation to her confused husband.

It only took a few minutes, and they were racing to the hospital. Derm clutched the steering wheel with all the force of a man who hates driving in a hurry.

Compressing her nerves by force of sheer will, Rhona kept still and didn't disturb his concentration. Speculation wouldn't do any good anyway, but her stomach had churned like steamboat paddlewheels as they zipped down country roads toward the highway.

Two hours later, after slogging through rush hour traffic and then a mind-numbing wait in the appropriately enough named "waiting room," she glanced aside at the large industrial windows, startled to see the nearly empty parking lot glowing under brilliant street lights, while the surrounding neighborhood rested in somnolent twilight.

The first frost wasn't expected for another few weeks, and the temps hadn't dipped under fifty yet, but her body felt frozen in place on the steel-framed chair. She could hardly move, much less think. A hundred questions swirled in her mind like a cloud of demonic gnats.

Gentle hands began to massage her shoulders. Being the kind and reasonable man he was, Dermid tried logic to bridge the gap between her originally peaceful day and their present distress. "Nia and Andy are going to be fine. The front desk said the doctor will give us an update soon. It's Syn we need to worry about."

Incomprehension met foreboding, and Rhona's fifty-seven-year-old body ached in weariness. She wanted to lie down, preferably in her own bed at home, in peace and quiet.

Finally, as the doctor approached their small group, she and Dermid stood up.

The doctor and nurse stopped before Zhang and his elderly parents.

Mr. and Mrs. Wei stayed seated, clearly too encumbered by their grief to stand.

Hesitantly, Rhona inched forward and positioned herself at her brother-in-law's side.

Zhang's face was locked in icy rage, adding to Rhona's confusion. *Who is he so angry at? Me, for being here? He called me! Nia, for the accident?* Part of her wanted to take a step back, but the stubborn part of her refused to budge.

The nurse glanced over and graciously widened the circle, allowing Rhona and Dermid to join in. Despite the serious expression on her face, her blond ponytail danced as she glanced from Rhona to Dermid and kindly recapped what the doctor had said. "Nia is doing well and is ready to go home. She has some bruising but nothing is broken. Andy is also ready to leave. Remarkably, he barely had a scratch on him. Syn is out of surgery and resting comfortably. It will be some hours before she is ready for visitors."

Without premeditated thought, Rhona's voice rose. "But how is she? Syn, I mean."

After a throat clearing and a significant glance at the nurse, the doctor faced Rhona head-on. "Physically, she'll mend in time. She had a severely dislocated shoulder and a broken right arm. We had to anesthetize her to relocate the shoulder and straighten her arm. She'll be in a cast for several weeks. Depending on how she recovers, there is a chance she might need some physical therapy." His gaze swept over the elderly couple and then landed on Zhang. "You'll have to make some follow-up appointments for her long-term recovery."

Suddenly, Rhona knew why autumn had come early this year. She had been able to freeze gallons of spicy salsa, the kind that Syn loved, ahead of schedule. The garden was winding down, and winter was coming but that never bothered her because she and Dermid loved each season in turn. They prepared for each as if they were high holidays.

Even still, she had never prepared for this.

Or had she? Had a crisis been brewing for so long, she had accepted it as a part of family life, refusing to accept that, when it erupted, she would have to play her part?

Zhang dropped onto the chair next to his mother. Irritation rather than concern etched his features. His mother patted his leg as if he were a pouting child, encouraging him to buck up under difficult circumstances.

Stupefied, Rhona blinked back tears. *Why is he so angry? Shouldn't he be running to his wife's side…to his daughter's side?*

Just then, a young, handsome man strolled into the waiting room, an unnaturally wide smile plastered over his face.

Andy didn't appear as if he'd just been in an accident. Not a hair was out of place. He lifted a hand as if to ward off any unwanted concern, setting the stage for his latest joke. "Hey, it's great being an adult now. I checked myself out. Now, if I could only get a beer, it would make this day perfect." His eyes did not match his smile.

Like an arrow loosed from a bow, Zhang rushed to his son, his arms wide and welcoming. It was a heartwarming hug, certainly. The elderly couple stayed in place, waiting their turn, their eyes glimmering with tears of relief.

Rhona didn't know what to do. Part of her dearly wanted to speed over and hug her nephew, glad that he was looking so fine, but something about the scene choked her mind and stalled her momentum.

Having no such qualms, Dermid stepped over and took his turn. He shook the young man's hand, saying something about the boy's uncommon good luck.

Andy found that funny and slapped his uncle on the back with a hearty chuckle. Then he remembered his duty and stepped over to his grandparents and gave each a gentle hug.

Her voice rising, Rhona ran over the happy reunion and felt like slapping someone. "What about Nia and Syn?"

Andy straightened and shrugged. "Mom is coming. She put up such a fuss, they have to wheel her out."

No mention of his sister. Rhona sucked in her breath and held off any judgment until she knew more, but mental alarm bells clanged for attention.

Before new worries could hit the family like a tsunami after an earthquake, the nurse lifted a hand to hold off panic. "Nia can walk; she's just feeling a little weak. Nothing a few days of rest won't mend." Her eyes narrowed at Andy as if considering him with some doubt.

The doctor fixed his gaze on Zhang. "You can follow up with your primary care physician for any further concerns. Let the nurses know if you have any questions." With a goodbye nod, he started down the corridor.

After glancing around, as if waiting for questions but meeting only silent stares, the nurse backed up, ready to leave.

Rhona stepped forward. "Wait! When can we see Syn?" The urgency in her voice made it sound high and scraggly as if she was lunging for a safety buoy.

A pause, a discerning gaze, and the young woman seemed to understand more than if Rhona had revealed dark family secrets. She gestured down the white corridor. "I'll take you. She'll need to stay for another hour, so we know she's safe to release. But you can wait in her room if you like." She glanced at Zhang, asking silently if he wanted to come along, but Syn's father either didn't see or refused to understand.

Rhona didn't know his mind, but she could guess. Her blood boiled.

A strident "Hey, did you all forget about me?" broke the tense moment.

Being steered into the waiting room by a grinning CNA, Nia clutched her purse on her lap as she sat ensconced in the wheelchair the way queens of old might have perched on a throne. Her head up, her chin jutted forward, she swung her gaze over the quiet room. "I really thought someone would come in and help me!"

Zhang sprang forward, an expert at tempering his wife's moods; he reached for her hands and soon crouched at her side. "I wanted to, but they said it was better if I waited out here. And Mama and Papa couldn't go in." His face twisted into a penitential plea for forgiveness, his hands clasping hers over her purse, making for a cinematic event.

Rhona's stomach tightened. She glanced aside at the nurse.

Astonishment filled the pretty face.

Refusing to give in to a head shake, Rhona merely pursed her lips into a hard line. She glanced at Dermid, who had eyes and sense enough to know the truth of the situation.

"I'll stay with Syn, no matter how late." Rhona bit her words off one by one, trying mighty hard to keep her opinion out of her tone. "I'll bring her to my home after she's released if you all want to go now and get some rest. You must be exhausted."

Andy's smile grew wicked. "I'll go home now—so long as Dad drives."

Without actually snarling, Nia whipped her words at her son. “It wasn’t my fault! You knocked my arm!”

“Only because Syn attacked me!”

In his best I-should-have-been-a-wrestling-coach manner, Dermid stepped into the fray. He lifted his hands. “This isn’t the time or place. You’re all worn out and need a good night’s sleep. I already called a tow and the car is at Mike’s Repair Shop. He’ll give you an estimate in the morning.” He bore down on Nia and Zhang. “We’ll take Syn home with us for the night and bring her around sometime tomorrow.”

Her shoulders relaxing, Rhona’s heart swelled as she squeezed her husband’s hand in silent gratitude. *Thank God I married this man.*

Leaving the rest of the family to sort itself out, Rhona and Demid followed the bobbing ponytail down the hallway. They made their way through the labyrinth — around a corner, passed through swinging doors, then turned to the right. Finally, they stepped softly into a dimly lit room.

There, on a steel frame hospital bed, a white gown barely giving her the modesty she never knew, lay a fifteen-year-old girl connected to various tubes, her arm encased in a protective cast. Her thin, pale face, not a hint of her father’s Asian heritage revealing itself, was splotched by bruises.

Even as she registered the oddity, Rhona brushed it aside. She gripped Dermid’s hand tighter, but there was nothing she could do to stop her heart from bleeding all over the gray tile floor.

As he pulled her into a hug, Dermid’s soft breath wafted across her cheek. “Poor Sparrow. I’m afraid she is broken pretty bad.”

A poem Rhona had discovered the same year that Syn was born gave her niece the special moniker,

Sparrow. She couldn't recall the exact words, though the refrain sang in her ears. An image of sparrows fluttering about her garden floated before her wide-awake eyes. The last of the tomatoes, peppers, cilantro, and the spice packets had been left, silent and waiting, on the kitchen table when she and Dermid had raced to the hospital.

Somewhere deep inside, Rhona knew that it would take many seasons and a whole series of gardens, but healing would come. With a dirt-stained hand, she patted her husband's arm. "Someday, Sparrow will fly again."

Mid-September

In the early morning mist, Rhona surveyed her dead garden with satisfaction. Weeds had sprung up faster than she could pull them from the hard-baked ground, but now, they were yellow and limp. All bold proclamations of taking over were as crumpled as the cucumber vines. Her basement freezer was stuffed full of summer produce: frozen bags of asparagus, zucchini, cherry tomatoes, green and yellow peppers. Containers of salsa were stacked on the right side, while home-grown spice packets made a mound on the left, ready for whatever winter soups and stews she had in mind to invent.

In a cardigan sweater she knew she would pull off in a few minutes, leaving her in a short-sleeved shirt, work jeans, and a heavy pair of clogs, she tugged on her thick gardening gloves, ready for a serious autumn clean-up.

In the north part of the garden, the St. Francis birdbath was overgrown with pumpkin vines, all tough brown ropes leading nowhere. Not a decent pumpkin in sight. She scowled at St. Francis. *What, you gave them to the blackbirds?*

With a harumph, she glanced to the east field where she had set out birdhouse gourd vines in May. They had done a mighty fine job of spreading over the area she had fenced off from Dermid's weekly mowing madness. The image of placing Syn at the kitchen table with an array of gourds and boxes of colorful paints sparked her imagination. *Surely, her dad will let her come back by then. I'll even join her, and we'll have a contest! I'll tell Derm that first place wins an apple pie.* She could hear her husband's grumbled response even as his shoulders squared to the challenge. Her heart warmed, and she tossed aside the sweater despite a lingering chill in the air. An image of Syn's wan face, as she climbed the steps to her room after being dropped off at home two weeks ago, drove a sigh from her middle into the chilly air. *I wish Nia weren't so self-absorbed and Zhang so dang proud!*

Wading into the middle of the weedy jungle, Rhona attacked with merciless alacrity. Brown weeds, yellowed vines, and crumbly leaves flew through the air and landed in sprawled defeat on the brown lawn. The decrepit wooden swing sat rather than hung under the ancient grape arbor in foreboding silence. *Stop fretting; I'm not about to throw you out. Too big, for one thing. Too picturesque for another.* The high-pitched voice of Oldtown's busiest woman, Ada Alden, spiked through her mind. *Oh, Rhona, you've got to refurbish that thing! You'll get splinters if you don't. I know just the man to help you. He's done all my lawn furniture. Not terribly expensive. Though I always say, you get what you pay for.*

Rhona closed her eyes and tried to shake off disconcerting memories.

A school bus rumbled down the lane. She lifted her head and waved with a fist full of weeds. She couldn't see the kids, but she could imagine their mournful faces. It hadn't been like that when she was a kid. She squinted at the bright sun as sweat began to trickle down her back. *Or had it?*

Memories of hiding in the shadows of the playground when she was a skinny little girl slowed her fingers. She was never much of a talker, and the other kids always seemed to associate silence with stupidity. Funny, but she had always maintained the opposite position. Big talkers tended to expose their ignorance at alarming rates.

Once again, Syn's pale face sprang before her eyes. She had been a talker. Even as a baby, she chattered on for hours. Nonsense, mostly, but funny nonsense. A pity that her mom never saw it that way. Always told her to shush up and go play in another room. The irony that Syn's jabbering perfectly imitated her mother's example should have made Rhona laugh, but it was too sad.

The bus rumbled by again, its load increased by the twin teens who lived down the lane. Rhona waved again, though she figured they were all on their phones and wouldn't be caught dead waving to a middle-aged woman half-buried in weeds.

At least Syn won't be taking a bus anytime soon. She's still too weak to go to school. Surely, Zhang will let her stay home a bit longer. After all, his parents were living with them, helping Nia with housework and meals. Rhona snorted. Nia's clubs, shopping sprees, hair appointments, girls' nights out, and all the rest kept her sister quite busy.

Taking her annoyance out on the dead tomato vines, Rhona ripped their shallow roots from the dusty ground and sent them flying.

Loud squawking broke her concentration, and she straightened up on her knees, surveying the garden and then peering beyond, into the wood line.

There! The fluffy white cat Dermid had the temerity to name Prissy held her latest squirming victim. *Dang blast that cat!* Rhona leaped to her feet and sprang across the dead lawn. Before Prissy knew what was happening, Rhona had her work mitts on the animal's back and opened its jaws just enough to free the poor bird. A sparrow. Of course.

"You always pick on the weak ones, don't you?"

Prissy glowered at her with unrepentant displeasure.

The limp little bird didn't open its eyes, but its rapid heartbeat told her that it still had some life in it. Rhona glared back at the cat. "Oh, don't you get an attitude with me, you villain! Don't I feed you and your brothers and sisters—why, your whole cat clan—enough kibble to keep Feline Royalty happy? Who the heck plays all the bills around here? It isn't you, that's for sure!" Fully conscious of the fact that she was arguing with a quadruped, Rhona sucked in a deep breath and tried to regain some semblance of personal dignity.

Suddenly a strident voice rose and jerked Rhona to her feet. She pressed the little bird to her chest protectively.

One hand flapping and heaving deep breaths as if she had just run the Chicago Marathon rather than ambling across a rock driveway onto a level lawn, Nia, dressed in a cerulean blue sweater and tight black jeans, repudiating the silly notion that she was, in fact, middle-aged, called out, "Hey, Sis, you've got to help me!"

Rhona gave into an eye-roll, well aware that Nia wouldn't even notice. She waited, one finger gently caressing the little bird's head.

Like a ship coasting into harbor after being tossed about by storms, Nia flopped to a halt in front of Rhona. She pressed her hand to her chest, her ragged breaths making the world aware that she was a desperate woman on the brink of despair. "You've got to talk some sense into Syn!"

So many stinging responses crowded Rhona's mind that her tongue became tangled, and she couldn't speak.

Never able to read body language and forever taking silence as agreement, Nia launched into her this-is-what-I-would-say-in-front-of-a jury argument. "She's always been an unreasonable kid; you know that. Zhang can't handle her anymore. Andy thinks she's a brat, and he's too wrapped up in college life to care about anything else. But I just can't have her hanging around the house one more day. I told her she could have a week to recover from the accident. Which was all her fault, by the way, in case you didn't know."

A pregnant pause while Rhona just stared.

Nia hurried on. "Heck, she won't even talk to me. Won't work. Won't go out. Just sits in her room and mopes." She lifted her hands in surrender. "It's been two weeks! I'm done! I can't do anymore."

Another dramatic pause, as Nia's gaze searched for a hint of agreement.

Rhona refused to give in to pressure. Her thoughts were her own, and she wasn't about to share them. Not yet.

"Anyway, she says she's not going back to school. But she has to! She's only a sophomore, unskilled, and pretty much untrainable. She can't waste her life doing nothing."

"You're worried about her welfare?" Rhona tried to keep the sarcasm out of her voice, but she feared it might have slipped through a crack.

"She is my daughter!" A smile that resembled a dagger reshaped her face. "You don't have kids, so you can't understand, but I always thought you took your aunt role seriously. This girl is major drama, and I can't manage her right now." Pouty lips took their place on stage. "I'm trying to heal. PTSD is no joke. Nightmares every night. I still can't drive. Zhang's dad has to take me to my appointments."

With a quake of realization, Rhona knew that the bird's tiny heart had stopped beating. She lifted the fragile body from her chest, dread galloping over her. It had fallen limp; its small head lolled to the side; eyes closed forever. She whispered, "Oh, hell."

Nia squinted and leaned in, peering at the tiny corpse. Then, her nose wrinkled. "What are you doing with a dead bird?"

The fury of God rose inside Rhona, and she wanted to battle the forces of insensitivity that killed innocent birds and hurt young girls. Cupping the little bird to her breast, Rhona spoke with all the forcefulness of being an older and wiser sister who wouldn't take no for an answer. "Syn will come and live with me and Dermid for the term. We'll arrange online schooling so she doesn't get behind in her studies and take her to all her appointments."

The shadow of sly satisfaction that flittered behind Nia's eyes spoke of a hope that had panned out well.

Rhona didn't care. Nia and Zhang and Andy would take care of themselves. For some reason she could not understand, they didn't like Syn. Granted, the girl had gone through every teen stage in the book, even deciding to wear nothing but black and eating carrots for breakfast, lunch, and dinner, but her heart was sound. At least it had been. Before the accident. Now? Who knew? One finger caressing the soft feathers that would never fly again, Rhona stared her sister into submission. Not that it was much of a battle.

Though she normally liked to argue, Nia gave in quickly, undoubtedly afraid that Rhona might change her mind. "Well, that could work. I'll miss my little girl, but I have to think about what is best for her. I'm just not made for confrontations. She stares at me as if I'm some kind of monster."

Rhona could only imagine. She feared the truth of the matter. But as Nia's shoulders relaxed and she exhaled a long-relieved breath, Rhona admitted that her sister had no idea how to parent a child. Especially not a sensitive girl like Syn. Perhaps she wasn't made that way. Rhona wouldn't judge what she couldn't understand. With a gentle shoulder pat, she sent her sister on her way. "Have someone drive Syn over this afternoon, and I'll get the guest room made up for her. Derm does all his teaching online, so he'll figure out some way of setting her up with her classes."

Unexpectedly, Nia threw her arms around her sister and hugged her tight. Her words brushed Rhona's ears in a hot blast. "You are the best!"

Rhona pulled away, conscious that if the little bird hadn't been dead before, it would be now. "I don't know about that, but you know Derm and I will do what we can. We love that little girl."

With happy nods, Nia's whole face glowed. "I know you do." A ding sounded, and she pulled her phone from a back pocket. Her head bent, she scrolled through, her glorious red braid dangling across her shoulder.

A burst of poignant love flowed over Rhona. Nia was her little sister. Seven years her junior and the twinkling star in their late father's eyes, her natural beauty and personal charm worked magic on everyone around her. Most of the time. Until it wore thin. Rhona had always wished Nia well, even when she didn't deserve it.

By the time Nia had sped off in her newest Land Rover, waving as she went, Rhona had decided where she would bury the little bird. She grabbed a shovel from the shed, traipsed across the yard to an old apple tree by the stream that meandered through their property, and dug a small hole in the soft earth. She murmured her prayer on the edge of the quiet woodlands. "God, You know when any creature falls, so I'm sure you're as grieved as I am by this little one's early demise. But if there's a sparrow I can save, I will do my best."

She laid the little bird in its earthy nest and covered it gently with the soft blanket of soil. Then she went to make the guest bedroom as pretty as she might.

Rhona knew her husband was a good teacher, not because all his students passed their classes the first time around—they didn't—but because, despite past failures and frustrations, they always came back to him. And eventually, most of them did pass their classes.

He had taught in a local private school for over twenty-five years before a heart attack laid him low. Depression followed until he discovered that he could adapt his teaching skills to the online world. But it wasn't his teaching that made the difference in his students' lives; it was his personality. Calm and always composed. A man who clasped Scottish reserve to his bosom and kept it handy at all times.

He had only one serious fault: he hated being told what to do. It took a few years into their friendship, which eventually evolved into marriage, for Rhona to realize that a request would always be met with tight-lipped silence. With what her mother used to refer to as her "uncanny wisdom," she stopped asking for things and watched closely to figure the man out.

When a difficult situation arose, Dermid waited for an opportune moment and then solved the problem in his own way. If people had sense enough to leave him alone. Rhona eventually learned to state an unmanageable situation outright, not asking or cajoling, and let God and the force for good that rested deep in Dermid's heart handle it.

Once his students became accustomed to his style, they adored him. He never told them what to do. He simply showed them the material, outlined the steps to solve math problems, the proper procedure for chemistry experiments, and the kinds of questions to be expected on a test. He never told anyone to study. He never assigned homework. If a student did nothing, he gave them the appropriate grade and moved on.

When students did ask him for help, he asked what they meant, repeatedly, until they finally explained what they did not understand. Then he sent detailed, even color-coded, instructions for each step. But he never told them to do it. He never asked for anything.

When Rhona told Derm about Syn coming to stay with them, with the understanding that Derm would help her with her school work, she knew with perfect clarity that she'd have to tread carefully and let nature take its course.

Syn, with her right arm in a hard-shelled cast, hobbling like an old woman, her eyes perpetually unfocused, was dropped off by her dad at their ranch house two miles outside town. With grim determination, she climbed gingerly up the porch steps, nodded a silent hello, then ambled awkwardly to the guest room, and flopped down on the bed.

Zhang waved from the car and sped off, dirt flying from under his wheels.

Taking a cue from her husband, Rhona let the girl settle in without undue commentary or direction. At dinner time that first night, she set a crockpot of beef stew chock-full of fresh zucchini, green beans, and onions on the table, and let Syn know it was there, but she made no demands for her to attend.

Syn didn't.

Rhona and Derm ate the stew, shared a small loaf of sourdough bread, and chatted in their usual way, discussing local news, the weather, and the possibility of aliens landing on Earth within the next year. Derm insisted that invaders were on their way, eager to discover the secret to breeding hairless, miniature dogs, while Rhona held the position that aliens had taken over the world in the mid-sixties, but humanity had been too dense to notice.

After dinner, they cleaned up, went to bed, and slept like logs.

The next morning, Rhona did her usual outdoor chores at the break of dawn. She fed their sedate collie dog, Nes, their whiny assembly of cats, and filled bird feeders all over the backyard before they got to scolding her.

Then she returned inside, enjoyed a simple breakfast of cereal, fruit, and a bracing cup of hot coffee. To keep her immune system in a happy state, she also drank a large glass of orange juice.

Derm stumped into the kitchen, slapped together a peanut butter & jelly sandwich, poured a cup of coffee and then a glass of milk, set everything on a tray, and retreated to his den.

Rhona knocked on Syn's door, told her that breakfast was available, arranged a plate and glass, and left the bread, peanut butter, jam, cereal, milk, and juice on the table for an hour.

Syn slept till after ten, but when she arrived in the kitchen and there was nothing on the table but a ceramic pumpkin and a vase of autumn leaves, she returned to her room. She didn't say anything. Neither did Rhona. Derm didn't traditionally start speaking until after noon.

Since it wasn't cold enough to start up the wood stove, Rhona contented her outdoor-loving spirit with an hour of piling sticks in strategic, sheltered places, so as to be ready when it came to lighting fires in the woodstove on cold days. Then she hurried back inside, started up her computer, and did her formal work for the day. As a consultant, editor, and proofreader for a large multinational textbook company, she earned a decent paycheck. Though there were days when she wondered if it was worth her sanity.

By lunchtime, Rhona was hungry enough to fix grilled cheese sandwiches and tomato soup.

Slump-shouldered, Syn meandered in and slid onto the bench, hardly glancing up.

Derm came out of his den, his morning classes completed, and smiled with a mischievous twinkle in his eyes. "Tavish is bringing a load of straw over to the churchyard for their fall festival."

Syn's head snapped up; her gaze fastened on her uncle.

Rhona didn't need to ask if Derm's brother wanted help. He'd never ask. But Dermid would drive five miles to his brother's humongous farm, and together they would load the Ford truck and trailer with bales of hay, mumble a few words back and forth that no one else in the universe could possibly understand, rumble off to the churchyard, nod respectfully to Father Sawney, who would wave a shaky hand toward the back field, where the brothers would unload the bales, arrange them artistically for the pumpkins that would arrive the next day, then nod in farewell to the aged priest, who would wave them on as if they were twelve. Finally, they'd drive home in silence, too tired and thoughtful to waste their energy in useless conversation.

Rhona considered the girl with the dingy yellow cast on her right arm and a hopeful spark in her eye, then cast a meditative eye over her husband. "After you both eat lunch, you can take two jars of salsa along, one for Tavish, the other for Father Sawney."

The grilled cheese and tomato soup were consumed within minutes. After Rhona washed up the meager dishes, the drying towel limp in her hand, she peeked out the window. Derm's truck maneuvered around the circular drive. Then he rumbled off toward his brother's place. Syn's head silhouetted in the passenger seat appeared so small and frail; Rhona's heart ached with the memory of a little bird pressed against her chest.

That night, dinner was well attended.

As she sat at the foot of the rectangular wooden table, Rhona studied Syn's cast. "It looks no worse for wear. I thought for sure you'd scuff it up trying to help with the hay bales."

Syn and Dermid shared an eye roll. Then Rhona's husband kindly informed her. "Our Sparrow here is left-handed. And strong as an ox."

Accepting the confused imagery without blinking, Rhona moved on to the next important family consideration. She offered Syn a deadpanned stare while leaning back on her chair, cupping a mug of hot cider in her hands. "What's your opinion on aliens?"

Syn said she didn't believe in extraterrestrials. She said they were as true as Santa Claus.

A gleam entered Derm's eyes that Rhona had never seen before, but she knew better than to ask. They'd both find out when he was good and ready.

Late September

The last Friday morning of the month, after Syn had settled into an online school routine, pounding on the kitchen door disturbed Rhona from her morning editing. Knowing that Derm would probably wait until the stranger returned enough times to eventually—by sheer statistical probability—bump into him when he went outside, she hurried to the screen door.

Out of the corner of her eyes, she could see the desk, chair, computer, and shelving unit that had been arranged in the living room for Syn's daily school work, which the girl used faithfully. Still, she had a habit of sidling into the kitchen and leaning on the doorframe whenever anyone happened to stop by. *She's undoubtedly inching her way over now.*

Plastering her pleasantest face in place, Rhona shoved distracting thoughts away and pulled open the door.

A five-foot-nine, heavy-set woman wearing an eye-smacking sweater over bright orange pants towered on the porch with a box clutched in her hands.

Rhona's artistic sensibilities cringed. *Ada does so love dramatic color combinations.*

Shoving unworthy thoughts into the I'll-have-something-to-say-at-my-next-Confession box, Rhona shored up her wavering smile and tried to think up a suitable invite that wouldn't involve an actual conversation, taking up her precious work time. "Hello, stranger, what brings you out on this beautiful autumn morning?"

Unexpectedly, the box began to whine mournfully.

In a matter of seconds, Rhona lost control of the situation.

Syn sped into the room, the box was set on the floor, a puppy tumbled out, and everyone was flapping their hands.

Rhona stared in amazement. Despite the broken arm, the girl could somehow manage to wriggle and hand flap with all the excitement of a child on Christmas morning. The irony that she had started flapping her own hands wasn't lost on Rhona.

The darn puppy was cute.

Joy beamed from Ada's face as she flopped down on the bench at the kitchen table, her eyes glued to Syn, who sat cross-legged on the floor with the puppy squirming in her lap, its tail going into warp drive. "I was afraid she'd hate dogs or something. You never know with kids these days. But my heart told me to try." Finally, she remembered that Rhona owned the house, paid the taxes, and might like to have something to say about another dog on the property. "I hope you don't mind. But Mrs. Sorcha's dog was unexpectedly found to be in the family way and had seven puppies. You know, she's a nice woman and all, but the least thing rattles her. And puppies in the house were enough to send her to the doctor for a sedative!"

Rhona let Ada go on about all the amazing tribulations of finding homes for God's innocent little creatures and how her heart nearly broke at the idea that someone might not treat them right. "I just knew that you and Derm would open your hearts to a homeless wayfarer." She glanced at Syn.

Praying that Syn had not taken the comment personally, Rhona jumped into the abyss and hoped that Dermid would forgive her. "It was a thoughtful act, Ada, and we'll be happy to keep her…or him…" And so, her morning's work shoved aside, Rhona bid a kind farewell to her do-good friend and then conspired with her niece to arrange a doghouse, food bowl, and all the necessities of life for the puppy before Nes, the collie, discovered the intruder and had a tantrum.

The fact that the month had started with simple visions of making a final batch of salsa and putting the garden to bed and had ended with two new additions to the family didn't disturb Rhona's equilibrium as much as she might have thought it would. Had she had a hint of what life-altering events were barreling forward, she probably wouldn't have slept the whole month.

But as the details unfolded in digestible stages, she discovered that the grace to accept a new vision wasn't so hard.

She only hoped that Derm wouldn't invite aliens over to discuss the merits of stray puppies.

Chapter Two

Rhona Reconciles Her Husband to Being a Hero and How Costumes Can Free Creative Spirits

Early October

Trees like to dress well for autumn. Even Ada's eye-catching color combinations couldn't match the glory of maples in their full array. Rhona sat on a rocking chair on her back porch, wrapped in a long, gray shawl that Dermid had given her on their twenty-fifth anniversary, during his rehabilitation after his heart attack. *Was that only five years ago?* He had told her that whenever she wore it, she should imagine his arms wrapped around her, keeping her safe and warm.

She had appreciated his words when he said them, as she appreciated them now, but she never liked to think of a time when he wasn't around to hug her himself. They had married later than most couples in their social circle; certainly, they were older than their parents hoped they'd be when they finally tied the knot.

But getting to know each other had been a long process that neither had wanted to hurry along. Both were reticent people who had overcome childhood challenges—Derm's brother had inherited the family farm, leaving Derm to find his own livelihood, while Rhona knew to the core of her being that her manic-depressive dad thought the world of her sister, while her mom liked to escape into a demanding work schedule that would have killed the average person—neither Dermid nor Rhona wanted to rush into a lifelong mistake. Both had escaped the travails of childhood relatively unscathed, but each was aware that most everyone had troubles to sort through in life.

As a Monarch butterfly wafted across the sunlit yard, Rhona marveled at nature's audacity. How could such a frail critter make its way from Illinois to Mexico over generations, covering thousands of miles? How did they know where to go? Did second and third-generation Monarchs have an inbred map, allowing them to continue the journey from wherever their parents had left off?

A mystery, to be sure.

Her gaze roamed over the bare fields, no less amazed by the human ingenuity needed to grow uncountable acres of crops and harvest enough food to feed a hungry world. Still marveling, she barely turned her head when her husband appeared at the bottom of the porch steps, appearing as glum as she had ever seen him. Her attention caught, she scowled. "What on Earth is wrong with you on this fine day?"

Dermid clumped up the steps, leaned on the railing, folded his thick arms over his chest, and swore, "A damned saint got me into trouble."

Rhona pondered this for a good moment before she returned fire. "That's highly unlikely."

As Dermid uncrossed his arms, a smile ghosted over his face. "Braden signed me up as Restful Glen's board president. He actually used Old Abe's wall mural on the Savings & Loan to set me up as a presidential hero. Can you imagine that? It was all Ada's brainstorm of an idea."

Picturing the peaceful cemetery, which resided on the east edge of Oldtown, Rhona considered what being president of a cemetery might entail. The idea of Dermid taking meeting notes was too absurd to entertain. Perplexed, she squinted as the morning sun peeked from behind her husband's broad back. "What will you do, exactly?"

"I'm supposed to run the meetings, suggest improvements, and be the caring face people come to when they want to bury a loved one or find the final resting place of a long-lost relative." He crossed his arms again. "I really need to unfriend Braden."

Spluttering, Rhona couldn't stop the laughter that bubbled up from her middle. Dermid's use of modern media terms was always a source of innocent amusement. She managed her online channels like a spy in hostile territory: confirming current relationship statuses, discovering unexpected road blockages, ascertaining public feuds, and generally determining the best way to sidestep emotional landmines.

Once she had friended Ada Alden, wife of Braden Alden, the manager of the largest grain-bin operation in the county, Rhona never had to add anyone. Practically the whole town added her within the week. The platform took on a life of its own. She would no more unfriend someone than shoot them in the middle of Main Street. She finally calmed enough to straighten her face and speak coherently. "Braden is your oldest friend in the world. And you have never spent a second of your life on social media."

His eyelids lowering to half-mast, Dermid sniffed his opinion. "Someone in this town will die, and their loved ones will ask me to find the right gravesite. I know where my relatives are buried, but I don't know about everyone else! And can you honestly say that this face is going to comfort anyone?" He waved in the vicinity of his nose.

Rhona scratched her chin. Something Ada had told her in one of their many conversations, herself only half-listening, tickled the back of her mind. Then the synapses sizzled in a connection, and she grinned. "It's all online."

Dermid glowered at a black cat that had decided this was a good moment to twine itself between his legs. "What's online?"

"Restful Glen. It was another of Ada's brainstorms. She got the whole cemetery mapped out on an online program: Find Lost Loved Ones. Or something like that." Another Monarch wafted by, and Rhona's gaze followed its undulating flight. "I'm sure that Ada can give you all the information, and you can log in and do pretty much all your work from there."

As the butterfly crossed Dermid's line of vision, his eyes started tracking its path. He tilted his head, his mind clearly appraising a new world of options. But then he sighed and fixed his sad eyes on his wife. "But what about being the caring face of Restful Glen?"

The Monarch fluttered around the corner of the house and disappeared from view. *Good luck, beautiful friend.* She studied her husband. "It's your kind, heroic heart they'll see; your face won't matter in the least."

Derm stepped closer, reached down, and hugged his wife, shawl and all.

She whispered through a smile. "I believe an apple pie might be a hero's reward."

Derm chuckled. "You're *my* hero."

Rhona laughed.

The first Sunday evening of the month, Rhona stopped by Syn's room and knocked on the half-open door. She peeked in.

Syn sat on her bed, slumped over a thick book. The cover was dark with a drawing of bare, black branches reaching like gnarly hands toward a shadowed moon.

A shiver ran down Rhona's back, but she readjusted herself and lifted her voice to the peak of cheerfulness. "The last of the fireflies and dragonflies are darting about in the yard. Derm and I are going to say our seasonal goodbye. You can come."

As if she had not moved in a month and needed to practice the art of locomotion, Syn let the book fall closed and slide off her lap, then she stretched every limb in her body that would straighten, and finally, with a ginormous yawn, she rose to her feet.

Rhona could hear the girl's steps padding behind her as she made her way down the hall to the kitchen porch and then around to the back lawn.

Derm sat perched on a tree stump that he had carved into a round seat with a short back. A pile of old paper, sticks, and branches in teepee formation filled the fire pit, with river rocks making an artistic border.

Three rough log chairs encircled the pit.

Rhona found a seat on Dermid's left, while Nes, the collie dog, staked her claim on his right.

The new puppy scampered excitedly in the back pen, where it had plenty of room but yipped in a demanding plea to be where the action was.

Before Syn could take a seat, Derm looked from Syn to the pen and lifted his eyebrows. No words were necessary.

With a huff, her shoulders sagging in typical teen style, Syn clumped to the pen. "Here ya go, silly dog. Now be good, Wilma." She unlatched the gate and opened it wide.

As soon as the pup saw the light of freedom, it streaked across the yard and barreled right into Nes.

"Wilma!" Syn chided.

Nes wasn't so nice. She rounded on the puppy, growling ferociously. She practically nipped off its little nose.

Panic in her eyes, Syn screamed.

Dermid leaped forward and grabbed Nes by the collar.

Rhona almost beat Syn to the frightened puppy, but when she saw the girl's terrified expression, she backed off, wondering who needed saving more.

Little Wilma shivered in puppy fright but soon comforted itself by wiggling into Syn's arms and then curling into a ball, making itself quite comfortable.

Derm had a little chat with Nes and then directed her to the front porch.

Nes glowered with revenge at the puppy and stalked off like a wronged woman.

With a sigh, Derm pulled out a box of matches and started to light the assembled kindling. "Might as well enjoy this beautiful evening." He eyed the yard. Not a firefly or dragonfly in sight. He shrugged off the disappointing fact. "Once autumn gets going, it'll be too dark and cold to stay out after dinner."

A choke and a sniff met this comment without explanation.

Rhona glanced from her placid husband to her distressed niece.

Tears spilled down Syn's cheeks.

Oh, dear. Her heart aching, Rhona reached over and patted her niece's shoulder. "Don't worry. Nes and Wilma will make friends. Sometimes it takes a while."

Syn's voice wobbled. "Nes hates her, and Wilma will never fit in."

Her mouth opening with a response she knew would start with a platitude, Rhona felt relief at the sight of Braden strolling into the yard. She hadn't heard his truck rumble into the driveway, but the dogs' quarrel and Syn's scream had probably deafened her to anything less than a blast of dynamite.

Derm climbed to his feet and then dragged over another stump, a half-finished chair he had been working on since spring and kept meaning to finish. He pointed his friend to the finished chair he had been sitting in with a welcoming smile.

Braden waved as was his style, the kind of motion that said, "Don't make a fuss; I can't stay, just came by to tell you something important."

Rhona darted a glance at Syn to see if her tears were still rolling. They weren't. The girl had brushed them aside with her sleeve and sat hunched over the puppy, hiding her face from view. Relieved that she wouldn't have to bridge the gap between Braden's news and her niece's meltdown, Rhona focused on matters at hand. "It's good to see you, Braden."

Gripping the back of the stump chair, Braden leaned forward and zeroed in on Dermid. "There's been a death. Hector Bean's sister's husband, who took that job in the city…well, poor man, he won't be making it to work tomorrow. Aneurysm! You ever heard the like? Young guy, only in his forties, and bam! Dropped dead in his yard at noon today. So, of course, the funeral home contacted Ada, and she told

Elspeth, and they're getting all the paperwork in order for state records, you know. But she'll need you to show the gravedigger where to dig. He'll be at Restful Glen early tomorrow. You got the map Ada gave you, so you can meet him and make sure everything is set for the burial. It's supposed to be Friday, if nothing gets tangled up."

If Dermid's jaw dropped any further, he'd have to wash dirt off his chin before bed.

Rhona glanced at Syn, hoping that she wasn't being traumatized by the news of a sudden death.

Unexpectedly, the girl's eyes were as wide as saucers, an eager gleam in them, as if she wanted more terrible news to feed a nefarious spirit.

Rhona's throat tightened. "Uh, I think, maybe, we should—"

Braden wasn't done. He straightened, shifted his stance, and suddenly altered the flow of conversation. "But that's not the only reason I came over." His gaze turned to Rhona. "Ada has had another brainstorm. A doozie this time!"

Derm picked up his jaw from the ground and clamped it shut. Rhona suspected that he might never speak again.

Syn's eyes narrowed in suspicion.

After sucking in a cleansing breath, Braden straightened and poured out his latest dispatch. "You know how St. Andrew's has their Autumn Festival? Well, Ada thought that it might be fun to have our own. So, she's working with the Quilt & Sew Shop to sponsor a costume party and parade for the end of October. Think how much fun that'll be!" He swung his attention to Syn. "You can design any outlandish costume you can think up, and the ladies at the shop will help you make it. Those two sisters love to have fun." Braden's eyes gleamed with what some might call maniacal joy.

How that man loves his wife's wild ideas. Though Rhona had to admit, it wasn't so wild and might actually be entertaining. She slid her gaze to her niece.

Joy beamed from the red-rimmed eyes.

Rhona's heart did a series of somersaults. There was more going on inside the child than she understood, yet if the idea of a costume party made her happy, then she'd do whatever she could to keep that spark alive. She leaned in toward Syn and patted her good arm. "I'll take you over there next week, and we'll talk it over with Lucia and Maisie." The image of what Syn would make of the polar opposite sisters brightened her mood. *We can all use a little fun.*

His announcements made, Braden offered a farewell salute and ambled back to his truck.

The fire had dwindled as a chilly wind rose.

With a shake of his head, Dermid stepped over to his niece. He crouched at her side and gently scooped the sleeping puppy into his arms. "I'll have a couple of training sessions with Nes so she understands her role as big sister better."

Syn let the puppy slip from her grasp in a manner eerily similar to the way she had let the book fall onto the bed.

Rhona watched her dear husband traipse across the yard toward the little doghouse in the secure pen, cradling the pup in his arms. Then she rose and clasped Syn's left hand, gently pulling the girl to her feet. "The fireflies and dragonflies are gone for the season. We wish them well. Now it's time for us to go in and get ready for bed. Tomorrow is another day."

Though Syn didn't argue and followed along at a sedate pace, Rhona knew that her words meant something quite different in her niece's head, and a shiver worked over her.

Mid-October

Rhona tugged the zipper up her heavy plaid jacket and pulled the hood over her head to keep the wind out of her ears. Nes jogged at her heels with the labrador pup darting from trees to bushes, attacking colorful leaves as they fell. With enough time and experience, Nes and Wilma discovered that they had a few important qualities in common. They both liked to jump into the air, zoom like crazy things all over the yard, and chew anything that even remotely looked like a bone. With these instinctual forces uniting them, and the fact that Dermid and Rhona gave them treats each day they played peaceably together, they joined Rhona and Syn on a Saturday afternoon sojourn through the woods.

Fresh memories flittered through Rhona's mind as she stumped along, brushing aside spider webs that threatened to entangle her. Their glistening threads danced charmingly in the golden light, while tiny, dangling corpses warned of doom to the unwary.

That morning, Dermid had finally gotten around to stacking a pile of chopped wood in the shed. Rhona decided to do her duty and started stuffing fresh hay into the dog houses, when suddenly, her husband began to dance, yelling loud enough to pique the interest of the next county.

Syn had been sitting quietly on the porch steps, studying her hands, when Dermid's racket caught her attention. She glanced up and, before Rhona could make sense of the situation, the child had ascertained the threat and taken action. She raced inside, grabbed a can of repellent, rushed out, took dead aim at the stinging beasties, and then drenched the hornets' nest hanging from the shed ceiling. Without hesitation, and while Rhona's heart practically burst out of her chest, Syn then grabbed a stick, swapped down the bubbling mess, and began to stomp on it with all her might.

Dermid stood aside, rubbing his arm where red blisters were rising, and stared in dumb amazement. It was only when the girl wouldn't quit stomping that he decided to take action. He called out, "Stop!" in the voice he used when the dogs rushed the mailman.

Uncertain as to who to attend to first, Rhona stood rooted in place.

Syn did as Dermid ordered and came to a complete halt, but her face made it clear that she wanted to stomp on every stinging insect in the universe. Laudable as her defense of her uncle had been, something about her reaction set off alarm bells in Rhona's mind. She stared at Dermid and tried to express her growing fear as puzzlement.

Dermid knew her too well. He started for the house. "I'm going to put something on these stings, and then I'll finish stacking the wood." He glanced over his shoulder, his eyes full of meaning. "It's a mighty fine day for a walk. The table could use some more fall decorations."

After tugging on jackets and plucking a cloth bag from the hook in the hall closet, Rhona suppressed a sigh and led Syn and the dogs into the woods. Only the dogs' excited yipping and the birds' exuberant chirping broke the silence for nearly half an hour.

Rhona kept her gaze fixed on the uneven ground as she tried to keep from tripping over tangled vines. "You know, when I get angry, I have to clean house. I mean deep clean—drawers, closets, cabinets, windows, screens, ovens, refrigerators, the inside of the wood stove, you name it; I'll clean it. When I'm peeved, I toss things out I may have been hemming and hawing about all year, stuff I didn't need but got all sentimental about." She rubbed her cold nose. "Anger really knocks the stuffing outta sentimentality."

Syn wasn't volunteering any opinions on the merits of house cleaning. Or anger.

At the sight of a fallen matriarchal tree, Rhona called for a breather and decided that the direct path would probably be the best one. She settled herself, half sitting, half leaning on the old broken trunk.

Syn hovered in the vicinity while the dogs raced around like they had never seen foliage before.

"What makes you angry, Syn?"

Her gray jacket hanging on her like a cloak on a scarecrow, Syn merely shrugged.

Rhona held firm and wouldn't answer the question for her.

An anthill took the brunt of Syn's feelings, and she began to talk. "I don't belong. No one wants me. Andy calls me—"

Rhona's phone buzzed. Exasperated, she shoved her hand into her coat pocket and tried to quiet it by squeezing the case. It sounded like angry bees under a blanket.

Syn gave one last kick to the anthill and marched away.

The moment broken and the phone silent now, Rhona wasn't sure how to work her way back to that sacred opportunity. She looked up through the light filtering through the golden canopy and begged for the proper words. *I don't want to do more harm than good here.* As if her editorial brain jumped into overdrive, succinct words flew from her heart to her mouth. "Please, tell me what's wrong, honey."

Syn's arms crossed, she leaned on the trunk and stared into the deep woods as slanted light sprinkled over leaf and bough, making everything appear magical. "I'm not who you think I am. I don't *know* who I am."

Not certain if this was a metaphorical discussion diving into deep philosophical territory, in which she was over her head at the first step, or if there was some hidden facet in Syn's relationship with her family that she didn't know, Rhona sucked in a bracing breath. "Can you tell me more?" Vexingly, her phone buzzed again. She yanked it out, ready to smack the caller at the first opportunity, but then thought of Dermid and all those stings. *Oh, Lord, what if he's had another...* She hit the green button without even registering the caller's name. "Hello?"

Ada's voice rose in near hysteria. "Rhona? Finally! I'm at my wit's end. We're having the bake sale this evening after Mass, and my volunteers can't make it. I'm supposed to be helping Braden at the Farmers' Extravaganza tonight, so I need someone to fill in. I know you usually go to the early Sunday Mass, but can you please, pretty please, go this afternoon and manage things at the table? It means so much to the whole community. You know, we've been falling short on our collections for the last two years, and our roof leaks like a sieve."

Slapping her forehead as the option of bi-location fizzled in her mind, Rhona nodded absently. She glanced at Syn, a corner of her mind praying that this wasn't another wall blocking honest communication but a bend that would lead to light down the road. She scraped her voice off the ground and assured her friend that she'd be there extra early and smile at everyone.

"You're a saint, Rhona. An absolute saint. God will reward your kindness."

Rhona grimaced at the greater likelihood that her thoughts would get her into the long-term rehab center in Purgatory. Once she pocketed her phone, Rhona turned and started homeward, whistling for the dogs and beckoning Syn with her arm. "I have to go to church and help sell baked goods. We better hurry if we're going to get there in time to arrange the table and stuff."

Syn balked; her chin tucked into her neckline. "I never go to church. Mom says she doesn't need God to be good, and Dad says it's the opiate of the masses."

Rhona spun on her heel, too exasperated to watch her words. "What do you think, Sparrow? Look around you, at all this natural wonder and living glory, and tell me what you make of it all."

Her back straight and eyes alight with a new fire, Syn smacked her hands together. "Why do you call me that? Sparrow! A weak little bird that dies at the least little thing." Her face tightened into a hard scowl. "I don't see what nature has to do with church or God for that matter."

Her stomach in a tight knot, Rhona knew she had blasted far and wide. She closed her eyes to find a calm space within herself. At the sound of shuffling footsteps and the dogs' distant barking, she opened them to see her niece tromping ahead. She scurried after her. "I call you Sparrow not because you're weak but because you're a survivor. Sparrows are one of the most adaptable creatures on the planet. Even in the coldest winters, sparrows find a way to endure." She stuffed her cold hands into her pockets. "I see God in every wonderful thing around me. I'm not telling you to believe like me. I'm just saying that you don't have to disbelieve like your parents. You can choose."

Syn paced ahead at a steady rate; her gaze fixed on the ground.

Oh, what the heck, in for a penny, in for a pound. "I could really use your help this evening at Mass. You don't have to sit in a pew and listen or anything. But part of Mass attendance is being with God, and part is being with other people trying to love God." She winced, her own struggles rising like shards of glass in her path. "No one is perfect. No one knows everything. We're all works in progress, trying to be better. Sometimes it's nice to not be alone."

Syn's pounding steps slowed; her face contorted in tangles of confusion. She swallowed a lump big enough to be a rock and shrugged her thin shoulders. "My right wing is still pretty useless, and I can't fly around or anything, but maybe this Sparrow can still hand out some stupid cookies."

Not daring to show how her heart bounced up and down, Rhona merely offered a friendly shoulder shove. "Wanna see if we can beat the dogs home?"

Late-October

Going to the Quilt & Sew Shop was always an experience. The sisters, Lucia and Maisie, had been running the store for as long as Rhona could remember. Back in the "good old days," they were enterprising young women who grappled with the modern world of fashion and set trends on their ears. They knew how to see the next craze a mile away and circumvent Oldtown from the hideous fate of being out of style. When they didn't like a coming sensation—they weren't too pleased with tie-dyes, hippie thigh-high boots, tube tops, or neon anything—they invented a variation of their own and started a new rage.

They knew how to make excellent use of accessories, including tattoos, authentic jewelry, colorful scarves, trendy hats, and footwear of all colors and sizes.

Originally, quilting wasn't an official part of their shop. In pure pity to the older generation, they sectioned off a small corner where elderly Oldtown ladies could sit and piece together family heirlooms—some went rogue and brought in their knitting—sip tea and chat about local events. Though the sisters knew it was gossip, pure and simple, they didn't complain. It kept them in the know.

Now that the worldly-wise sisters were in their seventies, with great-great-grandnieces and nephews who didn't care a hoot about style, they discovered that quilting and chatting made this rough world a saner, happier place. They also assisted select customers in the making of fancy costumes for parties and private events.

Rhona didn't consider herself a select customer since she had no aptitude for either sewing or quilting and rarely entered the shop, except to find fabric for such utility projects as curtains, party napkins, or to decorate an end table. She had made a brief effort in the early two-thousands when she thought that Derm might like a handmade quilt as an original birthday present, but when her completed project ended up being about three feet wide and seven feet long, he seemed just as happy with a miniature pizza oven. She went back to crocheting hats, scarves, and blankets thick enough to keep a bat warm in the Antarctic.

Ada, on the other hand, was as select a customer as one could get in Oldtown. When they reached the Quilt & Sew Shop, Ada promenaded inside, towing Syn along by her one good arm.

Rhona crept in behind, hoping that Syn's costume wouldn't involve anything more challenging than a straight stitch and a few button holes.

As if they were the only customers worthy of dedicated attention in the bustling shop on such a glorious Friday afternoon, Lucia's willowy form sashayed over, crooning her joy. "Oh, good! Sister told me that you'd be here today." She eyed Syn with the professional appraisement of a woman who knew clothing and shoe sizes to the nearest centimeter within seconds. Her voice perpetually just above a whisper, she leaned in confidentially. "I hear that you need something for the costume party, is that right?"

Rhona waited a long moment, hoping that Syn would find her tongue and explain what she wanted, but the girl stood petrified, as if she had just landed on another planet and wasn't sure if it was safe to breathe, much less talk. Like a good aunt, Rhona leaped into the breach. "We looked through a couple of stores in town and even searched online, but there's nothing that fits with what Syn has in mind, so we're hoping you can work your magic and help her fashion what she's looking for." She offered a humble smile. "You know I'm not much of a seamstress. Not a creative bone in my body."

As opposite in body shape as in personality, Lucia's sister, Maisie, boomed from across the room. "Don't be ridiculous. No one has taught you properly!" Weaving between customers, an autumn mountain came into range. The perfectly manicured, heavyset woman proclaimed her disgust, "Don't put yourself down, Rhona. You have sewing talent; you just haven't honed it yet. Anyone who can crochet those pretty blankets ought not to say she can't sew. It's the same part of the brain! Creativity flows through your veins. I remember your mama's paintings. Why, that woman had a love affair with color!"

Apparently rattled by the mere mention of family members, Syn found her vocal cords. "I want to look like a cross between a vampire and a werewolf. Something furry around my face and arms but dressed all in black with a long cape. Can you help me?"

The shop full of happily chatting, middle-aged women suddenly dropped to dead silence. Rhona didn't dare turn around, afraid that every patron in the place had turned into a wax figure caught in mid-motion. She wanted to say something but discovered that she needed to concentrate to stay on her feet.

Maisie recovered first. "Well, I always say, mix and match at your peril." Short and stout, she bustled closer to the girl. "But I sense a theme here. You want something scary, monstrous even, with a hint of villainy?"

Rhona leaned on the edge of the serving table, nearly sitting on a teacup, unconcerned that her pants might be absorbing the chocolate frosting in a three-layered cake intended for that evening's repast. She watched Maisie work her magic while Lucia hovered nearby, ready to gather the necessary material at a moment's notice.

Ada had frozen in place, a burgundy cloth clutched in one hand.

Eyes glowing with a frenzied light, Syn seemed ready to kneel at the foot of the artisan who could make her costume nightmare come true.

Three slow taps on her lips and the wheels in Maisie's brain were clearly turning. Her finger slid down to her chin, and then the force of nature locked her gaze on Syn and studied her as closely as a hound watches a treed possum. "But is that really *you*?"

Rhona heard the gasp before she realized it had come from her.

Violently, Ada shook her head, a leaf taken by the wind but not yet ready to fall.

A few of the other patrons tiptoed nearer, their hunched shoulders suggesting sincere efforts not to disturb a private conversation even as they listened in.

First annoyance, then confusion, followed hard on the heels by doubt, turned Syn's face into a cinematic motion picture show. She started to speak but then stopped, apparently stymied by the whole notion of personal identity.

Syn's confession during their walk two weeks ago, "I don't *know* who I am," replayed in Rhona's mind. *How can she not know who she is?* Her own struggles in that area notwithstanding, she could define Syn by the roles she played. The girl was her parents' daughter, her brother's sister, her and Dermid's niece, a sophomore high school student... The shallowness of such thinking astonished Rhona, and she wondered if she had slipped into senility sometime in the last hour.

A glance at the staring crowd, and Syn seemed on the brink of a meltdown that might take her all the way to the earth's core.

Rhona started babbling for all she was worth. "Dermid and I call her Sparrow because she was so tiny and frail when she was born, but her dark eyes reflected a strong spirit deep within."

Thankfully, Ada had stopped shaking her head, and some of the surrounding patrons seemed to be appraising the girl in a new light. Perhaps she wasn't one of those freaks who dress hideously to scare the heck out of everyone.

Maisie wasn't going to let anyone off the hook. A formidable frown building, she narrowed her gaze on Syn. "So, what are you? A scary, hybrid monster or a strong spirit?"

Her eyes wide, the girl seemed to be gulping for air. "Can I be both?"

Rhona figured that the entire congregation would toss them out in short order, but Maisie was full of surprises. She laughed! Long and loud. Slapping Syn on the back like a war hero returned from the front line, she nudged the child toward her sister and bellowed commands. "Find me that old lion outfit we used for the Wizard of Oz production a few years back, and pull the black draperies from the counter where we keep the leftover bits." She wiggled thick fingers in Rhona's direction. "You have any makeup at home?"

Rhona thought she might have some old stuff, but she wasn't sure it would be any good. She wasn't about to discuss how long it had been since she dressed up for a night out with Derm.

Ada sprang to life and hallooed as if she had a closetful of cosmetics to offer.

Rhona couldn't help but smile. *Perhaps she does.*

Instantaneous good cheer and the rising volume of happy customers who suddenly realized that their pathetically simple costumes could now break free of boring old routines rushed for vivid bolts of cloth and shelves of dangling accessories with fresh vim and vigor.

One woman called out, “You know, I’ve always wanted to do a mashup between Amelia Earhart and Madame Curie!”

Instead of being met with scandalized horror, fresh absurdities flew through the air with heightened relish. Lucia couldn’t sashay fast enough for all the new orders.

Her eyes glazed with a new passion and snapping phone photos of Syn, Ada babbled about all the makeup she’d bring over to get just the right look.

In the midst of a swirl of happy activity, Syn stood stock still, her mouth open, her eyes wide in blank astonishment.

Rhona edged over and wrapped her arm around the girl’s shoulder. “Look what you’ve done, Sparrow. Broken some old molds and set imaginations free.”

Without speaking, Syn blinked and then met her aunt’s gaze.

Huddled in the depths of the child, a spirit wanted to fly, but it couldn’t. Not yet.

As she hugged the thin shoulders of her perplexing niece, Rhona vowed that someday soon, she would know why.

Chapter Three

How Oldtown Became Famous and Rhona Discovered Unexpected Poetic Talent

Early-November

Dogs dig holes. It is as much a part of their nature as barking, chasing rabbits, and slobbering all over clean clothes. Rhona didn't mind their digging so much, though Dermid had a few things to say when his mower was nearly swallowed whole in the backyard. When they dragged bones to the house to show her, Rhona figured they'd unearthed the remains of a hunter's prize or an unlucky coyote and did little to encourage such skullduggery in its most literal form.

The collie dog, Nes, and the little labrador, Wilma, practically beamed when they dropped off their newest finds on the porch. Her protestations didn't bother them in the least. As far as they were concerned, humans were unappreciative, but they wouldn't let that dampen their enthusiasm.

An early morning at the beginning of the month, while Rhona was gathering kindling, the dogs returned to a hole they had started a few days before near an old fence line. Immediately, they began a frenzied barking. Not a possum or raccoon in sight to account for their silly excitement, Rhona ordered them to be quiet. It was too beautiful a day to be broken by such a ruckus. Surprisingly, they obeyed and began digging like fiends instead.

At least they're keeping themselves entertained.

She began assembling a tall pile of brush to use as kindling for the evening fires and, after an hour or so, had warmed up enough to make sweat trickle down her back. Feeling pleased with herself and the world in general, she took a breather and sucked in lungfuls of clean, crisp air. Contentment settled in her soul. Until she happened to glance over and consider how deep the dogs were digging their fool hole. *Derm will not be pleased.* Even if he never once in his life walked near that ancient fence line, he'd insist that someone could break a leg, and he'd grouse about it until he filled it in, glaring at the dogs every half-minute.

Shaking her head, Rhona hiked over to see what had caught their attention. Their coats were covered in dirt as they jumped in and out of their current excavation, barking like idiots. *They think they've discovered a mole community or something.* She hated to inform them that moles were solitary creatures and their united doggy efforts were in vain. Every mole on the property had heard about their digging prowess and moved to the next county by now.

She stared at them and then cast a lazy eye in the hole and nearly lost her balance. There, half sticking out of the hole, in a slantwise direction, poked the largest bone she'd ever seen in her life– outside a museum, of course.

If the earth had stopped rotating, she could not have been more surprised. Ignoring catastrophic earthquakes and what all might happen in such a case, she stared at the bone, feeling like the ground had shifted under her feet. It wasn't just any bone. If she had learned anything in her biology class, it was a thigh bone, maybe a femur, but the largest femur in history. Why, the part sticking out of the ground was a good three feet long and thick enough to support an outsized elephant.

Taking a step back so as not to fall in, she called for Dermid. Maybe it was a scream, but she thought it was important, so she ignored the dogs' glaring I-told-you-so expressions and bellowed again. No response. Flummoxed so badly that her hands were shaking, she rummaged through her pockets, found her phone, and texted her husband, "Get out here!!!" Three exclamation marks were excessive, but she could hardly think straight.

Later that night, as she tried to fall asleep, she wondered why she couldn't have just walked calmly into the house like a sane woman and informed her husband, in a matter-of-fact voice, that their two dogs had unearthed a giant femur. But the truth was that adrenaline had more power over her than she liked to admit.

As Derm hustled out of the house, stuffing his arms into his coat sleeves, Syn followed close behind, wearing only her jeans, a black sweater, and a worn pair of tennis shoes.

Fear of flu season jettisoning all other thoughts, Rhona waved at the girl. "Get your coat, child, before you catch something!"

Dermid chuckled as he wrapped his arm around Syn and promised to keep germs away. Then he saw the hole and annoyance clouded his expression.

Syn's gaze zeroed in on the bone, and she screamed. Then she jumped up and down as pleased as the dogs.

Trying to make up for her own momentary lapse of emotional balance, Rhona pointed at the two canines who were now relaxing beside the hole with simpering doggy smiles. "They dug up a big bone."

Syn went one better. "It's a mammoth bone!"

Rhona agreed that it probably was, but Dermid wasn't so sure. "We can't be sure of anything until we ask somebody who might actually know a thing or two about bones and mammoths."

Glaring with all the zeal of an I-know-the-facts scientist, Syn lectured for all she was worth. "There were giant sloths living here millions of years ago. And wooly mammoths lived in this part of the North American continent from three hundred thousand to ten thousand years ago."

Derm's mouth dropped open; his entire face becoming one big question mark as he stared at his niece.

A brief eyeroll and Syn exhaled a long-suffering sigh. "I've been studying ancient world history. Took a test last week and got an A, if you remember." She pulled out her phone and started tapping.

Dermid grimaced. "She'll pull up pages of world-renowned research, pictures even, and prove she's right before lunch."

At the mention of lunch, Rhona's mind somersaulted, and she remembered that she and Syn were supposed to meet Nia at the doctor's office at eleven to get Syn's cast off, and then they were going out to eat to celebrate. The idea that Syn's living arrangement might come up in general conversation had been shoved to the darkest corners of Rhona's mind. *I want her to return home, back to the bosom of her family...don't I? Why are my nerves as jumpy as a cat in a dog kennel?*

Leaving Derm to investigate mammoth authorities and somehow keep the dogs from dragging off their prize, which they would undoubtedly gnaw on in doggy delight, probably to their dying days, Rhona hustled Syn inside.

Driving just over the speed limit, but not so much as to set off police sirens or be a bad example for Syn, who would be learning to drive the next year, Rhona made it to the doctor's office exactly on time.

Nia didn't arrive for another half an hour.

Luckily, Rhona had been given authoritative clearance to oversee Syn's medical care, so their family doctor was happy to get the procedure done without a prolonged wait. With calm assurances, the doctor had an attendant cut off the cast, then he checked her arm and nodded thoughtfully several times as he had her move it in every position imaginable. He asked a few pertinent questions, which Syn answered straightforwardly. Since everything seemed to be in good working order, they were sent on their way with a colorful exercise sheet outlining a daily routine to strengthen the arm.

Nia met them as they exited the office. She seemed annoyed that they had completed the procedure without her. "I wanted to see him saw it off!"

Exasperated by her sister's petulance, Rhona turned the complaint into a joke before Syn took it seriously. "He said Syn's arm was fine, so he didn't have to saw it off." She nudged her sister on the shoulder to turn her around. "Let's go eat. I'm starving."

Nia's pouty expression led the way.

Surprisingly, Syn dragged her feet as she followed along behind.

Is her mom such a mood-buster that she's not even happy about being free of that cast? Rhona wanted to smack something, her sister foremost, but she refrained. Once she got Nia to agree to follow them to a family café down the road, she packed Syn in the passenger side of her car without asking if she wanted to go with her mom. It seemed an unnecessary question. Syn's feelings for her family were becoming increasingly obvious.

It was only a five-minute drive to the restaurant, but Rhona was determined to make the most of her small opportunity. She practically crawled across town. "It's nice to see your mom again."

Syn shrugged.

Rhona felt like the dogs digging for secrets. She squirmed and gripped the steering wheel tighter. "Are you angry with your mom? Or your dad, for some reason?"

Her pale arm resting across her lap as if it were still in a cast, Syn hardly moved.

"Has Andy said something? Brothers can be annoying. Well, I know sisters are. I assume the same is true for brothers."

Her voice low, Syn muttered, "He calls me Chinese Brain."

A sinking sensation nearly killed Rhona's appetite. Once she found a parking spot and did her best to stay within the lines, she tried on a reassuring tone. "I'm sure it was just a joke. Guys like to tease. Something in their DNA makes them act silly, but they think it's smart."

"I'm not a Chinese brain!" She darted from the car, her face red with suppressed fury.

After she got out and locked the door, Rhona pulled her niece into a side hug, then started toward the café's glass doors. "You're one of the smartest, most creative people I know, kiddo. Don't let anyone make you think differently."

Shaking her head, Syn pulled away and shuffled inside.

Knowing that she had just misstepped somehow, Rhona plodded along behind.

Nia scowled at them from a booth next to the front window as they bypassed the hostess. "What took you so long? Have to repair a tire or replace the engine or something?"

Ignoring the jibe, Rhona slid into place with Syn slipping in next to her. She kept her eyes fixed on Nia to keep her sister from focusing on the fact that her daughter had chosen to sit on the opposite side of the table. Rhona then plucked a menu from a metal stand and perused her options. "Hmmm, what sounds good on a chilly November day?"

Nia shoved her menu aside. "I already ordered lemon-lime sodas for everyone. I'm going with the vegetable soup and a tomato-cucumber sandwich. Anyone want to split with me?"

Rhona tilted her head as if that might help her decipher the strange logic of ordering drinks for people above the age of three and thinking that anyone wanted to eat half of a meal that wouldn't keep hunger at bay for an hour.

A waitress stopped beside the table, a smile signaling her readiness to serve.

Syn sighed. "I'll have some chips. Regular. Nothing else."

Leaping over her daughter's ridiculous menu selection and barely waiting her turn, Nia leaned forward, her full attention on the waitress. "You do have fresh tomatoes and cucumbers, right? I hate the stuff wrapped in cellophane."

Her eyes wide, as if she'd just been accused of drowning a cat, the twenty-something woman with flower tattoos up both her arms refuted the accusation with a glare. "Everything we serve is fresh." She turned her whole body toward Rhona, cutting off all visual contact with Nia.

The best smile she could muster in place, Rhona asked for a grilled cheese sandwich, French fries, and confirmed the lemon-lime soda. She dearly wanted to replace the cold drink with a hot cup of decaf coffee but knew all too well that Nia would take the change as an affront. *I need her in a good mood.*

Once the waitress had marched away, Rhona scoured her brain for a pleasant way to mine for information. *There has to be a reason why Syn is so easily upset. It's not just a teen thing—is it?*

Nia didn't have any such concerns. She listed in agonizing detail the recent shops she had visited, her latest massage therapy appointment, what her hairdresser had said about her newly painted nails, and how their neighbors had gotten a yippy little dog without even asking if the noise would bother them.

Keeping her honest reactions close to her chest, Rhona used every ounce of diplomacy at her command to appear to agree when she didn't and suppress eyerolls.

Syn played with the napkin holder.

When Nia took a momentary breather and decided it would be good to take a "stroll to the little girls' room," Rhona waited till she was out of earshot and nudged Syn. "Chips? Just chips?"

Syn rubbed her chin. "You'll end up paying, even though Mom and Dad have more money than anyone we know. No point in paying for food when Uncle Derm has a roast for supper. Besides, chips make me feel better." She looked out of the corner of her eyes. "You did say I could celebrate."

So many thoughts crashed in Rhona's mind that she wasn't sure she'd ever untangle them. Picking her niece's mood off the floor seemed like a good place to start. "I like comfort food, too. That's why I ordered the fries with my grilled cheese." A frown made her squint. "How do you know Derm is making a roast? I planned on egg salad."

"He said he wanted to surprise you. He put the roast in the crockpot and started peeling the potatoes when you ordered him outside." Deadpanned, she met Rhona's gaze straight on. "That man will do anything for you."

Not certain if she was joking or insightful, Rhona considered the girl at her side. "You're a considerate person with far too advanced observation skills for your age."

The first grin in ages wafted over Syn's face.

Beside the table, Nia cleared her throat, and right behind her, the waitress stepped forward with their food.

Once the plates were in place and the first bites enjoyed in silence, an itch tickled Rhona's mind. She took a sip of her warm soda, regretted it, and set it aside. "Tell me again why you named your daughter Syn. I can't seem to recall."

Syn choked and had to take a gulp of her drink.

Undisturbed, Nia's expression grew dreamy, as if remembering better days. "Syn is short for Synergy. You know, it means a harmonic relationship, forces working together, mutual good." Her smile widened as she retreated further into the past.

As if she had just struck the tip of an iceberg, Rhona dropped anchor, resolving to understand what was under the surface of her niece's identity. "It's odd, sounds nothing like Andy or Zhang. Or Nia, for that matter. What made you think of it?"

So completely immersed in a bygone moment, Nia's voice softened, a hint of yearning in her tone. "You remember Gustav? The handsome god-man from Venezuela who was trying for the principal position in Central? He couldn't find any place to stay, so he boarded with us for the summer."

If Syn slid any further down in the booth, she would be under the table.

One hand grasping the girl's sleeve, Rhona held her upright without letting a flicker of concern pass over her face. "Oh, yeah. I remember. Dermid thought the guy was full of himself."

Pouting lips expressed Nia's thoughts on Dermid's assessment. "He was a nice guy. A really nice guy. Dermid shouldn't be so judgmental."

Trying to steer the conversation back to solid ground, Rhona shifted enough to squeeze Syn in an upright position while keeping her eyes glued to her sister. "So, what does this have to do with Syn's name?"

"That was his favorite word!"

Rhona put every ounce she could into a pleasantly puzzled expression.

"Syn is short for synergy, Gustav's word. It was so cool! When she was born, it seemed so right. She had to have a name that meant all those wonderful things." She grinned at her daughter and stretched out her hand, though she never actually touched Syn's fingers. "See how much I love you, baby?"

Suddenly, her lunch option congealed into a knot in Rhona's stomach. She eked out her next words. "What did Zhang think of the name?"

Nia shrugged; her gaze refocused on the last bit of her sandwich. "Oh, he didn't care. He never even met Gustav. He was in China visiting his ailing uncle that summer, remember?"

Rhona did remember. A chill ran down her spine. "Why didn't you go with him? To China, I mean."

A pained expression marred Nia's beautiful face. "We stopped there on our honeymoon tour years before." Her scowl deepened. "I hated the place. His family treated me like a stupid servant. It was clear that they weren't pleased with Zhang's choice of a bride." A muttered huff. "I'm so glad his parents are going back at the end of the month." Squaring her shoulders, she waved to the waitress, then snapped her fingers. "The bill, please." In her typical alternating mood sequence, Nia picked up her designer purse and appeared as harried as a woman trying to catch a runaway bus. "I've got another appointment in half an hour, so I really must run."

Shocked, Rhona could hardly believe her luck. Nia wasn't even going to mention Syn's living arrangements? She could practically feel the wind of the metaphorical charging train as it rushed past her. *Thank goodness!* Syn wasn't going to be thrust back onto the rumbling track of Nia's passions. Her tongue started working as she grabbed her purse. "If you leave a tip, I'll pay the bill." She gestured to Syn to get her moving. Speed was everything. They had to get out of there before it occurred to Nia to ask for her daughter back.

As if reading her mind as well as her mood, Syn scooted out of the booth and bolted for the door.

Nia slid from the booth in her usual queenly manner. She left a measly tip.

Vowing to come back another time and make up for it, Rhona hurried to pay, glad beyond words that she could manage small, sudden expenses without the agony of uncertainty that the debt would clear the bank. It hadn't always been that way. *Nia must have forgotten. Or maybe she never knew.*

As they made their way to their cars, parked several spaces away from each other, Nia's face lit up with an announcement. "Oh, I almost forgot!"

Dread clutched Rhona's heart.

"Since Zhang's parents are returning to China, and he is going to some conference at the end of the month, Andy and I will be alone for Thanksgiving."

Uncertain where this was going, Rhona waited, afraid to breathe.

"So, I was wondering…" Nia blinked prettily, as was her way when she had a favor to ask.

Considering that the unpleasant prospect of having Nia and Andy over for Thanksgiving dinner was so much better than the horrible image of going to their house, or worse yet, having Syn go home alone, words ushered from Rhona's mouth as fast as she could articulate them. "We'd love to have you and Andy over for Thanksgiving. Derm bakes a delicious turkey, and I always make plenty of side dishes. You won't have to bring a thing."

Nia pshawed that thought. "Oh, I'll bring chips or something." She winked as if in naughty complicity with her daughter. "I saw you gobble them down in there."

Syn's face grew beet red.

Once again, Rhona wanted to smack something. *I'm back where I started.*

With fingers waving out the window, Nia rumbled off in her Jeep Cherokee.

As Syn slid into her seat in the old Ford Focus, Rhona patted her niece's arm. "Nice to have the cast off, isn't it?"

Syn nodded, though her gaze stayed fixed on her hands.

"And it'll be fun to get ready for Thanksgiving together, won't it?"

Another nod.

Rhona started the engine, backed the car out of the parking space, and then headed down the country road toward home. She reached over and nudged her niece on the shoulder. "Do you think Derm dug the rest of the mammoth bone out of the ground yet?"

A giggle burst, and Syn nearly laughed.

Relief sluiced over Rhona, creating a fair imitation of happiness.

Mid-November

Rhona's secret passion for poetry was a well-kept secret. She didn't have to work at keeping the secret because no one in her world honestly cared if she read poetry or trashy romances. Formal schooling hadn't instilled the love of literary narratives into her heart but rather a chance exposure to great books in an old house on the southeast side of town, opposite Oldtown Mansion Apartments. She had discovered the antique bookstore on the first floor of a classic farmhouse preserved in its antiquity on a quiet residential street. The perfectly plastered walls, wood floors, and high ceilings encompassed a universe of literary adventures.

Mr. Thompson's first love in life had been books. And that never changed, even after he married the second love of his life, a shy, retiring lady named Edith. She, a librarian at the same college where he worked, loved books, too, and in this, they united their passions with equal intensity. When retirement loomed, they hatched a plot to keep their personal vocations fueled for the rest of their earthy lives—they turned the first floor of their historic old house into a used bookstore. It flourished in the same dignified manner they did, quietly and with refined taste.

Even after Edith passed away, Mr. Thompson opened the store every Tuesday through Friday from ten in the morning to four in the afternoon.

When Rhona had hurried in one Wednesday a couple of years ago, her main intent had been to keep from being drowned in an unexpected deluge of rain. Mr. Thompson had merely waved to the placards outlining the literary sections and smiled. His glasses always glinted from the light of golden lamps hanging in strategic locations, giving the place a languid, relaxed feel. She had joked to herself at the time that the pacific atmosphere would take Derm's blood pressure down, even from his most aggravated state, in a matter of minutes.

Some force of grace compelled her to browse rather than stand by the front window and wait for the rain to slacken. An hour later, she had a stack of books on the polished walnut table near the front entrance and her wallet was wide open.

Mr. Thompsom nodded appreciatively at her choices. He even clucked his tongue at the heavy bound volume of poetry. "'Out to Old Aunt Mary's' by Riley is one of my favorite poems. Though I love everything that Longfellow wrote." He caressed the cover as he packed it into a brown paper sack. "Don't know how I would've faced the day without Babcock's 'Be Strong' to rouse me each morning."

Her heart singing a happy tune, Rhona had practically skipped between the last raindrops as she made her way to her car. It wasn't long before she was sitting in the living room with a cup of tea in one hand and the poetry volume open on her lap. After reading Mr. Thompson's suggested selections, she realized that the man was brilliant, for it took a genius to appreciate genius. Her world had opened into a beautiful literary garden, and she was welcome to roam at pleasure.

On a drizzly Friday afternoon in the middle of November, Syn dragged her lithe body into the kitchen and plopped down on the bench with the dejected air of someone with few reasons to go on living.

Rhona studied her for a long moment. Then, the marvelous idea of introducing her niece to Mr. Thompson filled her imagination. She would not take no for an answer.

Syn insisted that she didn't want to go out in the rain, that she'd catch pneumonia and die before Monday and thus fail her history test, ruining a perfect GPA, and besides, she could get any book she wanted on Kindle, so bookstores were irrelevant these days.

After wrapping the girl in one of Derm's old raincoats, tugging her across the room, shoving her out the door, and then towing her to the car, Rhona stayed true to her convictions.

With a desultory expression, Syn gave in to fate and her aunt's mighty determination. She muttered that she only hoped they both wouldn't regret it.

Rhona drove the short distance into town, wagging a finger at the limp figure leaning on the rain-glazed window. "Trust me. I know what I'm doing."

Silence.

A huff and Rhona plowed on. "You liked Maise and Lucia well enough, didn't you? They helped design the perfect costume that both charmed and horrified half the town when you went trick or treating and came home with enough treats to last through an apocalypse."

Syn offered a flat stare, but there was a hint of a smile behind it.

By the time she pulled onto a side street, found a parking place, got out, and pointed to the wrought-iron front door, Rhona no longer had to drag anyone. Once they got inside, it became a matter of keeping up. Delight suffused Syn's face as she ran her fingers along the wooden shelves, stopping every few minutes to pluck a book from its nest and peruse through the thick pages.

Deciding that a fifteen-year-old girl was safe to leave in the mystery section, Rhona moseyed over to the poetry corner, where a strangely familiar figure met her eyes. "Ada?"

Startled, worried eyes looked up with a guilty expression peering from their depths, then recognition followed. "Oh, Rhona! Thank goodness, it's you!"

Rhona snuck a glance at the book in Ada's hands and was only slightly taken aback by the colorful cover of an Amish romance staring back. She held her head still by sheer force of will. A headshake would not do.

Tugging a folded newspaper from under her raincoat, Ada leaped onto a new topic. "You have got to see our newest endeavor in Oldtown!" She practically smirked as she unfolded the paper and held it high, bold headlines declaring the latest in community news: *Poetry Contest Winners Declared Each Third Wednesday of the Month.*

Rhona's heart began to race. *How is it possible? I've kept my secret for so long. Who else has been keeping secrets?* She eyed Ada carefully, one eyebrow rising to new heights.

Ada waved her hand in frantic denial. "Oh, not me! I can hardly write a check; much less be creative with words. But, you know, dear Mr. Thompson said that there were a surprising number of sales when it came to poetry books. He thought that there might be some hidden talent tucked away in Oldtown. So, I suggested the contest, and he said he'd sponsor the effort. Even got the college to appoint three students from their senior literature classes to act as judges each month, September through May."

Syn meandered nearby, her head tilted in the right position for someone trying to eavesdrop on a conversation.

Rhona waved her over. "You remember my niece, Syn. I think she'd like to join in. When is the next deadline?"

Syn's eyes goggled as she stared at her aunt.

Never one to miss an opportunity to get the young people involved, Ada slapped her newspaper to her chest and acted as if her finest wish in life had just been granted. "Oh, would you, dear? That would be perfect! We've only had two submissions, and the deadline is Sunday, so you'd have plenty of time to think of something." Her gaze reverted to her friend. "Literary endeavors take time to catch on. They're not like bake sales where everyone has to have dessert anyway, so might as well buy a cake on the way home; you know what I mean?"

Flapping her arms like a flightless bird, Syn groped for words. “But I don’t know anything about poetry! I’ve only read a little of Emily Dickinson, Browning, and Emerson, though I did start something by Whitman and couldn’t finish it.” She frowned, her gaze turning inward. “Poe is pretty cool, though. He’s more than just a poet, more like a storyteller in poetical form.”

Rhona didn’t have to glance aside to know that she and Ada were a matched set, both with mouths gaping, eyes bulging.

As if he hadn’t been eavesdropping as well, Mr. Thompson drifted closer with a thick, blue-covered volume tucked under one arm and another book clasped with both hands. He smiled at Syn. “I don’t often do this, but every now and again, I get a little wild, and I give a couple of books away.” He bowed formally before the elfin girl as if she were a princess hidden in the oversized raincoat. “I would be honored if you’d take these as nourishment for your muse.”

Hesitant, a couple of glances at Rhona to make double sure that it was okay, then Syn reached out and accepted the two books. Finally, she smiled.

Ada’s eyes glimmered in the golden light.

Rhona breathed through a silent prayer of gratitude.

By Sunday evening, Rhona was ready to burst at the seams. She hadn’t dared ask how the poem was coming along as Syn trotted back and forth from her room, one of her new treasures pressed to her chest like a soldier carrying a shield on a battlefield. Rhona had to check the online link three times to assure herself that submissions could still be made until midnight.

Dermid, apparently sensing the tension of creative talent and Rhona's scattered mind, decided that a simple supper of fried chicken, potato puffs, and green beans would have a stabilizing effect. He was right.

After the dishes were washed and put away, Rhona made two cups of herbal tea and invited him to relax on the couch with her.

Dermid stretched out on the couch and sipped his tea with all the composure of a man with no expectations, merely wanting to keep his wife's frayed nerves from falling to pieces before bedtime.

To get her mind off the contest, Rhona scootched next to him, cradling her cup in her hands, and asked for an update on the mammoth bone.

Derm chuckled. "Oh, it's been confirmed pretty much. A guy is coming out in early December to take measurements and figure out the best way to transport it to the city museum."

Surprisingly, disappointment kicked Rhona in the gut. "We're giving it away? I thought we might like to keep it."

Derm's mouth twitched. "It's lucky it has survived this long! What with the dogs and all the critters that make free on our place. No, the guy said it's a historic treasure and belongs to humanity, and I agree."

"You didn't think to ask—" Out of the corner of her eye, Rhona noticed Syn sidling into the room, her hands suspiciously behind her back. Rhona swallowed down rising anxiety, sat up, and swept her gaze over her niece. "Have you something to show us, sweetheart?"

Derm hitched himself into a more upright position, his eyes sparkling with expectation.

Syn inched into the room and stopped beside the old upright piano that hadn't been played in decades. "I can't read it out loud. But here." She thrust her hand out with a wrinkled paper, pointing in their direction.

Rhona grabbed it and started to scan.

Dermid cleared his throat noisily. "Well, that's not fair. I want to hear it."

Locking her eyes on her niece, Rhona received silent permission to read it aloud. She sucked in a deep breath and took her time with each line, forcing herself to keep her voice steady.

Into the Woods Go I

Cawing, screaming, alarming meaning,

Winged whirlwinds scatter and fly.

Into the woods go I.

Sighs rise; steps pound the ground.

Crackling leaves rustling relentlessly.

Chattering, pattering, running feet.

Scurry in hurry, away, never meet.

Mounds plowed in sinuous rows, shallow and deep.

Creatures unseen and unseeing,

Toil and boil below as above.

Into the woods go I.

Shimmering lines woven of light,

Catching the unwary in the night.

Fluttering, buzzing, whispering, blurry waves,

Darting and parting

Undulating clouds abound.

Into the woods go I.

Alone in a crowd,

The wild world makes way,

Into the Woods go I.

Amazed, Rhona gripped the thin sheet as if it might take flight, leaving her heartbroken forever. She studied her niece, fear battling expectation in the child's eyes. Rhona's voice dropped to a solemn whisper, "Sparrow, this is one of the most beautiful poems I have ever read."

Derm, in his usual silent style, did one better. He rose from the couch, strolled over with his arms out, and embraced the girl in a tight hug. His voice was gruff but full of meaning. "My Sparrow."

When a tear slipped down Syn's face, Rhona was not a bit surprised.

Late-November

Advent means preparation. Since Rhona couldn't make the world behave itself for the Second Coming, she decided to do what she could and that meant cleaning the house top to bottom before her sister and nephew showed up on the Wednesday before Thanksgiving. Doing her best to endow the holiday season with cheer and goodwill, she ensconced herself at the kitchen table early Tuesday with a fresh cup of coffee, hummed a happy tune, and checked through her to-do list one last time.

When Derm stepped into the room, bleary-eyed and unshaven, she smiled and held up her list.

Waving her organized chores to oblivion, Dermid insisted that his students needed him more than Andy or Nia ever could. Besides—he used his most cajoling tone—Thanksgiving was supposed to focus on gratitude, and Advent meant preparing for Christmas, the season of love. For him, being one with the spirit meant helping his students get As.

Unable to argue his point, Rhona just watched him and his peanut butter-jelly sandwich retreat to his private study—which she never entered for fear of hyperventilating at the sight of his natural untidiness—and focused on what she could control. Her to-do list.

She ticked her completed items off for the third time that week because it brought her a pleasant sense of accomplishment. At seven in the morning, facing two difficult guests for three days, Rhona could use all the pleasantness she could get.

The brush piles had been broken down and stacked by the back door so she could get kindling at a moment's notice. The wood racks had been filled to the brim, and more wood leaned against the wall next to the kindling. For the next few days, the house could never get under seventy degrees, or Nia would call the cops and report abuse. Not that Syn or Dermid cared. They preferred the house temperature around sixty-five, but apparently, Andy was a hothouse flower and would wilt if he caught a chill.

A mental headshake and Rhona went back to her list. The back guest bedroom had been fixed up with fresh sheets and new pillows. Nia would notice if they dared to present her with decade-old pillows.

Unexpectedly, Syn had offered her room to Andy and moved a few of her things to a closet in Derm's study. She said she'd be happy to sleep on the couch in the living room. Considering the situation and knowing that Derm wasn't going to offer the master bedroom, it was the only logical solution. Part of Rhona wondered why Syn made the offer when she clearly didn't like her brother. *She's a generous spirit. Most kids would demand that their older brother sleep on the couch.*

Derm somehow managed to dig out space in his office for her school desk and books. Syn had been as grateful as a shipwreck survivor upon being dragged on board. Rhona lifted her head. Syn was in with him now, and the sound of a ball bouncing off the wall alerted her to non-academic activities. She rubbed an ache in her neck. *Four more days. I just have to live till Friday at noon, and then everything can get back to normal.*

She sucked in a cleansing breath and returned to her list. Andy would have fresh sheets on his bed, but Rhona used the pillows that had been stuffed in the back of her closet for the last eleven years. Once they had clean cases, he'd never know the difference. He was a teen boy, after all.

The huge frozen turkey was thawing nicely in the refrigerator, the ingredients for the feast were arranged in the refrigerator and pantry according to their respective recipes, and she had an apple pie and a pumpkin pie ready to heat up at a moment's notice.

What else? Oh, the dogs would have to be tied up and food and water bowls arranged near them. Nia had a thing about loose dogs. She thought it was bad manners to leave animals unchained in her presence. Rhona had no idea what Andy thought about domesticated pets since he ignored them absolutely. The only animal he was inclined to notice was the one served to him on a plate.

Rhona dropped her head on the kitchen table and whispered a prayer. "Please, God, keep me from saying out loud any thought in my head. I want everyone to have a good time. I don't want Syn to be embarrassed. Help me live through this!"

By Wednesday morning, she was convinced that life as she knew it was over. Her nights had been haunted by nightmares of burned turkey dinners arriving on the table, with Nia wrinkling her nose in disgust and Andy ordering fast food to be delivered by sled dogs.

Two minutes after she awoke, she realized why Siberian Husky dogs had predominated her dreams—the house was way too cold. The log fires had gone out during the night, and the inside temps had dropped to fifty-eight. A headache pounded on her brain, and it took forever to find a pair of thick socks.

Derm was kind enough to get the fires going properly while she downed a cup of hot coffee, thanking the good Lord for automatic coffee makers, and then made eggs and toast for Syn's breakfast.

Syn dragged herself to the table, limp and hardly responding beyond a nod and a murmur. Rhona was relieved when the girl retreated to Derm's study to do extra algebra problems.

The day went by in a blur of last-minute preparations unhampered by any extra assistance. Why Rhona felt the sudden need to clean under the refrigerator was a mystery she left for the End of Times Revelations. She simply couldn't be busy enough. For some reason, her conscious mind would not explore; she felt the need to keep as busy as bees in springtime. It helped calm her. Some. By the late afternoon, she was so tired, Chariots from Heaven could have rolled across her front lawn, and she wouldn't have missed a heartbeat. As far as she was concerned, if her heart was still beating, that was about all she could ask of it these days.

Nia and Andy were due to arrive at four in the afternoon, but they didn't show up until five-thirty. It was already quite dark by the time they pulled into the driveway, but Nia didn't seem bothered by the fact that she had missed the pre-Thanksgiving dinner Rhona had prepared.

As she stepped onto the porch—Rhona held the door open for them—Nia called out for all the world to hear, "Hope you didn't wait on us. We stopped and had burgers on the way. Andy had to meet up with some friends this afternoon, and they were late getting back."

Rhona merely nodded. There wasn't much to say.

As they entered the warm kitchen, Nia ruffled her fingers through her son's thick black hair, her eyes twinkling in private delight. "He's a selfish brat, but I can't get mad at him. Gets great grades, is president of the Debate Club, and runs track like a pro."

Andy shrugged, lifting his hands in a surrender fashion, like a guy who can't deny his own magnificence.

Rhona could hear Syn's tentative steps creeping forward from the living room.

Thankfully, Derm turned everyone's attention as he entered the kitchen from the hallway, a grand smile plastered over his face. His graying beard was cut close and neat; he'd put on a fresh shirt and even smelled of aftershave.

Falling in love with the man for the umpteenth time, Rhona had to drag her gaze to her sister. "Well, we waited for a while but finally gave up and ate. We did save dessert just in case you showed up before bedtime."

Nia offered a sad face to make up for being such a bad girl.

Andy leaned to the side, his head severely tilted, and grinned at Syn. He offered a polite wave. "Hey, Brain. What are you doing, hiding? Mom doesn't bite." His eyes crinkled with amusement. "And Dad isn't around to quiz you."

Swiveling, Rhona clasped Syn protectively by the shoulders and gave her a warm side hug in front of everyone. "She's been such a big help. I couldn't have gotten everything ready for tomorrow without her. She even made the dessert for tonight."

Nia's beaming expression radiated toward her daughter. "That's my girl! I guess I'll be needing you home to cook for me now, won't I?"

Rhona wondered if she had fallen off a cliff; the jolt hit her that hard.

Syn froze in place.

As usual, Derm ambled in to the rescue. "Well, I, for one, am ready for that chocolate cake. I enjoyed the tuna casserole most definitely, but my heart has been longing for dessert all day." He rubbed his hands together and started giving orders. "Syn, it's your creation, so bring it out to the living room. We'll enjoy it in front of the fire. Rhona, why don't we use paper plates so you don't have to do any more dishes tonight? Tomorrow's a big day." He waved Nia ahead, then clapped his nephew around the shoulders and propelled him forward.

Derm should have gone into diplomacy. Could have avoided a few wars with him around.

It took a few minutes for the sweet delight to work its way through Rhona's system, but eventually, her goodwill returned, and she accepted her sister's witless attitude with all the indulgence of a doctor in a psych ward. *She's not capable of being sensible. Can't help dominating conversations and going into vivid details about nail polish and whatnot.*

Derm managed Andy like the expert he was, asking about college life, guy friends, and what track meets were like. Derm had never played sports himself, but the man knew how to ask the right questions, and Andy had no problem talking about himself.

Perched carefully on the old piano stool, Rhona assessed the six-foot, black-haired, black-eyed, handsome, outgoing eighteen-year-old, as he lounged on her couch. He scattered crumbs as he chatted between bites of cake, then brushed the bits from his lap to the floor without a thought. His self-absorption was obvious. *Takes after his mother that way.* She glanced at Syn who sat huddled in an armchair, apparently afraid to move. *She looks like a rabbit hiding from a hound.*

Suddenly, a crack of laughter caught her attention, and Andy jumped up from his seat. "I want to see it!" He swung his gaze at his mom. "Did you hear that they found a mammoth bone out back?"

Nia waved the old news away. "Oh, yeah. Rhona told me." Her face contorted in disgust. "Can you imagine how many germs must be all over it, being buried in the ground for so long? I wouldn't touch it with a ten-foot pole! I don't even want to see it." She waved her son back to his chair. "Sit down and relax. It'll be time for bed soon." She cut her eyes toward Rhona. "I suppose you all still get up at the crack of dawn?"

Andy's mouth turned down into a displeased pout. "I didn't ask you to show me." He pointed to his sister. "Brain can do it."

Syn's naturally pale face blanched even whiter, her eyes stretched with worry. She cast her gaze between Derm and Rhona as if begging for a lifeline in a shark-infested sea.

Rhona got to her feet to head off any objections and pointed to the kitchen. "Syn's going to help me clean up, and then we'll head off to bed." She tried to smile through her dictatorial commentary. "We do get up early, and tomorrow is a big day. Everyone should get some rest." She swiveled her gazc to her husband and implored his intercession. "Derm, can show you the bone tomorrow."

Any doubts about such a prospect were buried so deep in Derm's eyes that anyone less than his wife couldn't see them. He merely smiled, climbed to his feet, and pointed down the hallway. "Let me show you to your rooms."

Nia checked her watch. "Lord, it's only seven! You guys must be Amish or something."

Andy swiveled around his mom and took his sister by the arm. "At least Syn can help me get our bags from the car, right?"

Before either Derm or Rhona could alter his plans, he had tugged her out the door and pounded down the porch steps.

Rhona told her heart to stay put while Derm followed at a sedate pace. Neither wanted to show the alarm they exchanged in a brief glance.

Oblivious, Nia stretched out on the couch. "I'm going to call Zhang from here. You all can talk to him if you want. He's probably tired, but he might want to say hi."

Since Derm had stationed himself by the door and was watching through the window, Rhona defaulted to clean up. She collected the paper plates and cups and carried everything into the kitchen, wishing that she had told Nia to make her own Thanksgiving dinner.

By bedtime, Rhona understood what a wrung-out washrag felt like. She snuggled beside her husband and rested her head on his chest.

Derm wrapped his arm around her and grunted, a familiar sound that assured her of his love and devotion in abbreviated form.

She couldn't help but ask, "Why does Andy call her Brain all the time? It doesn't make any sense.

She's a smart kid but not exactly a brainiac. She doesn't typically act like a smarty-pants or anything. I don't get why he does that. It obviously makes her uncomfortable."

A shrug and another grunt spoke of irritation. Derm ran his hand through his hair. "I watched out the window, and I could see Andy talking a mile a minute. Syn just stood there as he loaded her down." Another shrug, but this time it seemed to suggest a desire to get up and smack something, a feeling Rhona well understood. "He said something that made her drop her head to her chest. When she came in, I looked at her, but she wouldn't lift her eyes. I don't think she was crying, but then she wouldn't be so obvious in front of her mom."

Rhona snorted. "Nia wouldn't have noticed. She was whining to Zhang on the phone, telling him all about some issue she was having with the power company. Some guys were trimming trees and dropping limbs in her yard, but they didn't clean them up instantly." She sniffed. "You know how she is. Excruciating details about stuff and nonsense that isn't a big deal."

Derm's breathing had steadied, but his eyes were still open, so he hadn't fallen asleep. "Andy has something on Syn, some kind of secret he's using against her. The girl was loaded down like a pack horse, and he sauntered in behind with only his phone and his laptop in his hands."

Rhona nodded in silent agreement. Perhaps tomorrow, they would understand better. If nothing else, it would be one day closer to being free of her sister and nephew. She snuggled up closer and felt Derm's grip tighten. Their fear of losing Syn remained unspoken but shared.

Thanksgiving Day arrived sunny and cold. Before Andy could corral his sister into anything, Derm took over as personal manager and kept Andy so busy that the young man could hardly take a breath without Derm giving him something new to do. They ate a late breakfast with Rhona and Syn.

Nia slept in. When Rhona called for her sister, Nia mumbled from under the covers that she wasn't interested in birdsong or sunrises and would get something later. Rhona was fine with that and served up a healthy breakfast of scrambled eggs, hashbrowns, and whole wheat toast, and everyone—except Syn—ate heartily.

Once Derm had ushered Andy out the door to view the mammoth bone and do a "few more chores," Rhona got Syn busy with peeling potatoes, making deviled eggs, and various other meal preparations. She even made up a few jobs just to keep the kid close at hand and away from her brother.

By the time Nia made it into the kitchen, one hand rubbing her back but emphatically refusing to say why she'd had a rough night's sleep, Rhona had prepared another repast of eggs and toast. Nia scarfed them down with three cups of coffee as she checked her social media channels and ordered Syn to get her makeup kit.

Trying to hold her amazement in check as she watched Nia "make up her face" in the kitchen, Rhona continued with the dinner preparations as if she didn't really need the dinner table in the middle of the kitchen.

Syn and Rhona worked in tandem, and by the time everything was ready—the turkey roasted to a golden brown, potatoes mashed, sweet potatoes sprinkled with brown sugar, cranberries jelled, green bean casserole heated through, corn on the cobs boiled to perfection, rolls baked, and the pies heating—the guys stomped in with happy smiles and cheeks flushed with fresh air and hard work.

Derm clapped his nephew on the shoulder and shoved him in the direction of the hall bathroom with a hearty laugh. "Get cleaned up before sitting down at this fine table."

Nia had finished putting her face together, cleared away her case, and dressed as if royalty were attending the meal. She swept into the room and hesitated.

Probably awaiting applause or an awed gasp or two.

None forthcoming, Nia made her way to the table and waited to be served.

Andy sat at her right and narrated his entire day as if she really cared.

Rhona directed her husband to the head of the table and set the roast turkey in front of him. Then she nudged Syn to the side of the table opposite her mother and brother and finally slipped into her own seat at the foot of the table.

The meal was devoured, as so many Thanksgiving meals are, in a fraction of the time it took to make them. Rhona chatted amiably with Andy, asking any questions that popped into her head about college life, leaving Derm to chat with Nia, or rather listen to updates on Zhang's conference and her sister's itinerary for the coming week.

By the time the pie slices were being served, Rhona's heart rate had settled into a pleasant rhythm. The meal was almost over, and it was just one more night and a quick breakfast before she could see her guests out the door. Then, she could breathe free air once again.

A sudden quiet made her glance up, her gaze searching. *What?*

She glanced at Syn, and her heart stopped beating. The girl's eyes were full of tears. Tearing her gaze away and swinging it at her sister, her body went cold.

Nia was smiling, a teasing grin meant to allay any blame. She smacked Andy on the shoulder playfully. "Stop being a bully, you heartless thug."

Andy actually giggled and lifted his hands as if in self-defense. He turned his gaze on his uncle in a beseeching manner. "Hey, man, help me here. She's beating me in public!"

Nia took that as permission to swat him again.

Rhona wanted to back up time and hear whatever it was that she had missed. Though she knew she didn't have parenting privilege, every mothering instinct roared to life. She glared at her nephew. "What did you just say to Syn?"

Still grinning, one hand on the shoulder where his mother had barely touched him, Andy protested with fake cries of pain. "Oh, ow! Golly, you'd think it wasn't true!" He leaned toward his sister, who sat opposite, and dropped his voice to add vehemence to the moment. "You are a Chinese Brain, aren't you? That's how you IDed the mammoth bone, right? How you get straight As and impress the heck out of your uncle?" He leaned back and crossed his arms—suddenly shifting from innocent victim to a prosecuting attorney bent on making an airtight case. "You told them how you're the reason the car crashed, right?"

Syn glanced from her mom's pursed lips to Andy's tight grin and slipped from the table. She padded to Derm's study, opened the door, walked in, and shut the door behind her.

Nia shook her head. "That girl is too sensitive for her own good." She frowned at Rhona. "I hope you aren't encouraging her in that mopey, little girl 'tude she gets." Her natural pout outdid itself. "It *was* her fault. She needs to get over herself."

Andy dug into his apple pie as if prosecuting his sister had renewed his appetite.

His face a stern mask, Derm's fingers drummed the white tablecloth. Clearly, he couldn't decide whether to go along with the pretense or go after his niece.

Rhona leaned back in her chair and stared at her sister, a hundred conflicting thoughts battling in her brain. If she demanded to know what was really going on, Nia would just take on an injured tone and deny that anything was wrong other than Syn's being bratty. She turned an appraising gaze on her nephew, a strong young man who apparently hated his sister. Any comment in his direction would just make matters worse.

She met her husband's gaze and then pointed to the apple pie. "There's ice cream in the refrigerator."

Derm accepted that isolated fact and shoved his chair away from the table. Then he rose, retrieved the ice cream and a metal scooper, slapped them on the table, and then strode toward his study door.

Less than twenty-four hours. I can live through that. Rhona stared as her nephew scooped a healthy dollop of ice cream onto his wedge of apple pie and prayed that Nia had forgotten that her daughter could cook.

Chapter Four

Dark Secrets Revealed and How Tavish Dewar Makes the Most of Superstitions

Early-December

It was cold. One of the coldest December evenings that Rhona could ever remember. Despite heavy gloves, her fingers felt numb, so she shoved her hands deep into her coat pockets as she stood by her husband on the frosted lawn, peering at the night sky. Her teeth chattered as she lifted her voice against the biting wind. "What did you see? For Heaven's sake, be quick, before I catch my death out here!"

Syn trotted across the backyard, her jacket unzipped and fluttering against her arms. The grin that spread across her face could have warmed an iceberg. "It's not aliens but almost as good! It's the new satellite they're putting up to help rural communities get better service." She craned her neck back further than Rhona had thought anatomically possible and pointed at the night sky twinkling in all of God's glory. "Keep watching! There are a whole series of them, and one will make another pass in an hour or so."

A white cloud billowed in front of Rhona's face as she snorted. "I'm not staying out here another minute, much less an hour. It's too darn cold! Penguins have better sense than you two."

Syn drew her gaze level with her aunt. "Penguins love the cold. In fact, they—"

Reluctantly, Rhona pulled one hand from her comforting pocket and waved it in the air. "Save the lesson for another time and a warmer place. I'm going in." She cast a disparaging glance at her husband. "You really thought we were being invaded by aliens, didn't you?"

Derm had the grace to shuffle his feet and look a smidge embarrassed. "Well, how was I supposed to know that red glowing orbs in the sky were a sign of good fortune? They could have been the portents of disaster. Good Lord, woman, what did the natives think when European boats sailed toward their shores?"

"Uncle Derm!" Syn's voice had taken on the disappointed tone of a pedagogue who has repeatedly tried to pass on an elementary point of cultural sensitivity. "Not all natives had the same experience, and you can't just—"

Derm shouted so loud that Rhona jumped, and Syn lost her train of thought, which was probably his intention. "Look! There's another one coming. Now tell me that it isn't just like something out of that alien movie Syn made us watch and kept you as skittish as a mouse under a cat's paw for an entire week?"

Rhona glanced up, considered the tiny red orb, decided that it wasn't going to give her nightmares, and crept carefully up the porch steps. "I'll make some hot chocolate to thaw out and if you two bring in some wood and get the fire built up, I might consider sharing. There are oatmeal cookies I hid away that I might bring out, too."

Derm called after her, "You're a grand woman, Rhona Dewar!"

Feeling warmer already, Rhona managed to turn the door handle with her gloved hands and hurried inside the comforting kitchen. Her husband had undoubtedly tucked Syn under his arm to keep her warm, and they'd chatter about the night sky for another few minutes before icicles growing on their faces would force them inside. In the meantime, she could take her time and get a pot of homemade cocoa nice and hot.

She had just grabbed the package of cookies in the pantry when her phone chimed. It lay forgotten on the counter when she had gone out to investigate claims of alien invasion, so she had to jog around the kitchen island to snatch it up before it went to voicemail.

An urgent voice cried out, "I need you!"

Rhona's heart thumped, and she almost dropped the cookies. "Nia?" She clutched the package to her chest. "What's wrong? Is Andy okay?"

A spark of annoyance ignited; Nia's tone turned brittle. "It's not him! It's Zhang."

Imagining everything from business failure to a sudden heart attack, Rhona's mind raced through dreadful possibilities at full speed. "What happened?"

With a deep exhalation, Nia undoubtedly prepared herself to divulge dreadful news.

Rhona could picture her sister in widow's weeds, playing the mournful wife who had just lost her soulmate, all the while casting her eyes over the pallbearers for future possibilities. She shook herself. *Stop being so mean! Nia is hurting; I can hear it in her voice.* Rhona stiffened against the coming onslaught.

"Well, it's this way. Zhang has an opportunity to open a new dealership on the east end of Oldtown, just off Lincoln Way, leading toward Millsboro, so he's meeting with the president of the town board on Wednesday, and he really needs some family support."

Rhona wasn't sure whether to laugh at her rampant imagination or cry at falling—once again—for her sister's dramatics. She chose silence.

Nia didn't notice. "If you and Syn come, it'll make all the difference in the world. The whole town thinks so much of you, and Syn can dress nice and look like a little elf. She's cute when she tries."

Rhona's eyes narrowed, fully aware that her sister couldn't see her through the phone. She wanted to get out of this situation as fast as possible. "Well, I don't know a thing about cars, new or used, so I don't see how I can help. And Syn has her online classes, so she is very busy."

"Oh, don't be ridiculous, Rhona! Really. Do you honestly think for one second that Zhang wants you there to talk about cars and trucks? He knows more about automobiles than you ever could. So that doesn't matter. He just knows that you represent the town's interests, and the board will be swayed in a positive direction if you support your brother-in-law."

There was that. Though Rhona never felt comfortable around Zhang. His flagrant showmanship never impressed her. Still, the man did seem to know his business. It wouldn't do Oldtown any harm to develop the east side since most of the original businesses had died out generations ago. She shrugged through an uncertain hum. But then she remembered Syn. The girl definitely wouldn't want to attend the event. "Why can't Andy go? He's the heir apparent for the family business, right?"

Taking on a petulant tone, Nia snapped her words. "Are you going to help me, or are you going to argue with everything I say? Andy can't go. He's at the university now and has a lot of work to do. Zhang expects a perfect GPA, or the boy won't be finishing college, much less joining the family business. Syn has to do this." The needle stabbed deep. "Unless you don't want her to for some reason. I mean, I thought letting her stay with you and Derm would be a good arrangement while her arm healed, but I don't want you to get any crazy ideas. She's not your daughter; she's mine, remember that. Perhaps it's time for her to come home."

Well and truly outfoxed, Rhona knew she'd better take on a cheerful tone, or her sister would make good on her threat. And it was a threat, though Rhona couldn't understand why it should be. Why did the idea of sending a fifteen-year-old girl home to her parents feel like she was throwing a baby to wolves? She softened her voice. "I'm sure that Syn will be happy to come. What time do you need us on Wednesday?"

The relief in Nia's tone practically bounced in the air, though she did have to add a parting sting. "I suppose a noon luncheon does need to be clarified. We're renting the back room, so just go directly back. Zhang plans on taking the old coot someplace fun afterward, so everyone should be in a good mood."

Rhona had no idea what the town board president might consider fun, but she figured that Zhang was an expert in playing games—he certainly knew how to play the business field well enough. "We'll be there."

Nia sighed. "And make sure that Syn wears something nice. She's representing the family. It isn't all about her and her moods."

As Rhona sat on the embroidered living room chair by the window on Wednesday morning, the dryer rolled for the fifth time, nearly dropping her internal barometer through her toes. If the weather was bad—with gray skies and impending snow—her mood predicted a snappish attitude and short patience with Zhang at the luncheon.

She tied off the thread and clipped it so the coat button would hold through the next century. Then, she got up, traipsed to the front hall, and hung the dark blue wool blend on the wooden peg. She yelled in the direction of Syn's room, "Your coat is hanging in the front hall, ready for you anytime."

Syn's outerwear options had ranged from a stained jacket with a broken zipper to an old plaid coat of Derm's that he had hung onto since he was a teenager and could never fit into again this side of the Pearly Gates.

For Zhang's formal luncheon, Rhona had dug out her extra "good coat" and quickly realized why she had been ignoring it for the last five years—two buttons were loose. There was an easy remedy, but she had never cared enough to get to it until now.

The dryer slowed to a squeaky halt. Her nerves snapping in all directions, she marched to the laundry room on the south side of the pantry room, jerked open the door, and bundled the warm laundry into a basket.

Syn trotted into the room, holding the repaired coat out like a snake that might bite. "I can't wear this! It's for an old woman."

Rhona gripped the basket and her temper and hefted both to the kitchen table.

One arm flailing, Syn shook her head. "You shouldn't have told Mom I would go. Dad won't want me there. I'll say something stupid."

Shooting a glance at the kitchen clock that happened to be shaped like a crowing rooster, Rhona calculated her moves for the rest of the day. "We have exactly half an hour. Fifteen minutes to dress and fifteen minutes to drive to town, push our way through the lunch crowd, who'll want to chat about nothing and tell me everything, get into the back room, take off our coats and sit down, and look like we haven't hurried a moment in our lives."

She leaned in and stared Syn straight in the eyes. "You don't have to say anything if you don't want to. If someone asks you a direct question, just smile and say a word or two." She shrugged. "I don't see any way of getting out of this, short of murder—then I'd have to do time in the State Pen, and who would feed the dogs and keep Derm from strangling Ada when she comes up with her next great idea?"

Refusing to smile, Syn pursed her lips in annoyed defeat.

Rhona and Syn arrived at eleven fifty-seven and swept into their seats just as Zhang's throaty laugh announced his arrival. As he strolled into the room, he had his arm around the shoulder of a gentleman decades older but clearly his match in the charming department. Late forties with black hair and black eyes, six feet, and a well-defined body, Zhang appeared every inch the successful businessman.

Mr. Stewart, however, seemed too relaxed to worry about being successful at anything. He came across as a take-it-or-leave-it kind of guy. The mantle of responsibility as the town's board president resting lightly on his shoulders, he paced complacently at Zhang's side. Not that he could avoid it, as the younger man had a firm grip on his shoulder. Tall, slim, with gray hair and a bald spot on the back of his head, Liam Stewart appeared happy to go along with anything, though anyone who really knew him had learned that his perceptions were razor sharp and his decisions ironclad. He was a great friend to have on your side, but once betrayed, he strolled away and never looked back.

Nia followed the two men into the room, playing the subservient wife to the hilt.

It was all Rhona could do not to stare and ask if her sister was feeling all right. She comforted herself by ordering a turkey sandwich and nodding appreciatively when Syn followed her example and chose a simple sandwich rather than copying Nia, who ordered the most expensive meal on the menu. *She doesn't even like seafood!*

The men ordered the second most expensive meals—prime ribs and T-bone steak.

Zhang was at his salesman's best, laughing, chattering about sports teams one minute, then deftly switching to the high cost of everything, closures, lack of good jobs, and looming economic disasters. With uncanny agility, he swiftly transitioned to new business opportunities and how his dealership would alter the trajectory of Oldtown from doom and gloom to a vibrant new future.

His brown-eyed gaze fixed on Zhang, Mr. Stewart let the man make his case all the way through the main course.

Nia nibbled her food and watched the proceedings out of the corner of her eye, smiling any time anyone looked her way.

Rhona enjoyed any meal she didn't have to make for herself and even had a cup of decaf coffee to celebrate getting this luncheon off of her to-do list.

Her head down, Syn alternately took a bite, chewed slowly, swallowed, took a sip of water and then repeated the procedure until she set her napkin on her cleared plate and folded her hands in her lap.

Finally, just as pie slices were arranged in front of them and the deal seemed as sewed up as the buttons on Syn's coat, Mr. Stewart placed his napkin on the table and looked around at the assembly as if seeing them for the first time. He smiled at Nia. "You're always a breath of fresh air, Nia." He grinned at Zhang. "You're a lucky man, as you well know."

Liam's eyes wandered to Rhona, and he tipped his head. "Sure hope that Derm would be okay with a new automotive dealership in town. I know how he likes the Oldtown style and doesn't take to change too readily."

Is this a test? Is he trying to feel out how the "old-timers" would react to the news? Rhona straightened and cleared her throat, doing her absolute best to accept the responsibility as representative for nearly half the population. "Derm and I want what everyone around here wants—to see this town thrive. Good business means increased revenue, which will mean better infrastructure, and that could set a trend toward more investments, leading to a more prosperous town." She smiled her nicest smile. "You can trust that Zhang is a great businessman, and he will bring in good business."

An agreeable nod and Mr. Stewart turned his steely-eyed gaze on Syn. "So, what do you think about your dad, Syn?"

Rhona's breath caught in her chest, and she wasn't sure she could get her lungs to inflate any time soon.

Both Nia and Zhang bore down on Syn as if they were interrogators waiting for a prisoner's confession.

Syn all but melted into the chair. Finally, she lifted her head, blinked, and whispered, "He's okay, I guess."

A long silent moment while everyone waited for more.

Nothing forthcoming, Mr. Stewart laughed and slapped the table. "Well, nowadays, it's practically a miracle if you can get your kid to say *anything* good about you."

Rhona watched the rest of the proceedings with half an eye, one hand ready to grab Syn in case she slipped under the table.

Zhang carried off the rest of the meeting with his usual flair, and when Mr. Stewart agreed to bring the idea to the town board with his blessing, Nia all but kissed them both.

They all stood up, ready to leave. Mr. Stewart nodded in a courtly manner at Rhona and Syn, then passed through the doorway.

Nia thrust her arms into her heavy coat, wrapped it snugly around her body, and then sauntered ahead, talking to her husband over her shoulder. "I'll get him primed for the show tonight. It got rave reviews. We can stop and have drinks at that place on the north side first."

Rhona had just gotten her coat on and was watching Syn button hers, satisfied that nothing had popped off unexpectedly when Zhang rounded on them.

He leaned in and glared at Syn, hissing his words as vehemently as any snake. "Okay? That's what you say to an important businessman about me? That I'm okay?"

Her hands trembling, Syn attempted to tuck them under her arms, but the coat was too thick to allow such maneuvers, so she thrust them into deep pockets. She stared at her boots.

"Say something!"

Syn swallowed and tried to speak, but her words bubbled out incoherently. Her squeak sure sounded like an apology.

Rage filled Rhona. She wanted to shove her brother-in-law backward, but she didn't want Nia coming in and accusing her of assault. She thrust aside her indignation and intervened in a shaky but determined voice. "She's shy, and I know that Mr. Stewart was more pleased with her humility than if she had chattered on about what a great guy you are. Trust me, he's already planning the speech to convince the board to accept your business into Oldtown."

Exhaling a long breath, Zhang straightened and, with one last snort of disgust, let his daughter off the hook. "He'd better be."

Nia stepped back into the room and frowned. "What are you all waiting for? It's starting to snow out there, and it'll be a foot deep before we get to the city."

Following along behind, Rhona watched Zhang march after his wife, squeeze past her as they went out the door, and then take the lead to the car. He didn't open the door for her.

Mr. Stewart was already seated in the passenger side, patiently waiting.

Rhona shook her head as she stepped into the crisp air full of falling snow. *Don't think for a minute that Mr. Stewart didn't notice that omission, Zhang. Syn was being generous when she said you were okay.*

Without a word, Syn paced to Rhona's car and got in.

Nothing was said on the drive home, but Rhona could hear Zhang's words replay in her mind. She looked over at Syn, who sat hunched in her seat. *The girl should be excited by the first snowfall of the year, happy that her dad got his business deal through, pleased that Derm is making his famous pot roast for dinner. Something!*

But the dark cloud of unhappiness didn't budge an inch even when they pulled into the driveway.

Finally, Rhona pulled the key from the ignition and placed her hand on her niece's shoulder. "He didn't mean to sound so angry. He's under a lot of pressure." Rhona shrugged as if that explained everything.

Syn opened the door and squiggled her lithe body out of the car. "He hates me." Her voice dropped to a leaden sigh as she turned toward the house. "It's just as well."

Rhona stepped away from the car, then let her head fall back so the snow could fall onto her face. She peered at the swirling white flakes dropping from the gray sky. *I do not understand.*

Mid-December

Getting the Christmas tree was a traditional celebration. Rhona didn't want to get it too early because the needles would then turn brittle and start falling off, making a mess on the floor that she could never completely sweep up, no matter how hard she tried. But Derm didn't want to wait too long, or the season would fly by so fast that they hardly got used to the tree lighting up the northeast corner of the living room before it was gone.

So, they compromised and got it the second Thursday evening of December and decorated it the following afternoon. With the promise of hot cider and buttered popcorn afterward, the drive through back roads to a local Christmas tree farm was always a special event.

Derm drove his old pickup truck with one hand resting on the steering wheel and the other around Rhona's shoulders. He was the most competent driver she had ever known; so calm and collected, she often wondered if he was communing with the car. She loved the bench seat in the old Ford that allowed her to snuggle up next to him on the cold drive.

But on this perfect snowy day, when all should be right with the world, his shoulders were bunched into tense knots, and he acted as if he had a thorn pricking inside of his boot.

She glanced back at Syn, who was bundled up in Derm's old plaid coat, a garment that would've kept a naked bear content.

The girl had plastered her face against the window, devouring the scenery. If there were ever a contest for who loved the natural world, Syn would win first place. When she took a break each morning, noon, and evening and went exploring or for a run with the dogs, she soaked up every ounce of sunshine and particle of fresh air, noted the different bird songs, studied the various kinds of trees growing in the woods, took samples of everything, and had long conversations with squirrels, deer, owls, and hawks. She once mentioned a short interaction with a vulture that ended when the huge, smelly bird carried off the remains of an old raccoon. Syn looked like an elfin spirit who belonged to the woodland hills of a dreamy fairyland.

Rhona smiled at her niece. "Think you can pick out the perfect Christmas tree this year, Syn? I've been doing it for so long, I need a break." She twitched her husband's sleeve. "And I'm not sure I trust Derm to get it right this year. He's a bit of a grouch today."

Derm grumbled in his chest, turned the wheel, and pulled into the long, winding driveway that led to Henderson's farm.

Gladness filled Rhona from head to toes as they pulled into the old, classic-styled farmyard. Cut and bundled trees leaned on the wood rail fence before the low porch, and all varieties of Christmas decorations and colored lights hung in every available spot. She practically jumped out of the car, ready to soak up the spicy scent of pine resin and the comforting smell of a big outdoor wood fire that stayed lit throughout the holiday season.

Syn trotted forward and stared at all the decorations, ecstasy burning in her eyes.

Her own happiness bubbling, Rhona started to follow when a firm grip held her back. Derm leaned in and whispered in her ear. "Andy is coming."

Rhona froze stock-stiff.

Derm's rumbled voice stayed low. "He called yesterday and said that his mom told him to meet us here and get what we got." He rolled his eyes. "Apparently, Nia thinks that we have outshone her Christmas tree pick every year, and she's tired of it. Zhang doesn't care, but Nia ordered Andy to get them a good tree, like what we get, no matter the cost."

Her hands propped on her hips, Rhona seethed with all the indignation of a cat whose tail had just been stomped on. "If she wanted a good tree, she could've picked out something herself rather than sending her son to spy on us. Besides, it isn't just the tree, it's the decorations and the spirit of love that goes into everything. She can spend a thousand bucks and never get a tree to match ours because she'll just throw a bunch of store decorations on it, take a couple of pictures for social media attention, and then forget it—until she shoves expensive presents under it, which will be opened in a flash and forgotten even faster!" Her face felt hot, and a few heads had turned in her direction.

Derm stared at her as if she had just recited the entire Declaration of Independence in one breath.

She glanced over and saw horror ripple over Syn's face. *I wasn't that bad! A little frantic, but nothing to ignite such fright.*

A truck door slammed and a deep voice rose. "Hey, Brain! Picked out the perfect tree yet?"

All her giddy happiness evaporated, and Rhona was left with cold dread.

Dressed in a well-tailored long wool coat, Andy strode over to his sister and slapped her on the shoulder, nearly dropping the kid to her knees. With a grin, he leaned in and whispered in her ear. Her eyes squeezed tight like a dog about to be kicked.

Before Rhona could jog to the rescue, Derm was at the girl's side. "Hey, Andy, we were just about to check out the trees on the south field. Come along with me, son, and tell me how things went with finals." He nudged him playfully. "Any memorable date nights yet?"

Thank You, good Lord, for that man. Rhona muttered under her breath as she wrapped her arm around her niece and led her inside the holiday shop. The scent of cinnamon, nutmeg, and pine filled her nose as they walked around the perimeter, ogling all the candles, baked goods, and tree ornaments for sale, the miniature Santa and reindeer decorations, elven toymakers, and twenty other Christmas scenes artfully crafted.

Syn didn't say a word. She didn't look outside as Derm and Andy rounded the corner of the barn in search of this season's Christmas trees.

Rhona wanted to ask Syn if she'd like to choose the tree, but she knew as well as the gloom in her own mind that the joy of the day had been ruined. The girl would no more follow after her brother than engage in a fistfight with King Cobra. So, Rhona led her around the little shop, bought a small praying hands decoration, a jar of raspberry jam that Derm might enjoy, and a little candle held in the paws of a sweet ceramic mouse.

Syn watched but said nothing.

"Would you like the praying hands or the candle? The jam is for Derm, though I know he'll share."

Her gaze switching back and forth, as if struggling with the choice, Syn finally tapped the mouse and whispered, "Thanks, Aunt Rhona. You are always kind."

Rhona's heart nearly turned to goo right there in front of everyone.

A burly man wearing outdoor work overalls shuffled in, sending the tinkling chimes into a panic, and pointed outside at Andy and Derm standing beside their trucks with trees bundled, ready to be stowed on board. "Fifty-nine, ninety-nine each."

The cashier, a young woman with red cheeks, blinked in surprise. "Exactly the same?"

The man shrugged as if the world never made much sense, and he didn't expect it to ever change. "That's what they wanted. Did the best I could."

After Rhona had paid for everything, including the two trees, since Andy didn't come in and offer to pay, she escorted her niece back to Derm's truck.

Andy had his tree in his truck bed in short order and then ran over with a raised hand. "Hey, thanks, you guys. Mom would have my head if I failed her on this mission." He laughed and a billow of frosted air floated in front of his face. He directed his gaze at Syn as she gripped the door handle. "I heard you told Dad that he was okay. I burst out laughing so hard Mom almost had apoplexy." His grin widened even as his eyes narrowed. "I always knew you were a Chinese Brain. No one else in the world could've gotten away with that!"

With a sob and a jerk, Syn scrambled into the truck. She slammed the door shut and turned her back on her brother.

Rhona thrust her hands on her hips, wishing she had a hot spotlight for a serious interrogation. "What was that all about?"

Derm fluttered a hand at Rhona. "Not now, honey. It's a family matter. Brothers like to tease." He turned and slapped Andy on the back hard enough to make the young man step forward to keep his balance. "Glad we found what you were looking for. Say hi to your mom and dad from us."

Before Andy could respond, Derm was hitching himself into his cab and Rhona was forced to forgo her justified grilling and open the passenger side door.

As Andy returned to his truck, Rhona dearly wanted to yell at him— "Big brothers are supposed to take care of their little sisters, not make them cry." But the words never got out of her indignant mind. She slammed her door for effect, but it caught on her coat, and by the time she had adjusted herself, Andy was roaring down the road.

Derm's grip on the steering wheel was just as tight going home as it had been on the drive in. But at least he wrapped his arm around her again. When she laid her head on his shoulder, he grunted in satisfaction. "Well, we got a good tree. Syn can decorate it and make it a great tree."

Neither of them looked back. The silence was too loud.

That night, Rhona climbed into bed beside her husband and asked him the question that had been on her mind for months and had started screaming at her on the drive home. *It's been eating at me for years, really.* "What is wrong with my family?"

No need to clarify, Derm sighed. "I don't know." Despite the late hour, he shoved back the blankets and thrust his feet into his slippers. "But I won't sleep until I know more than I do now."

Though her heart knocked against the walls of her chest, Rhona paced quietly behind her husband to Syn's bedroom door.

Derm knocked softly. "Syn, can we come in? We have something we need to ask, or we'll never sleep tonight."

A small voice answered, "Come in."

Derm led the way. He pulled out the wooden chair that was too small for him, dragged it beside the bed, and managed to sit down without breaking the fragile thing. He leaned forward with his hands clasped.

Rhona perched on the edge of Syn's bed; one leg lifted as if she might stay the night. She glanced at Derm, waiting to see what would happen next.

Derm nodded for her to go ahead.

Startled, Rhona reached out, but Syn's hands stayed on her lap. Rhona let her hand fall onto the folded covers. "Why does Andy call you Chinese Brain, and why does that upset you so much?"

Squeezing her eyes shut, Syn struggled for control, but then she sucked in a deep breath and exhaled shakily. "I knew you'd ask. There's no way out of this." She pointed to her face. "Look at me. Do I seem the least bit Chinese?"

Derm scowled as he appeared to scrutinize her features.

Rhona braced herself against rising dread. "Not all children of Asian parents look Asian."

Syn shook her head in apparent disbelief. "But I should a little bit, don't you think?" She waved the uncomfortable silence away. "It doesn't matter. Andy always said I didn't fit in." She started to pick at her fingernails. "I always thought it was because he had trouble in school." She swallowed hard and took another deep breath. "But that doesn't matter either." She lifted her gaze. "The only thing that really matters is that I'm not Chinese. Not a bit."

The teacher in Derm took over as he crossed his arms over his chest. One leg crossed over the other was swinging idly as if he had all the time in the world to discuss his niece's current identity crisis.

Syn forged on. "Right before Andy started college, he said he wanted to do something nice for my birthday. I thought it was strange, a real one-eighty since he had started acting seriously mean during his college search. I guess he had trouble getting into the one he wanted. He had planned on going to someplace in California or New York but that didn't happen. He was stuck with a state college right here, near home."

Confused by all the Andy detours, Rhona held up her hand to stay on track. "So, what did Andy get you for your birthday?" *It couldn't have been anything nice.* She forced her mind away from some of the more unsavory possibilities.

"A DNA test."

Derm looked like he might have a coronary as he jolted upright. "A what?"

Finally letting the dark secret out of the family closet seemed to have ignited Syn's old spark. Her voice rose in indignation. "Yeah, right? And I thought it was a nice idea! But Andy knew what he was doing. He said it would show me where my ancestors came from…you know, like what part of Scotland Mom's parents came from. All that."

Rhona had to force out her next word. "And...?" She tried to lighten her tone. "It'd be interesting to know where my grandparents came from. Might be fun to go back and trace our roots."

"Well, my roots aren't in China. They're in Venezuela."

Rhona froze, so stunned she wondered if time itself had stopped. Words flooded her mind. *Synergy! You know, it means a harmonic relationship...his favorite word!* She nearly slapped herself. *How could I have been so blind?*

Derm dropped his head onto his chest, probably considering the futility of trying to make sense of a crazy world. Finally, he lifted his eyes and locked them on Syn. "So that's why Andy calls you Chinese-Brain, to emphasize the fact that you aren't Chinese, but he is?"

Syn's shoulders sagged. "It's not all his fault, I suppose. It's the pressure of being Chinese. He's supposed to be the smartest, the best of the best. Dad tells him that. Our grandparents didn't need to say it, they thought it at us every time we walked into a room, a demand for perfection." She scratched her head as if considering the situation from a new angle. "Andy has never been good at school. He has dyslexia. I never really understood why it was a big deal until I realized that I was never going to need a private tutor like he does."

Puzzle pieces slid into place, creating an ugly picture. Rhona ran her fingers through her hair, wanting to tug some out of her head. "So, he's punishing you for being smart by calling you what he knows you aren't and, in some twisted way, getting back at you for being free of the stereotype?"

"Oh, I'm not free of it. I'm just better at school, so it doesn't create so much conflict. Mom and Dad still think I'm Chinese."

Oh, Lord, help me now. Rhona had never had her mind go completely blank, but she understood the concept now better than ever.

Derm scraped his voice clear. "Your parents don't know—that you know—that you aren't Zhang's child."

"My parents don't know that I'm not Dad's child."

Rhona closed her eyes to keep the room from spinning.

Relentlessly, Derm pushed forward. "Nia doesn't know that she had a child with her Venezuelan lover?"

Syn shrugged. "How could she face that? And Dad? He'd never let me in the house again if he knew I wasn't his. It's easier for everyone if I am just what they have always said—Nia and Zhang's second kid." She rubbed her eyes against tears. "If I'm not, then they named me right, just spelled it wrong."

Despite tears in her eyes, Rhona saw through the lies to the truth. She studied her niece and then reached out and hugged the thin, brave child. "You'll always be my sparrow."

Derm closed in with an all-embracing hug. "Our sparrow."

Late December

As far as Rhona was concerned, it was a relief to tuck Christmas day away and enjoy the rest of the season with all the happiness of a woman who gave gifts that people seemed to enjoy, received things she didn't have to hide in the closet, and could settle down before the fire with a good book and a cup of hot tea. Jesus was in His crib, humanity had hope, and life was good.

Happily, Nia, Zhang, and Andy had flown out west on a skiing trip over the holiday break. Nia had made a half-hearted attempt to get Syn to join them, but when Syn said that she planned on helping Derm work on his old truck in the garage, Nia accepted her odd pronouncement with barely concealed delight.

Rhona had puttered around the kitchen when Syn discussed the matter with her mother—on speaker phone, thankfully—her heart jumping at every other word while pummeling the dough with far more force than necessary. Would the child feel guilty about skipping an opportunity to be with her family during the Christmas season? No need to fret. Having divulged her dreadful secret to Derm and Rhona, Syn appeared more confident than at any other time in her life.

The truth can do that to a person.

Relaxed, Syn lay stretched out on a wooly mat in the living room with a huge lion pillow meant for lazing around on long winter evenings. Wearing thick gray sweatpants and an oversized green sweater, one leg was crossed over the other as she propped a book on her lean stomach, Syn's eyes were glued to the page in front of her. The book's cover was dark, but the characters' clothes looked charmingly medieval, and their faces were far from scary. Derm had given her the first in a series, reporting that it had rave reviews for best in literary fiction and historical accuracy.

Rhona smiled as she glanced up from her own book, a mystery novel that involved nothing more mystifying than an oil painting and a suspicious antique dealer. She considered the absorbed expression on Syn's face. *Medieval, eh? Might be something I'd like to read.* Holding a finger in place in her book and a question on the tip of her tongue, Rhona had to switch gears when a knock sounded on the kitchen door. *Who could that be at this hour?*

It was only six-thirty, but on a winter evening with the dark coming so early, any time after nightfall seemed late. She roused herself from the couch and considered calling Derm in from his study, where he said he had gone to catch up on a little work but was probably sorting through the old truck manuals that his brother had given him.

With a sigh, she lumbered to the kitchen and swung open the door.

Speak of the devil! There before her wondering eyes stood Tavish Dewar, Derm's older brother. Six feet five, with salt and pepper hair, a neat mustache and longish beard, blue-gray eyes, wearing overalls, and a heavy overcoat, he stood there like a mountain that could only be moved by the will of God. The man hardly spoke at all. His expressions said everything that needed saying. Or so he supposed. One of the largest landholders in the county, he had inherited the Dewar family farm and added to it over the years. He didn't farm all his land, since hunting and grazing cattle added spice and variety to his existence. A man with heaps of common sense and not an iota of patience for fools, he was respected by the Oldtown population in general, though few would dare to attempt a conversation.

Rhona swung the door wider and waved her brother-in-law into the room. "Get in here, Tavish, before you freeze."

Lumbering forward, he followed Rhona, his head hanging low on his shoulders as if the mound of snowfall on his shoulders weighed him down. He swept off his wide-brimmed hat just as Syn moseyed in the kitchen. Her face lit up at the sight of him.

Rhona could never understand the effect the huge man had on women, children, and dogs. They all seemed to love him as if it were the most natural thing in the world, though he did nothing to draw anyone in. In fact, his quiet nature would seem to push people away. But not so. *He may not be handsome, but he sure is attractive.* It was a fact Rhona had accepted long ago.

Tavish glanced in the direction of Derm's study.

Syn spluttered, "I'll take you, if you want to see Uncle Derm."

Wringing his hat in his hands, Tavish seemed on the point of releasing a torrent, but he just strangled a few words to their death. "Well, there, Syn, I've got a problem I just can't solve."

Rhona's eyes widened. *What on earth could have unnerved this prominence of self-determination?* Before she could splutter her own question, Derm trotted into the room, waving to beat the band. Rhona had no plans on leaving the scene unless carried out bodily.

After a silent discussion, Rhona's eyes maneuvering adroitly between Derm's private study to the public kitchen table, Tavish made his decision, pulled out a chair, and plunked down with a heavy sigh. More than snow weighed down his shoulders.

For the first time in her life, Rhona felt sorry for the man who had never needed anyone or anything. Blessed in the arts of mechanical repairs, land development, and swerving around every attempt to get him married off or involved in social circles, Tavish managed his daily affairs with all of the aplomb of an archangel who did his duty without regard to weather conditions or foolish commentaries.

Derm sat on the bench and clasped his hands in an unnaturally tight squeeze, his gaze fixed ahead, no overt concern marring his congenial face.

Rhona knew him well enough to be certain that he was tapping his foot under the table.

Syn leaned against the door frame, attentive but expressing no opinions.

Too smart to jump to any conclusions. Considering recent revelations, Rhona's normal serenity jumped ship, and butterflies took the helm. *Is Tavish sick? Did he finally go to the doctor and get bad news?* Reverting to the stabilizing comfort of polite protocol, Rhona brought out the leftover pumpkin pie, set it on the table, and put the kettle on to boil. "In case you'd like a little something on this cold night."

Tavish smiled grimly. Then he leaned forward, ready to divulge the purpose of this evening's visit. "A dead crow, a black cat, a cracked mirror, and if that wasn't enough, my clock stopped!"

Jerking back in his seat, Derm appeared as stunned as Rhona felt. She honestly had thought it had to be some dreadful medical diagnosis. But this just plain flummoxed her brain. *When did Tavish become superstitious?* She pursed her lips tight as she glanced at Syn to make sure the girl understood her feelings on such ridiculous goings-on.

With a long inhale and then an even longer exhale, Dermid flattened his hands on the table. It had to be a man's way of signaling that he was going to get right to the point.

Tavish straightened, his eyes narrowing like a man waiting for a verdict he wasn't sure he wanted to hear.

Derm cleared his voice. "Well, I can see how such signs and portends would seem alarming, but Tav, you know as well as I, that all sorts of things happen in the natural world that bar human understanding." His gaze plumbed the depths of Tavish's eyes as if trying to infuse his brother with deep meaning that couldn't be grasped any other way.

Tavish kept his voice as steady as the rock on which Rome was built. "Perhaps. But I fear that I may not live to see the new year."

Derm squirmed in his chair, his knee bouncing so hard it was a wonder that he didn't hit the underside of the table. "Now, Tav, no one knows if we will live to see another day." He leaned in and dropped his voice, a hint of anxiety behind it. "I had no idea your imagination could go to this length." He straightened and his voice returned to its normal authoritative tone. "It's your birthday that's doing this—turning seventy? Heck, man, you're as strong as any ox I've ever met. You'll live to be a hundred and five, and it'll take ten pallbearers to carry you to your grave!" He bounced a glance off Syn.

Probably worried that this'll scar her for life, but he ought to know how tough she is. And wise. She's not going to fall for superstitious nonsense. Studying Tavish's face closely, Rhona could barely make out a hint of appreciation behind his eyes. Otherwise, he remained completely still and clearly unconvinced. Rhona practically had to grab her head with both hands to keep from shaking it in bewilderment at the two men. Without anything better to do, she pushed off from the counter and, while the men noted that it had snowed but it was due to warm up tomorrow, made four cups of chamomile tea, in the hopes that someone might sleep tonight, and passed them around.

Derm cut the pie, placed a slice on a napkin, and slid it over to his brother.

With a nod, Tavish offered his thanks and leaned back in his chair. "I know that you think I'm being ridiculous, but I found the dead crow on my back step when I awoke this morning. I didn't think a thing about it and just tossed it into the woods and went about my work. But just as I lugged my ladder to the east side of the house, where a gutter had broken free, a black cat skedaddled right underfoot. I laughed. Stupid cat almost got itself knocked on the head." He took a bite of pie that demolished it by half and then took a sip of the hot tea.

Syn slipped in closer and perched on a stool at the edge of the conversation.

After wiping his thick mustache free of pie crumbs, Tavish sniffed and continued the longest speech he'd made in years. "By noon, I was hungry as a wolf after a lean winter and went inside to make me some lunch. As I passed the hall mirror, I noticed it was cracked down the middle." He shook his head. "I can't think how it could've happened!"

Rhona leaned on the counter and thought of a dozen possibilities but didn't dare lift her voice. This was Derm's family, he would manage things.

Rubbing his bearded chin, Derm looked honestly perplexed, a studied expression he had perfected to express sympathy with a bewildered student. Not offering any possibilities, he opened a space for Tavish to ponder the matter with a clear head.

Tavish obliged. "Of course, it could've been the new guy…he's as clumsy as a sloth on stilts. Been in and out of the house all week, trying to learn my way of things." He jutted his chin out nearly a mile. "I'm too nice for my own good." His gaze turned inward, pondering his extensive generosity, no doubt.

Syn's voice wavered as she cupped her tea mug in her hands. "What about the clock?"

Derm's eyes traveled over her, no opinion offered, just waiting, patiently.

Rhona's mind traveled over Tavish's house. The only clock Tavish owned was ten times the clock of any other man. It was one of those old-time grandfather clocks that stood in the corner of his living room. It was astonishing that the thing kept time, but Tavish tended it like a loving father, so its pendulum continued to swing as rhythmically as a human heart.

As succinctly as possible, Rhona described the clock, making sure to give it all the honor it was due without anthropomorphizing the thing into a living spirit.

Her face alighting, Syn smiled. "Can I see it sometime? I've never seen a real grandfather clock."

His head tilting to the side as if the world needed to be considered from a new angle, Tavish peered at the girl. "I suppose so." He stroked his chin thoughtfully. "Could be that you and I could figure out why it stopped and get it started up again. Break this bad spell." Then he smiled.

In a flood of relieved understanding, Rhona knew exactly why her sensible brother-in-law had shown up on a cold winter evening, telling absurd tales of superstitious agonies. He no more feared the new year than he feared a long-horned bull in a bad mood.

She shifted her gaze to her husband and appraised the blush working over his face. *Why the old coot told his brother about Syn's secret and this is Tavish's way of helping out.* If the broad-shouldered Scot had suddenly discovered that his lineage was a lie, he wouldn't want sympathy, he'd want a problem to solve, a way to recover his dignity.

The joy on Syn's face gave the benediction to Tavish's offer.

As if settling the matter, Derm slapped the table authoritatively. "Well, I have a little time in the morning, so Syn and I can come by after breakfast and take a look at that clock. Rhona's got an old mirror in the basement I can finally be rid of, if you're willing to take it off my hands."

The smallest hint of a grin shone in Tavish's eyes. "Looks like my luck has changed for the better."

Rhona wanted to hug the man, but she refrained. She decided she'd make Tavish's favorite carrot-nut muffins and send them along with Syn tomorrow.

Chapter Five

Future Plans and Wrangling with the Truth

Early-January

Goals helped Rhona make it through life. She viewed her to-do list as stepping stones to higher self-actualization and a closer communion with God. A clean, well-tended home set the stage for a calm, flourishing family. Healthy meals made for strong bodies that could plow through winter and tend the gardens of life. Sensitivity to the natural world not only cultivated a happier balance between humanity and the environment but also grew the soul in boundless directions.

With all the vim and vigor of a newly evangelized zealot, she sat down at the kitchen table early Monday on a cold January morning with her second cup of coffee and arranged her calendar, a notebook, a black pen, an assortment of colored markers, and her cell phone in a neat semicircle.

Dough rested in bread pans, the yeast's magic working in its mysterious way to leaven the mixture; the rooster clock ticked the seconds in a rote rhythm; a layer of snow softened the outlines of trees and outbuildings, and Derm and Syn worked on their individual projects in companionable quiet in his study.

It was the perfect day to organize her life.

Her hands practically shook with anticipation as she opened the bright yellow notebook to the first page and headed it with the words: Goals for the Year. Then she wrote the name of each month in big, bold letters on the following pages. She'd followed this process in various forms until she had perfected the calendar and notebook combination to get her ideas from her crowded brain onto something solid in a systematic manner. As far as she was concerned, technology was great for gathering information, phone calls, and social media connections, but when it came to the big life issues, a creative, hands-on approach was needed. Pages she could feel as they slid between her fingers, the permanence of ink, and the pungent scent of markers stirred the whole body response, awakening her senses and stirring her creative energy. She was not only proud of herself for being self-disciplined, for her to-do list was law, but for having the wits to prioritize things according to importance and seasonal time limits.

First off, she tapped her black pen on the main Goals page. *What do I really want to accomplish this year?* The thought of Syn's revelation surged through her mind. She sighed. *How can I turn that tangle into a goal? For goodness' sake, is it even my mess to manage?* Her eyes strayed toward Derm's study. The girl was living with them. Nia was her sister. Syn's life was intertwined with her and Derm's now. She didn't want that to change. The threat of losing her hung over all of them like the Sword of Damocles.

She pressed the pen to the page and wrote in big bold letters: Keep Syn Safe Here at Home. How she was going to manage that, she had no idea. Perhaps it was an impossible goal. But she had made many impossible goals throughout her life and, though they didn't always come out as she planned, the ideal behind them usually started her in the right direction.

That's something.

She tapped the pen, stymied. Her brain couldn't think of any particulars. She took a sip of coffee, hoping to compel her synapses into firing. The phone chimed. She squinted at the caller ID and answered it with a question in her voice, "Ada?"

"Yes, it's me, Rhona…Ada…" A prolonged hesitation and then the sound of dogs barking close at hand.

Confused, Rhona tried to make sense of the notion that her dogs were barking on the porch and also through the phone. She narrowed her gaze and stared at the receiver. "Where are you?"

"On your porch." Ada yelped and then spoke in a rush. "They won't bite me? Your dogs, I mean."

Rhona was at the door and swinging it open before she could take a breath to answer the fearful question. No, the dogs wouldn't bite, but they'd sure enjoy interrogating anyone who got to the door without their express permission.

With the door swept wide, Nes and Wilma took their positions on either side of Ada, appearing to all the world like faithful guards just doing their duty. Nes's collie grin seemed to suggest that she wouldn't mind rounding up a few sheep if there happened to be any about the place, while Wilma's steadfast stare promised that she'd stay close at hand if the strange woman needed to be seen off the premises.

Rhona waved Ada into the kitchen, stood back a moment, and then snuck a pat on each doggy head, before following her friend inside.

At about five feet nine and twenty pounds overweight, wearing boots that could handle a Russian winter and a huge, puffy red coat with bright green pine trees imprinted over the surface, Ada appeared more imposing than usual. Until Rhona met her gaze.

The dark brown eyes were full of grief, pressed down and flowing over.

Is she about to cry? Ada was one of the most exuberant people Rhona had ever known, so this peek into a vulnerable interior came as a shock. *She can panic, whine, and wheedle a merchant into giving away half his wares. Didn't think she ever cried. Not for real.* Shaking off her foolish thoughts, Rhona pointed to the kitchen table. "You want to sit down in here or go to the living room? It might be warmer in there."

Ada plunked down on Dermid's chair at the head of the table and dropped her blue handbag with a long dangling strap on the table. "Whatever you like is fine with me."

Rhona considered the obvious lie and decided to put the kettle on to boil. She snatched her coffee mug off the table and set it in the sink. "I'll make us some tea, and if you don't mind, I think this dough needs a little kneading before it's ready to bake."

Ada sighed through a nod, slumping dejectedly on the chair.

Rhona leaned toward the hall and glanced at Derm's study door, surprised that no one had come out to investigate. *They can hear Ada's voice a mile away, probably hiding in there like mice waiting for the cat to leave.*

Once the cups were set on the table, Rhona placed a box of assorted teas on the table and let Ada choose what she wanted. Then she plopped the dough out of the first bowl onto the counter and started kneading it slowly and gently.

Ada's gaze zeroed in on the calendar and the notebook. "Oh, you're a planner too? I should have figured as much. We're kindred spirits then."

The notebook heading about Syn—a bold declaration for all the world to see—sent a shock wave over Rhona. She hurried to the table and was just about to close the notebook when she noted her sticky fingers covered in dough.

Ada waved off her attempt at secrecy. "I'll shut it if you want. I'm not a snooper, if that's what you're afraid of. Your goals are your own."

Abashed, Rhona met Ada's steady gaze. "It's okay. I just have a situation with Syn that's a family matter. Not mine to share."

Ada accepted the truth of it with graceful dignity and, with one finger, flipped the cover over the page. "Well, I might as well tell you why I've come." She took a long breath.

Her anxiety receding, Rhona returned to the bread dough. She dusted her fingers with flour to combat the stickiness and started kneading again, bracing herself for one of Ada's brainstorm ideas that probably meant extra work from either her or Derm…or both.

"There's a new guy in church, a Mr. Callum Knowles. He's disabled. Diagnosed with Lupus a few years back and has been fighting the good fight ever since. Went from being a guy who never thought about God to a man who wonders what comes next after this earthly journey is done. Seems book smart without being a showoff."

Rhona pummeled the dough a little harder than necessary. *What the heck am I to do about that? I'm not a doctor or a spiritual director.* She refused to glance Ada's way for fear she might shoot daggers at the woman.

The kettle whistled. In an attempt to catch her emotional breath, Rhona dropped the warm, smooth dough into bread pans, rinsed off her fingers, and started to prepare the tea.

Ada's voice rose and wobbled on the edge of a precipice. "My mama had Lupus." She sniffed. "She was diagnosed when I was little, but it didn't get really bad until I was eleven."

As if the ground trembled under her feet, Rhona gingerly made her way across the room and set the two cups of hot tea on the table. She slid the brown sugar dispenser a smidge closer to Ada.

Mechanically, Ada scooped a spoonful of sweetness into her tea, stirred, and then took a tiny sip. Then she leaned back and sighed. "I understand what the man is going through, at least a little. Back in the day, they didn't have all the medicine they have now. But still, it's dreadful to deal with an autoimmune disorder. Any disorder, really."

Rhona nodded. She knew the truth of that well enough. An image of her dad on one of his bad days flashed through her mind. She forced her attention back to the woman in front of her. "How did your mom…mama… handle it? Was your dad supportive?"

Ada's gaze dropped to the table, and she blinked in such a way that Rhona was certain the woman was battling tears.

"Mama killed herself that year. She couldn't face such a future." Ada swallowed hard. "Daddy was a bit of a drinker before, but he became a binge drinker afterward."

Terrible scenes rushed through Rhona's mind: Ada finding her mother's dead body, burying a woman who had given in to despair, and an incapacitated father, drinking himself into a stupor. Hurriedly, she wiped her hand and then reached out and gripped Ada's limp fingers. "I'm so sorry. I had no idea."

The large woman shrugged. "I never talk about it. What's the point? No going back. No fixing what can't be fixed." She lifted her gaze. "It's probably why I'm such a do-gooder."

Rhona's eyes widened, horrified at the idea that she had let the unflattering term slip out in public and Ada had heard about it. A hot flush worked over her cheeks.

A wave and an abrupt snort, Ada made light of the matter. "Oh, I know what people say, that I do good by getting others to do my bidding." A half smile lifted her face from gloom. "Braden was my salvation. He called my ideas 'brainstorms,' but he meant it in a nice way." Her face relaxed as her mind traveled into happier memories. "He knew that attempting to do something right in this oh-so-wrong world was the best way for me to overcome my depression."

Rhona offered another squeeze, then let the woman's hand go. This was no baby who needed to be coddled. Here was a seared soul who had traveled through the fires of hellish pain. Rhona took a sip of her tea and tried to contain the tears rising in her eyes.

Ada swigged back the rest of her drink and straightened. "I didn't really come here to tell you about my gloomy past. That's done and over, though it still haunts me in some ways, I suppose." She regarded Rhona closely. "I just want to know if you and Syn would sit next to Callum at Mass. He likes to be near the middle, as you do, and he attends at the same time. His hands don't work so well these days, so he just needs help holding the book and turning the pages. His eyesight was never good, but her does like to read and sing along." She flapped her hands. "I understand if you'd rather not. After all, he is a stranger, and—"

"I'll do it."

Rhona's head whirled around fast enough to impress an owl. She stared at the young girl who, though dressed in old jeans, a baggy sweater, and Derm's plaid coat, stared through penetrating eyes, more like a woman than a child.

With a thick book under her arm and a granola bar in her hand, Syn was ready to head outside, find a dry spot on some log in the woods, and read under the winter sun. She said it was her way of keeping in touch with nature and letting the dogs and cats know that she hadn't forgotten them. She nodded vigorously, as if to dispel any doubts. "I'd be happy to sit by your friend and hold his book and turn pages or whatever." She darted a meaningful look at her aunt. "It's kind of the point, isn't it?"

Feeling chastened by an unspoken challenge, Rhona nodded. "It is."

With a deep sigh, Ada rose ponderously to her feet and tossed her purse strap over her shoulder. "Good. Well, that's settled." She reached out for Syn's arm. "How about you see me to my car? I know that your dogs probably won't eat me, but I'd feel better if I had a little protection, just in case they get any funny ideas."

Grinning, Syn marched forward and opened the door to the cold winter world.

Hurrying to her feet, Rhona promised that she'd be at church a few minutes early and save a seat for Callum.

Then, as she closed the door against the frosty air, she peered out the window and watched Syn's lithe form holding the large woman's gloved hand, leading her down the porch steps with all the care of an experienced nurse. They were a mismatched pair, to be sure, but somehow, they were suited to each other in ways that Rhona could never have predicted. With peace settling in her heart, she collected the cups and washed them in the sink, a happy tune rising from her chest. Finally, she returned to the two batches of dough. Mysteriously, they had risen and filled out the bread pans, ready to bake.

After setting them in the center of the oven, she returned to her notebook and calendar, new goals for the year swirling in her head. *I'm almost as bad as Ada.* She smiled at the thought.

Mid-January

Taking their new Labrador, Wilma, to the vet was supposed to be a simple affair. Rhona always did what was necessary for pet care—vaccinations, flea and tick prevention, and spaying or neutering, so as to take proper care while avoiding an unmanageable abundance of animals scarfing down the dog and cat food she bought each week. She and Dermid had cared for numerous dogs and uncountable cats over the years. The cats came out of nowhere, lived in the outbuildings, devoured kitty nuggets left in dishes scattered about the place, and generally paid for their room and board by keeping the rodent population from taking over and establishing a vermin kingdom. The dogs were often gifts from neighbors with too many pups to manage. Nes had arrived on the scene just after their oldest hound made his way to the Happy Hunting Grounds.

She never paid much mind to recent trends, and when it came to pet owning, her resilience to marketing tactics designed to ensnare pet owners into lavish nonsense remained firm. Her Scotch thriftiness could not assent to spending hard-earned money on brightly colored dog food in miniature "fun" shapes that the dogs couldn't see, much less appreciate, and might give them a rash from all the food coloring or invest in dog clothes—vests, sweaters, and designer collars— which every dog with an ounce of self-respect would tear off as soon as it could. Besides, Rhona was on a tight budget, had always been on a tight budget, would probably be buried in the cheapest coffin available, so she couldn't see spending money on something that fed human vanity and little else.

The elderly vet who had taken care of Oldtown's four-legged friends for nearly fifty years had retired, and a trendy new outfit had opened up, calling themselves, "The All in the Family Clinic." Taking the name literally, Rhona had wildly misunderstood their true purpose and called them to see if she could get Derm in for a skin check since he had a festering sore where he had been stung back in the fall. The receptionist had giggled good-naturedly and confided that lots of folks made the same mistake, but they were, in fact, an animal clinic and could only see non-human family patients.

Disregarding warning drums beating in the back of her mind, Rhona changed her trajectory and made an appointment for Wilma to get spayed. She asked Syn to help since driving with an opinionated Labrador loose in the back seat didn't seem prudent.

As soon as they walked into the clinic, Syn's eyes lit up at all the animal-themed decorations covering the walls, spread across artfully arranged tables, and on inviting shelving units. Wilma charged for the bowl of dog snacks like a kid going for the candy selections.

The receptionist, wearing a blue lab coat, checked them in and recorded Wilma's weight, though the reluctant dog fought getting on the scale as if her honest reputation was at stake. Then they were led to a room with adorable dog and kitty pictures painted on the walls, a beautifully curved dog bed and smaller cat bed on opposite sides of the room, a steel fold-down table for serious medical inspections, and an assortment of bowls brimful with treats, animal apparel, and other items that Rhona could only shake her head at.

Syn did her best to comfort Wilma, who shivered in the middle of the floor.

Rhona sighed. *Probably still embarrassed by her staggering weight gain. Can't explain growth charts to a dog.* She clenched her teeth against the anthropomorphic influences all around her. *Now I'm doing it! She's shaking because the floor is cold, and she's scared of a strange place stuffed with doggie treats she can't get her teeth on.*

When the assistant finally walked in, chatted about the procedure, and then handed over a price list, offering all the extras to go along with the procedure, Rhona took one look at the fees and nearly had a coronary. The procedure alone was going to knock their budget into a hole that would take months to crawl out of. She had to swallow her pride, look the assistant in the eyes, and tell the honest truth, "I can only afford the spaying and nothing else. Really." She had kept her chin up and refused to drop her gaze. She might as well accept it; her identity as a cheapskate pet parent would be written on official medical charts forevermore, probably in bold letters.

She let the assistant lead Wilma to the back, silently assuring herself that though they may be pet-

marking zealots and she was a penny pincher, they would undoubtedly take excellent care of her innocent, good-natured dog.

Syn stared out the window on the drive home, while the empty backseat practically climbed into their laps. “She’ll be okay, won’t she?”

Rhona glanced over and appraised the girl who had filled out almost as noticeably as the puppy. “She’ll be fine. They are a quality clinic by all accounts and take great care of the animals in their care.”

Syn’s head swung around as she faced her aunt, her eyes inquiring while she crossed her hands over her lap. “You could spend a fortune in a place like that, couldn’t you?”

Rhona tilted her head. “Someone could.”

“But it’d be silly because Wilma wouldn’t even care about most of it.” She cracked a smile. “She’d rip a fancy coat to shreds, gobble down treats till she was sick, and drag half that stuff around the yard till it was ragged.”

Rhona nodded through an assenting nod. “She acts like a dog.”

Syn’s soft smile shone through her eyes. “I love Wilma because she is a dog. I wouldn’t want her to be anything else.”

Her nose nearly frozen, Rhona rubbed it with one hand as she directed the car into the driveway. “You are a sensible person, Syn.”

Syn stayed seated and silent as Rhona parked the car. Then she grabbed the handle and got ready to launch her body back into the winter world. “Guess that’s why I make Mom and Dad so uncomfortable. Because they see me as someone I am not.”

Rhona stayed in the driver's seat even after the passenger door shut with a click. She dropped her head onto her hands. *Oh, Lord, help me.*

After finishing her supper that evening, Syn retired to her room early to work on a history paper about the War of the Roses, giving Rhona an opportunity to tell Derm all about their vet visit and the return trip to pick up their sedated pet. She tried to play it off as a funny incident on a typically random day. "Despite everything, Wilma handled it well. Didn't moan or cry one bit. She's got the brave Dewar spirit."

Derm cut a glance in her direction as he sopped up the last of his stew with a chunk of homemade wheat bread. "You personify the animals around here every bit as much as any vet clinic. I'm surprised you didn't get the breath mints."

Stymied, Rhona had to ask, "What breath mints?"

"Syn said there was a whole selection of doggy breath mints on the counter. Plus, there are dental care packages, apparel for all kinds of weather, and mood enhancers for when the pet parent has to be away for a prolonged time…" He scrunched his brows and waved erratically. "Weren't you paying any attention? I hear their ads all the time on the car radio. I wasn't even there, and I know all my pet-parenting options!"

A bit frazzled, Rhona wasn't sure if Derm was joking or had gone insane. She was just about to think up a stinging reply when her phone chimed.

Nia? What does she want on a Wednesday evening? She tapped the phone. "Hey, Nia, what's up?"

A sing-song voice barely repressed inner bubbles rising to the surface. "Oh, nothing much. I just happen to be in the neighborhood, and I thought I'd stop by. I've got some news to tell you."

In the neighborhood, my eye. We live on a dead-end lane outside of town. Rhona swallowed down her plans for a quiet evening snuggled on the couch next to Derm while they both read their latest book finds. *News? Probably got a new full-page ad for Zhang's business or something.* "Sure, come on over. I'll put the kettle on."

"Oh, don't bother about that. I can't stay. I'm just pulling up now."

True to Nia's word, a bank of headlights flashed over the room, then a car door slammed.

Shaking his head in an exasperated manner, Dermid shuffled to the door, shoved the curtain aside, and peeked out. "She's here, all right. Just her. No Andy or Zhang in sight."

Rhona exhaled a breath she hadn't realized she was holding. She motioned for Derm to open the door.

With annoyance written in a bold scowl over his forehead, he motioned that he'd get to it eventually.

Once the door was opened, Nia swept in on a wave of frigid air. Before the usual hellos could be exchanged, she dug two red tickets out of her purse and waved them in the air. "Guess what I got?"

Rhona glanced over to Derm but only his back was visible as he escaped to his study, leaving her to deal with her sister's radiant happiness. Taking up the only shield at hand, she grabbed a dish towel off the drying rack, threw it over her shoulder, and stalked to the table, where she began gathering up the dirty dishes.

The scent of jasmine billowing from her long fur coat, Nia followed behind, her heels clicking on the hardwood flooring. "Aren't you even curious? These are great tickets! Well, the actual tickets are on my phone. These are just for show."

Rhona could hardly have cared less if Nia had gotten tickets to the next presidential ball, but she knew that Nia wouldn't let bragging rights go down in silent defeat. She spoke through tight lips. "Going to a big concert or something?" She had tried to imbue her tone with a lilt of interest, but it sounded forced. *Well, it is forced! Why does she do this to me? She knows I don't care about balls, dances, concerts, or any of her other social functions.*

Her voice pitched to a euphoric high, Nia pranced about the kitchen as she sang out, "They're for a Caribbean Cruise! It's a business thing for Zhang, but I get to go along as his significant other." Suddenly halting, with her hands clasped and her gaze fixed on the ceiling, it almost appeared that she was thanking God. But then she prattled on and ruined the effect. "I'll have to buy a whole new set of swimwear and a couple of dancing dresses, sandals, things to go with the Caribbean theme, you know."

Rhona's flat stare impressed no one since her sister wouldn't have noticed an enraged ox crashing through the front door. She went about her business of scraping off the plates and stacking the dishes in neat order. Then she ran the hot water and filled the sink, adding enough detergent to fill the entire room with sparking bubbles. If she could just pretend that Nia was a bird twittering in the trees, it would cancel the nerve-wracking effect of the woman's strident tone.

"...check in on the house and water the plants, not overwatering them, of course. Make sure no water pipes have broken and everything is nice and secure so—"

Rhona swirled on her feet so fast she splashed soapy water across the floor. "What? You want me to drive all the way to your house and keep tabs on things?"

Nia's eyes widened in honest surprise. "Of course, who else? You know Zhang is very particular about who he lets in the house, and I wouldn't trust anyone but you to water the plants."

Fearing that her jaw might crack if she clenched it any tighter, Rhona dropped the sponge in the sink, rubbed her forehead with the back of her hand, and tried to get a grip on herself. *Enough. Time for a reality check.* She pointed to one of the kitchen chairs. "I know you don't have much time, got to write up your shopping list and all, but I need to understand some things."

With a martyr's air, Nia plunked down on the offered chair and dropped her gold purse on the table with a decidedly impatient thwack. She raised her hands in supplication, making her thin, silver bracelets jangle. "What don't you understand? Zhang and I have the chance of a lifetime, and I'm asking you for a simple favor."

To keep from exploding into messy pieces all over the room, Rhona sat to the right of her sister, grabbed the towel off her shoulder, and strangled it quietly in her lap. She cleared her throat and enunciated her words clearly. "So, when is this trip, and how long do you plan to be gone?"

Responding to the need for facts, Nia got down to business. "It's in three weeks, early February, the perfect time to get out of this frozen tundra before I go mad. The cruise is ten days but with arrangements to meet people before and after, it'll extend to two full weeks." The attempt at dry composure dissolving, Nia's face practically glowed as she hugged herself. "I can hardly believe it! I wanted to go on a cruise for our honeymoon, you remember? But Zhang had to go see 'his people' in China. It was the worst honeymoon in history! Those people treated me like a stupid servant." With a dangerous gleam in her eyes, Nia's tone turned from bubbly to barely above a growl. "I'll never go back there." Her eyes narrowed. "I deserve this, Rhona. I really do."

Do I even know this woman? Fighting a desire to run outside for a breath of fresh air, Rhona struggled for words. In the corner of her eye, she saw Syn's head poke into the room, her eyes unnaturally wide and fearful. One look at her mother and she retreated faster than Derm had skedaddled.

If steel had been mystically infused into her spine, Rhona suddenly sat up straighter. A surge of conviction filled her. She fastened her gaze on her sister. "What about Andy?"

A huff and Nia flapped her hands impatiently. "He's in college. What about him? He's a big boy and can take care of himself now."

"And Syn? She never gets to go anywhere special. Have you even considered taking your own daughter with you on such a wonderful trip?"

A long pause while Nia's gaze swept over Rhona, her mouth turning down in petulant disgust. "You want to ruin this for me, don't you?"

Acid surging from her stomach, Rhona felt her insides burning. She clipped her words off like snipping dead branches off a tree. "Why would taking your own daughter on a family trip ruin it for you, Nia?"

A malignant glare and Nia didn't bother to hide her fury. "I'm not blind. She'd always been a difficult child, but ever since her birthday, she's become impossible." She leaned in and hissed her words. "You did something; I know you did. She always liked you and Derm better than her own flesh and blood, probably because you spoil her and tell her how great she is and swell her egotistical little head!" Her voice rose. "You practically rewarded the little brat for nearly killing me and Andy by inviting her to live in the countryside and take online classes—the special child who gets to have her aunt and uncle all to herself."

Up to this point, Rhona had no intention of revealing what she knew, but the ugly hate spewing forth from her sister removed whatever charitable hesitations she had. "I didn't turn her against anyone. You did that all by yourself. You and your deceptions. Andy helped, of course, by giving Syn the DNA results that proved that she isn't Zhang's daughter." Rhona shook her head. "How could you have been so stupid? You think Zhang can't see that the child doesn't have a particle of Chinese blood flowing in her veins?"

Under the glare of interrogation lights, Nia could not have blinked with greater stupefaction. She opened her mouth, but no words came.

With a deep sigh, Rhona climbed to her feet and returned to the sink as if it were the last bastion of sanity left in the world. "Andy has been teasing her for months, calling her Chinese-Brain, to emphasize what she is not." She peered over her shoulder, her heart unmoved by her sister's stricken expression. "What is it with that boy? So, he has dyslexia. It's hard, but it can be managed. Lots of people have learning challenges. It's no reason to treat his sister with such cruelty."

A barked laugh and Nia slapped the table. "Are you telling me that I don't even know my own daughter?"

Rhona whirled around. "Whose fault is that?"

Rising like a sprung jackknife, Nia stood and glared at her sister. "Who is she then? What did the DNA test say? Did they mix her up in the hospital or what?"

Rhona couldn't believe her ears. "She's your daughter, Nia! No doubt about that. But her father is Venezuelan!"

With her head snapping back as if by a blow to the face, Nia fell onto the chair. She clapped her hands onto her head. "Gustav?"

"Unless you have had affairs with other Venezuelans."

Her eyes remarkably dry, considering the situation, Nia lifted her head and stared back at Rhona. "Don't get all high and mighty with me. It was a one-time deal. And hell, it was good! The best time I ever had. I don't begrudge a minute of it, and if you think I'm going to apologize for enjoying myself, really being happy for the first time in my life, you've another thing coming. I loved that man. He was so good."

Rhona gripped the edge of the sink for support and dropped her voice to the arid expression of a woman who just wanted a few logical points clarified before she faced eternal judgment. "If he was so good, why didn't you divorce Zhang and marry him?"

A long, exasperated eye-roll and Nia played for all the sympathy she could get. "He was married, of course. He came over to see if he could land a teaching position before bringing his family. He had a couple of kids and wanted a better future for them. That's when he told me about Synergy, and I knew he was a beautiful heart wrapped in a gorgeous body."

"So much goodness and beauty that you had to betray your marriage vows." Rhona suppressed every nervous anxiety rioting in her mind and took her best shot. "So, Zhang really doesn't know?"

The first hint of fear rippled over Nia's face. Her grip on her purse tightened as she pressed it against her chest, the red tickets safely inside, waiting. "You won't tell him, Rhona. You can't! It would tear my family apart. You want to be responsible for that?"

"Andy is doing a fine job all by himself. It's him you should talk to."

Still clutching her purse, Nia started for the door, her head held high. "I can't expect you to understand. You never did care about me. Andy would never do anything to hurt me. He loves me. I've done everything for him."

Rhona merely watched as her sister swung open the door and stood on the threshold, one arm out for dramatic effect. "Oh, and forget about coming over to check on the house. I'll find someone else to help me." Her eyes flickered to the hallway. "You've got Syn now, and there's nothing I can do about it. Especially if she's holding a grudge about this." She paraded out the door with the injured air of a defamed woman.

Rhona sagged against the sink and dropped her face onto her hands. Only when Derm came over and wrapped his arms around her did she move, resting her head on his chest, her eyes shut tight.

Syn's voice rose from the darkness. "I'm glad I don't have to go on that cruise. I'd probably shove her overboard."

Late January

Burying herself in work, helped Rhona heal from emotional trauma. It was a Band-Aid she had used throughout her life. As a kid, her dad's spikes from delirious highs to suicidal lows left her as nervous as a treed squirrel with three hounds drooling below. She never knew what he would do next. What mood he'd be in.

Her mom worked long hours at the courthouse as a stenographer, making a decent living, no matter what condition her dad might be in. Somehow, they had managed to make their marriage work, neither demanding much from the other, two ships that sailed right past each other day in and day out. Her dad adored Nia, treating her as a princess who could do no wrong, while her mom taught Rhona the inherent value of hard work. A decent job not only paid the grocery bill, but it shaped a corner of sanity in a mad world.

When it came to managing her sister, Rhona chose the best of both worlds—she ignored the woman as much as possible and kept her own life as productive as circumstances allowed.

In silent support, Derm rarely offered an opinion on her family. Even when her father passed away several years ago, he kept his thoughts to himself while he labored to shift her mom to a nursing care facility to manage the old woman's increasing dementia. He went to every visit with Rhona twice a week and carried in whatever surprise Rhona had thought to bring—cookies, flowers, even a new pillow to support an aching back. When the old woman passed away, in due course, he followed established procedure and stood at Rhona's side at the funeral, just as she had stood at his side at each of his parents' funerals.

Aiding each other throughout their thirty years of marriage meant a whole lot more than working together to build a home life. It meant walking through the valley of death hand-in-hand as loved ones passed on, not offering callous platitudes—*It's a blessed release* or ignorant promises—*He's winging his way to Heaven now.* They both understood the price of life here on Earth was dealing with death here on Earth.

So, when Dermid tromped into the kitchen on a late Thursday afternoon at the end of the month dressed in his outdoor overalls smudged with grease and dirt and announced that he had invited Andy over to help work on his truck, she took a long breath before responding with every objection she could think of. "Why would you do that? You know how he treats Syn! She loves working on that truck with you. Now, the whole experience will be tainted by Andy's touch."

Leaning against the counter, the overhead kitchen light pooling a golden aura over the table where Rhona had been rolling out pie dough, he crossed his arms over his chest. "I think that Zhang has a right to know that Syn is not his child. Nia will never say anything. She's hoping to wring another cruise out of him before the year is over. But Andy knows the truth, and he's the one who created this mess, so he ought to tell his father, man-to-man."

The pastry dough now resting comfortably in the pie dishes, Rhona straightened and considered her husband a moment, the rolling pin swinging at her side. "Technically, Andy didn't create this mess. Nia did. Sixteen years ago." She set the wooden pastry roller down and huffed a stray hair out of her eyes. "I don't see the benefit. What good would it do if Zhang knew the truth? He'll probably want to kill Nia, and only the Lord knows what he'll say to Syn."

A grunt and Derm stared at the ceiling, praying for assistance or considering new spider webs, she wasn't sure. He dropped his gaze, his mouth as set as she'd ever seen it.

"Syn's father has a right to know the truth."

Glad that Syn was out playing with the dogs, Rhona shook her head. "Zhang doesn't care about the truth! Look at the way he wheedles deals to build his business. That man wrangles truth the way an insurance company cites exemptions."

One eyebrow rising as if in salute, Derm refused to budge off his point. "I don't just mean Zhang. How about the Venezuelan guy? Syn is his child. Maybe he'd like to know he has a beautiful daughter."

The risk of the notion sent shivers over Rhona's spine. She sat down and considered the idea before nausea forced her to stop. "No, I can't think that it would be a good idea. At least not yet. Maybe someday. When Syn is older and on solid ground. Right now, she feels rejected by both her parents and her brother. We can't set her up for rejection by her biological father, too."

A somber nod and Derm's eyes dimmed with sad agreement. "You're right. But I already invited Andy over for dinner next week, so we'll just have to deal with him." He scrunched his face like a man on the brink of sending soldiers into battle on the frontline. "I know it's hard, but Andy is her blood brother, and if we don't help manage the situation between them, no one else will. I still think Zhang has a right to know. As long as Syn is safe with us, he can't hurt her any more than he already has. If anything, it might clarify her position in this house. We want her here. If he doesn't want her there, well then, that'll be settled once and for all."

For pure logic and bold action, Rhona couldn't beat her husband. He took the lead in moving her mom to the nursing home where the frail eighty-five-year-old was well cared for during the last days of her life. He was the one who cleared out the clutter and helped to sell the old house, despite Nia's protests that she would manage it when she had time.

Rising from her chair, Rhona snatched a glance at her soulmate before the kitchen door swung open, and their red-cheeked niece bounded in with all the freshness of a cold winter evening. Her eyes danced as she unloaded her heavy plaid coat on the peg next to the new fluffy parka that Nia had brought but she refused to wear. "Owls were hooting up a storm out there, and Nes and Wilma thought they found another mammoth bone, but it was just the hind leg of a buck from last hunting season."

In silent agreement, Derm nodded at his wife. They'd prepare Syn for Andy's visit another day. Tonight, they would enjoy each other's company without anxiety.

Rhona pointed with her rolling pin at Syn. "If you get the pumpkin filling out of the fridge, I'll show you how to spice it up for the pie. Then we'll get started making biscuits."

Derm's soft smile warmed Rhona's heart as they watched their little sparrow dart around the kitchen in fluttery happiness.

Chapter Six

Unexpected Guests, New Revelations, and Old Truth

Early February

Rhona hated to admit that she didn't like some people. For a Christian woman who prayed for people daily, it hurt to know that the worst influences in her life had been members of her own family. Preparing for Andy's visit, which had grown into a full-blown Sunday afternoon mechanics' lesson, with him bringing a buddy from school and dinner afterward, she tried to marshal every virtue known to humankind. She practically ticked off the official Seven Heavenly Virtues on her fingers as she bustled about the kitchen, adding spices to the chili and getting the cornbread ready. Her hair was a mess after chasing the dogs off a new excavation project, this time in the *front* yard, and her jeans showed the effects of carrying a load of wood inside after a snowmelt had turned the yard into a slushy mess. She would deal with her appearance later.

Focus! She tromped to the stove and lifted the lid on the bubbling mass of ground beef, chili beans, tomato sauce with hot salsa mix, loaded with enough peppers, onions, and tomatoes to keep a horde of raccoons happy. Her mind wandered to bigger issues—her sanctity, for one.

Virtues? Heck, I've got 'em in abundance! Temperance has never been a problem. She and Derm enjoyed an occasional wine cooler in the summer, especially if he was barbecuing, but, heck, there wasn't enough alcohol in the thing to get a flea inebriated. *My mind and body are clean enough for a temperance society interrogation.*

She clicked the garlic salt bottle shut, picked up the chili seasoning bottle, snapped it open, and poured a healthy dose into the boiling pot.

Marital chastity was a no-brainer as far as she was concerned. Derm was her man, and she was his woman until death do them part. *Who'd want to mess with fidelity?* Nia's face came to mind, but she shoved that image away.

A little cumin and paprika and the spices were done. She scraped the big metal spoon against the edge of the pot, lowered the heat to simmer, and turned to the blue and yellow corn muffin boxes.

She bit her lower lip. Now, humility had its challenges, especially considering the snide voice in her head that often remarked on the stupid choices other people made. Online media didn't help one bit in this regard. *Small wonder that trolls rule the comments sections.* In her heart, she knew she was as fallible as the next person, but in her mind, she railed against human weaknesses as if she didn't have any. *Well, okay, maybe I do need to work on that one, but it's hard to live in a world where people do stupid things and then scream about the consequences.*

She sighed as she ripped open two packages, poured the yellow crumbly flour into a medium red bowl, measured out the oil and water, then added each in turn. She stirred at a rapid pace.

As for patience, that was easy enough. *Long as I don't have to deal with telemarketers, online surveys, jury duty, rampant scammers, skyrocketing food costs...* She considered the golden batter and decided that it must be ready. *I don't have all day. They'll be here in less than an hour.* Pursing her mouth, she had to admit that her patience was in short supply these days.

Pouring the mixture into the muffin tin felt like reaching the end of a dark tunnel until she realized that she had forgotten to spray the pan. Growling, she poured the sticky mix back into the bowl, washed the muffin tin, dried it, sprayed it with enough oil to last into the next century, then sloshed the batter into each muffin cup and slipped the sticky tray into the hot oven.

Huffing stray hairs out of her face, she paraded the last virtues through her mind like a general coming to the end of her inspection, displeased with what she'd seen.

Wisdom remained elusive, hiding itself just beyond reach. It certainly wasn't something she could pick up at the store like vitamins, but she wasn't sure how else to get some. *Well, I'm not alone. Can't think of a soul with a superabundance willing to share.*

She grabbed a stack of dishes out of the cabinet and set one plate at each place on the table. Then she went for the glasses and plunked them in front of each plate. *I want this to be a nice dinner; why am I so annoyed?*

Keep moving… Charity and kindness. It wasn't too hard to be charitable unless someone annoyed her. Then kindness was kicked down the road.

Flatware and napkins were doled out in quick order, followed by a couple of snowmen potholders strategically placed at each end of the table. She stood back and considered her work. The chili smelled delicious, the muffins puffed in golden glory, and the table looked neat.

She glanced at the clock and wiped her hands on her jeans. If her pants were a mess, her shirt was worse. She'd have to change before Andy's visit. He'd called at noon, informing her—not asking!—that he was bringing his friend Renzo.

Fine. She and her pathetic virtues could handle Andy and a stranger named Renzo. Two college guys who probably thought they knew everything and wanted to learn about old trucks by telling Derm how to manage every detail.

If she had been a chicken, her feathers would have been severely ruffled as she hurried down the hallway.

The guys were laughing as they entered the warm kitchen, which was fine with Rhona as it gave her a moment to consider the stranger before he sat down at her beautiful table. Short and stocky with dark brown hair, the young man's almond-shaped, gray-green eyes sparkled with the joy of youth and high spirits. *How on Earth did a meanie like Andy make friends with this guy?*

Derm seemed to be having a good time, too, which was another surprise since he never felt comfortable around his nephew. As she placed a butter tray on the table, she zeroed in on Andy. His face crinkling in amusement, he laughed heartily at Renzo's comment, something about accelerators and girls. It wasn't particularly funny, but since she hadn't heard the whole conversation, it wasn't fair to judge. *Yet.*

Syn hung on the door frame, apparently waiting for permission to enter the kitchen.

A quick glance and Derm, standing at his place at the head of the table, waved her into the room. "Come on, sweetheart. We're just waiting to say grace, and we'll eat."

A barely perceptible eye-roll from Andy as he gripped the back of the chair at his place.

With the naturalness of a man who says grace every day of his life, Renzo pulled his gaze away from Syn and bowed his head.

Rhona held up her hand. *First things first.* "I'd like to be introduced if you don't mind."

Derm cut a glance at Andy, who lifted his hands helplessly. Apparently, introductions weren't needed in his world, but he would play along. "Oh, yeah. Aunt Rhona, this is Renzo, a college buddy. He's going into chemistry. A brainiac." Smirking, his eyes slid over to Syn, who now stood before her chair opposite Renzo. "You'll get along great, Syn. Two brains—"

"Time to pray." Derm's expression had morphed from pleasant to barely contained fury.

Uncertainly, Rhona grabbed the lifeline offered. She clasped her hands, bowed her head, and started the prayer.

Derm's voice joined with Syn's, Renzo's baritone flowing smoothly with theirs. Andy kept his mouth shut in a firm line.

Didn't like his stupid joke being cut off. As soon as everyone was seated and Derm started serving the chili from the black pot on the stove, Rhona tried to pick up the pieces of their broken introduction. "So, what kind of chemistry are you interested in, Renzo? You hoping to work for big pharma?"

She ignored a cutting glance from her husband. If the guy was a money-making fiend, she wanted to know right off and excuse herself from the conversation. She'd set her aim to making it through the dessert with as much charm as her limited virtue allowed.

A head shake and Renzo held a scoop of chili balanced on his spoon. "No, not me. Pharma may have the big bucks, but I'd rather concentrate on the relationship between farming and our environment."

Derm's eyebrows simply could not go any higher. He stared, his spoon stuck in mid-air.

As she listened to the young man describe the chemical combinations used in modern farming, how plant and insect life had been altered throughout the land, and the necessity of understanding ecosystems and delicate balances, affecting far more than crop productivity, a joyful light cast its invigorating beams right into her heart. *He's not accusing or blaming, not angry, just knowledgeable, considering better ways of improving farming for everyone.*

She snuck a glance at Derm and saw approval in his eyes.

Before her husband could follow up with a question, Syn shifted in her seat and cleared her throat. "Do you know why they stopped rotating crops like they used to? I read that there are a whole variety of plants that help heal the soil, but we hardly ever grow them. We use chemical sprays instead."

Amazed, Rhona passed the muffin plate to Andy without taking her eyes off her niece. But suddenly, the plate slipped from her fingers, and the muffins rolled in all directions. Chagrined, she tried to play off her clumsiness with a comment about not looking at what she was doing.

Derm's previous frown returned with a vengeance. His glare should have knocked Andy into the next room.

With flailing arms, Andy was too busy elbowing his friend in the ribs. "Hey, we can't stay all night. You better eat up, buddy."

He knocked my arm, that idiot. Just to ruin the conversation.

Syn jumped up from the table and made a dash for the pantry.

Rhona knew what she was doing, and her heart stretched across the room, trying to protect her niece. She plastered a smile over her face and challenged her nephew. "We've got pie, made especially for your visit, so you have to stay for a bite." She pointed at Renzo's second helping of chili and half-eaten muffin. "And Renzo has just barely had time to get dinner in him."

Andy patted his friend on the back with an over-hearty thwack and affected a jocular tone. "Well, if he didn't talk so much and take over the whole conversation, he'd have time to chew his food."

Renzo's face turned crimson.

Dermid's expression darkened as well.

Luckily, Syn reappeared, balancing the pie in one hand and the gallon of vanilla ice cream in the other. Rhona was only surprised that the girl didn't have the scooper between her teeth.

Derm waved his hand. "While Syn does the honors and cuts the pie, I want to hear how you two met. I mean, Andy is in business, and you're in chemistry; what brought you two fellows together?"

His face as frozen as the bottom of the ice cream bucket, Andy's eyes seemed to search frantically for a plausible lie.

Keeping her composure as smooth as silk, Rhona turned to face Renzo. She wanted to hear from him. *Might learn the truth that way.*

A humble shrug and Renzo's embarrassed smile spoke volumes. "I don't remember how it happened, exactly. Andy just came up to me one day in the student lounge and offered me a cola. His math teacher had been giving him a hard time, and since I'd placed out of that class, I was able to give him a few pointers. Wasn't long before we were meeting twice a week and doing homework together." Renzo grinned. "He's always bringing something to eat. I told him that he didn't need to bribe me to help him with—"

"Hey, you slicing that pie or turning it into mush?" Andy's finger pointed accusingly at Syn.

Startled, Syn glanced up, but her gaze didn't leap to Andy but to Renzo. She stared at the young man a moment before she sat down, setting the pie cutter on the edge of the dish.

Derm shook his head slowly, which was never a good sign.

With the charm of a knight in shining armor, Renzo shoved his chili bowl aside and leaned forward. "I'd love a slice. My mom used to make pumpkin pies when I was a kid, and I've dreamed about them in my sleep ever since."

With hesitating motions, Syn gripped the pie cutter, sliced a neat piece, slid it onto a dessert plate, and then met Renzo's focused gaze. "You want some—ice cream?"

The smile spoke for itself, and suddenly Syn's hands worked eagerly.

Andy sat back, his arms folded across his chest, though when it was his turn, he accepted his share of pie and ice cream with a formal nod of approval.

Maintaining a smile through the silent dessert stretched Rhona's facial muscles until she thought they might crack. Syn's wide, innocent eyes darted to

Renzo every few moments, while Andy's glower deepened into a full-blown snit.

A soft knock on the door broke the tension.

Rhona rose from the table and answered the door.

Callum stood on the porch with the two dogs on either side, looking like proper guards just doing their canine duties. With a brace under each arm, the man could hardly keep himself balanced, but he managed to offer a quick, reassuring pat on each doggy head. "You've got two great watchmen here. Good thing I knew the password, or they'd never have let me through."

Too astonished to laugh, Rhona merely waved the man inside.

While Andy and Renzo hung back, shoving their arms into their coats, Derm chuckled as he pointed to the kitchen table. "Come in and have some pie. These young fellows are heading out, but there's a piece left with your name on it."

His braces clacking as he made his way just inside the doorway, Callum smiled a greeting to one and all. A strikingly handsome man with red-gold hair and blue eyes, his face commanded attention. But it was his soft-spoken tone that kept eyes glued to him. "Oh, no, I can't stay, but thanks for the offer. It's tempting. I love pie of any kind." Shuffling awkwardly, he balanced precariously and managed to rummage through his coat pocket with one hand. "It's in here, just got to…" With a grunt, he pulled out a small box, his gaze searching the room. "Is Syn around?"

An insecure mouse could not have stepped any more hesitatingly past the two young men and stopped in front of Callum. "Hi, how you doing?"

With a firm nod, Callum held the box out to Syn. "Doing great. But I'll be even better if you take this as a thank you for your kindness in church. I know it's a distraction helping a guy with the missal and finding the right page, even getting me on the right line in the song." He glanced to the guys who had positioned themselves between Derm and Rhona. "I'm off-key, but Syn here just braves through and just keeps pointing out the right spot, so I don't throw the whole congregation off."

Her face alight with the first honest joy of the evening, Syn playfully smacked Callum on the arm. "You're a great singer. Well, better than me. And it's fun to have someone in church who is as confused as I am. I can never kneel at the right time."

A snort and Callum pretended to smack her right back. "I'm with you, sister. Up and down! With these crutches, I'm always two steps behind and sound like the Tin Man from the Wizard of Oz besides."

Shared laughter soothed the uneven mood in the room.

Syn cradled the box in her hands.

Rhona nudged her. "Go ahead and open it."

After plucking the cover off, Syn's eyes widened. A golden bookmark in the shape of a sparrow glittered from the filmy white paper. "Oh!"

"It's nothing much, but I heard Rhona call you Sparrow one time, and I thought it was the perfect name for you. And I know you like to read!"

More laughter brought the evening to a close. Callum made his way out the door first, but Renzo was quick to follow and offer an assisting hand.

As Andy headed out the door, Derm grabbed his shoulder and held it in a firm grip. "Real glad you brought your friend. Bring him back anytime."

A shrug and Andy headed into the cold night.

Once the door was closed, Rhona leaned against it and exhaled a long, relieved breath.

Derm started stacking the dishes, his frown reflecting serious thoughts

As she filled the sink with bubbles, Syn's eyes radiated the happiness of awakening dreams.

Closing her eyes through a sigh, Rhona could only thank the Lord that though her own might be in short supply, virtues still abounded in men of goodwill.

Mid-February

Rhona tossed her bedraggled kitchen dishtowel aside and strode into the living room to check on her injured husband. One leg propped on the ottoman and his face a mask of indifference to his injury, Derm was doing his best to act as if his life had not changed one iota. Rhona could have laughed if she hadn't been so near a meltdown when she found him strewn like last season's scarecrow in the backyard the evening before. Derm knew better than to climb a ladder in freezing temperatures, but being a man with a job to do, he thought that necessity justified the risk. One emergency call later and with Tavish's assistance, he had been whisked to the nearest hospital, declared alive but with a severely sprained ankle, and fitted with a black brace. Derm hadn't said much and fury warring with frustration had choked off Rhona's attempts at conversation.

She shook her head as she stared at the oversized black boot encasing his right foot and propped her hands on her hips. "Well, you might as well get comfortable. Syn is bringing out your desk, and we'll get your computer set up out here until you can walk without stumbling over everything. Your study is a danger to circus acrobats, and with that thing on, you'll likely fall down and break every other bone in your body before nightfall."

It was useless to argue since he could hardly cross the room without falling down, but the way Dermid's eyes locked onto Syn dragging his desk into the living room—a castaway hoping for salvation—made her pause. "It's only a few weeks, for Heaven's sake. Syn managed with a cast on her arm for longer than that and never complained once."

Restraining her gasping breaths, Syn waved toward the sinkhole that was Derm's study. "I've got your computer all unhooked, and it'll just take me a minute to bring it out here, too."

Rhona cast a gaze over her husband and waited. Normally, the very idea of anyone else arranging his computer would have sent him into panic mode—he'd be crawling across the room military style to do the job himself.

Eerily, he held himself erect on the couch, his hands stiff on his lap, and merely offered a tight smile.

Has he gone catatonic on me?

Refusing to waste any more time babying a man who so well deserved his fate, Rhona started for the kitchen. A polite knock on the door made her pause. She looked over her shoulder. *The front door? No one uses the front door.* She glanced at Dermid, but his eyes were fixed on Syn as she set his precious computer on the desk and began to plug wires into various ports.

A dismissive wave and Rhona left her husband's technological fate in the competent hands of her fifteen-year-old niece. She turned and swung the front door open ready to tell the Jehovah's Witness that she was Catholic born and bred, but she'd be thrilled to have them attend Mass with her this Saturday. That usually ended the conversation pretty quick. Her smug grin faded as she stared at her brother-in-law dressed as primly as any evangelist. Even his long, wool coat asserted higher values. "Zhang? What are you doing here?"

The forced grin on his face hardly faltered. "Hey, Rhona, good to see you, too."

Heat flushing her face, Rhona stepped aside and did what she practically never did, led a front door visitor inside. She called over her shoulder, "Honey, guess who stopped by for a visit?"

Dermid got his feet faster than Rhona had thought possible and stretched out his hand. "Hey, Zhang, how are you?"

Zhang laughed and shook a finger at Derm's injured foot. "Better than you, it seems." He looked around and his gaze landed on Syn's pale face peeking around the newly installed computer. He waved like a good-natured stranger. "Hey, kid."

Syn lifted a hand and waved back, but her eyes pleaded permission from Rhona to leave the room.

With a nod, Rhona aided her escape. "That's enough for now, Syn. Uncle Derm can get the rest set up later. You go out and get some fresh air before the sun goes down and it drops another twenty degrees." Her composure back in place, Rhona motioned Zhang toward the kitchen. "You want some coffee? I can make fresh."

Zhang waved off the offer as his eyes followed Syn's dash out of the room. Then he refocused on

Dermid. “Actually, I don’t have a lot of time. I just wanted to ask a favor of Derm here.”

Rhona knew better than to stick around where she wasn’t wanted, but she’d be hung for a horse thief before she missed what Zhang had to say. She sidled to the doorway and hid from view by the wall, her hearing as good as any four-year-old listening for Santa Claus on Christmas Eve.

With just his legs in view, Zhang perched on the arm of the chair next to the couch. “I hate to have to come right to the point and admit this, but Andy isn’t the brightest bulb in the room if you know what I mean.”

A pause. Clearly, Derm wasn’t about to jump in and make things easier.

Zhang cleared his throat. “He needs help to pass one of his classes. The teacher is a jerk who won’t let him do take-home tests, but with his issues, he blanks out when faced with an exam in class.”

A low rumble and Derm mumbled something that Rhona couldn’t hear but imagined was the teacher side of her husband asking questions about what issues Andy had.

Mumble, mumble, and the two men seemed bent on keeping Rhona in the dark about Andy’s learning challenges. Disgusted with her low attempt to hear what was clearly not meant for her ears and an overpowering desire to better understand her family dynamics, she turned, ready to make a mid-morning cup of chamomile tea to calm her rattled nerves.

A voice rose and she froze in place.

Derm’s tone had altered considerably. “I understand that you want to help your son, Zhang. I just don’t understand why you seem so oblivious to the way that Andy treats your daughter.”

His voice moving across the room, a man pacing before his interrogator, Zhang's voice rose several notches. "Syn's not my kid! Andy is. I take care of my own. If Andy has a problem with her, he probably has his reasons. It's not my problem."

A streak of incredibility pierced the air as Derm's voice matched Zhang's. "You know about the DNA test?"

The pacing stopped, and Zhang's voice turned icy. "What DNA test?"

"The one Andy arranged for Syn on her last birthday that ended up proving that she wasn't Chinese. Doesn't have a drop of Asian blood."

A thick silence reached across the room, around the wall, and practically choked the life out of Rhona.

Then an unexpected laugh and the sound of a smack.

A goose chased by a fox could not have bustled into the room faster, as Rhona clenched her hands into fists, ready to finally have it out with her brother-in-law.

Zhang's hand, flat against his thigh, announced where the slap had come from, but his twisted smile didn't reassure her one bit. The man practically giggled. "So that's what's been going on! I should have guessed. That boy may not be smart, but he sure is clever."

Rhona maneuvered to her husband's side, still wary, with anxiety lifting the hairs on the back of her neck. "How did you know she wasn't yours?"

Spluttered breath and Zhang waved both arms at the obvious. "Think, man, she looks nothing like me or anyone in my family. I knew that from day one. My parents figured it out pretty quickly, too." He shrugged. "So, Nia had an affair. As long as she was discreet, and it was over by the time I came home, I couldn't have cared less. Hell, I was gone for over half a year. I even had one myself. But it would have been simple courtesy to honestly inform me that the kid I've been supporting for the last fifteen years wasn't my responsibility."

Rhona dropped her gaze. She took a breath and expelled the bare facts. "Nia didn't know. Not until recently."

Despite his unsteady footing, Derm rose and put his arm around his wife. "Why didn't you talk to her about it? I mean, this is a momentous issue to ignore for so long."

Deadpan, Zhang waved off the comment. "What was I going to say? Hey, Sweetheart, did you cheat on me and pass your adulterous offspring off as my kid? I figured I knew the truth, and Nia did her best. She'd never win any mother-of-the-year awards, but she tried, you know." He rubbed his forehead, a man trying to keep a complicated meeting on schedule. "Listen, I came to ask for your help with Andy. If you know any online programs that might help him manage these tests better, great. His friend Renzo does what he can, but he's no miracle worker. Just a kid himself."

Rhona shook her head, dumbfounded. "How about Syn? Don't you care that Andy has been taunting her for months about not being Chinese, using that DNA test to hurt her whenever he can?"

Shrugging that concern off his shoulders, Zhang retreated to his humble-guy persona, the one where he's selling you the best car on the lot and won't make a cent off the deal. "Andy is going through a hard time. Syn has a lot of advantages he doesn't. It's not fair, but life isn't fair. Ask my parents." His gaze turned inward, stark with naked grief. "They could tell you..."

An image of Mr. and Mrs. Wei filled her mind, and doubt clouded her soul. *I've never even asked them...* She swallowed uncomfortably.

Derm dropped his arm from Rhona's shoulder and hobbled forward, his hand extended. It was time to make the best truce he could. "I'll send some links that should help. But I'd appreciate it if you have a talk with your son. Syn is very important to us, and we'd rather she not get hurt anymore."

Zhang nodded at Derm and accepted the armistice. On his terms. "Thanks. Anything to keep Andy at the top of his game will be great." He turned and faced Rhona, his eyes narrowing. "Don't forget, I'm the victim here. Your sister cheated on me and then presented me with a kid that she's passed off as mine for fifteen years. Now that the truth is out in the open, I have no animosity toward Syn. She's a decent kid, but I'm not going to keep up the lie. It's a good thing you took her in." He glanced at his watch. "I've got to get going. I'm going to be late for an important meeting in town."

Derm and Rhona walked behind as Zhang made for the door. They stopped and watched him open it with a flourish and then dash down the wet steps to his red sports car.

Exhaling a long breath, Derm turned and hobbled to the couch. He flopped down and rubbed his face as if trying to wipe all traces of recent negotiations from his mind.

Rhona stood by the door, her hands clenched helplessly, as her brother-in-law zipped away.

Late February

Rhona's mom used to say that a house would grow old, but it could never grow up. The thought baffled her until she and Derm became homeowners themselves. Despite the many improvements they made, they'd still end up making more the following year. The house got older and needed new parts, but it never grew up and became self-reliant.

The previous year, a flooding rain broke through a basement wall, forcing them to relocate a number of electrical lines and rebuild the wall with expensive expert help. Derm hated to call in experts. Usually, he and Tavish could manage any problems that came up—but not always.

When Rhona heard Syn screaming about a downpour in the basement, she remembered the last expensive expert repair, and her heart sank.

Luckily, Derm had learned to maneuver so well in his special boot, that he beat her to the basement and dissolved her anxiety with a smile. "Just a leaky pipe." He squeezed Syn's neck playfully as she held up a blue bucket under the dripping pipe.

Syn glared in mock fury. "It was a waterfall! It gushed all over the floor! Look around. Good thing I came down to see what was hissing, or we'd all be climbing on the roof for safety."

Smiling, Rhona batted Syn's shoulder, but as she took in the scene, she had to admit that it was a bigger mess than *just a little leak.* She frowned at her husband. "What are you going to do?"

"Turn off the water, of course" He sighed. "I'll call Tavish and see if he has a few spare parts. We'll have it fixed by this afternoon."

Syn's face blanched. "Andy is bringing Renzo over for another truck-repair session with you. I'm making spaghetti and meatballs and a yellow cake!" Her voice has risen higher than the roof.

Oh, boy, she has it bad. In the most reassuring tone she could muster, Rhona directed Syn to set the bucket on the floor under the leak and then wrapped her arm around the girl. "No worries. Tavish and your uncle will have it fixed in plenty of time. And I think it would be great if Andy and Renzo got to meet Tav. He's a pretty good mechanic himself. He might have something to teach the guys."

With a smile fixed in place, Syn set the bucket on the floor. "I'll go work on dinner." She clasped her hands beseechingly as she stared over her shoulder at Derm. "You'll have it fixed in time, right?"

Derm pulled out his phone. "I've got Tav on speed dial for just such an emergency. Heck, he doesn't have anything important to do this time of year. He'll be glad to stop by."

Rhona led Syn up the rickety steps and leaned over, dropping her voice to a conspiratorial whisper. "He'll mention that you're making yellow cake, and Tavish will be here lickety-split. That man has a sweet tooth like no one I ever saw."

A genuine smile broke over Syn's face; she nearly giggled.

If Syn glanced at Renzo one more time before dinner was over, Rhona thought she might break out in hives. The spaghetti was delicious and the cake sweet enough to satisfy Tavish's most toothsome desires, but every time Renzo asked Syn a question,

Andy intervened with an abrupt remark, derailing the flow, and forcing Derm or Tavish to redirect.

Syn's gaze darted toward Renzo as if trying to ascertain his next move or figure out if he'd simply given up trying to talk with her.

After Tavish demolished his second piece of cake and pushed his dessert plate aside, he leaned on his elbows, an uncouth habit that he managed with calm authority, and took the situation in hand, challenging Andy with a bold stare. "I heard about some DNA test you arranged for your sister. A real thoughtful gesture." His bushy eyebrows bunched like mountains suggested the opposite.

Rhona's eyes nearly popped from her head as she dagger-eyed her husband. *What is he doing?*

Derm's fixed expression stated plain for the world that he wasn't saying anything without more information and a good lawyer.

Though Syn couldn't actually melt to the floor, she slid far enough to practically disappear from view.

For a kid habitually annoying the adults in his life, Andy didn't recognize the danger signs. He smirked and leaned back, tipping the legs of his chair like a child comfortable with pushing his boundaries. "Yeah. Can you imagine my surprise? Shocking to find out that your sister is really your half-sister and no one seems to know her true parentage."

Derm's head snapped up. "Your dad knew."

With a slap on the table, Andy exemplified his profound disgust with the situation. "Yeah, right, hey? He's a smart guy, I should have asked him first off and saved myself fifty bucks."

Rockets had nothing on Syn at that moment, and Renzo's imitation of a heat-seeking missile was nothing to be sniffed at. She was through the doorway in a second flat, but Renzo's call caught her before she got to her room, "Hey, Syn, wait a sec."

Before Rhona could think what to do, Tavish had risen from the table and cornered Andy neatly. His large hand on the young man's shoulder in a proprietary grip, announcing that Andy's interference was over for the evening.

Derm waved Rhona on, but where she was supposed to go, she had no idea. Finally, her husband took mercy on her bewildered soul and gave detailed instructions. "I think Syn and Renzo would like to see the old photos in the living room, dear."

A salute superfluous, Rhona charged into the living room to do her duty. *Okay, yeah, that'll work. Maybe.*

In a matter of seconds, Renzo and Syn stood before the mantle. Renzo held an old wedding photo in his hand and Syn was pointing. They were both smiling.

Rhona held back, not wanting to break their first moment.

Barely above a whisper, Syn relayed family history. "Uncle Derm said that he never wore that suit again so as to preserve the sacred honor of the day. But Aunt Rhona said that it itched so much he practically danced through their ceremony."

Renzo's laugh was like a refreshing shower on a hot summer day.

I like this kid. Ready to step in with her own welcoming charm, something squashed all during the dinner, Rhona ran her fingers through her hair in preparation for a fresh start.

Renzo turned toward Syn and pressed her shoulder, his head tilted down, looking her in the eyes.

Rhona froze.

Syn's gaze fixed on the young man before her.

"Hey, I know Andy can be a jerk sometimes. It's how he is. Insecure really, though he puffs himself up." Renzo glanced aside, noted Rhona with a small nod, returned to Syn, and hurried his words. "He told me about the DNA thing. But, get this, he's not making himself look good. Seems to me it was a rotten trick to spring on you. Still, you should take it in the right light."

Apparently, Rhona was invisible to Syn as she stayed focused on the young man in front of her with only a shake of her head. "Right light? I'm an illegitimate kid—"

"No!" Renzo's voice took on the first hard edge of the evening. "You're Syn, or Sparrow rather. I like that name better. You make your DNA mean something, not the other way around. Heck, my grandmother was Chinese, and she married some Peruvian guy, so my mom has mixed blood. She married my dad, who says that he has so many lineages flowing through his veins he might be descended from Martians and not even know it." His eyes crinkled in laugh lines, shaping his face into a wreath of inspiring cheerfulness. "I love your name. Remember, it's *you* that make your DNA special." Syn stared, mesmerized. "My mom always says that life challenges aren't dead ends but ladders. And she's recovering from cancer, so I believe her when she says it."

If Syn's face glowed any brighter, she'd rival the sun. Swallowing down the lump in her throat, Rhona stepped in.

Renzo dropped his hand from Syn's shoulder as Syn turned to face her aunt. "We were just looking at old family photos."

"Then you're probably all dusty now." She smiled to break any tension.

The murmur of voices drawing near turned her attention.

Derm stuck his head into the room. "Tav already left, and Andy is ready to head home now. He's got a test he needs to prepare for."

Rhona didn't care if it was a truth or a lie; her relief at Renzo's good-hearted comments had salvaged the evening. She accompanied the two men to the door and said goodnight with Derm on one side and Syn on the other. Finally, she turned around and faced the kitchen cleanup, one thought uppermost in her mind. *Please, God, don't let Syn's heart get any more broken.*

That evening, Rhona snuggled under the covers and tried to steal as much warmth from her husband as she could without leaving him an iceberg. Renzo's face rose in her mind as she murmured her summary of events. "Renzo seems like a nice boy. I hope Syn's crush on him doesn't set her up for heartbreak.

A rumbling volcano, Dermid gave his version of events, "I lost my composure and told Andy that he was an insecure brat who needs to get off his high horse and start treating other people, especially his sister, better."

Jerking upright, one hand propping herself on his chest, Rhona stared down at her husband. "I'm surprised that he didn't crash through the wall to get out of here."

Derm adjusted his pillow with one hand, sitting up straighter. "Not him. He had to let loose with a little name-calling, suggesting that my abilities to judge were compromised by my parentage."

Rhona froze.

After a long, cleansing breath, Dermid laughed. "My ability to think straight compromised, Tav took over."

With a little pressure, Rhona let her husband know that her sanity hung in the balance. "What happened?"

"Tav is a man of few words. He just asked Andy why his grandparents and dad had come to the Midwest if China was so great. Then he went for the jugular and asked how Zhang had managed to build such a thriving business without any financial backing."

Too many answers flooding her brain, with no certainty about anything, Rhona circled her hand in a hurry-up motion.

Outright laughter and Dermid sat up straighter, forcing Rhona to the side. "Don't try to intimidate me!" He crossed his arms over his chest and lowered his voice, a glance at the door reminding them both that they weren't alone in the house. "Look, it all happened in a matter of seconds, but when Andy tried his cock-and-bull routine about his dad's innate business sense, Tav cut in with a clear-cut fact. *He* had funded Zhang's business from the outset. Andy's grandparents were as broke as plates after an earthquake, and Zhang had no resources except his quick wit and charm, but he needed money, and, because he cared about us, Tavish helped him with some ready cash."

Utterly flabbergasted, Rhona didn't know where to start. "Tavish funded Zhang's first business?"

Derm nodded.

She rubbed her forehead, a headache building on an accumulation of shocks. “I had no idea. Nia never told me a thing.” She locked her gaze on her husband. “Do you think she even knew?”

A shrug and Dermid did a fair imitation of his nephew feigning innocence. “Honestly, I didn’t know until that moment. Tav was never one to brag. But he would do something like that, thinking he was helping us out by getting your brother-in-law on his feet financially.” His lips flapped in exasperation. “I should have said thanks or something, but Andy’s antics cut off all reason. I just wanted him out of the house.” He sighed. “Maybe he’ll realize that his father had no business demanding perfection, especially when he was trying his best under difficult circumstances and should have known how it felt to struggle.”

Confused, Rhona shook her head. “You sound like you’re on Andy’s side.”

“I’m not on anyone’s side. Or I’m on everyone’s side, rather. Insensitivity is practically programmed into some of these kids by how their parents treat them. They think that’s how adults are supposed to act. Andy couldn’t be the man his father wanted him to be, so he deflected his feelings by making sure that Syn wasn’t the daughter his father thought she was. Dragging another down makes a person feel that they aren’t so low on the totem pole.”

Rhona rubbed her eyes and resettled herself into a comfortable position. “Your psychological insight is beyond admirable and your metaphors delightful, but I’m exhausted by the convolutions in this family. Rather than scaling a totem pole, I think we’ve been on bucking broncos the last few months.”

Derm snuggled down in the blankets, drawing his wife in close. “Remember, Zhang’s parents probably suffered a great deal, too, perhaps at the hands of their parents who tried to make them feel powerful even when they weren’t.” He shrugged. “Hurt people hurt people, they say. Maybe even when they don’t have a clue they are doing so.”

Despite the fact that Derm had warmed her body head to toes, the vivid image of Syn’s sweet eyes fixed adoring on Renzo sent a shiver over Rhona’s heart.

Chapter Seven

How Derm Earned Heaven's Reward and Why Nia May Need New Shoes

Early March

Rhona sat on a hard chair in the corner of the town hall and prayed that she had somehow managed to acquire the invisibility superpower kids were always going on about these days. For all intents and purposes, she didn't exist, since all eyes were focused on her husband. When a glance fell her way, it was not to make human contact; it was to discern if the heater above her head was still working. The temperature could hardly be more frigid, no matter how much hot air blew into the room.

Derm sat at the head of a long plastic table, his face set in the mask she knew so well. He was trying to keep his temper from erupting all over the room. His fingers drumming on the tabletop could have clued in anyone who wanted to know, but considering the matters at hand, no one would have noticed if Derm exploded into tiny bits.

A matriarchal grandmother, a nervous middle-aged man, his two sisters, and twin teens made up the Hutchenson family group. The funeral director was due at any moment, but it was Derm's job to ascertain where—exactly—the man's wife would be buried. Gravediggers like to know these things. It should have been an easy matter. Next to her husband, of course. But poor Richie was slumped to the right of Derm, looking like something the cat dragged in after a hurricane.

Grandpa Hutchenson had bought five burial plots eons ago and had the temerity to be buried in one. Grandma had arranged a tombstone to be put on the site, staking her claim to the left of her husband, as tradition demanded, naturally giving her the willies every time she visited the gravesite and saw her name etched in black marble. She said so in a strident undertone to Richie, with her hand cupped over her mouth as if no one else in the room could hear in the deathly silence.

The three sites to the right of Grandpa remained free and clear. Richie didn't want to cause any trouble, but he did want to see his dear, departed wife buried in the family plot, next to his dad, leaving the next plot for himself. One spot remaining.

The two sisters glared dagger eyes at each other.

Unobtrusively, Rhona scrolled through social media updates, a source of the latest emotional maelstroms going on all over town. The sisters had made their positions clear before the eyes of the world, demanding that the jury of popular opinion vindicate their inherited rights. In order to fit everyone in the family plot, someone was going to have to be cremated. The question was, who?

Joan, the elder sibling, thought it mighty unfair that a sister-in-law got the prime position next to her dad, while the youngest child, Elaine, proposed that everyone get cremated to keep everything fair and save funeral expenses. Like a well-versed lawyer, she had done her research: "One full burial with two cremations, head and foot, are allowed on each site. If we mingle Mom and Dad's ashes in one vase, we'll have tons of space!"

Rhona shuddered at the word vase.

Dermid's eyes rolled Heavenward and then landed on Rhona just as she lifted hers to check, once again, what planet she was on. The anguish in Dermid's eyes bespoke his own struggle with death and burials and the whole notion of cremating bodies. He had sobbed like a baby at his mother's funeral, relieved only by the thought that he and Tav had done everything humanly possible to respect his mama's last wishes, which included cremating her remains so as to avoid extra expense. He would have willingly paid the cost to save himself the image of her body burned to ashes. Tavish's naturally taciturn disposition gave him the strength to accomplish the sad mission and bury her urn at the head of his father's plot.

Knowing how Derm's parents had lived out their sixty-eight years of marriage, Rhona considered the image of Gracie's urn on Tom's head appropriate. He may have been the man of the house, but she had always been the woman managing the man.

Imbuing her expression with every ounce of comfort she could, Rhona slipped her phone back into her pocket and prayed that Dermid would remember what she'd told him as they drove over. "You're not there to heal family feuds but to give the gravedigger accurate directions. Heck, it's a no-brainer; the next spot over is open. He just needs to know if he has to bring in heavy machinery or a posthole digger. After that, we're going to the café for our lunch date." She had practically begged, "Please, sweetheart, don't let other people's problems ruin our day."

Entering with a gust of late winter chill, the funeral director, Mr. Ives, sent relieved sighs reverberating around the room. His booming tone, "Hello, everyone!" incongruous with current events hardly seemed out of place, as his broad shoulders appeared solid enough to manage the weight of ten funerals plus one.

Negotiations were soon underway, and Derm's clasped hands stayed on the tabletop even as his knee jiggled at the rate of a teen at his first prom.

Rhona wondered if his face had frozen in place; his expression was so fixed.

The sisters wrangled back and forth, heartlessly poking their depressed brother, eliciting eyerolls from the second sister's teens as she called upon the Almighty to redress the wrongs being perpetuated upon them this day. "Lord Almighty! My boys want to be buried with the rest of us! You're being selfish, leaving them out in the cold like this. Might as well boot them out of the country while you're at it."

Finally, Derm's composure broke, and he smacked the table. "You could buy more plots."

The elder sister's ramrod spine leaned like the Tower of Pisa as she peered across the table at Derm, her eyes narrowing. "What plots?"

His hands shaking in this sudden need for salesmanship, a skill he lacked to the utmost degree, Derm yanked out the cemetery map, folded it to section F, and smacked the area in question. "There are three more plots available to the south of what you already own. Buy them, and you'll have enough for everyone, and you can always buy a section to the north, a few rows away, but close enough for Memorial Day gatherings."

Mr. Ives's face glowed in appreciation, and Rhona knew that Derm had just won favor in the eyes of one of Heaven's most trusted servants. She gathered her purse off the floor and stood up, forcing an end to Derm's position in current negotiations.

Poor Richie finally realized that he might live through his wife's funeral and grabbed the offered life raft. "I'll buy all three, and Gina will be buried next to my dad like we wanted. I'll order a tombstone for us tomorrow." His darting gaze reminded Rhona of a chickadee fending off hawks.

About time.

Fifteen minutes later, Rhona and her husband were seated at the Let's Eat Café, lunch specials were being prepared, and her chilled hands cupped a frothy mug of hot cocoa.

Derm leaned back, looking all the world like a wrung-out dish rag. "That's the part I hate the most. When families haven't settled the burial details and bring old feuds into what should be a simple matter."

"Burying loved ones is never a simple matter. Brings up all sorts of—"

Braden, in a plaid cotton shirt and jeans, shuffled over and, without an invite, dragged out a chair and plunked down. A man uncomfortable in anything less than a suit jacket over a well-pressed white shirt and tailored pants hardly looked himself in such casual attire.

Rhona narrowed her eyes in consideration. *Body Snatchers?* Syn had pleaded with them to watch the "old classic" with her a few nights ago, and Rhona knew she would never see the world the same. Now, whenever anyone did anything out of the ordinary, she had to consider the possibility that the person in front of her was really an alien inhabiting a human body.

Dermid's noisy throat-clearing yanked her back to reality.

"Hey, Braden. How are things?"

A slow shake of the head and Braden prepared them for grievous news. “Ada got me signed up for a fishing contest in Honey Bee Valley.” His eyes roamed over Dermid, beseeching commiseration. “You know the place, by the Wananana River? It’s got a resort and people from all corners of the globe come for the first big fishing of the season.” He rubbed his nose. “Only thing I’ll get is a cold and be as sick as a drowned dog. I can feel it coming on already.”

Derm’s lips quivered, though his eyes couldn’t hold back laughter. “So why are you going? Tell Ada that she’s barking up the wrong tree; you’re no outdoorsman. She’s been married to you long enough to know that.”

A pronounced nod and Braden agreed with his friend. “She’s trying to widen my life vision. Make me into a bigger man.” A wobbly hand motion before his chest, Braden clarified his thoughts on that matter. “I’m five foot six and always will be. Maybe lose an inch to old age, but I sure am not getting any bigger, no matter how many trips I go on.”

But he’ll go along and pretend to enjoy the experience just to see the glow of satisfaction in Ada’s eyes. Rhona reached out and pressed Braden’s limp hand resting on the tabletop. “You’re a man in a million, Braden Alden.”

The noisy chatter of incoming patrons filled the room until the rambunctious assembly found seating in a back booth and focused on the menu.

Apparently moving his thoughts onto other depressing topics, Braden tapped the napkin dispenser and glanced between Derm and Rhona. “Word is that Zhang’s dealership isn’t doing too well.”

Surprised, Rhona leaned back and tried to focus on her cocoa. Dermid was better at ferreting out the truth of such matters. She had a habit of asking about people's problems, while her husband got to the bottom dollar issues right from the start.

Lowering his voice, Derm allowed for confidentiality. "Not enough sales?"

Braden leaned in and dropped his tone to match, making them look like two spies in foreign territory. "He sold a flooded Ford to a couple who gave it to their daughter for her eighteenth birthday. She was going to use it for college in the fall."

Her interest quirked at the mention of a daughter, Rhona had to ask, "Flooded?"

In his typical abbreviated explanation, Derm clipped his words. "It was submerged in a flood, which no car can handle well, and then resold."

Her knowledge of cars being small enough to press into a tuna can, Rhona had to follow up to clarify. "Is that legal?"

Braden took pity on her abundant ignorance and decided to educate her. "It is—if you show the damage on the title and report all the issues that may stem from it." His gaze shifted to Derm, and his voice hardened. "The odometer had been set back, too. When the daughter drove it on the highway, it stopped cold in the fast lane, and she nearly got rear-ended. It was pure mercy that she didn't get killed. The parents had the car evaluated by experts and discovered the truth. Zhang's in the hot seat now, and no one in town will buy from him again."

The cocoa had gone cold and so had Rhona's frigid body. She thought of Syn hiking in the park woodlands with Renzo and a couple of her high school friends, grateful beyond words that the girl wasn't here to hear this. *No reason to add fuel to the fire.* She glanced at Derm, and they practically telegraphed an entire conversation. *Another blow to Andy.* Then she remembered the sisters fighting over grave sites, and her heart twisted. *Why can't people do better?*

Braden rose from the table and patted Derm on the shoulder in the comforting manner of an old friend who will be there when you need him. "We'll talk after I get back. Assuming that I make it back."

A gleam in his eye, Derm jutted his chin in a commanding gesture. "Get out there, man, and hook the biggest fish in the river. If anyone can, it's you."

A return smile and Braden nodded his goodbye, then headed toward the door.

The server ready with their specials, Rhona leaned out of the way, her eyes still on her husband. They both knew that Zhang's troubles would become their troubles. She sighed as the plate of fish and chips was set before her. Tantalizing aromas filled her nose, and with nothing better to do, she dug in with all the relish of a hungry woman who knew she'd need plenty of sustenance for the coming days.

Mid-March

Derm's 62nd birthday on March 16th was always a cause for celebration. Though not quite spring, it still felt like the harbinger of seasonal good news. Maintaining traditions long established, Rhona had invited as many family members and close friends as would fit into their small house. Then she and Syn prepared enough red meat, spicy snacks, and side dishes to keep a grizzly bear happy. Everyone would have a good time, even if it did clog their arteries.

Despite a brisk breeze, Braden did his best to grill three racks of ribs on the fire pit out back. The blaze that Dermid and Tav had built under the iron framework could have done for a controlled burn in a national forest.

Andy, Renzo, and Callum offered supportive directions while swigging beers or sodas and crunching Chex mix from a large bowl balanced on a stump. In expert moves, Callum used his braces to keep the cats from knocking the precious cargo to the ground.

While Tavish, dressed in overalls, a plaid shirt, and work boots, assisted Braden's attempts to keep the fire under the meat and from igniting the backyard, Dermid leaned against the large, colorfully decorated picnic table. Andy roamed between the snacks and the beer. Renzo practically tap-danced before them, playing the comedian, though his eyes strayed to Syn every time she came outside to refill the snack bowl.

Watching the outdoor action, Rhona held the kitchen curtain aside as Syn nonchalantly topped off an already full bowl. Renzo immediately sidled over to her as if his hands weren't already full of the mix. Heads bent, they were soon chatting like best buddies. The rest of the world had conveniently evaporated.

A hard tap on her shoulder nearly sent Rhona right through the window. She spun around and faced Nia, hoping that her heart had followed her trajectory.

Hands on her hips, a glare that could possibly have won an award for glariest expression in a contest, and a huffed breath stated her sister's mindset all too well.

"Something wrong?"

Nia pointed to the living room. "That woman! No, I mean those women!"

Blinking rapidly, as if that might give her time to decipher meaning from Nia's hieroglyphics, Rhona held her position. "Ada? The sisters—Lucia and Maisie?" She swallowed. "You can't have a problem with Elspeth Gillis. Why, that woman is the gentlest spirit God ever created, the secretary of Restful Glen, for Heaven's sake."

Her head high, Nia let loose. "The mousy one with the mouth—teetered over wearing an ugly throwback dress and ridiculous heels, like something out of a forties movie, and asked me how I was bearing up. I asked her what the h—heck she meant, and she practically simpered. 'Oh, I didn't mean to speak out of turn. Just wanted to offer my condolences.' Condolences? I asked, and that other one, the barge in bright colors lumbered over and tut-tutted me!"

Trying to get the players in the right position, Rhona spent much too long trying to figure out the identity of the bright barge.

Nia smacked her on the arm.

Rhona wasn't sure that she was okay with that. She took a defining step forward and spoke each word carefully. "I know you're upset that Zhang couldn't come, but you better control yourself, Nia, or you can go home right now."

Nia clapped her hand to her chest as if she had been shot through the heart. "You're going to throw out the victim? How perfect!" She threw her arms wide and encompassed the whole world. "Everyone hates us. Just because Zhang is Chinese, people get suspicious and think the worst things. Well, it's not true! He's a good man. I wouldn't have married him if he wasn't." She shook her head. "For Pete's sake, I'd think you'd love your own family enough to protect us."

Tired after a long day of party preparations and weary of family issues that never seemed to end, Rhona pulled out a chair and plopped down. She tapped the table in an effort to get her sister to stop glowering over her. "Sit down and let's talk. I have no idea what is going on. Fill me in."

Nia dropped onto the chair and then propped her head on her hand. "It's this town, these people. I know you think that they're open-minded and nice, but I hate to disillusion you. They are a bunch of narrow-minded, prejudiced idiots!"

With no emotion to squeeze into her words, Rhona followed up like a police detective trying to ascertain the truth behind a double murder. "What makes you think that?"

Her eyes as wide as they could go, Nia stared at her sister and then slapped the table. "They won't buy Zhang's cars or trucks. A rumor has been going around that he sold some kid a faulty car, and she nearly died in an accident. Pure exaggeration! Zhang never even saw the title report until they told him about it. They were so eager to get the car that they bought it right off the lot shortly after it came in. How was he supposed to know its history? He's not God!" Her fist swept through the air. "Oh, no, these people around here want to find fault. They want to believe that he's some sly Asian guy who will send kids onto the highway to die."

Rhona chewed her lip. It was true, she had been all too willing to believe the worst. The man was a used car salesman, after all. *Might as well be a lawyer as far as reputations went. Does the fact that he's Chinese play a part in this?* She shrugged. *Never trust anyone who says they're not prejudiced. We all have our blind spots.* She considered her sister for a long moment. "I think you're right. At least in part. As far as I can tell, no one ever asked Zhang his side of the situation."

The surprise in Nia's face made it clear that she didn't expect to be believed, much less that anyone would defend her husband's position. "So, you'll talk to them?"

Chagrined, Rhona clenched her hands in her lap. "And say what?

"What you just said! That no one is listening to his side."

Oh, Lord, how do I get myself into these things? "Well, I can go in and chat with the gals. I was going to do that anyway, and we'll see what happens, okay? I'm not charging in there like a defense attorney bent on hell-fire justice."

Nia regained her footing, her chin as high as it had ever been, and led the way to the living room. "Just plain justice would be enough."

The sisters stood in the middle of the room, laughing together, while Elspeth and Ada sat on the couch and sipped from dainty teacups. All joviality came to an abrupt halt as Nia and Rhona entered the room.

Her heart picking up speed, Rhona tried on an innocent smile and started toward Maisie and Lucia first. *Might as well get warmed up before I tackle Elspeth directly.* "How is the sewing world coming along? Lots of spring dresses to fashion, I bet."

A slow nod and exchanged glances between the sisters alerted Rhona to sharks in the water. *What is going on here?* Her nerves snapping, Rhona leaped over polite conversation and jumped off the deep end, unmindful of the blood already in the water. She threw her focus onto Elspeth and Ada. "Is there some concern about Zhang's business dealings? I vouched for him myself, and I'd be sorry to hear that my friends were jumping to wild conclusions."

Ada's "Oh, my!" was just barely audible over the startled silence.

Elspeth stood and teetered over, her petite frame wrapped in the long mauve dress, looking like an eighteenth-century schoolmarm. She glanced from Rhona to Nia. "I'm so sorry I offended you, dear. That was not my intention at all." She licked her lips and glanced back at Ada, who now stood with a petrified look in her eyes. "I heard about the car incident, and I'm very sorry that some people have taken it into their heads that one mistake means that your husband doesn't know his business. I'm sure he does. He certainly has that reputation." She swept stray hair behind her ear, her hands shaking. "I wasn't referring to that."

Nia crossed her arms over her chest. "What were you referring to then?"

Ada stumbled forward, one hand up in referee fashion. "It's my fault. I shouldn't have said anything. But Braden was so upset, and then I was so upset. I thought that Elspeth might help out somehow. Though I don't know what I was thinking. It's not like we have a body to bury or anything."

Clamping one hand on her forehead to keep her head in place, Rhona practically blew steam from her ears. "What on God's green Earth are you talking about?"

Convulsive swallows and the sisters moved in, their hands out as if to catch whoever fainted first.

Rhona glanced from woman to woman and finally smacked her gaze on Ada. "Tell me!"

Ada's eyes swam in tears. "When Braden stopped in to check in on Zhang, to see how business was going, the way he always does, you know, well, Braden mentioned what a wonderful young woman Syn is growing into, and Zhang laughed like a maniac. That's how Braden put it. Like a man gone pure crazy. Zhang said that Syn wasn't his kid, and he didn't care what she grew up to be. In fact, he was thinking of moving to Chicago—alone—where he could set himself up in big business, not like here."

All eyes swiveled to Nia.

It was a good thing the sisters had their hands ready. With all four women helping, Ada murmuring, "I'm so sorry, so sorry," in their wake, they managed to get Nia to the couch, where she flopped down like a rag doll with half its stuffing falling out.

Rhona knelt by the couch and held Nia's cold hand while the sisters stood guard in case anyone else felt weak in the knees. Ever practical, Elspeth poured fresh cups of tea. Ada stood back and wrung her hands in mute misery.

Her eyes closed, Nia appeared to have retreated into an inner sanctuary.

Taking a long cleansing breath, Rhona tried to figure out how to get Andy in to help his mother to her car without ruining her husband's party. She caressed Nia's hand and whispered in a hospital tone. "I'll get Andy, and you can go home if you want."

Nia shook her head. "Not yet. Give me a moment."

They waited in unified commiseration.

Suddenly, Syn and Renzo bustled into the living room, their happy chatter breaking the soothing quiet.

Rhona glanced over and put a finger to her lips.

Syn tiptoed over; her eyes wide with alarm. "Mom, what's wrong?"

Nia's eyes flashed open, and she immediately pulled herself to an upright position. She tugged down her cable knit sweater as if to make sure that it hadn't hiked up. "Nothing, honey. Just a spell. Didn't eat all day, and then I tried…I drank…" A suitable lie not forthcoming, she staggered to her feet. "Better now."

Rhona gripped her sister's elbow and turned to Syn. "I think she might need some rest. Tell Andy to come in and take her home."

The concern in Syn's eyes morphing to panic, she glanced over her shoulder at Renzo and back. "But he brought Renzo, and we haven't even eaten yet. That's why we came in, to tell you that everything's ready. Uncle Derm and Renzo and I got all the side dishes set on the table, and Uncle Tavish helped Braden get the meat from the pit to the platter. Didn't spill a thing." A smile ghosted over her face as she implored her mother. "You can't go now. I can help you if you want."

Renzo jogged forward. "I'd be happy to assist you to dinner, ma'am."

Ignoring the knight-in-shining-armor persona before her, Rhona studied her sister. "What do you want to do?"

Unexpectedly, Nia squared her shoulders and reached out for Renzo's arm. She plastered a pleased expression on her face. "Ribs sound great. I would be honored, sir."

Glowing, Syn ran ahead, ready to bash open the door and negotiate the path to the loaded picnic table.

Once Nia, Renzo, and Syn were out of earshot and before the others could slink away in turn, Rhona cleared her throat, halting every attempt at escape. She considered each woman in turn. "I know you probably meant well, but this is a family matter." She sighed. *There's no point in trying to cover things up now.* "It's true. Syn isn't Zhang's child. Andy gave her a DNA test for her last birthday, proving that. Lots of hurt and mistakes and muddles have made this a trying time for everyone." She shook her head. "But I'm not sure who to blame. And I really don't want anyone else to get hurt."

The four women stared at Rhona, compassion in their eyes.

With nothing better to do than follow her sister's brave example, Rhona led the way through the kitchen and out the door into the blustery March day.

Seated at the head of the picnic table, Derm glanced her way, concern narrowing his eyes.

She smiled and waved as she made her way over the uneven ground.

Late March

Nia never used to come over for tea, but suddenly, Rhona's kitchen became her go-to destination the last two Thursday afternoons in March. Despite her busy schedule, Rhona found ways of working around her sister's visits, so she wouldn't fall too far behind. It was impossible to edit with her sister's non-stop commentary, and besides, it would have been unkind to push the point. Nia couldn't possibly understand what earning an income meant. She had gone from being her father's pet to being her husband's toy.

As Rhona gathered the matching creamer and teapot—emptied of her latest spicy chi-chamomile tea blend—she considered her sister's new red-blond highlights, perfectly made-up face, revealing blouse, tight jeans, and the jangly bracelets dangling from her wrists. *She's still playing dress-up.*

Despite her sister's chic dress, once the cups were emptied, Rhona saw no reason that her sister couldn't help with a simple outdoor chore. On the pretense of "showing her something," she led the way to the back garden plot, retrieved two shovels from the shed, and handed one to Nia.

Nia squinted at Rhona in the slanting afternoon light. "What am I supposed to do with this?"

With a sigh, Rhona considered her sister's leather moccasins. "You're not really dressed for it, but I don't think you'll hurt anything. Just smack the shovel in the ground and swivel it around to loosen up the topsoil. I'll hoe it later."

A mammoth slug could not have elicited a more disgusted expression as Nia snorted. "I'm not here to prepare your garden soil! I came to visit you. My sister. The one I *let* take care of my daughter." She arched one eyebrow meaningfully.

Exhausted by the old threat, Rhona struck the earth with the tip of the pointed shovel, bent low, lifted the broken soil, and then flipped it on its back. It took three shovelfuls before she thought of a suitable reply. "Syn lives at my home because she is happy here. And doing quite well in school, I might add. Zhang has made it clear that he doesn't care to have her around. Andy made her life miserable for long enough." Her back demanding a breather, Rhona leaned on the shovel. "You never talk about anything real. Hair appointments, shopping sprees, and what all, I can never remember; it's all so supercilious." She leaned in and scooped up another mound of dirt. “Why are you here, Nia?”

Outrage pouring from her eyes, Nia smacked the shovel on the ground, where it stuck fast. “Supercilious? How’s this for supercilious—Zhang is leaving me!”

Her heart squeezing tight, Rhona let the shovel fall from her hands. Her shoulders hunching in defeat, she pointed to the bare wooden picnic bench that had served so well during the birthday party. “Come on. Let’s sit down.”

Oddly, Nia yanked her shovel from the ground and brought it with her, using it like a crutch at each step. She leaned it against a tree and plunked down on the far side of the bench.

A cat jumped on the table and demanded immediate attention.

Rhona grabbed the animal and set it on her lap. She stroked its fur as it settled in a purring mound.

Nia plucked a brown oak leaf from the tabletop and rubbed it between her fingers. “Dad always treated me like a princess, and Zhang treated me like a queen. I guess it never occurred to me that I might have to take care of myself someday.” She shrugged. “Maybe that’s why I never understood Syn. That girl always ran ahead of everyone, wanted to learn everything, see what was on the other side of a fence, be the first to race down a trail. I could never keep up with her. She was too quick and didn’t understand that everyone wasn’t like her.”

Rhona considered the images her sister brought to mind but only agreed in part. “She’s a smart girl, but she’s never been insensitive. Not that I’ve seen. I would have thought that you would bond well with her since she cares so much about people…and animals…and causes." A memory brought a smile to her lips. "Remember when she became vegan?"

Nia slapped the table, her eyes rolling. "I thought I'd go mad! The girl wouldn't eat anything. She kept asking, 'Is it right that someone has to die to keep us alive?'" She pressed her hands to her face. "Zhang wanted to strangle her whenever she talked like that, and Andy only egged her on, making everything worse. I felt so guilty."

"Guilty? You mean about her not being Zhang's child?"

Wrinkling her nose, Nia shook her head. "I never considered that. Never entered my head. I should have thought of it, of course. No, I felt guilty for eating a hamburger after she told me about feed lots. I had never thought about things like that before. And then she got on that craze about how poor kids in third-world countries were being forced to make our clothing, and I was supporting systematic abuse. Remember that? I couldn't buy anything nice, and she'd be quoting these terrible statistics. Heaven forbid, I bought a fur coat or fur anything! She tried to make me give back the one Zhang got me for Christmas five years ago; remember that?"

Rhona shook her head. She didn't remember that exact incident; all their crazy altercations had become blurred over the years. Nia had always played them off as silly family quirks.

The cat had fallen asleep, its body heat warming her lap. She let her hands rest on its back. "Do you really think Zhang will leave you?"

Blinking, Nia stared at the leaf in her hands. "In a way, I think he already has." She swallowed. "The whole Oldtown business venture was one last gasp, a wild hope that we could make our family a success."

Puzzled, Rhona tried to fathom her sister's reasoning. "His business had to succeed for your family to succeed?" She leaned in. "You knew about Tav helping him out?"

Nia nodded. "Yeah. I thought it was only fair. Tav inherited so much. You and Derm worked hard all these years, and the least he could do was help out his brother's family. Extended family, I guess."

"Tav told Derm that Zhang paid back the loan with interest years ago. Zhang has been a success for a long time. At least, in business."

Her voice cracking, Nia met her sister's gaze. "But that's just it. He never felt like a success. Not deep down. Not the way he needed to. His parents always wanted him to add on more stores, to get bigger, to do better. I never understood it." She shook her head. "As long as we had what we needed….yeah, I know. I've always had expensive needs."

"Zhang married you, knowing that's what you wanted, lots of nice things. He was okay with that. Is it because of Syn? Because you had an affair?"

A shrug and Nia's mouth drew downward. "He said he had an affair of his own, and it didn't bother him since I was discreet and all. But that he raised Syn as his own kid for so many years, well, that was unfair. Apparently, his parents were livid. They had always suspected the worst. Called me all sorts of nasty names."

The cat's weight becoming uncomfortable, Rhona carefully lifted the hulking white fluff ball and set him on the ground. Grumpily, he stalked away. She wiped her hands on her jeans and tried to think of something positive to say.

Nia sucked in a deep breath and shuddered. "Well, that garden soil won't turn itself over. We might as well get to it. I told Zhang I would have something special for dinner tonight. Who knows, he might change his mind if I try hard enough."

Alarm zipping through her, Rhona shot to her feet. "You'd better get going, or you'll never get anything cooked in time."

Nia waved her sister's concern into the backwoods. "I ordered the dinner special from a place near home. I'll pick it up on the way." She grabbed her shovel. "I may not be able to do much, but I can turn over a patch or two. My shoes will die an ugly death, but, honestly, I'm not sure I care anymore." She stared at her shoes. "Maybe they deserve it."

Her eyes dry but her heart overflowing, Rhona led the way to the ragged patch of ground she could only hope would one day be a garden.

Chapter Eight

Literary Risks, A Cry for Help, and A Surprising Answer

Early April

Rhona sat by the large bay window in the living room, her laptop on the table beside her chair, and munched a handful of peanut M&M candies. She liked to console her health-conscious spirit with the notion that peanuts and dark chocolate were actually good for a person, but she knew perfectly well that it was a bribe, pure and simple. Her muse demanded treats—preferably chocolate ones—and she had to give in or sit like a dolt in front of a blank screen.

A poem she had started during the winter had been hammering at the back of her mind, and with Syn with Dermid and Tav on one of their jaunts into the deep woods before summer vines took over, she figured she would finally face her Inner Artist and let it have its say.

It demanded M&Ms.

Weak in the face of her own creative limitations, she gave in.

Bracing herself with a couple of yellows and a red, she straightened, scraped her throat clear, and gently murmured her poetic outpouring, glad that no one else was around to hear.

She Stands Upon

She stands upon a

Frozen, snow-covered land.

Mesmerized by shining sparkles, white drifts,
heavy laden bushes.

Brown sparrows and red cardinals flitter and fluff
under a cold sun.
Survival
Pumps blood,
Gives hope to flight.

Last season's garden forlorn in broken stems
unplowed.
Slippery roads, frostbiting chill, warning clouds.
Stillness and quiet.
Nowhere to go.

Remembering,
Golden yesterdays bring warm thoughts.
Traveling over seasons long ended, ever renewed
in poignant dreams.

Splat.
Melting drops slide down rooftops, forming icy
puddles on the barren ground.
Snow clusters wave upon bowed branches.
And fall.

Rays of strengthening sunlight reach out.
Taking hold of the cold.

Memories give way to present glory.
Seedlings in cups set by a warming window.

Bare branches freed from snow prisons

Bounce in a promising breeze.

Sparrows join in fluttering flight.
Cardinals pair up in nesting union.

Underfoot the hard soil softens.
Gardens await seedlings.

Trailing softly away from memories to present moment,
Ever active even in stillness.

Yesterday's rebirth,
In hoping hearts.

Sleeping gardens and soon-to-be nests
Play their part.

Before she could change another word or delete the whole thing in a fit of anxiety, she pasted it onto an open submissions page. She listed the author as "Anonymous" and hoped that Ada would never know the truth.

Her friend's newest brainstorm—***Oldtown's Artists' Club***—was open for offerings the entire month of April. Rhona hadn't really planned to submit anything. She had hoped that Syn would come up with an idea, but the girl was suffering from Renzo-obsession and could hardly think of anything else.

Poor Ada seemed so discouraged when nothing showed up in her inbox this week.

So, Rhona had grabbed a large bag of peanut M&Ms off the store shelves, raced home, put all the groceries in their proper place, sat at her work desk, retrieved the half-completed literary piece on her computer, and bribed the heck out of her Muse.

She sighed in relief as the computer reported the success of her mission. *It's done. At least Ada can say she got—*

Bling!

A return message from Ada:

"Hello, Creative Spirit!

Thank you for contributing to *Old Town's Artists' Club*. I know your efforts will add to our community endeavor as well as encourage other latent talents to blossom in the light of recognition and well-deserved praise.

Your friend and Club President (Temporarily),

~Ada Alden

P. S. We now have two paintings, a children's book submission, one sculpture, and there are RUMORS of a band starting up, possibly performing at the Sewing Shop one night a month.

P. P. S. Can you ask Syn to stop by the Literary Enlightenment Bookstore on Friday at four? I want to enlist Mr. Thompson's help and maybe get Syn involved, too. If that's all right, of course. See you at the cookie table on Sunday!

Rhona's mind blanked for longer than she thought possible, barring a stroke. *I thought you didn't have any submissions! How did you know it was me when...*

Then she looked at the address bar with her name prominently displayed and slapped her forehead. *My brain does not think like technology thinks!*

She reread the postscripts, and her heart lightened. *Might do Syn good. It certainly would give her something besides Renzo to think about.*

A chime on her phone alerted her to a new message.

What now?

"Good afternoon, Rhona! Would you ask your sister, Nia, to stop by the next time she is in town? It's been hard to reach her these days. She ordered a new dress, and we just finished it—a little behind schedule, I'm afraid. Too busy for words!

Happy Springtime!

Maisie

Rhona supposed she could call Nia, though dealing with her sister wasn't at the top of her to-do list today. She sighed as she realized that reprioritization might be in order. *She probably ordered it before the big blow-up with Zhang. May not be many opportunities to sport a fancy dress this summer.*

Since she had just done one hard thing, it didn't seem impossible to do two more. Rhona messaged Mr. Thompson first and set up the Friday meeting. *I'll figure out how to get Syn there later.* Then she shut her computer and stepped onto the porch. Bright rays of sunlight revitalized her waning spirit. She hit Nia's number and prayed that her sister wanted a new dress.

On Friday afternoon, despite spitting rain, Rhona decided to stop off at the Let's Eat Café before taking Syn to the bookstore. Her head stuffed and her throat aching, a night off cooking duty would do everyone good. Besides, the café advertised a new fish and chips carry-out that she had been meaning to try.

Surprisingly eager to get to the bookstore on time, Syn asked to be let out on Main Street. She wanted to walk the rest of the way, while Rhona ducked into the café to put in her order.

In no mood to argue with the silliness of walking in the rain on a fine April afternoon, Rhona parked the car, waved her niece on, and then trudged through the front door, doing her best not to sniffle or cough.

Elspeth Gillis stood in line; her handbag neatly tucked under one arm.

A sneeze exploded before Rhona could stop it. Chagrined, she practically buried her head in her purse, searching for a tissue. A hand gripped her arm.

With the fiery eyes of a martyr facing the plague on a mission of mercy, Elspeth held out a pink plastic tissue bag. "Oh, my dear, you do not appear well."

Just what I wanted to hear. Her fingers slipping every which way but the one needed to unpeel the plastic wrapper, Rhona could feel her pulse throbbing in her temple. "Oh, just a little cold. Spring, you know. Happens to everyone."

Apparently unable to watch her tissues mangled, Elspeth snatched back the bag, opened the slit, dragged forth a single tissue, and waved it like a white flag at a finishing line.

Another sneeze threatening, Rhona didn't waste time with pride. Pretending that her nose blowing didn't sound like a flock of geese honking irate directions to the lead goose, Rhona eventually got her nose to behave properly in polite society. For a moment, anyway. She blinked through watery eyes. "You here to get the fish and chips, too, eh?"

Beaming, Elspeth proclaimed her culinary mission. "Oh, yes! I had them for the first time last Friday, delicious! I vowed I'd return every Friday this month. So good to support local businesses." As the customer ahead dealt with debit card issues, her gaze roamed over Rhona as if her friend were hiding something. Or someone. 'Where's your darling Syn?"

"Oh, she's gone ahead to the bookstore. Meeting Ada there with Mr. Thompson. A new project, of course. The Artists' Club, you heard about it?"

Gleaming eyes—typically just a literary turn of phrase—suddenly took on a literal meaning as Rhona assessed the woman before her. "Elspeth? Is something wrong?"

The hostess was ready for their order.

Naturally, Elspeth went first.

It only took a moment as the shining-faced hostess handed over a red striped box. "We had it all ready for you!"

Beaming back, Elspeth paid with a perfectly well-behaved debit card and stepped aside.

Her turn, Rhona ordered three Fish and Chips Delights, and the shining face clouded. "You'll have to wait. Our new batch of fish needs a few more minutes."

Question marks doing a jig on her aching brain, Rhona steered Elspeth to a quiet corner of the café. "Are *you* okay?"

The petite woman stared into Rhona's soul and begged, "Can I come? Please?"

Taken aback, Rhona rubbed her nose to keep another sneeze at bay. "To the bookstore? To see Ada about the club?"

"Is Mr. Thompson going to help out?"

"That was Ada's plan. To rope Syn and Mr. Thompson in…" Rhona squinted at the woman she realized that she hardly knew. "What's going on?"

A quick glance around and dropping her voice to the barest whisper audible to human ears, Elspeth leaned in practically nose to nose. "I'd like to get to know Mr. Thompson better."

Comprehension filling her, along with a hot blush that may or may not have anything to do with a rising fever, Rhona held her grin in check. She returned to the counter, told the hostess she'd be right back, and steered Elspeth and her box of fish and chips out the door.

A spring lamb could not have been more obliging.

As they stepped into the warmly lit bookstore, Rhona sighted the three conspirators standing together next to the mystery section. Even Agatha Christie had a sly expression on her face. Rhona led her charge to the small group and lifted her hand in a salutation. "I've got another club member for you." Then she sneezed.

Mid-April

When it came to springtime planting, Rhona tended to get ahead of herself. She had vowed to wait until the ground had thawed and the winter clouds had cleared before planting seeds in the waiting trays by the south window. She stuck to her promise.

On a sunny afternoon in the middle of the month, she shoved the couch two feet from the big bay window in the living room, centered a long plastic table before the bright pane of glass, and then gathered her planting cups, trays, garden soil, and seed packets. In control of her universe, she laid everything out in neat order, as light rays streamed into the room, warming her spirits. She hummed in proud satisfaction as she labeled each seed cup: Bell Peppers, Jalapeno Peppers, Cherry Tomatoes, Big Boy Tomatoes, Zucchini, Acorn Squash, Green Beans, and Cucumbers. She shook her head at the cucumber cup. *Didn't do too well in that raised bed last year. I'll have to find a better spot—*

Her phone chimed, and it took a good five seconds to wipe the dirt off her fingers, check the name, control a jolt through her chest, and answer in some semblance of a calm voice. "Andy?"

No soft intro. "Mom wants to kill herself. You better get over here."

A tangle of images racing through her mind, Rhona felt a sense of déjà vu as she bustled from the living room to her husband's study. Both he and Syn turned with startled expressions when she burst in; it didn't take long to explain.

Derm wanted to go with her, but she insisted that he stay with Syn. Nia's house was over an hour away, but she had made the drive enough times to find it without worry. And if there was any real danger, she'd call for emergency backup.

Syn rose shakily to her feet. "But I'm her daughter! I need to be there."

Hesitating, Rhona wasn't sure what to do, until she met Derm's unswerving gaze as he wrapped his arm around his niece. "It's probably best that your aunt talks with her first and see what's going on. She may be talking crazy, but likely this is a call for help, and the fewer people muddying the waters, the better."

Though his words reasoned the situation clearly enough, it was his expression that spoke a deeper truth. Syn didn't need to experience her mother's meltdown and threatening suicide was a whole new level of trauma.

Throughout the drive, Rhona's mind wandered from childhood memories of Nia wearing her star-studded tiara as she paraded in front of a mirror to the little gasps that escaped her chest when she tried to turn the soil in the garden. *She didn't try very hard for very long, but she did try.* That was enough to make Rhona hope that her sister might consider life beyond dress-up and shallow relationships.

She pulled into Nia's driveway; her stomach tied into sickening knots.

Andy jogged forward and intercepted her as she got out of her car. "She's in her bedroom, resting. I gave her a little wine but added some Nyquil to make her sleepy."

Rhona reared back. "You did what?"

"I read it in a book. It seemed like a good option." He shrugged. "She wouldn't listen to reason."

Taking slow steps, Rhona started for the ornate front door. "What started it? I mean, she didn't just wake up wanting to kill herself."

Andy halted, his head falling back, his gaze on the bright blue sky. "Dad moved out last night. He's got a new job in Chicago. Finalized the sale of his local businesses earlier this week. Took a loss but said he didn't care. He wants to start fresh."

Rhona gripped her nephew's shoulder. "And you? How are you doing?"

"I got finals coming up next month. Renzo has been helping me." A long shudder worked over his body. "I don't know what I'll do if Mom leaves me."

Rhona leaned in for direct eye contact. "Your dad is going through a hard time; give him space to get his life sorted out. Hang in there. Right now, your mom needs you."

Andy didn't follow as she made her way up the porch steps and inside the house.

A lavish entryway with cream tile flooring and white walls startled her with its opulence every time she came. The front room, with an oversized entertainment center, steel framed couches, two leather recliners, and three modern paintings that represented nothing but splashes of dull hues, made her think of a futuristic dystopian novel—cold and sterile, not a particle out of place, unmoving, unloved.

Rhona crossed over the beige shag carpet and grabbed the curved banister for support. She called out, "Nia? I'm coming up. We need to talk, okay?"

Nothing. Not a breath stirred.

Dread filling her, Rhona climbed each step as if she were that much closer to her own beheading. Finally, she paced down the hallway to the Master bedroom and knocked on the closed door.

Nothing. Not a peep.

After turning the handle and opening the door, Rhona poked her head into the room. "Nia?"

Her sister lay in a sprawled heap, half-dressed, on a king-sized, unmade bed. The room was a mess, with drawers drooping open and the closet door half closed, articles of clothes strewn over a chair and across the floor. Some of them were Nia's and some Zhang's. Apparently, her sister had tried to pack her own bag as a large suitcase sat propped on a chair with high-heeled shoes and a couple of dresses on the zippered top.

Rhona sat on the bed at her sister's side and felt for a pulse. Still there, strong enough. So was the acrid scent of alcohol. Her sister's grunted snore brought Rhona's anxiety levels back down to earth.

After clearing a space off a chair, Rhona sat down and texted Derm. She told him that Nia was sleeping, and she'd stay for a few hours to see if there was any chance of talking sense into her.

Derm texted back a simple red heart.

That was all she could stand at the moment. While her sister snored in oblivion, she let herself have the first good cry in months.

Three days later, Rhona parked outside the Quilt & Sew Shop on Main Street. A light rain fell from an overcast sky, but it was warm enough to promise brighter days ahead. She gathered her courage and got out of the car and faced the quiet street. To the north, Restful Glen resided in mid-afternoon peace. A few pedestrians came and went from the Old Courthouse to the Let's Eat Café. They may be kitty corner from each other, but the traffic between the two remained steady every workday. The Do Unto Others food pantry was closed, but the Savings and Loan appeared busy enough. *Spring always enlivens adventurous spirits.* An elderly gentleman led his muscle-bound Boxer into the vet clinic. She only hoped she had a good hold on his leash when the canine spotted the breath mints.

Thoughts of Nia swirled through her brain. Her sister had arranged a meeting with a realtor to sell the house. In hasty messages, Zhang had insisted that he would need every cent he could get to establish himself in Chicago. The hurry was ridiculous, but Nia didn't want to argue. He was blaming her for the divorce, citing her infidelity and the deception about Syn's true identity.

Rhona sighed and turned her mind from her brother-in-law to her sister. *At least I can do something about her.* Once Nia sobered up and got a good meal in her, she admitted that she didn't want the house, the furniture, or anything that would remind her of Zhang. Except for Andy, of course. *Thank goodness for that.*

In the ensuing days, Rhona had rescheduled her editing assignments and helped her sister navigate various complications involving the divorce, selling the house, and finding a new place to live. Maybe even a job. *She doesn't get up until after nine; how on Earth will she manage a work schedule?*

Trying to keep the horror of her sister staying at her home for an undefined amount of time at bay, Rhona squared her shoulders, swung open the door to the sewing shop, and prepared to lie through her teeth.

Maisie, dressed in leggings and a light sweater, rounded the counter at the speed of a woman half her age. "How is poor Nia doing?" She shook her head. "We were so sad to hear the bad news." Her hands clasped in a death struggle, as her sister came up behind her, their eyes matched in grievous concern.

Rhona attempted to exude confidence. "Oh, she'll be okay. Upset, of course. Lots of changes to think about." Her gaze swept over the counter to the rack of new dresses awaiting their owners. "Which is what brings me here today. I'm afraid that Nia won't need her new dress any time soon, but I'm going to pay for it, and we'll hold on to it for better days ahead."

Lucia stepped beside her sister, her blue eyes oozing compassion. "We know this must be such a challenging time. But…we were wondering if she might be interested in a job."

Unable to hold back a strangled sound, Rhona tried to form words as quickly as her throat would allow. "Nia? Work here?"

Her voice growing formal with the hint of a prepared speech, Lucia stepped closer. "Yes, well, it so happens that sister and I have been worked off our feet this season. Not exactly spring chickens anymore, you know. Nia loves quality clothes, and she might need a little cash these days."

Maisie broke in, wagging finer, "And a place to stay."

Reasserting her role, Lucia swiveled and pointed to the back room. "We have that extra suite, just two rooms really, but they're just waiting for someone to make them home. Grandma Turner used to stay there, but she passed on years ago."

Her heart leaping like a happy kangaroo, Rhona wasn't sure what to do next. She was about to hug the sisters when the memory of Nia's unpredictable, stubborn streak slapped her joy to the ground. She yanked out her phone and waved it at them. "I'll call and see if she's open to the idea. Would that be okay?"

Stately nods and the two women discreetly stepped back behind the counter, suddenly absorbed by bolts of cloth and fiddling with a canister of scissors.

Her gut twisting, Rhona tapped Nia's number on her phone. *Please, don't be a stupid head!*

Her voice as lifeless as last year's hair styles, Nia answered, "Yeah?"

"Hey, I am in the Quilt and Sew Shop, and Maisie and Lucia just mentioned an offer they'd like to—"

"Tell them that I'm sorry, but I can't pay for the dress. An impulse move. They can sell it to whoever. I don't have two pennies to rub—"

Frustration tightening the death grip she had on her phone, Rhona overrode her sister's self-pity in a decidedly firm voice. "They want to offer you a job and a place to stay."

Silence.

Rhona closed her eyes and prayed that her sister hadn't fainted. She snapped her words, "Nia, are you there?"

Audible swallowing. "Yeah. I just had to think. What would I be doing…in their shop? I don't know how to sew or anything."

Lumbering over, Maisie wiggled her fingers at the phone, mouthing the words, "Let me explain."

Glad to get out from the middle, Rhona passed over the phone, only slightly concerned that she had broken out in a sweat and might faint with joy.

In an amazingly short time, Maisie outlined a mild training program, a decent pay scale, with raises if proceeds allowed, and the dimensions of the back suite with an attached bathroom, which would be a part of the package.

Nia promised to meet the sisters the next morning and work out the details.

As she slipped her phone into her purse, Rhona hadn't realized that she had been holding her breath. After a long exhale, she inhaled free air once again.

Then she hugged the sisters.

Late April

With only mild trepidation, Rhona stepped into the Literary Enlightenment Books Store with Syn as jittery as a new job applicant in tow. *Lord, what have I gotten myself into?*

Rhona hadn't known Elspeth Gillis well, but once the woman got her foot in the literary door, so to speak, her true colors came to light. She was a huntress on a mission to find herself a man. Not just any man, but a well-educated, soft-spoken human being who wasn't afraid to take a chance in life. Mr. John Thompson fit her ideal perfectly. Rhona couldn't help but smile every time she saw them together in the bookstore, strolling down Main Street, or at the café enjoying a light luncheon together. *Perhaps she fits his ideal as well.*

Though she had nudged Syn into helping with Ada's newest brainstorm and had even won an honorable mention for her own poetry submission, Rhona had successfully avoided direct contact with Oldtown's Artists' Club. *I've got enough with my work, helping Nia, and the garden is depending on me.*

Syn had stayed in the shadows, hardly saying a word, until Callum approached her after church the last Sunday of the month and asked if she knew any guys who might want to work with him on a "great idea" he had. Syn's face had lit up, fireworks shooting from her eyes. Quick texts back and forth between Syn and Renzo, and Callum's wish was granted. She knew just the right guy to help out with a great idea.

As Rhona tread carefully into the bookstore, avoiding eye contact with the Thrillers section, Callum rose from his place and sat at the head of a long wooden library table. At Callum's right, Renzo jumped to his feet and hustled over to intercept Syn.

Mr. Thompson and Elspeth conferred at the far end of the table

Afternoon light streamed in, highlighting the golden surface and the edges of the gleaming shelves, filling the quiet room with calm luminescence.

I can't take on another thing... The memory of last night's dinner flop sent a shiver down her spine. *Certainly, editing and cooking don't mix.*

As Renzo led Syn to the chair beside his and Callum resituated himself at the table, Mr. Thompson offered an intimate hand pat to Elspeth and rose to his feet.

Hovering between shock at the scandalously fast romance and giggling at the very notion of these sweet souls finding happiness together, Rhona bit her lip to keep from expressing anything too obvious. *He might as well declare his intentions now. The ring is practically on her finger!*

Unmindful of what his gesture had done to at least two hearts in the room, Mr. Thompson offered a welcoming smile. "Are you going to join the team, Rhona? We'd love to have you."

Trying to decide in a hurry forced a decided retreat. Rhona waved as if the Huns were scaling the walls, and she really couldn't deal with them now. "Oh, I'd love to, I've got so many chores at home and behind in my work and..." Syn's eye-roll at Renzo brought her babbling to a halt. "Maybe you could give me a run-down, and I can give Derm an update?"

Mr. Thompson nodded at Callum and took his place at Elspeth's side, where her hand waited patiently for his.

Grinning, Callum rose, exchanged a meaningful look with Renzo, and then focused on Rhona. "Well, we've got some great plans, and since Syn is joining us, I think we have a real opportunity to bring our community together this year."

As the young man outlined their ideas for a summer artist exhibition, outdoor movie nights at the park with free popcorn and a snack vendor, and a community clean-up day, all eyes focused on the young man.

Her pen racing over a page, Elspeth took notes. Mr. Thompson's eyes roamed freely from her to Callum in equal measure.

Syn's shoulder rested against Renzo's with all the innocence of best friends who love being together.

Hope bursting into flower, Rhona found a place at the table and sat down.

On the last day of the month, Rhona shoved Nia's glossy end table against the wall in the Quilt & Sew Shop backroom suite, pinching her fingers between the table and a wood-framed chair. While trying to shake off the stinging pain and cross the room, she tripped over the chair's ornate claw foot, sprawled half a yard, and barely caught herself. She swore under her breath, then glanced through the open doorway, hoping that her sister didn't hear her.

Nia's face, twisting with the effort to squeeze between her dresser and makeup table in the bedroom, suggested that she was struggling with a few bad words of her own. Eventually, she popped like a cork and shot into the living room, both hands out to catch herself as she hit the wall.

A gentle tapping on the door frame stopped them both in their tracks.

Lucia's tremulous, "Hello, are you girls okay?" clearly hoped they hadn't died in the attempt to fit Nia's furniture into the compact space.

Nia's chest heaved as she staggered into the living room, gesturing for Rhona to answer. The battle-weary warrior had to catch her breath.

Rhona barely had enough energy to open the door.

In a sincere act of mercy, Lucia dared to enter the bulging confines, bearing a tray of tea cups and cookies. Maneuvering between unpacked boxes, she set the tray on the end table, neatly sidestepping the clawed foot that nearly broke Rhona's neck.

Not normally a drinking woman, Rhona wished the seventy-year-old had brought in a whiskey bottle, glasses optional. *But tea will do.*

Nia's eyes bulged as she eyed the tray on the end table.

The chocolate chip cookies never had a chance. Nia snatched two.

One hand pressed to her frail chest, Lucia suppressed a gasp as she surveyed the overcrowded space. Then she grinned good-naturedly as she carefully backed up to the doorway. "My grandmother stayed here for weeks at a time, using it as a second home." She sniffed at the walls, now blanketed in modern art. "A beautiful cabinet stood about there," she pointed at the north wall with a shaky finger, "with three shelves lined with homey knick-knacks, and a handmade Afghan always lay on the foot of her bed." A baleful sigh. "So quaint."

Fully aware that there was no way in the universe that Nia could compete with anything resembling quaint, Rhona changed the topic as fast as possible. "Are you and Maisie done for the evening?"

Her gaze retrieved from her charming memory, Lucia nodded with a I'll-get-used-to-it smile. "Yes, sister and I are going to the café for an early supper and then off to bed. I've got a new book Mr. Thompson recommended that I'm dying to break into—a springtime mystery on Cape Cod involving a sewing shop." Her face glowed in anticipation.

Flopping on her one plush chair, Nia waved a languid hand. "Knock yourself out." A brief smile in Rhona's direction. "We already are."

With a cackled guffaw, Lucia left them to pack the place to the rafters and shut the door.

After scarfing down both cookies, Nia pointed to a cheese-encrusted pizza container on a stack of packing boxes. "Leftovers or tea and cookies?"

Rhona retrieved a cup and one cookie, then settled on the couch, letting relief flow over her body. *The hardest part is done. She can do the rest herself.*

In something of a yoga pose, Nia sat on the floor with a cup in one hand and a third cookie in the other. Sip. Bite. Repeat. Finally setting the cup on a stack of paperbacks, she dusted her hands free of crumbs and leaned against the entertainment center, facing the couch. Her gaze seemed to consider Rhona for a long moment.

Becoming unsettled, Rhona munched the last of her cookie, slurped the dregs of her tea, and then set her cup on the tray. Where it belonged. She pursed her lips and stared back at her sister. *What?*

Mind reading the way only siblings can do, Nia answered the unasked question. "I always wondered why you and Derm never had any kids. Of your own, I mean."

Slapping her forehead, Rhona wondered why people couldn't just be nice, say thank you, and wish you a good day as you headed out the door. Finally, she leveled her gaze at her sister. Questioning eyes wanted to know. "Because we couldn't. I told you that we tried. For years. Then we gave up. We still hoped, but it never happened."

"You could have gone to one of those clinics and had one started in a lab and implanted… You know what I mean."

Her jaw clenching and the tea and cookie threatening to do something ugly, Rhona took a deep breath and let it out slowly. "That's not us, Nia. We were open to having children, but we were never desperate. Can you understand that?"

Nia shook her head. "Not really. When I want something, I get depressed until I get it." She shrugged. "I didn't really want kids that much. Zhang wanted a son. I wanted to make him happy. Luckily, we had a son right off the bat." Her lips flapped as she exhaled a long breath. "Syn was obviously a surprise." She squinted in the failing light. "How did you and Derm manage to make it work for so long? I mean, you didn't get what you wanted, but you stuck together."

A scream bubbled from deep within. Closing her eyes, Rhona counted to ten before she opened them and shot a glance through the ceiling to Heaven above, though her words were directed to her sister. "I think you mix up happiness with getting what you want. Happiness comes from inside, not outside." A sudden image of Syn chattering at a squirrel on a perfect winter day blasted her anger into oblivion. "Syn knows how to be happy."

"With you." Nia's gaze swerved across the room. "I want her back, you know."

Deadpanned, Rhona waved to the cramped space. "Here?"

Nia tapped her chest near the location of the human heart. "Here."

Rhona sighed. "That's entirely up to you."

Squinting at a new insight, Nia moved to safer territory. "She's in love with that Renzo boy."

"She thinks she is in love."

A frown and Nia folded her arms over her chest. "I suppose you think there is a difference."

"All the world."

"Well, I'm her mother, and I think her love is real." She could have stuck her tongue out and added, "So there!" like a ten-year-old.

Rhona sighed as she staggered to her feet. "Never said it wasn't. But real love takes time. Actions bring it to life." She ignored the nagging fear that Nia might make the connection to her failed marriage. *Not now. I'm too tired.* Hurrying on, she pulled out her phone and checked the time. "I told Derm I'd be home for dinner."

Using the entertainment center for leverage, Nia managed to get to an upright position. "You can eat?"

In mock outrage, Rhona made it to the doorway. "Hey, I worked hard enough to win the Hauling-Stuff Award for the month. Every calorie from that pizza was gone by midafternoon, and the tea and cookie will give me just enough steam to drive home on."

Nia limped over and dropped her hands on Rhona's shoulders. "You are the best sister I ever had."

It was an old joke between them, but one that still brought a shared smile. "Love you, too." As Nia's hands dropped to her sides, Rhona headed for the door. "I'm leaving before I fall over."

Nia laughed. "Don't worry; I'd get you to your home."

Rhona smiled with a backward wave. *She'd try, probably kill me on the way, but she'd try.*

Chapter Nine

What Happens When Truth is Revealed and No One Can Handle It

Early May

Bright sunlight warmed Rhona as she turned the soil in her garden plot. Taking a breather, she rubbed the small of her back. Her oversized bib-overalls, old stained shirt, and worn shoes matched her rugged work mindset perfectly.

Birds trilled, warbled, and chirped in springtime joy. New nests had appeared in the tall pine tree beside the work shed, and the bird feeder was doing excellent business. Even a few hummingbirds had made an appearance, whizzing about, their pointy beaks darting at Rhona accusingly.

Better get those feeders filled before they tell everyone that I'm a bum.

Looking surprisingly elegant in jeans and a light green t-shirt, Syn stumped forward, her arms full of old notebooks and a torn folder. "What do I do with these?

"What are they?"

"Old school papers. Uncle Derm said I could get rid of them. All my finals are on stuff I have online."

"If you are sure, dump them in the burn barrel. I've got trash to clear out this afternoon."

"You're not burning plastics?"

Deadpanned, Rhona leaned on her shovel. "Not since you threatened to inform the UN of my nefarious deeds."

"You were burning plastic bottles!"

Refusing to be tried, convicted, and probably sentenced to a year of community service by her environmentally-minded niece, Rhona clamped her mouth shut and pointed to the burn barrel.

In pure stubbornness, Syn crouched down and started tearing the notebook pages off the metal spirals. "Can't burn metal either."

Rhona smacked the shovel into the soft ground and changed the topic. "What do you want for your birthday?"

"Not a DNA test, that's for sure."

Rhona suppressed an eye roll and decided it was time to draw a line in the ground. For the lettuce and spinach. She paced to one end of the garden bed, eyed the rectangular space, and slid the shovel tip into the dirt a few inches from the northern edge. As she dragged the shovel along, creating a neat furrow behind her, she spoke to her niece in the most conciliatory voice she could muster. "What's gotten into you? You've been argumentative for the last week. I could say the sky is blue, and you'd tell me—"

"It isn't."

Rhona stopped at the edge of the garden bed and scowled at the teen clutching a roll of papers in one hand and a wad of metal spirals in the other. "What isn't?"

Syn lifted her gaze. "The sky isn't blue. Not today. It's white. There's a chance of showers this afternoon.

"The very reason I want to get the lettuce and spinach seeds planted."

Her face blank, Syn had clearly lost track of her argument.

Rhona heaved a deep sigh. "Are you going to tell me what's bothering you?"

"Nothing."

"It's your birthday, your sixteenth, that's got you as riled up as a broody hen with a fox at the door."

Syn's head dropped to her chest. "Mom wants to have a party."

"Is that bad?"

"At her place."

Rhona played along with the image of her sister's tiny two-room suite overflowing with clothes and boxes strewn everywhere. She propped her hands complacently on the shovel handle. "Sure. You can have a party there with three and a half people. So long as no one sits down."

A fake smile and "Ha! Ha!" said it all.

"Look, do you want a birthday party? I wasn't going to say anything because I didn't want to push it on you. My mother had a party for me when I was six, invited my whole class, and by three in the afternoon, I swore off social activities forevermore. But if you'd like one, I'll tell Nia we'll have it here, and you can invite anyone you want."

"Just family. And Renzo, of course. And Callum. Maybe Mr. Thompson…" She shrugged. "You'll have to invite Elspeth and the sisters and…" She grinned helplessly. "Invite whoever you want." Her smile vanished. "Except Andy."

Rhona nodded, her mind filling in the blanks. "What do you want for a present?"

"To learn to drive."

Rhona's heart plummeted to the ground and tried to bury itself deep. She managed to squeak, "Okay."

Now humming a happy tune, Syn turned and headed to the burn barrel.

Rhona watched the slim young woman stroll away before lifting her eyes to the sky. A prayer was in order, but she wasn't sure what to ask for. *Strength? Escape?* Before she could identify her need, she blinked in sudden realization. The sky was white, and it would probably storm soon.

Saturday at noon on Syn's birthday, Rhona, dressed in light cotton pants and a bright yellow shirt, stood by the dessert table in the living room and poured equal amounts of soda and fruit juice into the punch bowl. It hadn't rained though a cold, spitting wind forced a relocation from an outdoor party to an indoor one at the last minute. *No big deal. Springtime is always unpredictable.* She snorted. *Heck, life is unpredictable.*

A snappy dresser in black pants, a dark blue button-up shirt, and black loafers, Renzo sauntered over, a smile lighting up his face. He stopped by the table and scooped up two plastic cups. "Syn asked if I had anything to liven up the punch, but I had to tell her that my idea of a lively drink is black coffee."

Her brain revving into high gear at the unexpected opportunity to weasel secrets out of the young man her niece had fallen for, Rhona took a casual tone, practically channeling a late-night talk host. "So, you're not a drinking man? I would think that you and the guys would enjoy a few beers now and again. No sin in relaxing with friends, right?" *Oh, that was smooth.*

Using the metal scooper from the ice bowl, Renzo filled the two cups with ice shards, his smile gone, a thoughtful expression probably trying to map out a path through possible landmines.

Practicing indifference, Rhona dabbed drops on the edge of the bowl as if it took every ounce of her brain power.

Renzo swirled the ice about in a decidedly leisurely manner. "Sure, I'll have a beer when it fits the situation, but I don't try to get drunk. Not the way some of the guys do." He leaned in. "Between the two of us, I worry about Andy sometimes. He doesn't handle it well. Gets pretty goofy." Enough said, Renzo held out his cups and waited like a good boy who had no further secrets to divulge.

Her heart rate spiking, Rhona fixated on making sure the cups were filled exactly evenly. "Goofy, eh? His dad was like that. Derm swore he'd never go into a bar with him. I guess the bachelor party was an eye-opener."

A chuckle and Renzo's smile lit up the room again. "I can only imagine." He glanced over his shoulder.

Syn perched on the edge of a large armchair in the middle of the living room, watching Renzo with eagle eyes.

Oh, well, no use interrogating the kid. This is Syn's day, after all. Rhona nudged Renzo gently so he wouldn't spill. "Tell Syn we'll cut the cake in a few minutes if she's ready."

Syn beamed as Renzo made his way toward her. Once he handed over the drink, she took a polite sip, set it aside, and started talking.

Probably wants a full report. The girl doesn't need cake; she's practically devouring Renzo. To distract herself, Rhona studicd thc room. Streamers and balloons dangled from the ceiling and people congregated in small groups, the sound of pleasant babble filling the space. Unlike her sixth birthday party, this one seemed to be going well. No fights over gift boxes and, so far, nothing sticky had spilled.

As expected, Nia took center stage before Mr. Thompson, Elspeth, Maisie, and Lucia. They chatted and laughed, clearly teasing Nia about her latest sales adventures. Her sister's blushing expression suggested that she couldn't be happier.

Center stage always did appeal to her. Never guess she was a recently divorced woman who had to make a living for the first time in her life.

Across the room, one arm propped on the bookcase, Derm stood next to his brother as Tavish chatted with Ada and Braden. Derm was usually quiet in social settings. The perfect audience, he always smiled at the right time and asked questions that showed he was listening.

Almost perfect. Except for those missing in action.

Callum couldn't come on account of a spring cold, and Andy hadn't been formally invited. Unfortunately, Nia had taken it upon herself to message him. Luckily, he claimed he had finals to study for and couldn't make it. Rhona shook her head at the near miss. No one mentioned Zhang, as if the man had never existed.

As she considered the friendly assembly, the relaxed atmosphere, the table of snacks and sandwiches, punch, and the sheet cake Ada had insisted on bringing over with HAPPY BIRTHDAY, SYN! in green lettering with pink flowers along the edge, she knew that a sincere effort had been made to celebrate Syn's happy day. A marked contrast to her last birthday.

Renzo's comment about Andy getting goofy with alcohol didn't sit well with her. She'd have to pry more information out of Nia. If the boy was drinking too much at nineteen, he'd be in serious trouble by the time he was ready to graduate.

One of Nia's more boisterous laughs split the air. Heads turned and smiles broke out at her deepening blush.

She really is having a great time. Almost as good as her daughter. An odd thought, considering the situation.

Rhona imagined Andy's face—the son left behind by his father, struggling in school, his sister blissfully happy in a new relationship, and his mom starting a successful job. Perhaps she knew why the boy wanted to drink. *He may be a mean kid...but he's still just a kid. Lord, what'll happen when he becomes a man?*

Mondays were always hard. It was a fact of life that had to be accepted along with death and taxes. Rhona stared at her little blue car and bit her lip. She knew how to change a flat tire. In theory. Derm had shown her at least a half dozen times. But her confidence in doing the job well enough to ensure that the spare didn't fall off while accelerating above five miles per hour dissuaded her from ever trying. She stood in the driveway beside the ailing auto and grunted appreciatively at her husband's skill. And courage. *How does he know it won't fall off?*

Derm huffed impatiently as he rose to his feet, the tire iron dangling from his fingers. "Can you drive it into Mike's Repair for me? I've got a student hyperventilating over finals, and I don't want him to expire before I remind him that he's already got an A in class and the test was not designed to kill him."

Hands on hips, her most agreeable smile in place, Rhona accepted the mission she knew would involve speed praying from the moment she left the driveway to the second she drove into Mike's Repair shop.

When Syn trotted over and offered to assist—perhaps even drive—a cold sweat broke over Rhona. "Not this time, honey. You've still got to pass the written test before you get behind the wheel." *Thank God.*

Leaving her burdened husband and moping niece behind, Rhona settled herself into the compact car, started her litany, and drove slow enough to get a few angry looks, but fast enough to get to Mike's before the café's luncheon special drew a crowd.

Tall and lanky, Mike's Repair owner was actually named Steve. He had taken the shop over from his friend and mentor and refused to change the name in honor of the man who had changed the trajectory of his life. Rhona didn't know much about Steve. No one knew much about Steve. He was a man of few words, and he didn't often voice those. Only a clipped newspaper article, yellowed with age, announcing the turnover of the shop from Mike to Steve, with Steve's one revelatory statement: "Mike changed the trajectory of my life," clued Oldtown citizens into the meaning behind the name and the deep feelings of the current owner.

Since Dermid had called ahead, Steve didn't stare at her as if she had arrived from another planet with an alien spaceship needing replacement parts. He merely motioned to the docking bay where he could accomplish his task in as quick and orderly manner as humanly possible.

Rhona knew the drill. She parked herself in the tiny waiting room just off the garage and studied the various auto parts for sale and notices about tires, once again humbled by her automotive ignorance.

In an amazingly short period of time, Steve ambled in, holding up a huge screw. "I'll keep it, if you don't mind."

Flummoxed, Rhona didn't know why the man would ask if he could keep a screw until it dawned on her that it might be the culprit in the flat tire mystery. "That's what was in my tire? That enormous thing?"

"Yep."

"You can have it."

"Thanks." Steve sat at his desk, a structure as yellowed at the old newspaper on the bulletin board, and wrote out the bill.

Rhona dug in her purse for her checkbook. Steve didn't bother with debit cards. He could. He just didn't.

"Fifteen dollars."

Surprised, Rhona changed direction and dug out her wallet instead. She pulled out a ten and a five. The only thing Steve liked better than a cleared check was cash. "You haven't raised your rates? That thing must have made a big hole. I'm surprised I don't need a new tire."

Steve shook his head. "The patch will hold. I appreciate the screw. It's just what I need for another project." He accepted the bills and tipped his head. "Thanks much." Then the service man she could trust with her life headed back to his garage, aiming for a tractor that looked decidedly needy.

On her way home, Rhona's heart settled into a peaceful rhythm as she absorbed the fact that the car was repaired, and she could relax her grip on the steering wheel. *Was I always so anxious?*

The sun shone on mountain-sized tractors in the fields as they planted a new season of crops, creating a gloriously pastoral scene. An open road before her, Rhona searched for inner gladness, but anxiety niggled at the edges of her mind. *The car is just the lightning rod. It's Syn and Andy and Nia I'm worried about. Any one of them might go off the road any day now.* The fact that it had been eight months since Syn's accident was not lost on her. *So much has happened...deep wounds with only patches to heal.*

Steve's honest face rose in her mind. He was the incarnation of silent strength. Her mother's oft-quoted saying filtered through her mind, "Least said, soonest mended." Something from a book her mother had read long ago yet remained eternally true.

Rhona pulled into her driveway and wished that life's patches were as trustworthy as Steve's.

That night, Rhona left the window wide open and reveled in the gentle breeze cascading into the room. She snuggled down next to her husband and hoped that sleep would come swiftly.

It didn't.

Derm lay with one hand under his head on his back, his eyes wide, facing the ceiling neither one of them could see in the dark room.

Her nerves, going from rattled at Syn's daily reminder that she needed to learn to drive to high alert at her husband's unusually quiet demeanor, sizzled like fried bacon on the edge of burning. Unable to stand it another second, she sat up and plumped the pillow behind her head. Once she settled back and clasped her hands on her lap, she readied herself for a heartfelt chat. "What's up?"

Derm didn't waste a second. "Syn needs to contact her dad. Her real dad."

Rhona glared at the ceiling. *What on Earth brought this on?* Keeping her mother's sage advice firmly in mind, she abbreviated her response to the fewest words possible. "Why?"

His head swiveling in her direction, Derm stared at her. "Because he is her dad. He would want to know."

Rhona's heart ached. "*You* would want to know. We don't know what Gustav wants."

"That's my point. He doesn't even have a say in the matter, and it isn't fair."

Silence as a refuge only worked for so long. After a few tense moments, Rhona sucked up her courage and did the needful. "What do you want me to do about it?"

"Talk to Nia. She needs to contact the man and let him know the truth."

"You don't want to talk to Nia?"

"She's your sister. If it were Tavish, I would talk to him."

"Tavish would no more have an affair than skydive."

A grunt approved of the metaphor.

"All right. I'll talk to her. But don't expect miracles. Not from Nia or from Gustav."

Derm shifted to his side and lay an arm over his wife. "I don't expect miracles. I just want to do the right thing, know we tried."

Suddenly, "Least said, soonest mended" seemed like a distant dream.

Mid-May

Lunch was always a casual affair, even when guests stopped by. Renzo had become such a common visitor, helping Derm in the garage and learning all there was to know about old automotives—while visiting with Syn on the side—that Rhona didn't bother with anything fancy. Since finals were over and spring was flaunting blossoms and buds all over the land, grilled cheese sandwiches, spicy tomato soup, and barbecue chips seemed entirely appropriate.

It wasn't until she started collecting the dishes after the meal that things turned weird.

Renzo's phone rang as he carried his plate and glass to the sink. He checked the caller ID, scowled, and then let it go to voicemail. A tight smile said he didn't want to talk about it.

In that case… Rhona pointed at Syn. "You two go ahead and help Uncle Derm with hauling the scrap metal to the recycling place. I don't want him straining his back."

Straightening like a soldier on parade, Renzo saluted smartly; grinning, Syn followed his example.

They're such a cute couple… Rhona sighed as she gathered the rest of the dishes and carried them into the sink.

Then her phone rang. She wiped her hands on a dish rag and checked the ID. Nia. Of course, it would be. But since her sister was deliriously happy at the shop, making a nice home for herself—decorated in her own tornado-original style—and earning her first real income ever, Rhona had ceased to react to her calls as if state troopers were banging on her door. She hadn't brought up Derm's concern about Gustav, hoping for a natural opening in some future conversation. Setting that alarming idea aside for a day when she didn't have a guest and a million other things to do, she swiped the green button. "Hey, Nia, what's—"

"You got to get over here!"

The question of how many times her heart could be shocked into stillness deflected Rhona's attention for a mere millisecond. She swallowed down rising panic and tried to formulate the level of disaster she was facing. "What's wrong?"

"Andy won't wake up."

Completely confused, Rhona tried to formulate a rational line of questioning. "Where is Andy?"

"He's here, at my place. He finished finals last week and came here since he had to be out of the dorm."

Rhona closed her eyes and sucked in a deep, cleansing breath. "Tell me what happened."

"He might be dead! You've got to get over here!"

A lightning bolt could not have electrified her any faster. Rhona jogged across the room, swung open the door, and screamed Derm's name.

After speeding from the garage doorway, Renzo, Syn, and Derm raced to the porch. Derm shouldered his way to his wife, his eyes scouring her as if to ascertain if she cut off a body part or something.

Rhona held out her phone. "Nia said that Andy might be dead at her place."

His face setting like quick-dried cement, Derm took the phone while Rhona folded her niece into her arms.

Syn mumbled into her chest. "I hate the guy, but I don't want this. Not really."

Formal prayers not forthcoming, Rhona swayed as she hugged the fragile child, hoping for a miracle they could all live with.

As the sun set that evening, Rhona ignored the glorious golden rays as she perched on a patio bench behind the sewing shop. With deliberate motions, she set her phone on the matching table and hugged herself, holding off a rising chill.

On speaker, Zhang raged in a high tone, his voice breaking at moments, barely touching her frozen heart. She waited for him to catch his breath and then spoke in the calmest voice she had ever used in her life. "This isn't all Nia's fault. You have had a part to play. When was the last time you talked with your son?"

The insulting verbiage that issued forth nearly forced Rhona's hand. Her finger hovered over the red button. As if shielding herself behind a storm wall, she waited for another opening and then reverted to the facts. "Andy is resting now. The medics said that he was out of danger but would need supervision. Physically, he should recover quickly. They advised counseling and possibly time in a rehab center."

A high-pitched scream. "My son is not an addict!"

"Your son mixed sleeping pills and alcohol. It was a deadly combination. He's lucky to be alive."

"I'll come get him and bring him here to live with me this summer. Nia is the one that's killing him. Her stupidity is enough to—"

"Nia is the one watching over him. Derm is with him. Even Syn tried to talk with him. Everyone here is offering support. Lucia and Maisie said he could stay with Nia if he wants to."

"Syn talked with him? Like that's going to help. The girl hates his guts and would love to see him dead."

Fury rising, Rhona couldn't keep her seat. She stood and towered over the phone. "Zhang, Andy says he wants to stay with his mom. I told him I would call you and let you know what happened, but he is the one who said that he doesn't want to go to Chicago. He said you are drinking too much and acting like a fool. He's blaming you!"

Silence echoed like a stilled heart.

Finally, Rhona snatched up the phone and dropped her voice. "I'm sorry, Zhang. But I don't think that Andy is the only one who needs help." She hesitated, not sure what else to say. Her throat nearly closing, she managed a few parting words, "I've got to go." With that, she hit the end button and dropped back onto the bench.

Flashbacks to her dad, his nearly comatose state when he would go unresponsive, tightened her stomach into knots. She wanted to cry, to rage, to let the bile out. But Nia and Syn needed her. She had to go back inside, face the situation, and take Syn home.

Home. She shook her head and headed for the door.

Late May

Rhona never liked showdowns or suspense dramas. Murder mysteries where the victim had no idea what was about to happen, but the audience knew, made her grit her teeth and wring her hands in helpless agony.

Sitting on the one chair in Nia's minuscule living room on the third Friday of the month, while Andy slumped on the couch, had her heart pounding at the rate of impending doom. Fight or flight were the only good options, but she couldn't do either.

Her hands propped on her hips, wearing a tailored gray pantsuit fit for an international executive meeting, Nia sported the determined mother look as she faced her son. "You have got to get a summer job and find positive ways to spend your time, Andy. Staying up half the night on your phone or playing games at all hours of the night with your friends isn't going to work." She tilted her head as if considering a new angle. "You might even think about a summer class, so you don't get so far behind like you did last semester."

Science fiction had missed Rhona's world by miles. Only Derm's occasional reference to a possible alien invasion made a mark in her conscious world. But as Andy rolled his shoulders and then stretched out, a cat getting comfortable, the term "transformer" suddenly took on new meaning. From slumped and defeated to masterfully in charge, the young man was now as relaxed as a lion after his latest kill. He eyed his mother through narrowed eyes, a smile hovering on his lips. "How you have changed, Mother."

Nia's swallow was loud enough to be heard across the room. At least, Rhona heard it from the doorway where she leaned on the frame, ready to intervene if claws came out. *Come on, Nia! Say something!*

In true Nia style, she did. Stretching languidly, she went right for the jugular. "I never wanted you. Zhang wanted a son. I got pregnant to please him."

Rhona imagined melting through the floor and oozing on down the road.

Andy's gaze hardened. "I didn't exactly choose you."

They might as well have flown at each other and started tearing each other's skin off. Rhona stepped forward, her hands up, much like a referee in a fight where people might actually kill each other. "Stop it, you two!" She swung her glare at her sister. "What are you doing? You know you wanted Andy from the minute you found out you were carrying him."

A shrug and pretended indifference. "Yeah, I did. But I didn't know he'd grow up to be such a pain in the—"

Andy rose to his full six feet, his hand clenched, looking remarkably like his father.

For the first time, Rhona feared a physical fight, and her voice shook as she tried to grab some control of the spiraling situation. "Sit down, Andy! This isn't settled." She swung back to her sister and screamed loud enough for everyone on Main Street to hear, "Nia, you have lost your daughter and your husband. Do you really, seriously, want to lose your son as well?"

Trembling, Nia did what she did best. She matched drama for drama and dropped to the floor, sobbing.

Gulping a breath to keep up her strength, Rhona gestured abruptly to Andy, motioning to the couch he had just vacated.

Surprisingly, Andy reached down, grabbed his mom around the waist, and helped her to the couch.

Once she was settled in an upright position, Rhona shoved Andy down beside her. "Okay, get this clear. I'm tired of this. So tired that I may do something drastic. I don't know what, exactly, but I'll think of something! Don't imagine I won't."

A similar mix of turbulent emotions on their faces, along with their matching eyes, made them appear like upset book ends.

Nia pouted. "He started it."

Before Andy could respond in kind, Rhona jumped in. "I'm stopping it." She folded her arms over her chest and focused on Andy. "What your mom suggested wasn't bad. You do need to do something productive over the summer. And drinking can't be a part of it. But—" she glanced at Nia and back at Andy, "it's up to you what to do. You're a grown man, almost. You need to decide the direction you take in your life. Neither your mom nor your dad can live your life for you. What do you want to do this summer?"

Andy shrugged, sitting forward with his hands clasped, his voice entirely reasonable. "Maybe get a job in town. Mike needs help at the repair shop."

Rhona nodded. "That would work. Though it might help if you call the owner by his right name. He's Steve. A good man."

Staring out of the corner of her eye, Nia's lips still trembled. "I didn't mean it. I did want you." She wiped an errant tear from her cheek. "It was Zhang's idea to have a baby, and I wasn't so thrilled. But the first time I felt you kick inside of me, I knew there was a little person inside, and it was the most amazing thing that ever happened in the whole world. It felt so right and wonderful." She reached out tentatively and pressed his shoulder. "You believe me, right?"

Offering the universal wave, meaning don't-worry-about-it-I'm-not-upset, Andy lowered the tension in the room, allowing for free air to flow once again.

With visions of going out to the garden and spending time with seedlings, worms, and other harmless members of God's creation, Rhona took a step back toward the doorway. She was about to say something about everything being settled when Andy straightened, a curious gleam in his eyes.

"You wanted Syn, though, didn't you? She was always the special one."

Convulsive swallowing and Nia resembled a fish out of water.

Sighing at her failed escape, Rhona decided not to intervene.

Squeaking, Nia lifted her hands in surrender. "I didn't know she was Gustav's baby, but somehow, after being with him and feeling…well…being in love the way I was, being pregnant was like another gift. Like I was going to be able to keep part of him with me."

Rhona jumped in before she thought. "So, you did know that Syn was his?"

"No! Not really." She slapped her hands over her head to keep shards of reality from crushing her. "I never thought about it. I just pretended that she was. In my head. I imagined that I had married Gustav, and we had a little girl together, and then he died or something, and I was with Zhang, making the most of life, and I had this adorable little girl with his eyes…"

A disgusted snort and Andy shook his head. "I must have been such a disappointment. Not only the son of a guy you don't love but stupid to boot."

Nia flung her arms around Andy, her words coming in choking sobs. "Never! I felt so bad for you. You were such an adorable kid, energetic, and eager to please. When you had trouble learning Chinese, I tried to shield you from Zhang and his parents. They may have loved you, but they judged everyone. You were either fit or not fit. There was no other way to be. It was like some kind of caste system. I never belonged. Not really."

Andy stared ahead. "Did I?"

Nia's eyes searched the ceiling, tears held back by sheer gravitational force. "I don't know. I don't understand Zhang. Never could. It's all so complicated. His family back in China had expectations, and his parents were determined that he would carry out those expectations come hell or high water." She blinked as she leveled her gaze at Rhona. "People here didn't help. So many preconceived notions. Always live up to the image! The brilliant Asian guy married to the beautiful American woman."

Rhona didn't dare say one word. There wasn't a right one to say.

One hand gripping Andy's shoulder, Nia's voice turned fierce. "You need to forgive Syn. I didn't even realize that I held it against her, being who she was. It's not her fault. If you have to blame someone, blame me."

And Zhang Rhona wanted to scream.

"When your dad found out about Syn, he wanted me to get rid of her. He said he didn't want another kid. One was enough." Nia's face flushed, and she dropped her hands. "I wouldn't. But after that, when I realized that you were having trouble, I worried that he might reject you, too. So, I did everything I could to hold you up, make you look great, ignoring Syn. I wanted to keep his attention off her and on you—in a good way. To protect you both."

His voice as vacant as his stare, Andy leaned back on the couch, all pride gone. "You make my dad sound like a monster."

Her head propped on her hands, Nia peered into memories. "Sometimes, the right circumstances can make monsters of us all."

Aching behind Rhona's eyes threatened a downpour, but she would not release it. *This isn't the time. I'll cry later.* She shivered. *I'm not sure who I'll cry for most.*

By the last Saturday of May, Rhona had recovered enough to attempt a driving lesson with Syn. When her niece jerked to a standstill at the end of the driveway, Rhona knew she had misjudged. But it was too late to convince Derm to take over. Syn's face glowed with happy expectation as she pressed the accelerator, narrowly missed the mailbox, and then rounded the curve onto Main Street.

Fifteen heart-stopping minutes later, her foot pressed firmly against the floor and her hand strangling the door handle, Rhona directed Syn onto the circular drive of Oldtown Nature Park.

A smooth landing, Syn turned off the ignition and faced her aunt, beaming. "Pretty good for my first time, right?"

Never a great liar, Rhona just nodded and hoped that would be enough. Then released the door handle, relaxed her foot, and leaned back, practically melting into the seat.

A petite woman in leggings and a tank top, leading a dog that looked remarkably like a child's toy, strolled by.

Syn laughed delightedly. "I wish wc could get something like that. Nes and Wilma would have their own little dog to play with."

Rhona mumbled under her breath, "Nes and Wilma have plenty of squirrels, raccoons, and possums to play with." She tried to assure her heart that the drive home wouldn't be nearly as traumatic.

"Can I get out and walk the path?"

A little fresh air and a stretch of legs might be just what this old body needs. With a nod, Rhona opened the passenger door and met her niece on the path. They meandered along the trail that wound around a playground filled with little kids and attending adults.

Syn pointed to a small boy who hovered on the edge of a slide, undecided if he wanted to risk letting go, while a woman waited with outstretched arms at the bottom, calling, "Come on, Geo! I'll catch you. Don't be afraid."

Her voice suddenly serious, Syn kept stumping forward, her gaze averted from the boy. "Guess that's how Andy must have felt."

Rhona kept pace, silent, waiting.

"You know, Mom told me about it. How she wasn't sure she wanted Andy but then was glad she had him and how she wanted me but then had to act like I didn't exist to keep peace."

A question popped out before Rhona had a chance to vet it properly. "How does that make you feel?"

A sniff and a long hesitation while they both stopped and watched two squirrels race up an enormous oak tree. "Zhang probably had a rotten childhood. I don't know. Maybe he was spoiled rotten. Could be. I just can't figure him out." A shrug and she moved to a bench as if she might sit down. "Same with Andy. I don't know. Was he the favored child or a misfit kid who tried to cover up his failings?" She squinted at the treetops and then swung her gaze at

Rhona. "What was Mom like as a kid? Was she the favored girl or…?"

Rhona lifted her face and stared at the treetops but couldn't catch sight of anything to hold her attention, so she dropped it to the ground and slid onto the bench. She took her time, formulating an answer that made sense. "It all depends. My dad certainly favored her. He treated her like a princess and gave her whatever she wanted. His mood swings were legendary, and alcohol was not his friend. My mom worked hard and kept the ship afloat, so to speak. She and I got along quite well. I never felt like her daughter. I was always Mom's best friend."

Syn collapsed onto the bench and leaned forward, propping her elbows on her legs. She squinted at her aunt. "So, you actually got the better deal."

Surprised, Rhona had to admit the truth of it. "Yeah. In many ways, I think I did. Though that didn't stop me from being jealous of Nia for years. She always knew how to dress well, attract attention, and make people laugh. All gifts that missed me by a mile."

Syn threw her hands up into the air. "So, how am I supposed to judge my family?"

A chuckle bubbling up, Rhona smiled innocently at a passing couple. "Perhaps it's best you don't."

"How about my dad—my real dad, I mean?"

Rhona met Syn's gaze straight on. "You want to try that? He might not be receptive."

"He might. I won't know unless I try." She flapped her arms. "Everyone is so crazy and mixed up, I might as well know the truth about him, too."

Rhona nodded. "Ask your mom, and we'll send him an email or something."

Syn pulled out her phone. "I already asked and got his number. We can text him now if you want."

If I want? Rhona watched a squirrel on a high branch wave his tail frantically at another squirrel nibbling a nut on the ground. An unleashed dog romped nearby. *Get going, you fool. Get up that tree!*

Syn held out the phone with Gustav's name and number in her contact list.

Her heart writhing, Rhona nodded. "Okay, but let me see it before you send it."

Syn opened the message system, tapped her lips with one hand, and then tapped onto the phone for a heartbreakingly long stretch of time.

Before Rhona's nerves broke all to pieces, she had to ask, "Are you writing your biography?"

A wry expression and Syn waved her off. Finally, as shadows lengthened across the park, Syn handed the phone to her aunt.

Rhona squinted in the angled light.

Hello, Mr. Gustav Sanchez,

My name is Syn Fortune-Wei, and you knew my mother, Nia Fortune-Wei when you stayed at our home sixteen years ago. It turns out, after confirmation by a DNA test, that I am your daughter.

Mom didn't know until after I had the test done. So, it was a surprise to my whole family. Especially to me.

Anyway, I thought you might like to know that you have a daughter. I am open to exchanging messages with you if you are interested.

I will understand if you can't communicate with me. Maybe another time, then.

Wishing you all the best,

Syn

No words to express her pride and anguish, Rhona wrapped her arms around her niece and hugged her tightly.

Syn hugged back for a long moment. Then she pulled back and tapped the send button. Finally, she slipped her phone into her pocket, and a saucy smile spread over her face. "You ready for me to drive home now?"

"No, but that doesn't matter." Rhona rose to her feet and figured that if her heart hadn't given up the ghost yet, it was good for another twenty miles.

Chapter Ten

Can Rhona manage Stumbling Blocks, Altered Personalities, and Cruel Storms?

Early June

Early June and it was already hot. Rhona, dressed in loose pants and a baggy shirt, slipped from her bedroom just after the neighbor's cock began crowing, before stifling heat made outdoor work pure drudgery, and plodded her way to the garden. The sun, still hidden behind the tree line in the east, sent slanting rays ahead, highlighting sparkling spider webs and green tree tops.

As she tromped across the dewy grass, a stench assaulted her nose. She halted, spying out the landscape. *Erch! What is that?* It didn't take long before her nose and eyes met the source of the stink—a dead raccoon with half its innards splayed across the new grass.

Oh, my. Rhona's heart sank as she changed direction and headed for the garden shed. She snatched up a shovel and stomped back to the scene of the crime, or at least where the latest body lay—the third raccoon this week. *It's only Wednesday. What are those dogs doing? Trying to set a world record for the most raccoons slaughtered in a season?* She glanced around. Ness and Wilma lay sprawled on the ground in front of their dog houses. *Probably exhausted by their night of skullduggery and evil deeds.*

Huffing with effort, she scooped the carcass off the slippery grass, balanced it so its innards didn't leave a horrific trail behind, and carried the appalling load to the compost heap. Using a good portion of her precious cool morning time, she dug a deep hole to the south of the compost bin, tipped the broken body in, and then proceeded to cover it with fresh dirt and brambles hauled over from a winter clearing job. That done, she wiped her sweaty brow and started back to the shed. *Are the dogs even keeping track, or is every night just a new murderous adventure?*

Syn called from the back door. "Hey, there are two dead mice here. You want them?"

Refusing to be drawn into an inane discussion of why it's best to think before you speak, Rhona clutched the shovel and repeated the burial process in a timely manner.

With the assault to her nostrils still in her mind, Rhona decided to take a quick shower and put on a clean outfit. Shorts and a T-shirt would do better than the long pants and shirt she had been wearing. A quick scrub up and feeling remarkably refreshed, Rhona padded into the kitchen. *Doing a hard task first thing in the morning always makes the rest of the day seem better—less grizzly, anyway.*

She met her husband in the kitchen and offered a brave smile. She wasn't about to detail her early morning escapades. Derm's glazed expression sent alarm bells ringing. *Trouble in the online world? It's summer vacation, for goodness' sake! He should be napping with an old truck manual slipping from his hands.* She grabbed a cup of coffee, dropped in a heaping spoonful of dark brown sugar, and then poured in enough creamer to satisfy her dairy requirement for the day.

Derm filled his cup, his brow furrowed, and his gaze fixed on some inner trouble.

Rhona leaned against the sink, her hands cupping the steaming mug. "Out with it. What's wrong?"

Derm clumped over to the kitchen table and plopped down on the sturdy bench. He gripped his cup like a lifeline. "I got a message from Renzo this morning."

Uh, oh. Rhona made her way to the table carefully and sat on the chair at the head of the table, close enough to hear a whisper. "Yeah? What about?"

"He wants a letter of recommendation."

Relief seeped through Rhona. "That's nice. You can give him a great one. He's always friendly, helpful, and on time when he sets an appointment to meet you. There are lots of good things you can say about him."

Derm shook his head. "That's not the problem."

Rhona took a comforting sip of the liquid energizer and waited, her muscles tensing.

A long sigh and Derm unburdened himself. "Turns out that he applied for a study-abroad program last semester, but it was full, so he didn't get in. But somebody just dropped out, and the university wants him to send along one more character reference, and they will decide between him and another guy to fill the vacancy." Derm set his cup aside and leaned back, his gaze wandering the room as if he had never seen it before. "It's a fantastic opportunity, a chemistry program for potential PhD students where he'll get to meet some of the leading professors in his field. It could lead to a fully funded advanced scholarship at a big-name university."

Rhona shook her head. "So why do you look as if the sky has fallen?"

"It's in Germany."

Her stomach souring, Rhona set her cup aside. *Syn will not take this well.*

Derm leaned forward, and his gravelly voice took on a more determined tone. “Listen, it’s only for one semester, and it’s a fantastic chance for the kid. I had to write the best recommendation I could. He deserves this.”

Rhona nodded, her words just barely scraping the audible range. “Yes, I agree. Renzo must want to go, or he would never have asked.”

They sat silent as bright morning light streamed through the kitchen window. A songbird fluttered about the sky and then settled on a high branch of the apple tree in the middle of the yard. It began to sing its heart out.

If she really loves him...

After Renzo called two days later and told Syn his wonderful news—he’d been accepted into the program, Rhona thought she might lose her mind. *Dead raccoons and now this!*

Sitting at the table with a nice lunch of egg salad and carrot slices waiting, Syn clutched the phone to her ear, faked enthusiasm as well as any Emmy award winner—practically screaming into the phone with excitement—then let Renzo hurry off to a thousand details that he needed take care of before his departure in August. As soon as she hit the end button, Syn ran to her room and slammed the door. Muffled sobbing issued forth for the rest of the afternoon. By evening, Rhona and Derm were tiptoeing around thc house, fearing that a wrong step would set off more wailing.

The next morning, Rhona’s nerves beyond frazzled, she completed her garden duties—relieved that not one dead animal required her burial services—caught up on her editing assignments, and then, deciding that twenty-four hours was long enough for a girl to go without eating, she ordered Syn to come out, eat a good lunch, and do something useful with herself.

When Syn flopped down at the table, the girl's depressed attitude rivaled a deflated Santa balloon three days after Christmas. Not knowing what else to do, Rhona excused herself with a meaningful glance at Derm to make sure that every particle of the healthy meal made it down Syn's throat. Then she sped to the store, bought four gallons of gray paint and a good brush, raced back home, and lugged them onto the porch. Then she called her niece from her sarcophagus, where she had retreated once again, and set her to painting the porch railings and floor. The ceiling was white, and no one had walked on it, not even the cats, so it was still in good shape. The Lord knew that the old wood needed a fresh covering, and Syn needed something to keep from any further deterioration. Leaving the girl to manage without any overzealous advice, Rhona went to her computer and buried herself in household finances.

By the time she had wrestled her monetary accounts into proper shape and set a pot of chili simmering on the stove for dinner, Rhona decided to check Syn's progress. She halted just outside the door, stared at the uneven splotches across the floor, and wondered if she had made a mistake. Her beloved porch appeared to have a case of Chicken Pox, and there wasn't a thing she could do to rectify the situation, other than wrench the paintbrush from her niece's hand and add to the girl's growing list of reasons why life was no longer worth living.

On his way to help Tavish with a tractor issue, Derm leaned out his truck window, took a long perusing look at Syn's handiwork, and exhaled a low whistle. He locked sympathetic eyes on Rhona and dropped his voice to don't-want-to-alarm-anyone level. "There's a spare brush in my shed if you need it." A backward wave, gravel spitting acceleration, and he made his escape.

No other repair schemes coming to mind, Rhona stepped around the wet spots, tromped to the shed, dug through piles of unidentifiable things that her husband kept for uncertain future projects, found the dusty paint brush, clutched it all the way back to the porch, and met her niece slapping paint on a railing the way an angry woman might slap a sleazy drunkard. Rhona lifted the new brush in salute and forced a grin. "Fresh troops ready to serve."

Holding up a slathered brush handle with approximately three straggly bristles held together by gobs of paint, Syn stared deadpanned. She was not amused. Her expression insisted that she would never, ever, under any circumstances, be amused again, as long as she lived.

Gingerly, Rhona nipped the pathetic brush that had clearly gone well above and beyond the call of duty, dropped it on a pile of defeated paper towels, and gestured to the rocking chair on the other side of the porch. "Take a breather, sweetheart. I'll do my time."

After slumping over to the chair, Syn fell onto it with an oomph.

In a moment of insanity, Rhona thought a positive light on Renzo's opportunity might help her niece make the best of the situation. "I know you feel sad, honey, but think about what a great chance this would be for Renzo. He'll only be gone for the fall semester and be back for Christmas. We can have him over for dinner and make popcorn balls or something; how about that?"

Silence.

Rhona glanced over.

Her hands over her face as she crouched forward, Syn groaned in misery.

Just at that moment, Nia's matchbox mini-car pulled into the driveway.

Oh, Lord, here we go, Sensitivity Central. She'll find a way to blame this on me; I know she will. There was no point in putting the paintbrush aside. It would only dry out. Besides, there were just a few more feet to go and this side would be done. Acting as if her niece wasn't having a meltdown a few feet away, Rhona continued slathering the porch railing in healing gray paint.

Nia skipped up the steps—a happy kid home from school ready to tell mom all about her day. Her "Hi, all!" froze on her lips as she stopped on the top step, her eyes fixed on her daughter. "What?" Before anyone could respond, she flew across the porch, somehow managing to dodge the wet spots, and wrapped her arms around the slim figure. "Tell me what's wrong, honey. Has your aunt gone wicked and said something mean?"

It was the first good laugh Rhona had had in days. Once she got started, she could hardly contain herself. Chuckles turned into belly laughs, and she had to set the brush down or risk dribbles over her clothes.

The sight of Syn's astonished face morphing into a grin and then joining in the laughter and Nia's confused expression only added fuel to the hilarity bubbling up from inside. She tried to speak, but her words came out in gasps, "Yes! I've gone…wicked! Mean me!"

When Syn rushed from her chair and plowed into Rhona, her arms twining around her, hugging hard, Nia's baffled expression set off another burst of laughter. Honestly, Rhona wasn't sure whether she was letting off months of accumulated tension or having a nervous breakdown. Only Syn's murmuring, "Sorry, I'm not mad at you, sorry," brought Rhona to her senses. She smoothed down the girl's dark hair and heaved a long sigh.

Nia flapped her arms, ready for take-off. "What in the world is going on?"

Syn lifted her head and faced her mom. "Renzo is going to Germany in August to study abroad for a semester. It's a great opportunity for him. He may even get a scholarship for a PhD program when he graduates."

For once, Nia didn't interject her opinion on the matter. Her wordless, wide-eyed expression articulated her confusion.

Syn stepped back and wiped her eyes with the back of her hand. "It's just that I'm going to miss him. A lot."

Her arms out and moving with the speed of light, Nia embraced her daughter with a squeal, "Oh, darling! There are lots of guys out there! Renzo-boy isn't the only one in the world. Just wait till you start college. There'll be guys falling all over each other, trying to get your attention."

Rhona winced. This was not what Syn wanted to hear. It was what Nia would have wanted to hear if she was in a similar situation. Her hysterical laughter turned snippy. "Thanks, doctor. That's the perfect prescription for a broken heart."

Frowning, Syn started for the door. "I don't want another guy. I love Renzo, and I'll just wait to see how things turn out before I sell myself to the highest bidder! Besides—" She swung the screen door open, glared over her shoulder, and tossed a verbal grenade. "My own dad doesn't seem to want me since he never answered my text, so I doubt anyone else will either."

Before Nia could launch herself through the doorway after her daughter, Rhona grabbed her arm and held her in a firm grip, a scraggly hiss issuing from where her laughter had died. "Let her be. She needs time."

Least said soonest mended whispered in her brain like a demented demon.

Exhaling a huge huff, Nia limped to the rocking chair and fell onto it much the same way her daughter had moments before. She rocked in seething silence.

Rhona returned to her painting. Smoothing gray paint over tired wood no longer comforted her—not even while imagining how nice the porch would look when it was done. Now, it was just a job she had to endure—a price to be paid to keep the porch from rotting and falling to pieces under her feet. Sick dread rose, and she tried to push it away, but the idea that Gustav had ignored Syn was absorbed by her mind the way the wood soaked up the paint. Dabbing a touch of gray into a tough corner, she imagined an even worse response: "I don't know you. Go away."

Finally, Nia broke the silence. "She told me that she wanted to contact him. I encouraged her. I thought for sure he'd be thrilled. After all, it was so many years ago; his wife can't hold it against him now."

Rhona rolled her eyes and wondered if her sister was brain-damaged. She almost said, "Like Zhang?" but refrained.

"I told her to send a picture of herself along with her message. Once he saw that adorable face and perfect body, he could never refuse her. She looks so much like him. You'd think he'd be so proud."

"Of his illegitimate daughter he didn't know about for sixteen years?"

Nia picked at her nails. Not a hint of nail polish today. "I guess there is that."

Rhona finished the last section and decided that Derm would probably be willing to finish the other side if she promised to make strawberry shortcakes for dessert for the rest of the month.

A ragged breath and Nia slapped the arm of her chair. "Damn it, Rhona! Look what I've done!"

Squinting, Rhona searched her sister's hands, body, and then the chair, looking for a broken piece, something amiss. Nothing out of the ordinary struck her. She tapped the lid on the can and had to ask, "What?"

"What I did to our little girl. I really screwed up her life, didn't I?"

Astonished, Rhona nearly knocked the gallon of paint off the stool. In a quick save, she gripped the handle and the brush with one hand and her heart with the other. *Our?*

Nia wasn't crying, but her eyes bled haunting sorrow as if she knew that, for the rest of her life, she would have to live with painful consequences she had never considered before.

The first glimmer of real pity swelled in Rhona as she stowed the paint by the wall and wrapped the brush in an old rag. "Sixteen years ago, you loved a fantasy. You made an error in judgment, but Syn was never a mistake. Now you get to love your flesh and blood daughter." Still gripping the brush, she wiped a blob of paint off her nose with the back of her hand and turned to the door, visions of strawberry shortcake dancing in her head. "Go inside and listen to your girl; stop talking and just be there for her."

Nodding, Nia rose to her feet and held out her hand. "I'll wash out the brush if you want to work on dinner."

A nod and Rhona agreed to the plan. No need to ask. They both knew Nia was staying. The word "our" danced through her head all the way to the kitchen.

A week later, Rhona stood in the middle of Oldtown Main Street, blocked off for the first annual Art Festival the town had ever known. In jaw-dropping surprise, she watched the hustle and bustle of visitors from all across the county streaming in and out of booths lining both sides of the street.

Though she'd been to a dozen cities in her lifetime, Rhona had only visited a handful of museums and art centers. As far as Derm and most of their friends and family were concerned, historical sites, breweries, and natural parks were worth investigating. They could take or leave music festivals, but art shows left them cold. So, when Ada had announced her newest brainstorm—actually, Callum came up with the idea, and she acted a patroness, supporting it with all the vim and vigor of an Old Testament Zealot—for an Oldtown Art Show, Rhona was certain sure it would face a quick demise.

She was wrong.

Standing outside the Granary Feed and Seed building—a monstrosity painted bright red, with "Oldtown" spelled out in bold, black letters across the top—she watched as Callum, dexterously directing his braces, led Renzo toward a row of booths populated with clay sculptures, stone carvings, stained glass exhibits, and large wooden quilt blocks.

You're a genius. Never would have thought this possible.

A sprig of hope springing to life, Rhona stepped over to the table decorated with a miniature fantasy scene comprised of elves and dragons made entirely from natural objects and felt like a kid again. After a slow tour around the magical tent, a horn blast from the "Medieval Artistry" tent brought her back to the present reality. Gripping a pole, she figured that she might as well spy on her friends and neighbors while she waited for Derm to finish taste-testing the five varieties of relish being offered for sale. How relish got into an art festival, she couldn't say, but Derm sure seemed happy about it.

Before she knew it, Syn loped out of the last tent with one arm linked with Renzo and the other helping Callum keep his balance as they made their way across Main Street.

Rhona held her ground. Ever since Nia had stayed for dinner late into the evening, listening to Syn pour her heart out, the girl's mood had risen from the depths of despair to puppy eagerness. Perhaps it was Nia's comment about how an advanced degree would give Renzo options he might never have had otherwise, igniting the girl's imagination in a hundred directions. It could have been Renzo's text message—*I'll take my mind to Germany, but I'll leave my heart with you—* that had abolished her wretched anxiety. Whatever the cause, it was wonderful to see her smiling again. *Can't keep a good woman down.*

Just as Syn crossed in front of the taste-testing booth, she glanced aside and, before Rhona knew what was happening, the girl had flown across the street and grabbed her uncle around the waist.

Her eyes glued to the stricken expression on her husband's face, Rhona sped forward, her chest constricting. *Not again! Please, God!*

She reached Dermid just as Renzo took over and helped her husband land on a metal chair. Concerned looks all around, and at least fifteen people had their phones out, fingers poised over 911 buttons.

Derm waved everyone off and held up his own phone. "It's not me. It's Tavish. He's been rushed to the hospital." He tapped his chest. "Same thing as me. Bloody fool! I told him to stay out of the heat."

Closing her eyes, Rhona couldn't help but wonder why happiness was so fleeting.

Mid-June

Rhona loved Friday evenings with her husband. They were as good as any date night, but without a hint of nervous anxiety or an expensive dinner bill. A light supper of tuna salad with whole wheat bread and vanilla ice cream for dessert had put them into a relaxed frame of mind as they settled on their matching rockers, breathing in the warm summer air. The porch, now a smooth and pleasing shade of gray, gleamed in the slanting rays of light.

When Derm's phone bleeped, he squeezed his eyes shut as if to keep the larger world at bay.

Rhona thought of Syn on a date with Renzo and checked her own phone. No messages. Her heart unclenched, and she relaxed, glancing aside at her husband.

His phone now plastered to his ear, a trail of gray hairs fluffed along the side of his face, Derm's gaze stayed focused on the tree line straight ahead. A frown, then a smile, and he chuckled softly.

By the time her husband hit the end button and pocketed his phone, Rhona was ready to burst with curiosity. But she knew her husband too well to ask. *He'll talk when he's ready.* Her knuckles whitened as she gripped the arms of her chair.

Leaning back, Derm's gaze stayed focused on the trees, noisy birds flocking in for the night.

A billow of wrens fluttered about the maple in the middle of the yard, settling themselves down, an occasional squawk, alerting the noisy ones that the early birds were trying to get a bit of shut-eye.

Taking a deep breath, Rhona tried to imagine life in a noisy flock, always sticking together, darting about the same feeders, building similar nests in a copse of trees. *Do they ever get sick of each other? Might one independent fellow decide to fly off and be by itself for a while? What would happen then? Would they scratch his name off the family list or harass him till he rejoined the flock?*

Derm broke through her thoughts with a preliminary throat clearing. "Callum and Andy are coming over for breakfast in the morning."

Rhona's heart started wiggling toward her throat. "What for?" She really didn't want to hear the latest in family drama, though the idea that Callum was involved did nudge her heart back in the right direction. "You know that Syn isn't feeling particularly friendly with Andy, and she hardly needs anything to upset her delicate frame of mind these days. She may be acting happy, but she's still as nervous as a mother bird facing down a snake."

Derm nodded, though his gaze stayed fixed on the trees. "Andy wants to fix up that old UTV vehicle I have in the garage for Tavish."

As the birds quieted, Rhona tried to figure out Andy's angle. She blinked at the gold-pink sky. "Why?"

Scowling, Derm turned his head, his gaze now aimed at his wife. "What do you mean why? He knows that Tav can't get around like he used to and that the guy won't get himself a UTV, so he's going help me fix mine, drop it off, and leave it there with some excuse that no one will believe, but Tavish will understand."

With a shake of the head, Rhona tried to reorientate herself to this new vision of the universe. A world where Andy did kind and unselfish things. "Has he changed that much?"

"Nia hinted that he's been going to counseling. Maybe his counselor told him to do a good deed every day to feel better about himself."

"Sounds more like something Callum might suggest."

Derm snorted. Her husband probably didn't care if aliens from a distant solar system had convinced his nephew to do something nice. "It's about time he appreciated all that Tavish did for his family."

"You mean for Zhang's business."

His scowl deepening, Derm sat upright, no longer relaxed. "I mean for his family. Tav helped Zhang in his time of need so the man could provide for his wife and children. Zhang may be obsessed by his work, but he's not all bad. Tavish wouldn't have helped him if he thought the guy was nothing but a selfish jerk."

Rocking slowly, grieved by their misunderstanding and loss of tranquility, Rhona simply nodded. She couldn't reconcile the Andy, who mercilessly teased Syn, with this image of a reformed guy who wanted to help her brother-in-law without an ounce of self-interest.

Derm seemed to read her mind. "I know you don't trust the guy, but Callum is a pretty good judge of character. He must see something redeemable in the kid, or he wouldn't bother."

Rhona nodded again and spoke with all the hearty cheerfulness she could manage. "I'll fry up some bacon and eggs with hashbrowns for breakfast. That should give you guys enough energy to fix up any dilapidated vehicle. I'm sure Tavish will be pleased as punch. Though he'll act like he never noticed it even as he's driving it through the field to check on the cows."

An agreeable grunt and Derm rose from his chair. He pointed at the quiet treeline. "If I'm going to be managing two guys and a broken UTV tomorrow, I better follow their example and get some shuteye."

As her husband shuffled inside, Rhona watched the last spark of day fall into darkness. Syn would be home soon, probably happy as a lark after her date with Renzo, so she'd wait till morning to tell her that Andy was coming over. For now, she'd let her sense of disappointment over a non-existent rift with her husband and the loss of a pleasant evening in warm companionship fade. Tomorrow was another day.

She rose, stretched, and tried not to wake the birds.

Rhona thought about antiques the same way she thought about food. If it energized a person, great. If it cluttered life's arteries, leave it be. It wasn't that she failed to be charmed by vintage furniture, sparking visions of days long past when each household article was a treasure often made by a family member. Rather it was her utilitarian nature to appreciate things that served rather than objects that merely charmed. One of the reasons she saw no excuse for the existence of cotton candy.

Though anyone on the planet could see in a five-second glance that Nia's house was packed full to bursting, her sister insisted that she needed something "pretty and spirited" to add to her little home. Against all sane judgment, while the men spent a second Saturday working on the UTV for Tavish, Rhona allowed herself to be talked into visiting a local antique shop to see if Nia could find something in the right size physically and financially.

As Rhona scooted into the driver's side of her car, since she wasn't about to risk life and limb letting her sister drive, she peered across the yard at Syn reclining at the picnic table with a book in hand and the dogs sprawled on the green grass in the cool shade.

Nia bounced onto the passenger side seat like a kid getting on a school bus. "You ready?" She followed Rhona's gaze and immediately jumped back out of the car. Then she yelled loud enough to wake owls in three counties. "Hey, kiddo, come with us! We're going antiquing. I'll buy you something cute."

Her legs stretched out on the bench and appearing rather peaceful as she leaned against an elm trunk, Syn merely smiled and waved a pleasant goodbye.

Slumping, Nia reentered the car and flattened herself against the seat. A burst balloon if ever there was one. "I can never make her happy."

Rhona started up the car and drove it around the circular driveway shaking her head. "You can't make people happy. You can do nice things, be attentive, help out, even save a life, but happiness is a choice people have to make for themselves." She shrugged as she pulled onto the road leading to the shop Nia had picked out from the half dozen in the area. "Syn never heard from her dad—Gustav, I mean, and I think it weighs on her mind. Adding that to the fact that Zhang has never once reached out to her. Well, it might take a while to get past all that."

A pout and Nia hugged herself. "I miss him so much, I can hardly stand it."

Accelerating, Rhona kept her eyes on the open road as fields whizzed by and her heart began to race. "Who?"

"Zhang, of course. I mean, I know it's silly. He left me, right? But I made a mistake, and I understand why he's angry at me." Her fingers did a nervous dance on her handbag. "Still, he cares about Syn. At least a bit. He knows it wasn't her fault. He even told me that. He said he has no hard feelings toward her, he just wants to move on. But we had some fun times together. It's not easy to give all that up and have to work every day. I barely make enough to live on. Good thing Zhang's insurance still covers the kids, or we'd be up a creek."

Boggled, Rhona's mind bounced wildly. "Zhang still covers Syn on his insurance?" She hesitated a second, trying to think through the ramifications. "I never even thought to ask. I should have. Derm mentioned it once, but I just figured it was a family plan that would last…" She tapped the steering wheel. "Honestly, I don't know what I was thinking." Then she glanced aside. "What about you? What are you doing for coverage…in case something happened?"

A snort. “If I get into another wreck, you mean?” Nia dug in her purse and pulled out a small, white card. “Lucia showed me what they use and even called her insurance guy. He walked me through it. I don’t make enough to get a premium plan, but I got basic coverage, though the deductible will kill me.”

Trying to wrap her mind around Zhang’s unexpected generosity toward Syn, Rhona turned onto the road leading to the designated shop. A mile to go, but she wanted to clear her head first. “So, Zhang never told anyone else, at least not formally, that Syn isn’t his kid?”

Her eyebrows crunching together like furious wooly worms, Nia spat her words. “He’s not a total monster. He was angry, and he left me. Simple as that. He wasn’t perfect either, but I really think we could have lived the rest of our lives happily together if he had forgiven me. But he’s not the forgiving type. Still, that doesn’t make him evil. He says that Syn can stay on his insurance until she gets a real job and lives on her own. He’s even willing to help out with college, so long as she works part-time to earn her own money on the side.”

“Andy didn’t have to work.”

“He does now. Zhang said that he won’t tolerate stupid behavior, and when Andy messed up, drinking too much and all that, well, that put him in no man’s land. He’s still his son, but only sort of. On probation or something.”

A weathered red and blue sign hanging over an old barn announced their destination, “Antique Visions.” Rhona pulled into the gravel parking lot and found a spot near the door. Her head still spinning with conflicting images of her former brother-in-law,

Rhona tried to keep up with her sister, who managed to make it inside at record speed.

No museum she'd ever visited prepared her for the onslaught of personal history as this gathering of items frozen in time. Rhona wandered aimlessly with no interest in taking anything home when a familiar booming voice called from the other side of a shelving unit filled with glassware and a high-pitched squeal answered. Amazed that nothing had shattered, Rhona toured the labyrinth until she came upon Nia and Ada huddled before an arrangement of China dolls.

Ada turned as Rhona stepped nearer. "Oh, there you are! It's so good to see you. And this one!" She tapped Nia's shoulder playfully, "As beautiful as ever! The sisters brag about you all the time." She dropped her voice to a conspiratorial low. "If you keep on the way you are, they might make you manager so they can take that trip to Europe they've always dreamed of. Wouldn't that be fine!"

A tiny voice in Rhona's head sneered, *But she's missing her ex-husband so much she can hardly stand it.* She told herself to stop it and plastered a smile on her face. Ada was a dear, and Nia might eventually grow up and realize… *What?* Rhona wasn't sure. *I'm not sure what I know these days.*

When Nia held up a figurine of a woman dancing, Rhona merely nodded through a smile. When she caught sight of a beautiful figurine—a sparrow balanced on the edge of a nest, ready to fly—Rhona realized that though antiques may not make her heart beat any faster, visions did. She got out her purse and paid for both.

Midsummer's eve, being the longest day of the year, deserved some recognition. A simple barbecue of hotdogs and hamburgers, two poetry recitations—one read by Syn, one read by Rhona—and four jokes fired off by Renzo, Callum, Tavish, and Derm made for a memorable night.

Since Nia was working on inventory at the shop, and Andy was visiting his dad in Chicago, it was easy to keep the gathering small. Fighting a summer cold, Rhona cleared the table as soon as everyone was done, washed up the dishes, and then headed for the porch while the older men fixated on a new tractor model big enough to take over both lanes of traffic while roaring down the road.

Renzo and Syn had skedaddled shortly after the last joke. As she settled into her chair facing the glowing sky, she could hear their murmured conversation in the living room. *I should get up…announce myself…do something…*

As if her blood had been replaced with lead, Rhona's body refused to obey any direct orders. The house could have caught fire, and she wasn't sure she'd be able to do more than wave an arm and moan helplessly. She closed her eyes and tried not to listen.

Renzo might as well have been using a megaphone. "…a dream for so long, I can't imagine not following it. You've got to find your dream, Syn. I know you have one somewhere inside of you."

A murmur as Syn's voice complained, sounding eerily like her mother. "I don't know what I want, besides you."

"You've got to want something besides me." A spluttered breath. "Listen, when my mom got cancer, I thought my dad was going to flip. He depended on her for everything. He always said that life just happens and you can't change anything. But Mom believed in the power of faith and good works. In the end, he's miserable because nothing ever happens the way he thinks it should, even though he says he doesn't expect anything better. But Mom takes whatever life hands her, even cancer, and she turns stumbling blocks into stepping stones. It's her way. That's how I want to live. But it's a choice. You got to choose for yourself."

A long silence, and Rhona wished she could float over to the window and look in.

Finally, Syn sniffled, her cracked voice rose, gaining strength as she spoke. "Yeah. I like the way your mom thinks. Like Aunt Rhona and Uncle Derm." Another sniff. "But I'll still miss you. A lot!"

His voice strained—*with tears?* Renzo's devotion rose through his words. "I'll come back, Syn. I promise I'll come back to you."

The tromp of footsteps up the steps and across the porch, and Derm made his appearance. He scowled at his wife. "You look like death warmed over."

Rhona wanted to laugh, but a tear meandered down her cheek instead.

By sheer force of strong arms and determined love, her husband led her to their room, helped her tug off her day clothes and slip on a night dress, and settled her comfortably in bed. The sound of their guests driving off and Syn's door closing in her room, calmed Rhona's heart into a quiet rhythm. As night finally took over the longest day of the year, she could hear soft clattering of dishes as her husband put them away, then the snap of the switch when he turned out the light.

Late June

Rhona had to make peace with herself. Otherwise, she would go crazy or get sick again, battling self-accusations that she wasn't doing enough to protect those she loved from the dangers of love itself. *I can't save people. I'm not God, for Heaven's sake. A time-out is long overdue.*

She didn't know what was wrong with her. Gloomy and sad, she couldn't shake an oppressive weight that deadened her soul to any spark of hope. Was she responding to a haunting ghost from the dim past when her father had raged and her mother retreated? Her prickly conscience often shoved her into managing challenging situations no one else wanted to handle, but sometimes, she wondered if she wasn't in the wrong when trying to do right. *Am I getting in the way between actions and consequences, a reality check that everyone needs? I should step aside and just relax.*

She stretched out on the plastic lawn chair that Derm had dragged out of the shed and considerately dusted off and watched evening fireflies dance like fairies over the bright green lawn. She eased a long sigh, grateful for the end of another drama-less day.

Derm puttered about in the kitchen, fixing heaping bows of ice cream, with Syn undoubtedly adding dollops of caramel, sprinkles, chopped nuts, and even a few strawberries. She pictured them hunched over the bowls like happy witches over their latest brew. *They act like naughty children, outdoing each other in their extravagance.*

Rhona had no idea what they would bring her, though she doubted she would be able to eat half in one sitting.

When a truck pulled into the driveway, she merely turned her head. It sounded familiar, but she couldn't imagine what Tavish would be doing, coming over at this time of the evening. *He should be resting. Derm will have a fit if he's started another project.*

To her surprise, the sound of Callum's braces scratching over the gravel met her ears, and before she could yell out a hello, Syn was racing from the house, heading right for him.

Carrying a large tray, Derm ambled down the porch steps and stopped at the bottom. He waited for Callum, calling out something Rhona couldn't hear, though his smile was welcoming enough.

It didn't take long for another dish of ice cream to follow the first three, and they were all sitting before a flickering fire as dragonflies and fireflies framed a fairyland setting.

Amazingly, Callum did justice to his dessert in record time, while Syn nibbled hers as if she planned to savor it over the next week. Derm plodded along, slurping his drippy caramel-covered ice cream, nuts, sprinkles, and all, with the determination of a hound following a scent.

Rhona enjoyed a few bites and then asked Syn to put it into a plastic container and back in the freezer. If she ate all that sugar in one sitting, she'd go into diabetic shock.

While Syn hurried inside, leaving Derm to guard her dessert from nosey dogs and whining cats, Callum clasped his bowl in his lap, and leaned forward, dropping his voice low. "I'm moving in with Tavish this week, and I think it might be good if Andy joins us. He really wants to."

Derm reared back as if he had been struck. "Andy? He's up north with his dad. I thought he was having a high old time in Chicago, seeing all the sights and everything."

A mournful headshake and Callum dispelled any notion of a happy reconciliation between father and son. "Zhang's got a girlfriend, and Andy's not too fond of her. Apparently, she's pretty and ambitious, just the sort of woman that would appeal to Zhang."

Rhona closed her eyes a moment to stop the ice cream from churning in her stomach. By the time she opened them, Syn was back, standing next to her uncle, her eyes wide with questions.

Derm pointed to her chair, handed back the sticky dessert, and explained the situation.

Her chin raised in defiance; Syn's eyes blazed with moral indignation. "It's only been a few months, and he's replacing Mom already?"

Callum scratched a reddish beard sprouting over his chin. "I think that's pretty much how Andy sees it, too. He's rather upset and told his dad that he's coming back down here to help Tavish with his farming."

His gaze as steady as boulders at the base of a mountain, Derm stared at the young man. "What did Tav say about that?"

Callum sucked in a deep breath and straightened, his gaze darting from Derm to Syn. "I was kind of hoping you could help me ask him." He waved his free hand in the air. "I don't know what to do. I asked Andy to help with stuff earlier, and he seemed responsive. I think he's upset that Renzo is leaving. And now his dad, with a new gal, has pushed him back to the brink.

I really don't want to see him dive into drinking again."

Feeling more hardhearted than she ever remembered, Rhona sat up and dropped her feet on the firm ground. "That's never been our choice. Andy has always done what he wanted. He'll do what he wants now, no matter what we say."

The deafening silence that followed suggested disagreement.

Rhona pursed her lips. "I won't let Syn get dragged back into Andy's cruelty. It's bad enough that Nia will fall to pieces when she discovers she's been replaced. So fast!"

Derm's head shake wasn't consoling, and grief practically poured from Callum's eyes. But it was Syn's voice that rocked Rhona's determination.

High with strained displeasure, Syn's tone rivaled a school mistress finding a toad on her desk. "Andy is my brother, half maybe, but still, he's mine. I know he's been a jerk and needs to learn a ton of things about being a decent human being, but still, he's had a hard time. He didn't choose to have dyslexia, and his dad practically nailed him to the floor every time he brought in anything less than an A, which was most of the time. Mom may have loved him in her way, but she didn't really help. She just made everyone ignore the huge elephant tromping around the room." With an oversized sniff, she swung her glare at Callum. "If Tavish could use some more help, it'd be a great idea. Andy might as well have a good man in his life while he figures out how to deal with a terrible father."

A hot blush worked over Rhona as she tried to confront the shame that flooded her. *Was I that off the mark?* She glanced at her husband, whose head hung low, his elbows propped on his knees like a man wishing for escape.

A small grunt and Callum struggled to his feet. "I probably shouldn't have come over unannounced and dumped this on you. But I just got Andy's message this afternoon. He sounded so disheartened, without even thinking, I asked if he'd like to move in with me and Tavish. He texted back yes so fast; I don't doubt that he sees it as a lifeline. He can't stay with his mom. There just isn't enough room, and they get on each other's nerves." He sighed. "Sorry, I've made a mess of things. I just didn't know what to do."

Derm stood and took the empty bowl from Callum's hand. "I appreciate your coming by, and I think that Tavish would want to know your idea. I'll talk with him. He's the one who will have to live with the consequences if he takes Andy into his home." Derm squinted as the sun peeked around Callum's shoulder. "When are you planning on moving in?"

"My lease is up at the end of the month. Tavish suggested it. He's aware of his advancing age, and the doctors made some pretty clear recommendations. So, though I'm not able to do much physical work, I can help with bookkeeping and that kind of stuff." A soft smile drifted over his face. "The man has ledgers going back to before I was born! I told him that I could transfer everything from the last few years and going forward onto an online financial program. He seemed to think that it was about time he joined the twenty-first century."

Derm patted Callum's shoulder. "You're a braver man than I."

Slowly, Rhona creaked to her feet and raised her hand in a conciliatory gesture. "Sorry I was so snappish. I just hate to…well, I need to let some things go and see if we can make a better future."

Callum nodded. "Like you said, it's on Andy. If Tavish will have him, and he works hard, he might find some kind of fulfillment in life."

Derm frowned. "How about school? Isn't he going back in the fall?"

Callum shrugged. "That was the plan, but I honestly don't know now. I'll wait till he and Tavish talk things out and see what happens."

Syn had her arms folded high over her chest, her face set like flint. "When Andy gets back, tell him that we're having a goodbye party for Renzo at the end of July since he has to leave in early August. He's invited."

Callum locked his gaze on Syn, and his smile brightened. "You're a good-hearted Sparrow."

As Syn and Derm piled the plates on the tray and headed for the door, Rhona folded the lawn chair and stowed it back in the shed. *Time to face reality again. No more lazing about.* She watched her husband's slumped back as he climbed the steps and figured that he was practicing his line of questioning—how to ask Tavish about Andy without exactly asking.

Shaking her head, Rhona's gaze wafted over to the lithe figure tromping up the steps right behind her uncle with all the force of invading troops. Her spirit brightened. *I'll send Syn along with a cherry pie.*

Rhona hated it when Mondays turned out to be the precursor to a difficult week. By Thursday, she was ready to wave a white flag in surrender.

Another flat tire, a stopped-up sink, one dog wounded in a fight with something she could no longer identify, and worms attacking her zucchini plants had taken the joy out of living. To top it off, Ada had stopped by the day before to remind her of the next poetry submission opening and hinted that it would do Syn the world of good if she could "expel spiritual demons through artistic cleansing." Then, as the large woman lumbered to her car, she pointed out the green mold growing on the south side of the house. "There's a remedy for that involving a bleach solution, a spray nozzle, and a ladder." Grinning good-naturedly, Ada bundled into her car and drove away, undoubtedly on another mission of mercy.

Well aware that she wasn't going to win any "Housekeeper of the Year" awards, Rhona stood in her driveway, grimaced at the living microorganisms that were eking their living off the south side of her abode, and considered mentioning the incident to Derm to see if he would take the initiative.

Then her glance fell on the spot where Derm's car should have been but wasn't.

It was true, legally he had not moved in with his brother along with Callum and Andy, but he had been spending so much time there of late, she wondered if they were splitting the tax payments four ways yet. Honestly, she couldn't begrudge him the Good Samaritan award. He wanted to help his brother, which, as it turned out, also meant helping two young men turn vacant rooms into livable spaces after squirrels had declared squatters' rights decades ago.

Since she had been cajoled into helping out at a church fundraiser, and Syn had been doing extra duties for the Artists' Club, she had no right to complain that he was doing too much.

Heaving a long sigh, she decided that the green ooze wasn't going to magically disappear and tromped inside, got the bleach bottle, and called Syn out of her room for assistance.

Once outside and positioned on a ladder against the south side of the porch, she attached the bleach-solution bottle to the nozzle—after only three tries—gripped the hose with both hands and yelled at Syn to turn the water on full blast. She aimed the nozzle at the top of the house and hoped that the concoction she had made would be strong enough to dissolve the mold off the wall and blast Ada's comment into oblivion.

For about five seconds, she had control of the situation, then for the next two minutes, she did a high-wire dance, trying to keep the wriggling monster that had been an innocent hose from strangling her and then sending her plummeting to her death.

Down below, Syn's screams helped immensely.

It was only when she heard footsteps clattering up the ladder behind her, strong arms reaching around and grabbing the hose, and a man's voice yelling at Syn to turn off the water, did Rhona realize that Andy had possibly saved her life.

I could have just let go of the hose! Syn could simply have turned off the water! We didn't need to act like such nincompoops! Such thoughts racing through her mind kept Rhona from fixating on the fact that Andy helped her down the ladder as gently as a fireman trying to get a cat out of a tree.

Once on solid ground again, Andy grinned like a Cheshire cat. He actually patted Rhona's shoulder! "I saw you up there and nearly had a cardiac arrest."

Rhona deadpanned. "Not too far from that myself."

Perhaps realizing that a middle-aged woman wasn't beyond feeling embarrassment, the smirk disappeared, and Andy had the good grace to lift the hose as if it weighed a ton. "Hey, since I'm here, I'll just finish the job. Uncle Derm wanted me to pick up a few tools and ask if we all could come by here for supper tonight."

For the first time in months, a mountain that had weighed on Rhona's chest in the shape of her nephew budged. It practically toppled over. She smiled as she playfully smacked his muscled arm. "If you can wrestle that serpent and blast the mold off the side of the house, you'll deserve dinner *and* dessert." She looked over at Syn, whose gaping mouth could have caught an oversized dragonfly. "Text your uncle and tell him to bring on the troops. We're having fried chicken tonight."

Syn's mouth closed slowly, but before she could move her gaze off Andy, he smiled at her. For the first time in forever, she smiled back.

On the last day of the month, Rhona decided that she'd take another stab at a little me-time.
So, she gathered her latest mystery novel, a cold glass of lemonade, and a bag of peanuts and headed to the chaise lounge, now cleaned and situated under the maple tree at the back end of the yard.

No sooner had she crunched the last peanut, slurped down the dregs of her drink, and decided that she knew who had stolen the cake from the pastry shop—which was a strong hint at who was having the affair with the café owner, the town rival and a strong motive for murder— when she felt a shadow in the form of her niece fall over her book. She looked up and reflectively offered a smile, though her inner me snarled in the early stage of a leave-me-be-a-while-longer conniption fit.

Syn's expression banished her inner me to the lowest dungeons.

Rhona closed her book, one finger holding her place just in case. "What's wrong?"

"Gustav texted back."

The bookmark, shaped like an Alice in Wonderland white rabbit, her favorite, was nowhere to be found. Rhona closed her close without thought, sat up, shifted over, and patted the place beside her.

Dropping onto the frail chair, Syn nearly toppled them both, but her exhausted sigh suggested that she didn't care if she fell through the ground all the way to molten lava.

Rhona clasped her hands and hunched forward, trying to brace herself. "What did he say?"

Syn lifted her compact phone and held it out.

The words were small but readable.

"Syn Fortune-Wei,

I have no way of knowing if you are a real person or a scam. I searched your online profile and, yes, you do look like the picture you sent, and I can see a resemblance to Nia, but quite honestly, I am in no position to follow up. I have a wife and family and, though Nia was a special person in my life for a short time, barring a paternity test, which I will not take, I have no proof that you are my child. In any case, there's little I can do now. I have my own life, and you have yours. I can only offer my best wishes and, if you are a scammer, may you get your just desserts.

G. S.

Stunned speechless, Rhona could only wrap her arms around her niece and pull her close. Sadly, Syn remained as hard as a rock with no intention of budging. Sensing her niece's resistance, Rhona let go and clasped her hands, attempting to rise above the turmoil that had ruined her afternoon and, possibly, the rest of the year. She spoke in as neutral a tone as she could fashion. "How are you doing?"

Syn pulled back and straightened her shoulders. "It's okay. I never really expected anything. I just wanted to see what he said. Now I know." She rose to her feet and started pacing away.

Rhona leaped up. "Wait! Don't you want to talk about it? That's a huge shock to process. He was so cruel."

A shrug and Syn continued walking.

Though the sun shone from a bright blue sky, the dark thundercloud over Syn's head was as real as any natural formation. How Rhona would manage the next storm that would rage through their lives, she had no idea.

Chapter Eleven

Holiday Plans, Summer Pests, and Confrontations

Early July

The fourth of July never sparked much enthusiasm in Rhona's soul. It was a great day to honor, and she certainly appreciated everything the Founding Fathers did to shape her nation into the beacon of personal freedom and national unity it was meant to be, but she wished they had considered the heat when making their declaration. July was simply too hot to celebrate anything well.

She tried to get comfortable on the folding chair that Derm had kindly toted from his truck to the front lawn of the Quilt & Sew Shop. An empty seat on her left waited for her sister, who was late, of course. *If she didn't live a few millimeters from the shop, she'd never make it to work on time.*

Kids with sparklers ran up and down the sidewalk, chasing each other like frenzied Star Wars characters wielding lightsabers. Fireworks were set off each year in the field behind an abandoned warehouse situated between the All in the Family Vet Clinic and the U. S. Post Office. Though it was a magnificent show sponsored by local businesses, she felt for the birds who were probably scared witless by the enormous flashes of sparkling lights and loud bursts just as they settled down to sleep. A few howling dogs bespoke their attitude on the occasion as well. She didn't even want to imagine the snippy comments cats around town were making.

Besides that, poison ivy had attacked her ankles and burned with itches that she could barely constrain from scratching. Only a smug satisfaction that her bottle of poison ivy killer would have the last laugh saved her from utter frustration that after fifty-seven years on the planet, she had hardly known a few summers, probably in her infancy, without at least one poison ivy attack. *Bloody vines are relentless. Out to kill me, probably.* She imagined the forsythia bush they had invaded, which happened to be a favorite sleeping spot for the dogs, where the unwary canines rubbed against it, then promptly rubbed against her, spreading wicked poison onto everything she touched so that her washing machine had to do extra duty for a week to repeatedly cleanse her clothes and bedding. Her hand slid to her ankle; fingers poised to scratch.

Dermid tapped her arm. "Stop thinking about it and watch the show."

After a well-aimed glare, which her husband didn't even see, Rhona moved her gaze to Syn, sitting with Renzo just a few feet away.

Syn had a much worse case of poison ivy with boils on her arms and legs, but the girl pretended that it didn't bother her at all. Renzo wanted her to see a doctor, but she begged off, insisting that it would just take a few weeks, and they would disappear.

She's ignoring her feelings, pretending that nothing—

Another burst of fireworks exploded in the sky just as Nia flopped down on the chair beside Rhona. "I thought I'd never get my hair to behave. This humidity is disastrous on curls."

Stymied by her utter lack of interest in the subject, Rhona pointed to Syn and whispered loud enough to be heard through the next blast, "Syn's got a bad case of poison ivy. I think you should talk to her about seeing a doctor for some intensive cream."

Nia flapped her hand at mosquitoes who apparently wore earmuffs and would continue to suck blood from innocent victims if the world was blowing itself to smithereens. "Syn's not in a listening mood right now. I tried to talk to her about Gustav, but she just told me to forget about it. It didn't matter. Though she did have the temerity to ask if there were any other contestants for her DNA dad. Ended our conversation pretty quick, let me tell you."

Smacking a mosquito into a bloody pulp only slightly relieved Rhona's indignation. "That's not like Syn. Did she catch a cruelty bug and decide to spread it around?"

Her gaze straight ahead, but her eyes still, as if she wasn't looking ahead but into a distant past, Nia shrugged. "Could be. I never thought he'd be so mean. Now, I wonder if I really was in love with an illusion." She turned her head and met Rhona's gaze straight on. "It's not all his fault. Or even Zhang's. It's *me* I can't trust."

Rhona reached out and grabbed her sister's hand, offering comfort, when the last volley of fireworks filled the sky—and her ears—with blasts loud enough to freeze her in place.

Once it was over and the crowd clapped in jovial approval, Rhona tried to recapture the moment. She glanced over, but the moment was gone.

Nia had climbed to her feet and was grinning winningly as Tav strolled over. "Hey, stranger. Andy says that you've got him cleaning gutters, replacing roof tiles, and even fixing a toilet. Hope he's not getting too big for his britches. The kid will think he's ready to take over the whole estate if you let him."

A gleam in Tav's eye put that worry to rest.

Derm chuckled as he stumped forward and stopped next to his brother. "Tavish knows how to manage his men."

Tavish stroked his luxurious mustache. "Well, generally, I would agree, but in this situation, there are many angles to consider."

Just sitting there, Rhona felt small, so despite body aches after hours in the garden, she struggled to her feet and tried to smile her greeting. Her brows furrowed into question marks.

Tavish got the hint and shuffled his feet. "Well, it's just that Callum has a full-time job online, so when he's done helping me, he'd got plenty to keep him busy throughout the day. Not so with Andy. The kid is helpful, but he's taken to tagging after me."

Holding back a wince, Rhona imagined her brother-in-law's natural aversion to being followed around. He wouldn't even let a puppy do that for long.

Knowing Tav's shorthand for help, Derm interjected a question, "You want him to head back up north early? Get back to school before the term starts or something?"

A slow shake of the head, stroking his white beard in a thoughtful manner, his gaze downcast, Tavish hummed low. "Nope. That won't work. They wouldn't take him early, and to be honest, I don't think it's the right place for the boy. University life works for Renzo. That guy was made for academia. Not Andy."

Bracing herself, Rhona sucked in a deep breath and jumped into the deep end. "You want us to take him in?"

Another slow head shake. "Don't think that'll work, either."

His hands on his hips and his patience clearly running out, Derm rattled his words, "Well, what? You've got an idea, Tav. Spit it out."

"Community College. I think the kid would do well as an apprentice in something. He's good with his hands and takes direction well. He just needs someone to follow around, someone who can teach him."

Rhona's heart fell fathoms, dark water swallowing a faint hope of Andy leaving in the autumn and starting a new life with his dad. "A great idea, but I don't know how well he'd go for it. His head is full of some pretty big dreams. Zhang would probably have a fit if his son was anything less than the top of his class at the university."

Tavish tilted his head; his eyes could have become lasers with their searing intensity. "Whose life are we talking about here? Andy's or Zhang's?"

Derm nodded. He was stroking his chin now, though his beard wasn't nearly as bushy as Tav's. "Still leaves the problem of money. Community college costs, and Rhona and I have been trying to figure out how to make it work for Syn in a year or so. I'm not sure we could take on Andy as well."

Suddenly a voice cleared nosily, and Braden stepped into the circle of light under the old shed. "I just happen to know a construction guy, Wellington, who is looking for an apprentice. He'd be happy to interview Andy, as long as Andy went to school to learn the trade—you know, electricity, plumbing, air conditioning and heating. Stuff like that."

Tav nodded, approval in his eyes.

Derm held his peace.

Rhona nearly exploded. "How do we convince an ambitious young man who has been raised to think that he's supposed to take over the world that he should settle down in a community college and learn a trade?"

Braden's eyes practically glowed in the dim light. "You know my wife? Let Ada have a little chat with him."

The image of Ada tackling the young man and wrestling him into signing up for classes in a community college almost made her smile. For some reason, the idea seemed perfectly sane. She grinned. "That might work. Let her have ten minutes with Andy."

Tav's smile was barely concealed by his beard. "It'll only take her five."

Driving to Tavish's farm with Ada in the seat beside her sent Rhona's imagination into high gear. She wasn't much for time machines, but Tav's sprawling farmhouse estate set on a wooded hilltop with matching grain bins repurposed as medieval turrets with conical tops and flags flying certainly bespoke another era. It felt like she was introducing Daniel Boone to Neil Armstrong—except in reverse. How Ada had managed to live in Oldtown for so long and had never been to Tavish Dewar's house was a mystery. Though, Rhona suspected that Tavish's reluctance to get dragged into anything he didn't think of first may have been a big clue.

Ada could only gasp in turn as each grand aspect met her eyes. The winding path around aged sentinel oaks only hinted at what was to come. When the legendary trees gave way to a wide circular drive before a four-story house with a stone base, matching turrets, tall gables, rounded windows, and a wraparound porch, her extensive gasps nearly had the woman hyperventilating.

As Rhona directed her breathless friend to the side entrance, which led to the kitchen, she jokingly attempted to prepare her for the next shock. "Tav hardly ever uses the front door, except when politicians or clergy come by. Then he leads them through the foyer into the formal living room, which is attached to his extensive study. More often than not, he arranges for a farmhand to take the part of a servant, and he plays the role of landowner to the hilt." She stifled a giggle. "Since it's just us, we can go straight to the kitchen. Besides the library and barns, it's his favorite place when indoors. Usually, he prefers the outdoors, but ever since his near heart attack, he's been more careful. Not living quite as rigorously as he used to. A hard adjustment for such a self-determined man, but…well, we all have to make little sacrifices in life. Just be prepared; it's a smidge bigger than my kitchen."

Ada glanced over, her narrowed eyes suggesting that she believed only half of what Rhona said. Until she saw the room for herself. Only then did she start hyperventilating.

On the south wall, an enormous hearth allowed four iron pots to hang in various degrees over a log fire that could have roasted a full-grown stag. On the north wall, a stove with a high back had room for six burners and two ovens, a top and a bottom. On the west wall, an oversized refrigerator butted against a locker freezer, possibly containing a couple more stags. The last wall opened into another part of the house, with shelves on each side, housing everything from pots and pans and cooking utensils to an oversized, revolving spice rack. Ropes of onions and bunches of dried spices hung from a rafter while a narrow stairway led to a dim interior Rhona had never investigated. She hadn't dared.

Ada stood stock still in the middle of the kitchen, apparently afraid to move. Footsteps clumped forward and, before Ada could curtsy, Tav made his entrance. He grinned at Rhona as if to suggest that the cat had had its fun, now, it was time to let the mouse go.

Her head high with the natural dignity of a close family member, Rhona lifted the porcelain kettle off the stove and shook it to see how much water was in it. Nearly full, she set it on the front burner, snapped on the heat, and stared her brother-in-law in the eye. "I suppose you still have some of the peach turmeric tea I sent over?"

He nodded pleasantly and pointed to a canister on the tall wooden island in the middle of the room. Then he strode as smartly as any landed noble right up to Ada and pretty nearly bowed. "It was good of you to come, Ada. I'll get Andy. Like any sane man, he likes a snack in the midafternoon." He started for the doorway, then stopped and directed his gaze at Rhona in dead seriousness. "You know where the shortbread cookies are."

Once Rhona arranged the teapot, cups, cookies, and napkins, she finally took pity on her friend. She stepped over, took Ada's arm as gently as any qualified CNA in a nursing home, and directed her to the ladderback chairs around a round, wooden table on the right side of the island. "Sit down and relax. Do you know what you want to say? How to approach the sub—"

Bounding forward, Andy's glowing expression welcomed Rhona as if he had not just seen her the other day. Then his gaze bounced off Ada, and he lifted a hand in hello.

Watching her friend's frozen state, Rhona realized that she may have made a large mistake. *I should have done this at my house*. Guilt started to gush through her nervous system, twitching her skin like gnats with teeth. *I didn't seriously try to prepare her…kind of fun to see friends go into shock.* The gnats swarmed more fiercely, and her stomach hinted that tea and cookies were no longer welcome.

But Ada wasn't one to get stuck in a stupor. Adapting to the situation with uncanny aplomb, her shoulders straightened, and her face took on the expression of a pedagogue whose reputation was at stake. She had a mission to accomplish, and nothing would get in the way, not even a medieval kitchen!

Tavish took his place on a stool at the island, staring at the group as waiting for the first act of a play to unfold.

Rhona nervously nibbled a cookie between batting casual, "How are things going?" questions and answers between herself and Andy.

Finally, Ada took charge. She cleared her throat and leaned in. "So, tell me; what are your plans for the future?"

Darting an alarmed look at Rhona, Andy snapped a cookie in two and bit into one piece. He chewed for as long as he could hold out before answering. "I'm not sure I have one." He dropped the cookie pieces on the table, slapped his hands down flat, and heaved a long breath. "You have any great ideas? If so, I'd love to hear them."

Rhona figured that Ada had just died and gone to Heaven. She usually had to force her brainstorms on people, and here was an innocent victim asking for one.

Clearly undeterred by the unexpected turnabout, Ada grabbed the opportunity with the full force of her determined personality. She smiled disarmingly. "How about a trade? There's a local construction company that's been looking for good men. I happen to know the manager. Or rather, my husband, Braden, does. The man had been pestering Braden for leads. But Braden isn't about to send him just anyone. He wants a man willing to commit to proper training, work hard, and do a good job." She narrowed her eyes. "I told my husband that I might know of such a young man. You interested?"

Startled, Andy slid his hands back into his lap. "I don't know anything about construction."

Rhona bit her lip. Fear that he would reject the offer chilled the room temperature considerably.

Tavish's deep voice reverberated against the walls. "That's what training is for. I trained under my dad and a series of farmhands, mechanics, and carpenters who taught me everything I know. It's called being an apprentice."

Andy peered over his shoulder at the older man and then swiveled back to the table. His fingers ran along the grain of the wood, but he remained silent.

Rhona wanted to say something, fill the awful void, but Ada gave a short headshake, warning her off.

Finally, Andy straightened and stretched his hands on the tabletop, palming the surface. "You know, it's not a bad idea. I never fit in at the university, and I'm not even sure my dad is going to help me out anymore. Even if he did, I'd never please him. It's only a matter of time before he'll get mad and cut me off. I'll never be the guy he wants." He swallowed and ducked his head. "Only thing, I don't have a lot of money. Just a little savings Mom squirreled away. That won't pay for much."

Ada nodded. "The community college is not nearly as expensive as the state university, and since it's within driving distance, you can still live here and work for Mr. Dewar part-time. Plus, I'm sure that Braden's construction manager can pay you something through the training program. So long as you show you are worth the investment."

The expression "a new lease on life" animated itself across Andy's face. He glanced from Ada to Tavish and nodded like a little boy entrusted to mow the lawn the first time. "Hey, I'm not afraid of hard work. I just never liked to spin my wheels doing things that made no sense."

Tavish slid off his stool and clamped his large hand on Andy's shoulder. "Trust means you try even when it doesn't always make perfect sense. That's what a good education does—it makes sense of things. Takes time, though."

A sober nod and Ada agreed as she scooted out of her chair. "Come on, Rhona, I have a meeting at the bookstore, and then Braden and I are going out for dinner. It's our thirty-eighth wedding anniversary."

Surprised, Rhona clapped her hands. "Why, Ada, that's wonderful! I hope you have a great time. I feel bad having taken you away from your husband. You should have gone somewhere special for the day."

Ada's eyes twinkled. "Every day with that man is special. Kind of like you and Derm. Best friends forever, you know." She moseyed over to Tavish, her arms out. She clasped his arms and pressed them in a friendly, familiar manner. "I must tell you that I love your home. Took my breath away." She glanced at

Rhona. "I think my friend was having a little fun with me, but I don't mind." She winked. "Two can play at that game."

A chill ran over Rhona's spine.

Andy laughed as he walked them to the door. "Let me know what I need to do. I'll take any entrance tests you say and start at the bottom if I have to."

Ada chuckled as she faced the beaming young man. "You're a long way from the bottom, Andy. Remember that. No matter how hard things may get, you're among friends. We won't let you fall." Her gaze hardened. "Not unless you insist."

Amazed at her friend's uncanny ability to comfort and caution within mere breaths, Rhona followed Ada out the door, hoping that Ada's next brainstorm wouldn't have her hyperventilating.

Mid-July

Rhona preferred winter to summer, especially in the blasting humid heat of July. She stood staring out the window on her morning break and struggled to comprehend how her niece could lie on a blanket on the lawn under the full glare of the sun and read a book. *How does she concentrate when her brain must be melting?* She figured that it had something to do with magazine pictures of girls on beaches with a tall drink in one hand and a handsome guy holding her close. *People will put up with anything if it fits a fine vision.* The Princess Leia hairstyle came to mind.

Rhona retreated to her work desk with only a headshake at another of life's many mysteries. That afternoon, the temperature soared to rival Venus and, despite an old, overworked air conditioning unit at full throttle, sweat trailed down her back. It came as no huge surprise when Syn bounded into the living room, in the middle of chapter four of Rhona's latest editing project, and insisted that they needed a pool.

Rhona finished the line she was working on, trying to take a mental note in her brain to replace every misspelled version of complement in the document. Then she turned and faced her niece. "A pool?" Various images of pools ran through her mind, everything from a kiddie pool with colorful fish painted on the bottom to an inground, Olympic-size, with filters and pumps running twenty-four/seven. She didn't want to squish the idea, just keep it within the realm of both budget and feasibility. "What do you have in mind?"

Syn's gaze wandered to the ceiling as if she were considering the idea for the first time. "Oh, just the standard round thing, about four feet tall—not too big but a few people can have fun in it at one time. There are some on sale at the Big Store in Hillsborough. Maybe Uncle Derm and I could go, since he needs to pick up a few items anyway."

Oh, she's planned this out to the details. Not being opposed to slipping into a cool pool on a hot afternoon, maybe splashing Derm and having a little fun with Syn, she nodded agreeably. "You'll have to talk him into it. I'm not wrestling a pool into shape on a hot day like this. And you'll have to set it up by the garden well pump. We're not using up the house water."

On her toes and clapping in quiet glee, Syn's head bounced like a bobble doll.

Glad to see a happy expression on the girl's face, Rhona watched her hurry into Derm's study. *Undoubtedly conferring on their next move in the "get a pool" scheme.* Derm had mentioned a pool before, but there never seemed like a good enough reason. Now they had a life-size reason. Rhona returned to her work, a part of her brain trying to remember where she had put her swimming suit.

In another "no-surprise" moment, Renzo just happened to show up in time to help set up the pool. Between Derm, Syn, and Renzo, it only took a half hour to get it set up, the dogs from attacking the foreign entity, and a hose connected from the well to the pool.

Rhona finished her assignment for the day and made a simple lunch of turkey sandwiches, homemade pickles, and corn chips, along with extra spicy salsa. Bewilderingly, right after lunch, Renzo and Syn had to hurry away to help Mr. Thompson with a new shipment of books, and Derm wanted to get a few new supplies over to his brother's place. So that left Rhona to be the first to try out the new pool. She didn't mind. Just odd that the one person who hadn't lifted a finger should get the premier pleasure.

The temperature had risen to the high nineties, and the humidity was enough to drench a desert, so she finished up in the kitchen, then ran upstairs, searched through her drawers, and found a one-piece suit that wouldn't embarrass her too much, though she slid on an old pair of shorts to comfort her aging midsection, then donned her sandals, and marched across the lawn to inspect the latest homestead addition.

It took longer than expected to ease herself into the frigid water, but once in, she had to admit, relief seeped through her whole body. *So good to cool off my inner core.*

A rumble overhead turned her attention upward.

Dark clouds swirled in angry formations. Chagrined, she rumbled back at the sky, "It hasn't rained in over two months, and, today, right after I get into a new pool, you decide to—"

A flash of lighting and an alarming crack sent her scrambling over the wall. She slipped on her sandals just as heavy drops splattered against her skin. "Well, I'm already wet, so there." She practically shook her fist at the sky as she ran across the yard, slipped on the porch step, righted herself, and then made it inside.

It wasn't until after she had changed into dry clothes and gotten a cup of ginger tea that she could chuckle about her misadventure.

When Syn and Renzo appeared an hour later, looking as if they had jumped in the pool with their clothes on, Rhona merely pursed her lips and waved her niece to her room. "Get changed while I fix something for dinner." Then she appraised the muscled five-foot-nine guy and lifted her hands to the fate of clothing sizes. "Maybe Derm has something that'll fit you, Renzo."

Not quite dripping, but definitely leaving shoe marks on her otherwise clean floor, Renzo padded closer. "Oh, I can't stay. I've still got a ton of things to do before heading out in a few weeks, but I was just wondering if you and Derm would be open to meeting my mom. She's met Syn, of course, but I thought it would be nice if she got to know you guys before I left. She said she'd make whatever you'd like, and if you have any dietary restrictions, she'd more than understand. She's been battling breast cancer, you know. Treatment really did a number on her stomach for a while, but she's much better now—in remission, they say."

Rhona leaned against the counter, her arms folded comfortably over her chest. "Your mom sounds like a remarkable woman, and I'd be happy to meet her." She scrunched her brow meditatively. "I never asked about your dad. Where is he?"

"Oh, he travels a lot, for work. He's an inspector for industry food plants all over the country. Sometimes he's away for months at a time. His parents live in Minnesota, and Mom's mom passed; her dad remarried and lives in Colorado. We don't see either side very often. Everyone lives in their own worlds, it seems." His forced smile didn't match the strained look in his eyes.

Rhona unfolded her arms and launched herself from the counter toward the refrigerator. "Tell you what, rather than her cooking for all of us, why don't you bring her here? That way, she can see where Syn's been living, and you might even take her to Nia's place and, if she doesn't have a heart attack, then you all can come back here for dinner. Kind of gives your mom the big picture, so to speak. Plus, I'd enjoy giving her a night off. Anyone who has held cancer at bay must have a warrior spirit. I always admire that."

As Syn tromped in, wearing a dry outfit of jean shorts and a purple top with lacy sleeves, Renzo's smile finally found his eyes. Tearing his gaze away from her, he returned his attention to Rhona. "This means a lot to me. It really does. Mom's checkup is right before I leave, and I know she's anxious about it. This will give us both something to look forward to."

"Well, let's try for the end of the month then. Would it be better before or after the check-up?"

"Would the twenty-eighth work for you? The results should be in on the twenty-third, so that'll give her a few days to adjust to the news, whatever it is.

Plus, it's a Saturday, so she'll have the afternoon off from her job at the bank."

Rhona nodded as she patted the young man on the shoulder in approval. Then she pointed to the door. "Now go home and get yourself dried out before you catch something."

Syn's hands reached out, and she got wet again as she hugged Renzo's arm all the way to the door.

Rhona considered the extra wash she'd have to do, the special dinner she would have to prepare, and the muddy floor she'd have to mop, and realized that she didn't mind a bit.

Three days later, late on Friday evening, Derm carried a large tray with a bowl of popcorn and wine coolers to the porch, set them on a small plastic table, and settled down next to his wife.

Happy contentment sent Rhona's mood soaring into the sun-drenched sky. Everything seemed to be going well, and when Derm had suggested an evening of fun in the pool, followed by eating whatever they felt like—cake for dinner maybe—and relaxing in casual conversation on the porch without any interruptions, she agreed without hesitation. Syn had gone to a movie with Renzo, and the house was quiet. They both turned off their phones and leaned back in their matching rockers, determined to soak in the first decent breeze in weeks.

Rhona closed her eyes, listened to the birds fluttering around the tree, each trying to get the best accommodation possible, and even enjoyed the soft snore of one of the dogs asleep by the railing.

Then, a car drove down the road and turned onto their gravelly driveway. *Oh, no.* It sounded like a sports car. She squeezed her eyes tighter in the hopes that it was just an invading alien ship that had accidentally rolled onto their property and would soon be on their way once they realized that they were interrupting two old humans' nap times.

Zhang's voice rang out, and he didn't sound like a happy man. "What the hell are you two doing to my family?"

Sucking in a bracing breath, Rhona opened her eyes and quickly realized that Derm was already on his feet, fire in his eyes. Her stomach dropped to the floor, but she made herself stand up anyway.

Derm's soft tone belied his anger, but his clenched hand trembling at his side wasn't playing any games. "Your family? Zhang, I do believe that you disowned Syn some time ago, you divorced your wife, found another woman, and told your son to "Accept it or get out" if he remembers correctly. Am I right in assuming that he has to agree to your newest lifestyle choice, no questions asked?"

The sparks coming from Zhang's eyes could have ignited a forest fire. He cracked his words as if chipping granite. "Andy is my son! I can choose to have any girlfriend I want, and it's not his or your place to pass judgment on me."

Rhona tried to intervene, but the tension between the men created a sizzling barrier she wasn't sure she could safely cross.

Derm's rigid stance didn't alter a millimeter. "You're right. You can date anyone you want. But Andy does have a right to his opinion. And there was more to it, and you know it. Nia is his mother, for Heaven's sake. How should a son feel? How would you feel if you were in his place?"

An expert in deflection, Zhang did what he did best; he changed the direction of his attack. "You convinced the kid to quit the university and go to some measly community college and take a trade? A trade! For God's sake, my family didn't risk their lives to emigrate to this country so we could be lowly servants of the upper class."

Rhona swallowed a lump the size of a glacier. *So, that's what this is all about?* She started to mumble, "But if that's what he—"

Two glares cut her off. Apparently, this was going to be a gladiatorial fight between two men, and she had no part to play. A section of her brain wondered if she should just sit down and watch it from a safe distance, like a spectator. But a wrenching ache inside warned that it wouldn't take much to turn this showdown into a disaster. Derm wouldn't strike out, but she wasn't sure how much control Zhang had over himself. She stayed at her husband's side.

Out of the corner of her eye, she caught sight of another car racing into the driveway. *Oh, Lord, Andy.* Even as the full awareness that the tension just went up another notch, a sliver of relief filtered through Rhona. *Two against one are better odds.* Then she glanced at Andy to make certain she knew who the two would be.

Andy left no doubts as he clambered up the steps, pounded across the porch, and halted within inches of his dad. "What are you doing here?"

Now shooting laser rays at his son, Zhang backed up a step. "I messaged you. I wanted my things from the storage unit." He cut a glance at Derm and Rhona. "But I couldn't leave without asking these two bozos why they think it's okay to interfere in my family affairs. Because they have a long history of it, and, damn, but I'm tired of it." His hands swung at his sides as if rearing up for action.

Andy's jolt and the blank surprise on his face suggested that he had no idea who he was dealing with. "Have you gone crazy, Dad? Rhona and Derm have picked up the shattered pieces you left behind!"

Deflection now being his best friend, Zhang roared, "You will stay at the university and get your degree, or I will cut you off completely. And that goes for Syn, too. I'm not responsible for her. She can get her own health insurance and all the rest."

At that moment, Syn's face appeared in the window, then retreated.

Rhona's mind blanked. "I thought she was out with Renzo!" She closed her eyes. *Or were they going to the late show…?* Trying to keep an ice chunk from blocking her airway, Rhona considered swaying over to the door, but one look at Andy changed her mind.

The young man crossed his arms over his chest and suddenly seemed as cool as a cucumber in a crisper. "It's okay, Dad. I get it. You failed, and you have to save face." He jutted his chin north in the approximate direction of Chicago. "Go ahead and start a new life. Be a big success and marry your newest model girlfriend. I don't want your life, and I don't want your success. I'm my own man, and I'll figure things out my own way."

As cold as the arctic plain, Zhang glared at his son. "Without my money. Without my support."

Derm's gravelly voice had turned to bedrock. "He has support, Zhang. He'll get a scholarship, loans if he has to. It is his life—to own and to live—whatever the consequences." He leveled his gaze at the man. "Just like you."

An intense staring match broke only when Zhang spun on his heel and marched to his car. His tires spat gravel as he roared away.

Derm placed a hand on Andy's shoulder, but the young man was in no mood for comfort.

Andy merely nodded, jogged back to his car, and drove off in a decidedly more controlled manner.

Derm plunked down on the rocking chair and dropped his head onto his hands. He needed a few minutes.

Exhaling the breath she had used to keep the block of ice from choking her, Rhona pressed her hands to her chest and told her heart to settle down. The ice was gone, melted. It wouldn't be back anytime soon. Then she tromped inside and found her niece slumped on the couch. She dropped down next to her. "I thought you'd gone out with Renzo to see a movie."

"We were going to, but he was running late. I just texted him that I'm not feeling well. We'll do something tomorrow."

Rhona caressed her niece's limp arm. "Are you okay?"

A moment's pause as Syn seemed to be studying the braided rug under her feet. Finally, she sat up and cleared her throat. "No. I'm not okay. But apparently, that's not so unusual. Terrible dads might be more common than I previously thought. Maybe terrible people in general."

Rhona bit her lip before replying, "That's an awfully cynical view, honey. Not everyone is terrible. And even when someone does something terrible, that's not the whole person."

Syn nodded and staggered to her feet as if she had just been battered by a cyclone. "True. But terrible things happen—and not just to me."

Tears flooded Rhona's eyes. She racked her brain for wisdom and words of hope, but nothing seemed right and true at the moment. Grief colored everything.

"Still, I have to keep living, right? Might as well try to do better than terrible." Syn plodded down the hall to her room.

Derm stepped in carrying the tray of popcorn and coolers, and they shared a sad moment. He sniffed and nodded to the kitchen. "We'll try again another day."

Late July

By the end of July, Rhona's love affair with the garden was beginning to wane. It always did around this time, when summer heat turned the outdoors into a sauna, and the lack of rain meant that the baked ground clung to weeds harder than a collection agency grasped late payments.

Though she loved zucchini, there was so much she could do with it: fried zucchini, chocolate zucchini bread, cinnamon zucchini muffins, zucchini added to soups and stews and stir-fries. It was a versatile vegetable that never overpowered but added texture and flavor to an amazing number of recipes. But when her zucchini plants grew as tall as small trees, bushed out to the size of baby elephants, and produced enough zucchini to feed the nation, she wondered if she really loved it that much. *Enough is enough.*

She rose at the break of dawn on the last Friday of the month, soon after the early birds began warbling, dressed in light clothes, slurped down a mug of hot coffee, and then made her way to the garden just as morning rays highlighted pearls of dew hanging from spider webs looped all over the yard. Some of the webs were so large and intricate, she stopped and examined the handiwork. Of course, if there was something caught in the web, alive and squirming, she moved on quickly. More often than not, the spider had done its housekeeping and seemed intent on patching up tears and holes. Orb weavers were her favorite, with their bright-colored bodies and their huge, iconic webs that might stretch from one tree limb to another. It felt prayerful to simply admire the glory of creation, worlds within worlds, that asked nothing from her other than to be admired and left in peace.

She stumped along, marveling at the beauty all around and tried to formulate the perfect dinner for Renzo and his mom, set for the next day. A bee whizzed by, nearly missing her face. Startled, she followed its trajectory, and her eyes widened in horror as it landed on the edge of the pool. She dashed over.

Stop, you fool. You're supposed to be making honey someplace; now get out of there. That water is deep enough to drown your entire colony. She looked at the water's surface and gasped. There floated myriad dead and dying bees. *Oh, my. No!*

Leaping into action, she grabbed the pool net and started scooping and dumping the bee bodies on the grass. A few lay limp, never to buzz again, but more than a few roared to life and zipped away, undoubtedly writing up unfavorable notes, giving her pool the worst ratings possible as an insect-watering hole.

Once the water was insect-free, Rhona dropped the net and slapped her hands on her hips. "Fine. Go and tell everyone to stay out of my pool!"

A laugh and Nia's voice nearly sent Rhona zooming after the bees. She whirled around.

Smirking, Nia lifted her hands in surrender. "I wasn't planning on going in."

Trying to save a smidge of her reputation as a sane woman, Rhona wagged her finger. "Good. It's been infested with bees this morning, and there might be a few stingers loose in there." *Oh, that was good. Just the comment to assure my sister that early dementia hasn't set in.*

A small headshake and Nia dismissed momentary insanity. She pointed to the picnic bench. "I was just wondering if we could have a little chat before I head off to pick up some supplies for the store. The sisters usually have things delivered, but I know a place that's always willing to give me a discount, especially if I buy in bulk. I figured I could save them a few bucks and maybe find a new treasure, something for the shop window."

Relieved at the change of topic as well as Nia's benevolent thinking, Rhona gratefully dropped down on the bench and folded her hands together. "What's up?"

A long huff and Nia plunked down; her gaze wandered across the yard. "I still feel bad for the way Zhang talked to you guys, and the way he treated his own son was unforgivable. But I can't help myself—I still miss him."

Rhona's eyes widened. *Well, marriage is supposed to be until death do us part, so why does this seem ridiculous?*

Her hand up defensively, Nia spluttered, "I don't mean I miss how he acted. I just miss being in love, being with a guy that loves me. Is that so wrong?"

Fidgeting, Rhona didn't know what to say. Before meeting Derm she had dated a few guys, but no one had felt right, so she never let a romance develop. She always figured that it was better to be alone than be in a bad relationship. Since being with Derm, no other man interested her as anything other than family or friend. She felt for her sister without really knowing how she felt. Finally, she defaulted to the truth. "You have people who love you, Nia. And I believe you love them back. Romance is only one aspect of a relationship. Even if you found a man, there would have to be more to it than sex or passion."

Nia blinked, clearly confused. "What are you getting at?"

A huff and Rhona heaved herself off the bench and toddled toward the garden, one hand waving to her sister to follow along.

Once they stood before the four enormous zucchini plants, Rhona pointed to the abundant vegetables, some of which could rival battleships. "You need to make friends with yourself and your world, find fulfillment in the basics, like making food that you can eat and enjoy." She waded into the green jungle, wrestled five large zucchinis from their thick stems, then thrashed her way back to land. She bundled the green goodness into her sister's arms. "Aftcr you get back from shopping, look up a few recipes, pick something the sisters would like, and make them a treat."

Stymied, Nia stared over the pile. "I don't have a stove or an oven. I'm not a good cook. I burn things."

"Ask Lucia to help you. She's got culinary skills, as well as fashion sense. Maisie will probably turn it into a party. Just mention wine."

Nia made a feeble attempt to get to her phone but gave up after the mound started to slide. With an uncertain sniff, she turned and practically tiptoed to her car.

Rhona strolled alongside, selfishly grateful to have found a home for the five biggest monsters in her garden.

After Nia dumped the load into the passenger side and then dusted off her pantsuit, she backed up toward the driver's side. "You really think that zucchini will cure me of heartbreak?"

Rhona sighed and lifted her hand in goodbye. "No, but it'll give you something productive to do while you heal."

As soon as Nia was safely on her way, Rhona returned to the garden, faced the rest of the zucchini, and felt a kinship with spiders.

Syn was so excited to make dinner and dessert for Flora Fulton, Renzo's mom, that she nearly drove Rhona out of her mind. Apparently, lasagna was a Fulton family favorite that Flora hadn't made in ages. So rather than asking her aunt to do the work, Syn begged to drive to the store, get all the ingredients herself, and then make the whole dinner without any interference. Rhona only had to sit in the passenger side of the car on the way to and from the store, since Syn still didn't have enough hours to get her license yet. And if Rhona could manage to sit silently on a stool and say nothing during meal preparation time, that would be great, too.

Rhona did her best, though she couldn't help grabbing the car door handle every time they made a turn, pressing her foot to the floor a mile from a stop sign, and generally keeping her nerves from tearing themselves to shreds before, during, and after the drive.

When it came to unloading, Derm romped into the kitchen with the box of goodies in his arms as if he had just run to the store and back to deliver them to his favorite niece.

Syn became a mere blur as she unpacked the box, arranged the ingredients, and cooking utensils, snapped on the oven timer, and did approximately thirty-four things at once.

By the time the lasagna was cooking in the oven and a cake was cooling on a rack, Rhona had downed two cups of chamomile tea and then, in desperation, broke into the reserved bag of party pretzels.

Syn snatched the bag away and poured the contents into a fancy Christmas bowl, saying that the decoration was a reminder that Renzo would be back for the holidays. Relieved that the girl hadn't created a whole holiday theme sped over Rhona like a dodged bullet. With the main dish safely in the oven and the lemon cake iced and ready on the counter, Rhona decided it was time to retreat with whatever dignity she had left. She headed to her room to dress, snatching a couple of pretzels to take with her.

The lasagna was baked to perfection, and Syn was rightfully proud of her efforts. Renzo sat next to his mom, Flora Fulton, on one side of the table, while Syn sat opposite. Derm took the head, and Rhona sat at the foot. It was a small enough table that no one had to reach very far and conversation could be shared by all. After Rhona had been assured that Flora's recent test results were good, she gained detailed particulars on Flora's family of origin, going back to her mother's emigration from China to the US, her father's trek from the Peruvian mountains to California and their subsequent romance, Flora's early marriage, and her work at the bank. Rhona finally directed a pointed look at her husband.

Dutifully, Derm interrogated Renzo on his preparations for his trip, what classes he would be taking, any excursions he planned on the continent, and how on earth he would keep track of the currency rates.

Syn rolled her eyes. "Uncle Derm, most countries use the Euro."

Derm's fixed expression covered his surprise. But he had the grace to smile and shake his head. "Of course. Should have thought of that. I'm still back in another era."

After devouring two helpings, Flora dabbed her mouth and grinned. "I don't know half of what kids are talking out these days. They just get on the computer or their phones, and they seem to know everything."

Rhona swirled her last piece of lasagna around on her plate, trying to soak up the last bit of savory sauce, and shot a glance at Flora. "*Seem to* being the operative words. Knowing that you don't know is sometimes just as important."

A stalled silence fell over the room, and Rhona could have kicked herself. *No time for a philosophical discussion, you idiot.*

Renzo scooted back from his chair, a grin spreading over his face. "Since Syn did all the cooking, I insist on doing the dishes."

Syn flapped her arms, a killdeer trying to get your attention. "Dessert comes next. I made a cake."

Flora's choked laugh made every head swivel her way. She fluttered her hand. "Sorry! I just loved the way you almost took off." She set her napkin aside from her empty plate. “Renzo told me that he likes to call you Sparrow, a family nickname. I never understood why. But just then, I understood.”

Rhona laughed. “Yes, well, we didn’t know what a strong bird she’d grow up to be, but Sparrow still fits.”

Flora’s tone softened. “Can I call you Sparrow, too? Sometimes, maybe?”

Syn started gathering the plates, moving gracefully through a shrug. “My full name is Syn Speug Fortune-Wei. She stopped with a load of plates on her arm. “Syn is for Synergy, my biological father’s favorite word, a guy I’ve never met and will never know. Speug because mom thought it was funny to name me after a Scottish house sparrow since Aunt Rhona called me sparrow in the hospital. Fortune was mom’s maiden name, but I never knew my grandfather, and Wei was Zhang’s name, a guy who never wanted me in the first place.”

Silence filled the room.

Rhona’s mind went completely blank. She couldn’t think of a thing to say.

Derm fiddled with his fork, and Renzo rose to his feet.

Only Flora and Syn seemed unconcerned by the dramatic revelation.

Flora lifted her gaze and locked her eyes on Syn. “It’s the person that makes the name, not the other way around.”

Syn nodded. “You can call me Sparrow any time you want.”

By bedtime, Rhona was ready to collapse. She fell onto her bed and closed her eyes. “I may not have made dinner, but I tiptoed through every step till I thought my nerves would snap."

Derm heaved onto the bed, making the headboard smack against the wall. "I got to give it to our little Sparrow. She did us all proud. I'm starting to think the world of Renzo, too."

"Flora seems like a nice woman. Been through a lot but doesn't talk about it much. She's not a victim type."

Derm rolled onto his side, facing Rhona. She could feel him staring at her. She opened her eyes and followed his example, rolling over. They were as close as two peas in a pod. "What?"

"I think Syn's ready to fly soon."

"You want to kick the kid out?"

A snort and Derm gave her arm a familiar squeeze. "No. I just think that she's done so well in school online and, after one more year, she'll have enough credits to graduate. Maybe she should do what Andy is doing and start at the community college. It would give her a chance to meet more people, talk to her professors in person, get out into the world."

"She'd only be seventeen when she starts."

Derm shrugged. "She'd still live here, and Nia and Andy will help. It's not like we're kicking her out of the nest. Just let her have a chance to try out her wings a bit more."

"How about Renzo?"

"Derm's brows scrunched together. "What about him? He's a good kid."

"What if they want to get married or something?"

"They may. But that'll be their decision."

"The consequences could be ours." Rhona widened her eyes. "Babies happen."

“Still their lives. But I think they will take their time. No reason to rush things if they have plenty to keep them busy.”

Rhona rolled onto her back and stared at the ceiling. “Could she be lucky enough to find real love the first time at bat?”

Derm rolled closer. “If it’s real, then it’s not her first and won’t be her last. Why, woman, this house is just bursting at the seams with love.”

Rhona smiled, and then she laughed as her husband pounced.

Chapter Twelve

Sorrow Builds Strength, Love Matters, and Remember to Say You're Sorry

Early August

Normally, parties were a cause for celebration, but the farewell feast for Renzo on the first day of August had Syn moping around as if she were arranging a funeral dinner.

Since Rhona wasn't sure what Renzo wanted or needed, she had Syn act as a spy, and the girl had reported back that he could use one nice, large piece of luggage. He had some small pieces his dad didn't need anymore, but he wanted something of his own.

When she went online and compared prices, Rhona nearly had apoplexy. An urgent call and Nia's extraordinary shopping capabilities tracked down the perfect piece. It arrived the day before the party, and Syn hid it out of sight in the closet.

Then Syn went into her room and cried.

Rhona went about the party preparations, inviting everyone who even faintly knew Renzo. The fact that Tavish invited some friends from town, Andy invited friends from the college, and Derm invited pretty much everyone he bumped into during the week, it wasn't a huge surprise that there were nearly fifty people at the house on the hot August afternoon.

Derm and Tavish grilled burgers and hotdogs, chatting in a jovial men's conclave.

Ada had called everyone she knew and told them what to bring, so there was a vast array of side dishes.

Rhona practically staggered in amazement when Nia carried in a side dish of savory zucchini squash.

The sisters giggled as they set down their offerings of zucchini muffins and zucchini pie. Lucia's eyes crinkled with laughter as she gripped Rhona's arm. "Bet you didn't think you'd ever see your vegetable friends again!"

No, Rhona had not. But she didn't mind. So long as the chips and soda held out, the college guys would survive, and there was enough grilled meat to meet the town's protein requirements for the month. She bustled about, trying to keep the punch bowl filled.

By the time it came for farewell toasts, the guys were all in high humor. One joke after another with raised glasses and hearty chuckles dissipated any gloom, Syn's aura of despair and lowered gaze might have plastered over the event. Tavish and Dermid finalized their plans to drive Renzo to the airport, and Flora's eyes glimmered with gratitude.

As the sun hit the horizon and the last rays of light gilded the evening, guests began to gather their empty dishes, offer one last hearty pat on Renzo's back, and then head to their cars.

Flora was one of the last to leave. She hugged her son, dabbed her eyes, and thanked Derm for doing the airport run. "I just don't have the energy I used to, and I'd hate to make him late if I went to the wrong place. Scares me the way people dash around that place."

Derm assured her that he and Tavish were old hands at getting in and out of airports, and since Renzo was staying the night at Tavish's place, they would get an early start.

Perhaps in order of importance, starting with the least, Flora hugged Rhona, then Syn, and finally her son. For a young man, Renzo's gentle embrace of his frail mother appeared not the least awkward. *He must hug her a lot...* A warm thought flashed against a cold memory of her own mother's neat shoulder pat and her father's sloppy kiss.

The punch long gone, and the outdoor trash filled beyond capacity, Derm, Tavish, Callum, and Andy began the final cleanup.

Rhona pulled the plastic tablecloth off the picnic table and shooed the dogs from underneath. Guiltily, they scuttled away, still chewing leftovers they had snuck off unwatched trays and abandoned plates.

Syn stood with Renzo a few feet away, both still holding plastic cups, unwilling to admit that the party was over. His arm rested around her shoulder. She leaned into him, apparently studying her shoes.

Trying to hide tears?

Renzo faced the horizon, murmuring in a consoling tone.

Suddenly, Syn lifted her head and, using her cup, gestured to the sunset in a signature salute. "May you have a wonderful semester, learn everything you can, impress the heck out of your professors, and come home safe." Then she tipped back her head, gulped the dregs, and tossed her cup into a trash bag by the garage.

Renzo imitated her and his cup followed hers. Then he wrapped her in a hug, and they stood together, rocking in a silent goodbye.

If Rhona's heart had somehow managed to get caught in a mangle, she knew just how it would feel. To keep from bleeding all over the yard, she snatched up the garbage bag and started picking up anything that didn't look like grass or dirt.

After a private consultation, Derm nudged his brother forward.

Tavish smoothed his mustache, stepped closer to the entwined couple, and in the gentlest manner possible, clasped the young man's shoulder. He nodded politely to Syn. "It's getting late, and we have to be up early. Renzo should head out with us now."

In the driveway, with Callum at his side, Andy opened the truck door. The two men waited like an honor guard as Renzo gave Syn a final goodbye squeeze. Then they hustled to the truck and piled into the back seat.

Derm stood behind Rhona as they watched from the driveway.

In a moment, Tavish's truck, with the three young men's hands waving from open windows, rumbled into the falling light.

Syn hurried up the porch steps and into the house.

Rhona had to wipe a stray tear away as she leaned back into her husband's strong embrace. "I'll have a pie waiting for him when he comes home."

Derm chucked low, his body firm and comforting. "He said he'd really like to get your salsa recipe."

Four days of mourning was about all Rhona could stand. Then, she had to take action and save her sanity. Luckily, a mission of mercy took her out of the house. Lucia and Maisie were on a stir-fry binge and needed all the tomatoes and peppers she could spare. Practically rubbing her hands together in Reverse-Grinch excitement, Rhona bagged up two quarts of cherry tomatoes and nearly a gallon of green peppers, sweet and spicy all mixed together, and dashed out the door before she had to witness Syn's latest attempt at stoic bravery. Derm's insistence that even heartbreak gets boring after a month hardly encouraged her own spirits, which were wilting in the dry August heat.

She drove into town with the air-conditioning off and the windows open, just to feel the rush of air through the car and over her skin. Dreadful malaise had infected everyone. The pool sprang a slow leak, and no one bothered to patch it. The dogs shuffled across the yard and hid under the forsythia bush, the cats lay sprawled out in the old chicken yard, and even the garden plants drooped, looking as exhausted as Rhona felt.

The entire town seemed depressed, and on a hot Wednesday afternoon, it appeared about as somnolent as Restful Glen. After parking in front of the sewing shop with plenty of room to spare since the street seemed deserted, Rhona labored out of her car with her three bundles. Hardly refreshed by the short drive, she stepped into the quiet interior, uncertain what to expect, and glanced around. It was empty. Except for the standard goods, of course.

Bolts of cloth in a variety of colors lined the back shelves, four turnstiles showed off threads in vibrant hues, and lines of wall hooks sported a selection of rotary cutters, mats, seam rippers, and acrylic rulers. At least ten sewing machine models stood on side tables, jutting from the south wall. Clear containers of clips, pins, a fun assortment of pin cushions, and, of course, needles of all sizes were scattered on shelves and counters across the store. By the back door, twin mannequins wore cool summer outfits with signs hanging from their necks announcing that they were Quilt & Sew Shop originals and were now available by special order. The mannequins had been Nia's idea, and Rhona had to admit; they were eye-catching.

Lucia padded in on silent feet, her face crinkling with a smile. "So good to see you, Rhona! Every time you're here, it's something about Nia, and we never get a chance to catch up."

Rhona hefted the vegetable bags onto the counter and flourished her hands as if she had just done a magic trick. "Well, I came to bestow nature's bounty upon you. If you need any more, just let me know. I've enough salsa made to last into the next century, so I'll be glad to find a home for the extras."

Her face glowing, Lucia plastered her hands over her mouth and smothered a giggle. Finally, she straightened and shook her head at Rhona. "You're too generous. We have to pay. It's probably considered organic and worth a fortune." She glanced over her shoulder and lowered her voice. "Maisie is on a health kick. Trying to lose a few pounds before the big wedding." She nodded knowingly.

Rhona nearly staggered backward; one hand slammed against her chest. "What big wedding? Is Maisie getting married?" Watching the seventy-year-old woman in front of her howl with laughter only added to her confusion.

Heavy footsteps labored down the stairwell, and soon Maisie was charging through the doorway, her face scarlet as she waved a soup ladle. "What on earth!"

Fluttering her hands, Lucia's laughter subsided into gasps.

Fearful of Maisie's wrath, Rhona took another step back.

Lucia finally got a hold of herself. "Rhona thought you were getting married."

Her lips pursed, Maisie gestured to the stairwell with her ladle. "We'll talk upstairs. Hardly anyone comes in this time of the day."

Clasping the pepper bag to her chest while Lucia toted the tomatoes, Rhona followed along behind. She had never been in the "upper room," though she had imagined their place a thousand times. What she saw was like nothing she had expected.

One large room laid out with a couch, two recliners, footstools, and a coffee table in the center, a stove, refrigerator, cabinets, shelving units, and a low counter on the east wall, hanging pictures on either side of a door with a sign in the shape of a fish stating, "The Bassroom" took the south wall, while two stout beds positioned with an end table between them and an antique lamp hanging above made up the west side.

Hardly able to take it all in, her jaw undoubtedly on the floor, Rhona simply stared.

Maisie scurried over to the stove and dipped her ladle into a bubbling concoction that smelled suspiciously like salsa.

Rhona spoke before she thought, "You don't have to cook it!"

Maisie turned, her eyes wide, while Lucia set the tomato bags on the table.

Defensively holding up the peppers, Rhona tried to explain as fast as she could. "I only mean, that you don't have to cook salsa. You just cut everything up, add vinegar and spices, then freeze it or eat it fresh. That keeps all the vitamins and stuff…" *I'm babbling.* It was shock, she was sure. *Who is getting married?* Chagrin filled her.

Instantly, Maisie turned off the stove. "Well, that changes everything! I love to cook, but standing over a boiling cauldron on a hot day feels like one step too close to purgatory." She gestured to the refrigerator. "I made a nice pitcher of iced tea this morning. How about you sit and enjoy a respite? You look like you could use a breather."

Gratefully, Rhona accepted.

It wasn't any time before the three women had cold drinks in their hands and gossip pouring from their mouths. Lucia leaned back with a gleam in her eyes. "Maisie isn't getting married. But guess who is!"

Rhona hated guessing games almost as much as she detested scooping dead bees out of her mosquito-infested, nearly empty pool. She grimaced through a helpless shrug.

Maisie jumped in. "Mr. Thompson and Elspeth!"

Lucia leaped back into action. "They're going to Ireland for their honeymoon!"

Her hand fluttering, Maisie retook the lead. "For a whole month!"

Stunned, Rhona shook her head. *Why am I surprised?* She blinked as the ramifications bounced around her brain. "Who is going to manage the bookstore?" Then she spluttered, "And the Artists Club meetings?" Her plans of getting Syn's mind off Renzo derailed, and she nearly gnashed her teeth.

Lucia lifted her glass and glanced from her sister to Rhona, her eyes wide with innocence. "Oh, we thought Syn could take over for a bit. They're getting married at the end of the month and will be gone all of September. That won't interfere with her studies, will it?"

Rhona had to get her heart going again, but once she did, it was no trouble at all to smile, take a refreshing sip of tea, and answer with perfect honesty, "Oh, no, it won't be any trouble at all."

By Friday afternoon, with Callum, Derm, and Rhona acting as a united front, Syn had accepted to her new role as an apprentice at The Literary Enlightenment Bookstore. The gloom fading like a dissipated storm cloud, Rhona felt like doing something fun and different. A dinner date would be just the respite she and Derm needed.

Since Derm had to go to Restful Glen, meet a family, and direct the placement of a tombstone, and it was on the way to their favorite restaurant, Rhona thought she'd go along, and they could eat out afterward. *Finally, we can put other people's problems behind us!*

As Derm gripped the steering wheel, his gaze fixed on the road ahead and his brows scrunched in concentration, Rhona pulled her thoughts from Syn's near state of contentment to larger, societal concerns.

Whenever a call came in concerning a family plot, either to discern where to bury a loved one or to erect a tombstone, Derm treated the situation as a formal affair, following protocol and doing his duty like a good soldier. With the aid of the online program, he had little difficulty finding most gravesites. Only once had he been stymied by a request to determine on which site a body had been buried nearly a hundred years ago, an era when records were not always kept or were lost. He could find no documentation of this particular internment other than a yellowed obituary notice stating that the person had been, indeed, buried at Restful Glen somewhere in the northwest corner. Knowing full well that the body had surely decayed and there was no tombstone in place, Dermid was desperate to find a solution.

Braden had come to the rescue with the suggestion that he use witching rods to determine the burial site. The man swore by the method, and Ada supported him to the hilt. Since Derm had no other options available, he had Braden, clutching the rods, walk over the grassy area to see what would happen. When the rods moved over the second site, Braden determined that was where the body had been buried. Uneasily, Derm reported the findings to the family without offering extensive details. A stone was erected, and the family member's burial place was thus recorded. Fairly close, in any case, Derm had consoled himself.

Rhona peeked over at her husband and considered twitching his arm and reminding him of the incident to lighten the mood. But the dark cloud surrounding him stayed her hand. His spirits weren't going to improve until this latest quagmire was resolved.

A young man had called the evening before and asked if Derm would meet him and the tombstone guys at the cemetery at four in the afternoon. He had traveled in from out of state with his two daughters to mark the place where his dad had been buried nearly fifteen years previously. He wanted to make absolutely sure he had the right spot since he hadn't been to the funeral and wanted to get the whole thing over as fast as possible.

An unspoken history radiated the kind of tension that Derm normally avoided like the plague, causing him to drive the four miles to the cemetery at the speed of an inchworm. Once they pulled into the circular drive, it was clear that they were the last to arrive.

A truck and attached trailer with Memory Monument Company written in bold across the side were parked on the far east side. A small silver car had pulled up behind it, and three people stood in a huddle a few feet from the workmen.

Without a word, Derm put on his professional face and hurried out of his truck, leaving Rhona to watch from the window. He jogged over to the work crew, his map in hand, pointed to the exact spot, and nodded effusively as the burly foreman retreated into his truck and began to mechanically tip the trailer so the other workmen could set the flat base in its proper position.

The process went smoothly, and before Rhona got tired of watching the fascinated expressions on the two girls, teenagers both, who stood by their father, the workmen had started to maneuver the small tombstone onto its base. *Marvels of modern skill and mechanics.* The daughters appeared equally impressed and kept inching closer, with only one abrupt comment by a workman to stand back.

The girls' father had no problem watching from a distance. He stayed just in front of his car and hardly moved a muscle. His gaze stayed fixed on the proceedings, but his expression held not a smidgen of awe. Rather, his tight face bespoke barely controlled disgust.

Finally, when the workmen laid the stone in place and stepped back with satisfied expressions, the girls advanced, appearing more perplexed than satisfied.

Needing a stretch and more than a little curious to see the new stone herself, Rhona slipped from the truck and took one step closer.

The father's angry tone halted her progression. "Because, that's why!"

The taller daughter, perhaps seventeen or so, shook a finger at the stone accusingly as the workmen backed off. "But it's got nothing but his name and dates of birth and death! Surely, there was more to your dad than that."

The younger sister, hardly more than fourteen, propped her hands on her hips, her head tilted at an angle.

Off to the side, Derm shook hands with the workmen and waved at the north exit to the circular drive.

The foreman, thick with muscles that fit a stonemason, strode over to the family and spoke softly. "Everything okay? This is the stone you ordered, right?"

His face tight, the father nodded and reached out and shook hands with the man.

Their jobs done, the entire crew piled into their truck and, with the empty trailer clattering behind, rumbled out through the driveway.

The father turned and headed for his car, but the girls weren't budging. Their arms crossed over their chests, the younger shouted, "Even if he was as bad as you say, you could have written something."

His head down, Derm retreated to his truck and climbed in.

Slump-shouldered, Rhona followed his example.

A glaze of fury and hurt in his eyes, the father shook his head. "Sometimes, there just isn't anything good to say." He climbed into his car, started it up, and waited.

Since backing up wasn't an option, Dermid turned on his ignition and waited for the girls to join their father.

Her heart aching, Rhona watched the girls accept the fateful situation and plod to the car.

But as she went, the older shot her words like arrows across the quiet green expanse. "There's always something good to say! If not about him, then about you. Could have said you loved him anyway."

After a moment, the girls finally bundled inside the car, the doors slammed shut, and the family drove around the circle and out onto Main Street.

As their car followed in turn, Rhona glanced aside. "Another ruined date night?"

Gripping the steering wheel with one hand, Derm sat straighter than he had on the way in. "No, we'll go have a nice dinner and relax a bit."

Slipping her hand into his, Rhona exhaled a long breath. "The girl was right."

Derm nodded. "That's what I was thinking."

Mid-August

When Nia got excited, she tended to talk fast and bounce on her feet. As far as Rhona could tell, standing in the middle of the sewing shop, her sister was talking fast enough to get a speeding ticket, and her feet weren't even touching the floor.

A front-page article in the community paper announced that Maisie and Lucia were semi-retiring, leaving the store in the capable hands of their general manager, Nia Fortune. The news burned through Oldtown's gossip chain, electrifying everyone with unbounded joy for the two stalwart ladies who had dressed the town citizens, young and old, in proper style for so many years. Nia had already made a favorable impression with her fashion sense, so little anxiety dampened the celebratory mood.

When Nia had called, urgently insisting that her sister get to the store as fast as humanly possible, a hundred disasters threaded through Rhona's mind. But when she arrived and met the beaming smiles of Nia surrounded by delighted patrons, she had to step into the fitting room to regain her composure.

Once she came out and heard the glorious news in detail, Rhona could formally congratulate her sister without the burning desire to smack the woman for once again nearly sending her into cardiac arrest.

Across the room, Lucia and Maisie hunched over the counter with maps, pictures, and brochures spread across the surface, discussing their newest travel itinerary with Ada.

Ada beamed, as well she might, since she had talked Braden into making the October excursion into a foursome.

The poor man will probably come back wearing a tweed suit and leather brogues. She could only hope that what didn't kill him would make him stronger. Rhona's gaze darted from the conclave to her sister, well aware that her opinion wasn't needed.

Nia hardly noticed the gathering at the counter, since she was so busy outlining future projects. She waved at the west end of the store. "We're going to expand the girls' section and add a line of vintage clothes. You know all these estate sales that are around here? Tons of stuff at reasonable prices. I'll create a whole new line of vintage outfits, retro yet modern, with leggings and lace in a fresh mashup."

Before Rhona could nod in approval, one hand gripping the far end of the counter to keep balance, her sister zipped into warp speed as she danced around the store, arms spread toward the north wall. "We're going to create a snack bar here, nothing to rival the café or anything, just some herbal teas, exotic coffees, and a few light pastries. Pure fun for everyone! Maybe even seasonable fruit juices, what do you think?"

Hesitating, Rhona waited to be sure she could get a word in edgewise.

Syn swooped in like a bird snatching a ripe berry. Her phone camera positioned just so, she snapped pictures of the store from every angle. Then she righted herself and, face beaming, one arm swinging as if to encompass the whole place, she gushed in delight, "I'm getting before and after pictures, so we can make a big bulletin board and set it up at the Artist Club display at the bookstore, showing everyone what you're doing. We'll document every step, and that'll draw more customers and get other businesses excited about new ventures."

Despite the fact that her heart had stabilized from the earlier fright, Rhona found her chest heaving with boomeranging emotions. A flashback to nearly a year ago, when Nia had been wheeled into the waiting room, and Syn's bruised and broken body lay on the steel-framed hospital bed, her mind burdened with a terrible secret, filled her mind. These were hardly the same people. *It's not just Renzo's messages and her new role at the bookstore that has Syn so excited. She's really happy for her mom. And Nia isn't just jubilant with new plans, she's thrilled for the whole town.* Her throat tightening, Rhona nodded approval and kept her peace. They didn't need her. They were both flying high.

Thank God.

By the third week of August, Rhona was ready to clean up the yard and start preparing for winter. It had been a scorching summer with only a few spotty rainstorms, but a change was in the air. A few chilly nights and heavy morning mist hinted at an early autumn.

She awoke extra early on Friday and felt refreshed enough to slip from her bed before Derm awoke, pull on her work clothes, grab a quick cup of coffee, pace across the yard to the garden bed, and appraise the current state of leafy affairs.

The zucchini bushes were wizened and needed to be cleared out. Brown green bean vines trailed forlornly across the east end and might as well be pulled. The tomato and peppers would last a little longer. She'd pack a few more produce bags into the corners of the freezer and give the rest away. The food pantry was always asking for supplements. If her bones spoke true, the first frost wasn't too far away. It was time to clean up.

She tugged the wheelbarrow from the shed and steered it to the garden, then got to work. By the time Derm ambled out, holding out a fresh mug of coffee, his own clutched to his chest, the sun had warmed enough to send sweat trickling down her back. She grabbed the mug like a lifeline and met her husband's admiring gaze. "Thank you, sweetheart. I always knew you loved me."

He smiled in return and then faced the garden plot that now sported bald spots. "Well, you got your salsa done early this year, so no worries there. With Syn's help, we should have enough vegetables to last us through winter and bribe any incoming aliens."

A chuckle and Rhona savored the hot brew. Then she sighed. "With Renzo coming home in December, Andy and Callum coming over with Tavish at least once a week, and Nia dropping in whenever she feels like it, we'll need every scrap."

Derm's shoulder met hers in a gentle nudge. "You love it."

Gardening was a lot of work, and it had been a difficult year, but she had to admit that Derm was right. She did love it.

By mid-morning, she was tuckered out and ready to call it a day, at least as far as gardening went. Derm had retreated inside the house to start preparing for his autumn classes and then head over to Tavish's place to assist with a minor repair job. *And probably a bit of gossip.* As she steered the wheelbarrow across the yard, she remembered last year's gourds, forgotten and abandoned. With everything else going on, she simply didn't have the energy to deal with them. She wasn't sure what directed her steps, but she found herself heading to the old plot.

To her amazement, intertwining brown and shriveled vines revealed an abundant crop of birdhouse gourds, perfectly shaped and ready for harvest. *Glad I brought the wheelbarrow.* She closed her eyes, readying herself for one last push, when she felt a hand on her shoulder. She looked over.

Syn stood at her side, eyeing the gourds as if they might just be alien pods ready to unleash a War of the Worlds horror. She pointed. "Are they good for anything?"

Rhona huffed, relief giving her new energy. "Good? Why, those are the newest in bird housing. After we get them hung and dried out, we'll decorate them with paint and hang them outside for our feathered friends. Sparrows absolutely love them."

A slow grin wafted over Syn's face.

Its happy reflection brightened Rhona's soul.

Late August

By late August, the seasonal heat almost convinced Rhona that her internal weather forecaster had been wrong, and summer had decided to stay for the remainder of the year, maybe even burn them to a crisp before the end of the month. Despite what her body was telling her, her mind knew that the current heatwave was just an illusion. Autumn and bitter winter winds would return eventually, and the people in her care would need a well-stocked wood pile to keep from freezing. Tavish was a big help in this department since he had plenty of surrounding woods full of old fallen trees that hadn't yet rotted and were well worth cutting up for firewood. This year, with Derm's, Syn's, and Andy's help, he was able to get several trailer loads filled and sent over.

As the sun hovered over the horizon, Rhona stepped back from the woodshed stacked high with firewood, glad beyond words that this seasonal job had been completed without any splinters, wasp stings, or smashed fingers.

A few insects winged their way across the yard, crisscrossing the paths of birds in their evening flight. A vibrant blue sky shimmered above with a few cotton clouds wafting across, in no particular hurry, shifting and changing in slow motion.

His brow beaded with sweat and his gray hair sticking up at odd points, Derm tugged off his thick work gloves, leaned on the shed wall, and wiped his face.

An expression of glad wonder on her face when looking at nature, Syn stood aside, absorbed in the golden scenery. Her shape softer and less angular than it had been, she appeared older, more a woman than a girl, a glow of health adding benediction to her beauty.

A few feet away, Andy knelt on the brown grass, dangling orange twine before two fascinated cats who clutched at the string in alternate efforts to prove their quick reflexes. He laughed and then tousled one cat's head only to find himself ambushed by the two dogs who rushed him from behind. He rolled over, laughing harder than ever, possibly enjoying himself in youthful abandon for the first time in his life.

Not to be left out of a fight, no matter how innocent, Syn raced over and joined in, tackling Wilma, who took the game as seriously as an Olympic contestant. Clearly bewildered as to which side she was on—animal or human—Nes leaped into the fray and started tugging any article of clothing or clutch of fur she could get her teeth on.

Chuckling, Derm ran over and tried to wrestle the dogs off Andy, but before he could grip a collar, Syn suddenly had Andy on his back, sitting on his chest while the cats climbed over his head and the dogs tugged at his shirt and pants.

Derm halted, his eyes wide with surprise.

Rhona jogged forward, uncertain where this might lead. *What is Syn doing?*

Still half laughing, Andy tried to rise to his feet, but it was hard going with Syn straddling his chest and the animals now taking her part. Apparently, they liked to side with the victor.

Syn leaned forward, her hair curtaining her face, making it hard to read her expression, but her voice, hard and determined, was clear enough. "Tell them what really happened."

Andy made one more feeble effort and then lay still. If he was going to die, he would face it with dignity. "What? When?"

"The car accident. Tell Aunt Rhona and Uncle Derm what really happened."

His eyes flared in shock. Andy tried to shake his sister off, but the dogs started to growl.

Derm didn't move a muscle.

Rhona crossed her arms.

Blinking in surprise, Andy let his head drop back on the grass, his body going limp. "Okay. It was my fault. I kept teasing you about being a Chinese Brain, and you got upset and started yelling."

Syn leaned so far forward that her nose practically touched her brother's.

Rhona couldn't be sure, but the girl might have growled every bit as savagely as Nes.

Andy lifted his hands in surrender. "Okay! Don't tear me to pieces. I did it. I knocked Mom's arm. When you started to cry, I lunged for you; I was so mad. I didn't mean to hurt you, and your crying made me see red. I wanted to shut you up. But when I unbuckled and turned around in the front seat, I must have hit Mom, which knocked her aside and she turned the wheel, sending us over the embankment."

No dog could have snapped more savagely as Syn heaved up on her knees, pressing on Andy's chest. "You could have killed us all!"

For the first time since she had ever known her nephew, Andy began to sob. Slapping one hand over his eyes, he wailed, "I know! It was my fault. I was so angry; I couldn't think straight."

Syn didn't let up the pressure; she seemed to be waiting for something.

Rhona glanced at her husband, telegraphing the message that it was time to intervene.

Derm didn't shift an inch.

His shoulders heaving, it took a few moments for Andy to regain his composure.

Even the dogs and cats settled to the side as if declaring the battle won.

Syn glared down into his face.

A gulp of air and Andy nodded feebly. "I'm sorry, okay? I'm really sorry. It was my fault."

Slowly, with determined motions, Syn slid to the side and rose to her feet. She dusted imaginary dirt off her pants. Then she reached out to help her brother to his feet. "I forgive you."

Rhona wasn't sure how it was possible, but when Andy regained his footing and the two stood side by side, with Andy's hint of meekness and Syn's glint of pride, they finally looked like brother and sister.

Chapter Thirteen

Fly, Sparrow, Fly

September

The third Thursday evening of the month, yellow and pink highlights brightening the cottonwoods, ash, and elms, the great outdoors beckoned Rhona deep into their quiet embrace. Dressed in a warm sweater, long pants, and thick shoes, she set out along the tree line and into the woods.

Squirrels scampered in haste to finish gathering a stash of acorns and walnuts, stealing seeds from the bird feeder whenever Nes and Wilma weren't looking. Humming bees zipped from the last of the summer flowers, collecting the final ingredients for sweet winter survival. Spider webs glinted against long shadows as she sidestepped dying vines and prickly patches. Her mind traveled freely over fresh impressions and unprocessed revelations.

Nia's newfound purpose in life had altered her so profoundly that she hardly wore much makeup anymore, yet she appeared more vibrant and vivacious than ever before. Occasionally, she'd make reference to Zhang, her heart still longing for what had been. But as she sat on the plush chair she had added to the sewing room's new "social circle," her head bent over an intricate embroidery project, she had spoken with uncharacteristic calm, "He's his own man, you know. I can only hope for the best. Maybe this new relationship will work out. Maybe not. He said he was sorry about blowing up, and maybe he'd be willing to help Andy and Syn a bit—whatever that means. In any case, I still care about him. Probably always will."

Rhona had asked how he responded, and Nia had merely shaken her head. "I haven't been able to say that to him. Not yet. I don't think he's ready to hear it. Maybe someday."

Rhona had sighed, strangely relieved, and then admired her sister's fine stitches.

A flock of doves burst from the tree line and fluttered to high branches, safe from Nes and Wilma, who hurried on ahead.

Resettling her heartrate, Rhona curved along a creek bend and found a fallen log just on the edge of the field, overlooking the glory of a burnt orange soybean crop nearly ready for harvest. She perched on its smooth trunk while the dogs scampered in delight at old scents and new dreams of catching a rabbit. Her mind wandered over fresh territory.

Andy's classes, far more meaningful than those he had been taking, kept him plenty busy. With the support of Tavish, Derm, and Callum, his spirits had risen as he finally discovered the real meaning of pride. He had reported at dinner the previous weekend, "Mr. Thompson said—in front of a dozen other guys—that I'm a first-class apprentice!" Whether the spark of nastiness would return if circumstances changed, Rhona could not say. But that the young man had it in him to become better than she thought possible offered a buoy of hope she would cling to with all her might.

What will Zhang think if his son finds success to rival his own? Will he be happy for him? She set the question aside with a shake of her head. There was no knowing the labyrinth of human hearts.

A monarch butterfly flittered past, its golden orange and black winds fluttering lazily, as it didn't have miles to go before making it home. *If it makes it home. Perhaps it's just one member taking its own personal step in a long butterfly journey.*

The dogs barking brought Rhona back to the scene. They scrabbled at the base of a grand oak, drooling at the squirrel on a high branch flashing its tail at them tauntingly. The squirrel appeared to be smiling. Rhona considered the resolute dogs and chuckled. *Will they ever learn?* Her thoughts bounded to her husband's kindly face.

Teaching morning and afternoon classes, Derm's gentle yet determined love of excellence led yet another generation through the intricacies of advanced math and basic chemistry. He may cloister himself in his study with only his morning PBJ and a glass of milk to comfort him through the early hours, but his love for his students kept his spirit engaged the whole day. She could hardly wait to share tonight's pot roast and a fresh loaf of warm bread with him at dinnertime.

Syn's work desk, now permanently stationed in Derm's study, where she managed to bring order to a world Rhona had been forced to abandon years ago, gave her the structure to follow up on her online curriculum, heading for graduation the following spring. Texts flying from Renzo in Germany right to Syn's heart were a modern miracle that never ceased to amaze Rhona. *Back in the old days, young love would have died on the vine waiting for a letter to cross the ocean. Probably a strain on old love as well.* She sucked in a deep refreshing breath as she considered the wide fields and matriarchal woodland. *I'm glad I live now. Able to enjoy old treasures and modern miracles.*

Thinking of the old joined with the new, Rhona pictured Elspeth's shy face as she stood beside Mr. Thompson outside the bookstore. The middle-aged couple had been married in a private ceremony, witnessed by Maisie and Lucia dressed in perfect style, and soon winged their way to a honeymoon in Ireland. *Clearly, there's no age limit on love or adventure.*

Rhona had stopped by the store the week before and picked up a volume of poetry that Mr. Thompson had left for her. She had driven home pondering the power of poetry to grow spiritual gardens. That thought had kept her company all through dinner preparation and even led to a lively discussion with Derm about alien poetry and whether humans could appreciate it when we so often ignored our own. Syn had volunteered her opinion, saying that it depended on the alien, since they'd surely have free will, too. Derm had grunted in decided agreement.

As Rhona considered the growing beauty of her niece, she had to nod in acceptance. Appreciation, like love, was a choice.

Wilma's doggy head nudged Rhona's leg while Nes's deep brown eyes begged. A wind had picked up, and the sun would soon set. It was time to go. She patted each animal on the head, ignored the fact that they both could do with a few breath mints, and stumped her way over the uneven ground toward the porch light. Undoubtedly, Derm had lit it to welcome her home.

With Syn's help, Rhona pulled together an end-of-summer picnic, inviting all those who had time and energy to celebrate the changing season.

Nia arrived with the sisters, Lucia and Maisie, while Tavish brought Andy and Callum.

Derm had to show off his latest building project, a two-story animal house. The lower rooms for the two dogs and high rises for the cats. Everyone clapped. Except the dogs. Privately, Rhona knew they considered themselves well above cats.

Syn set the dried gourds on the picnic table, having cut an entrance hole big enough for a small bird in each, and had shaken the seeds on the old patch for next season's garden. Then she laid paints and an assortment of brushes on newspaper and invited each guest to decorate their own birdhouse.

Childhood rivalry between Derm and Tav added suspense to the afternoon.

A simple meal of taco wraps, salsa, chips, spiced cider, and s'mores was arranged in the kitchen. Food wasn't the point of the gathering, and everyone knew it. Most went in—more than once—grabbed a bite, and returned to their artistic endeavors, sticky fingers notwithstanding.

Rhona kept an eye on the food, wandered between the house and the yard, chatted with everyone, acclaimed Nia's eye-smacking efforts, patted Andy on the shoulder, his gourd more in line with a bat's taste than a bird's, laughed at the funny face Callum drew, admired the ability of the elderly sisters to make their gourds look like well-dressed, full-figured women, and hugged her niece who used a lot of blue and green—insisting that even in winter time, we have to remember spring.

As Rhona watched her family and friends gathered together in peace and creative harmony, her heart soared into the bright sky, somewhere between the sun and the moon.

So softly that no one could possibly hear but God above, Rhona whispered the words that had directed her soul to this one crystalline moment.

Be Brave
Be Strong
Do not Despair.

Fight the icy blast,
Scrounge for each repast,
Huddle under wing,
Let the furies sing.

Survive, Sparrow, Survive

Long past dreamy hopes of dawn,
The sun shines, breezes blow in a new song.

A revived spirit rises from your depths,
Hope blooms with flowers blessed,

On a new day,
You find your way.

No longer alone,
Flying becomes dancing as your skills you hone.

Your nest has room for more.
Go and find them,
Those who'll be
Your nestmates, your loves, your family.

Fly, Sparrow, Fly!

About the Author

A. K. Frailey, an author of a historical sci-fi and science fiction series, short story collections, inspirational non-fiction books, a children's book, and a poetry collection, has been writing for over ten years and has published 17 books.

Her novels expand from the OldEarth world to the Newearth universe-where deception rules but truth prevails. Her nonfiction work focuses on the intersection of motherhood, widowhood, practicing gratitude, and rediscovering joy.

As a teacher with a degree in Elementary Education, she has taught in Milwaukee, Chicago, L. A., and WoodRiver, and was a teacher trainer in the Philippines for Peace Corps. She earned a Masters of Fine Arts Degree in Creative Writing for Entertainment from Full Sail University.

Ann homeschooled all eight of her children. She manages her rural homestead with her kids and their numerous critters. In her spare time, she serves as an election judge, a literacy tutor, and secretary/treasurer of her small town's cemetery.

A. K. Frailey Books QR CODES

A. K. Frailey Website

Translated Books Page with Links

A. K. Frailey Interviews Page

A. K. Frailey Amazon Author Page

Reading Guides
Available on A. K. Frailey's Website/Blog

- **Promote conversation with family, friends, and students through reflective questions based on the characters and conflicts in the book.**

- **Journal your own thoughts and feelings to better process personal trigger points and journey through conflicts with greater awareness.**

- **Discover insights into admirable qualities, infuriating behavior, and why certain scenes have such a powerful effect on our emotions.**

- **Build stronger relationships through shared reading experiences, comparing and contrasting likes, dislikes, and avenues of interest.**

No right or wrong answers! Use these reading guides as aids toward greater personal insight.

Like a dream, stories highlight our unconscious, hidden selves and allow us to face our inner complexities.

The most powerful part of reading a good book is not meeting great characters but discovering a new facet of our true selves.

www.ingramcontent.com/pod-product-compliance
Lightning Source LLC
Chambersburg PA
CBHW070613310726
48982CB00001B/67

* 9 7 9 8 9 8 7 4 0 4 7 8 2 *